The Vexing

The Vexing

Age Of Faith: Book Six

Tamara Leigh
USA Today Best-Selling Author

Copyright © 2017 by Tammy Schmanski

This novel is a work of fiction. Names, characters, places, incidents, and dialogues are either the product of the author's imagination or are used fictitiously. Any resemblance to actual events, locales, organizations, or persons, living or dead, is entirely coincidental and beyond the intent of the author.

All rights reserved. This book is a copyrighted work and no part of it may be reproduced, stored, or transmitted in any form or by any means (electronic, mechanical, photographic, audio recording, or any information storage and retrieval system) without permission in writing from the author. The scanning, uploading, and distribution of this book via the Internet or any other means without the author's permission is illegal and punishable by law. Thank you for supporting authors' rights by purchasing only authorized editions.

ISBN-10: 1942326262
ISBN-13: 9781942326267

TAMARA LEIGH NOVELS

CLEAN READ HISTORICAL ROMANCE
The Feud: A Medieval Romance Series
Baron Of Godsmere: Book One
Baron Of Emberly: Book Two
Baron Of Blackwood: Book Three

Lady: A Medieval Romance Series
Lady At Arms: Book One
Lady Of Eve: Book Two

Beyond Time: A Medieval Time Travel Romance Series
Dreamspell: Book One
Lady Ever After: Book Two

Stand-Alone Medieval Romance Novels
Lady Of Fire
Lady Of Conquest
Lady Undaunted
Lady Betrayed

INSPIRATIONAL HISTORICAL ROMANCE
Age of Faith: A Medieval Romance Series
The Unveiling: Book One
The Yielding: Book Two
The Redeeming: Book Three
The Kindling: Book Four
The Longing: Book Five
The Vexing: Book Six
The Awakening: Book Seven

INSPIRATIONAL CONTEMPORARY ROMANCE
Head Over Heels: Stand-Alone Romance Novels
Stealing Adda
Perfecting Kate
Splitting Harriet
Faking Grace

Southern Discomfort: A Contemporary Romance Series
Leaving Carolina: Book One
Nowhere, Carolina: Book Two
Restless in Carolina: Book Three

OUT-OF-PRINT GENERAL MARKET TITLES
Warrior Bride, 1994: Bantam Books (Lady At Arms rewrite)
*Virgin Bride, 1994: Bantam Books (Lady Of Eve rewrite)
Pagan Bride, 1995: Bantam Books (Lady Of Fire rewrite)
Saxon Bride, 1995: Bantam Books (Lady Of Conquest rewrite)
Misbegotten, 1996: HarperCollins (Lady Undaunted rewrite)
Unforgotten, 1997: HarperCollins (Lady Ever After rewrite)
Blackheart, 2001: Dorchester Leisure (Lady Betrayed rewrite)

*Virgin Bride is the sequel to *Warrior Bride*
Pagan Pride and *Saxon Bride* are stand-alone novels

www.tamaraleigh.com

1

Normandy, France
Early December, 1161

W<small>OMEN WERE MORE</small> trouble than they were worth. Or so Sir Durand Marshal told himself each time one dragged him into a mess like this one promised to do.

Black hair and mantle shaking themselves out in the chill air stirred by her flight, the woman rode ahead of three riders who protectively fanned out behind her though they stood little chance of outrunning their pursuers—a dozen armed men who wore the colors of one who risked much in trespassing on King Henry's lands. And therein lay the mess, one that could see the crisp layer of snow splashed with crimson of sufficient heat to melt it through.

"Lord, protect us," he rasped and drew his chain mail hood over his head and gave the signal.

The men under his command did not hesitate when the thrust of his arm further delayed the promise of a warm hearth and hot meal denied them these past days of hard riding. They did as bid, following him from the cover of trees that reached wintry fingers toward a sky thick with clouds that resembled the billowing smoke of a great fire.

"King Henry!" he bellowed and drew his sword as he spurred his destrier forward.

His men repeated the battle cry, their voices across the frosted land causing those bringing up the rear of the pursuers to whip their heads around and shout warnings. But the one leading the pursuit, a broadly built knight whose beard jutted on either side of his face, did not surrender his prey. He and his companions stayed the course.

So be it. Durand had given King Louis's vassals a chance to withdraw peaceably from the French lands held by the King of England. If blood was the price paid for their trespass, it was on their heads. Unfortunately for their wives and children, the woman who evaded capture could not be worth their deaths.

No sooner did he think it than the one protecting her left flank was overtaken by the bearded pursuer. The latter swung his sword and landed a blow to the knight's chest, knocking him out of the saddle.

The other pursuers veered away from the unhorsed knight. Providing his chain mail deflected the blade's edge, he stood a good chance of survival.

It had, Durand saw as he passed near, the snow defiled not by the spray of blood but dirt flung by hooves and the knight's tumble across it.

Urging his destrier between two pursuers, Durand left them to his men the sooner to overtake the one who sought to unseat another of the woman's protectors. In the seconds required for the bearded knight to achieve that end, Durand was granted the time needed to draw level with him.

The woman's mare no match for their warhorses, they came alongside her, Durand on the right, the bearded knight opposite.

Gripping the saddle with his thighs, Durand released his left-handed grip on the reins and reached for the woman. It was his arm that hooked her, his opponent having failed to sooner transfer his sword to the opposite hand.

She screamed when Durand dragged her from the saddle, and hardly did he register she sounded more enraged than fearful than her pursuer caught her skirts and yanked her toward him.

The force of the pull causing Durand's mount to slam into the mare, he ground his teeth as ache shot up his leg.

Despite the woman's precarious state—suspended above her mare between two destriers—she flailed, clawed, kicked, and bucked so wildly Durand feared his mount would stumble and take them both to ground.

"Cease, woman!" he shouted and tossed aside his sword to take up the reins needed to better control his destrier. "I but give aid—"

One of her booted kicks caught the other knight in the face, and from his nose flowed crimson that ran into his teeth and beard. Spewing blood-colored curses, he once more wrenched at her skirts.

The sound of tearing fabric was met by her shriek. Still, the miscreant retained his hold—until she landed another kick that thrust him sideways. Then Durand had all of her.

Turning his destrier aside, he thrust the woman onto the fore of his saddle. Though no longer a bone tugged between two dogs, her disposition did not improve. As she continued to struggle, her long black hair whipping across his face, he hauled her back against his chest and glanced over his shoulder.

His men were routing the French king's vassals, including their bearded leader.

Still the woman fought, raking at the hand gripping her waist, jabbing her elbows into his mail-clothed ribs, reaching behind to scrape nails across his jaw and down his throat.

Feeling the great animal quiver and jerk beneath them, Durand shouted, "Behave, Lady! I am King Henry's man!"

That settled her. Whoever she was and whatever King Louis's men wanted with her, she would likely fare better with the English king across whose lands she fled.

Durand's breath of relief swirled white across the chill air. He had her in hand. Not a great feat compared to other services performed for King Henry and his queen, but—

She lurched forward against the arm he had begun to relax, kicked her heels into his horse's side, and slammed her elbow into her savior's left eye.

Durand was not one to ill-treat women, but as he reeled from the blow that threatened to unseat him, he had enough presence of mind to know his enraged destrier would not much longer suffer the lady. And that could prove deadly. Thus, he gave the vixen what she sought, flinging her away so she would not be trampled beneath frantic hooves.

The lady who landed face down in snow too thin to cushion her fall, cried out. The impact jarred her, causing pain to shoot head to toe and blood to coat her bitten tongue, but that did not keep her from rising. There was too much at stake to pity a body that would be heavily bruised within the hour regardless of how this day ended.

She made it onto her hands and knees, then her feet, and nearly toppled when her boot caught the lower edge of her bliaut that was more familiar with the ground than it ought to be. The count's man, Sir Renley, had done that, dragging at her skirt with such force the seams at her shoulders had torn through—not all the way, else her gown would be down around her feet.

Regaining her balance, she grimaced at the sound of metal on metal that evidenced some of the coins sewn into the hem of her mantle had worked free of their wrappings.

Blinking to clear her vision, she peered past the hair that had escaped its braid and saw the one who had tossed her to the ground was distant, evidence he was having difficulty calming his beast. But as she glared at horse and rider, they reined around and started back.

"Dear Lord!" She spun opposite. "I must—"

Must, but could not. Though the count's men, who had hounded her league after league, were pursued by a half dozen of those who had emerged from the wood, only one of the escort tasked with delivering her to safety remained astride. And he was in the midst of an abundance of knights who, like the one who had tossed her from his horse, were King Henry's men.

"So close," she whispered, then assured herself all was not lost. Plans had been made for such an occurrence. Now if *she of many words* could keep her mouth shut…

Holding her back to the knight who deserved whatever injuries she had inflicted, she smoothed her damp skirt, adjusted her skewed mantle, and draped the hood over her head in the hope that had she previously encountered any of Henry's men, they would not recognize her amid the shadows.

Lord, have mercy, she sent heavenward. *Save me from greedy men. See me safely to my father.*

Ignoring the pound of hooves behind, her next prayers were those of praise when her unhorsed escort were assisted to their feet. They stood no chance of taking a stand against so many, but she would not see them suffer for her. Hopefully, words would achieve what weapons could not.

Help me not speak where I ought to hold my tongue, Lord, she added. Then to aid Him in sealing her lips, she clenched her teeth so hard they hurt nearly as much as the rest of her.

The knight at her back slowed, but she kept her gaze on the others of his party. When the one who had tossed her from his horse reined in to her right, she did not look around. Her anger still boiled, and nothing good would come of unleashing more of that emotion. Better she seek to gain the man's favor—if such was possible in light of the blows she had landed to his body and pride.

In a civil, albeit sardonic voice, he said, "And here I feared you might have broken your neck, Lady."

Whose fault would that be, knave? she silently demanded, then compressed her lips lest her tongue tapped out the words.

Well done, her beloved Conrad praised from afar. *A civil tone across a civil tongue is full of the possibility of goodwill, my darling.*

A civil tongue was beyond her. Thus, a quiet tongue it must be.

"Are you hurt?" the knight asked as the others advanced.

Could so simple a word describe the discomfort felt in every joint, the sting of skin abraded by her bliaut digging into her shoulders, the ache behind her eyes?

Oh, Conrad, she silently bemoaned, *would that I were not so alone. That my world were yet the beautiful thing you built around me. That there was something true to laugh about. But the walls tumble down.*

"I hope you will forgive me for granting your wish to dismount," the knight persisted. "'Twas that or see us both beneath the hooves of a distraught warhorse." One that remained agitated, as told by its snorting and stamping.

She knew her struggles had so provoked the beast that the man and she could have suffered grave injury, perhaps even death, but she was in no mood to forgive.

She looked around and saw the knight had lowered his mail hood, revealing dark hair that sprang back from his brow. The side of his face into which she had thrust her elbow was livid and swelling around the eye. On either side of a short, trimmed beard encircling his mouth were bloody scores running down to his throat. And the hand he had dug into her waist further evidenced the rake of her nails. She had been vicious.

Though she told herself he deserved no better, remorse gripped her. If he and his companions had merely happened on the count's attempt to abduct her—had not been looking to do so themselves—gratitude was their due. If not for them, she would be Sir Renley's captive and once more torn from all she held dear.

Regardless, unless allowed to continue her journey, she would find herself in the company of King Henry, which could prove as detrimental as being held by the count.

As she foraged for conciliatory words, the knight's gaze probed her shadowed face, and he said, "I am Sir Durand Marshal. You are?"

He did not know? She narrowed her lids at the one who, until that moment, she had mostly looked near upon to note the damage she had inflicted. Many would think him handsome, and he was, but not to her taste. However, his golden eyes were captivating.

"As one who shall bear the marks of our encounter"—his mouth lifted toward a smile that made no sense in light of those marks—"I ought to at least have a name to blame them upon."

It might be his due, but he would not hear it from her.

"Sir Knight!" called the only one of her escort who had remained astride during their flight. "I am Sir Norris."

Relieved by his intercession, she looked to the middle-aged man flanked by King Henry's men. When he glanced at her, she discreetly inclined her head. All was in his hands, just as she had been instructed.

"I am Sir Durand of Queen Eleanor's personal guard. The lady is?"

"Of no consequence, Sir Durand. We—"

"Of no consequence? The Count of Verielle's men trespass upon King Henry's lands for a woman who warrants no name?"

Then he knew the identity of their pursuers. That boded ill.

With a smile so tight it looked more a grimace, Sir Norris dipped his chin. "I can but own I am charged with delivering the lady to her family."

"And yet you nearly lost her."

"Thus, we appreciate your aid. But now—"

"For what did the count seek her capture?"

Sir Norris's shrug was hesitant. "Who can say why men do such things? As ever, lawlessness abounds."

"Indeed." It was so drily spoken, she wondered why Sir Durand did not take the wineskin from his belt and wet his mouth.

Sir Norris sat taller. "As we are under the press of time, we must continue on our way."

"Which way is that?"

"'Tis of a private nature, Sir Durand."

"No longer. As it was across King Henry's lands you set your course, he will have the answers you refuse me."

Dear Lord, it shall come to pass, the woman lamented. *Out of the count's reach only to land in Henry's lap. And he and Eleanor shall know me.*

Anger was momentarily dampened by dread, but the former quickened. Being an emotion with which she had too little experience, she struggled to keep hold of it lest it made her situation worse.

"Sir Durand," Sir Norris said, "I am certain King Henry—"

"Nay, you are not." The knight looked past him. "Sir Jessup!"

A young man with a sword across his lap and one in a scabbard at his side, urged his horse forward. "Yours, sire." He passed the unsheathed blade to Sir Durand.

When did he lose it? she wondered. Whilst she fought Sir Renley and him as they sought to tear her in two?

"Retrieve the mare and see the lady astride." Her supposed savior jerked his chin at her horse whose flight had ended at the tree line. "Our dinner grows cold."

She caught her breath. Her life had taken another terrible turn, and he worried over stuffing his gullet?

Tongue, stay still, she entreated. *If not for me, then Conrad.*

Sir Jessup grunted. "If dinner is yet to be had."

I hope 'tis ice in your mouth, she fumed as that one moved toward her mare. *May it go down like fouled snow.*

"And here are the rest of us," Sir Durand announced as pounding hooves heralded the return of those who had chased away her pursuers.

Though the possibility of escaping an audience with King Henry had been slight, now it was hopeless. Unless God was of a mind to right this wrong, England might remain a distant shore.

Shortly, Sir Jessup assisted her into the saddle. Though she rarely required aid in mounting, being no slight thing and Conrad having come around to her way of thinking, she ached so deeply she was grateful for the aid—and that he did not appear to catch the ring of coins in her mantle's hem.

Accepting the reins passed to her, she peered out from beneath her hood at Sir Durand.

"To Bayeux!" he shouted.

Despite his yearn to fill his belly, he set an easy pace that, by the time the great fortress came into sight an hour later, had allowed her to calm her frustration sufficiently to play the role for which she was best known—a most unusual wife.

2

She was hardly petite and more pretty than not—providing she did not open her mouth without benefit of a smile. In terms of her prospects, that smile was so bright and broad it could be forgiven the small gap between her front teeth. But her laugh...

Ladies were not meant to express joy in that manner. It was too loud and quick, and when it eased, often it was but to take in more air with a gasp husky at its start and almost shrill at its end. Then more laughter.

From alongside the stairs on the eastern end of the great hall, Durand had watched her a quarter hour as she conversed with knights gathered around her before the cavernous hearth. Hers was a group absent other ladies, many of whom kept their distance whilst watching the peculiar one in their midst and speaking near with one another.

They could be excused their prattle, Durand supposed. The lady *was* fascinating.

Of course, he was interested in her only as long as she did not become interested in him. Though never had he been so often in the company of women than since entering King Henry's service three years past, and others envied him the opportunities for flirtations, kisses, and caresses, none of Eleanor's ladies moved his heart with longing as once—nearly twice—it was moved. And that was a good thing, for it kept beyond arm's reach the temptation and sin that had almost been the end of him when he served the Wulfrith family and felt for Lady Beatrix—

The woman laughed again at something a knight spoke at her ear, tossing her chin high and causing her veil to shift and allow a glimpse of dark hair.

Again, he wondered who she was and her purpose at court. A guest who had accompanied her husband to keep Christmas with their sovereign? The daughter of a vassal who hoped to add his indelicate offspring to the ranks of Eleanor's ladies?

That last made Durand chuckle. If the queen had agreed to take the woman into her household, she would soon return her. Indeed, were Eleanor present now, she would put an end to the lady's behavior.

He sighed. Having been absent a fortnight to attend to Henry's business in Rouen—a boon considering whose visit to Bayeux he had avoided—he would have to bring himself current on what had transpired. And the men entrusted with Sir Norris's party when the king had summoned Durand upon his return, would oblige him over tankards of ale. Providing they could be coaxed away from that woman.

He strode forward, and she glanced his way, glanced again, and lowered her smile.

His face, over which Henry had not been quietly amused, probably offended. But he did not care. He was simply grateful his eye had not swollen shut.

When he was a stride from the gathering, the woman turned to the knight who came alongside her.

"My lady." He bent over her hand. "I am Sir Oliver."

There was her smile again, bright even in profile, and it stayed Durand from ordering the knights behind whom he paused to take drink with him.

Sir Oliver straightened. "You are?"

She clicked her tongue. "Ah, Sir Oliver, do not pretend you have not inquired. I laugh too often and loud for the curious not to ask after me, even if only to know what name to pair with a curse."

Her admirers laughed.

Durand did not. As much as he did not care to be intrigued by a woman, he was—and appalled to hear her speak thus.

"A curse?" The knight's eyes lowered to her chest. Despite her bodice's modest cut, it did not hide that she was well endowed. "I cannot imagine cursing you, dear lady."

She slid her hand from his. "Oh do imagine, Sir Oliver. It makes for interesting thought which might otherwise be…dull." Another smile, but this one did not fool Durand.

The knight was misbehaving as much as she, and though it was unlikely the lady knew her would-be suitor was wed, it was obvious she did not care to be looked upon in such a manner.

One redeeming quality, Durand allowed.

Sir Oliver's brow rumpled, as if he questioned whether to be offended, but then the lady laughed, and he smiled.

She turned forward again and inclined her head. "Sir Durand Marshal."

Barely containing his surprise, he berated himself. Of course she knew him, just as he ought to know her. In his defense, he had not looked near upon the lady. Other matters had been too pressing—reaching her ahead of the count's men, snatching her from her horse, keeping them from landing beneath his destrier's hooves. And when he could have become familiar with her countenance, he had not been inclined and had allowed her to hide beneath the hood. Too, there was a marked difference between their first encounter when she had been quiet beyond the usual reach of a woman's tongue—except for screams and shrieks—and this encounter that exceeded the reach of any woman's tongue he had known.

Still, you are a Wulfen-trained knight, Durand Marshal, he silently chided. *Was not judicious observation among your lessons?*

The lady smiled at the other knights. Then with a rustle of unsullied skirts that showed her journey across Henry's lands were planned well enough to allow for a change of clothes, she stepped forward—stiffly, as expected considering the means by which she had dismounted his destrier.

The knights on either side of him moved aside, and she halted before him. Though she stood several inches shorter than he, she was no small thing, but neither was she of an ungainly height. And just as she was generously endowed above, her hips were defined past a slender waist.

Tilting her head to the side, she considered his bruised and scratched face. "I should apologize."

That he did not expect. Though irked by her resistance to his rescue, he understood she could not have known he spoke true in claiming to be Henry's man.

He summoned a practiced smile, just enough to appear genial without encouraging affection to which many of the queen's ladies were partial. "As should I," he said. Of course, in a manner, he had. After tossing her distant from his destrier's hooves, he had expressed the hope she would forgive him.

The lady raised her eyebrows.

He raised his.

When moments passed and neither voiced remorse and dozens of eyes made themselves felt, she laughed. But the sound that rolled off her tongue did not ring true.

Had it before? Had he been too distant to detect the false note? Or was this laughter exclusive to him? If not the latter and her mirth was forced, it was understandable considering how sore she must be.

Her laughter ended on a sigh that sustained the bow of her mouth. "It seems we are at an impasse, Sir Durand."

"You make it sound adversarial."

She put her head to the side. "What would you call it?"

He shifted his weight. Never had he met a lady so outspoken, albeit in a playful manner—

Deceptively playful, he amended. The woman he had wrested from her horse might be the same physically, but she was not the same in spirit. She had come about too quickly. But he would banter with her and discover what game she played.

"What would I call it if not an impasse?" He shrugged. "Perhaps 'tis more a matter of one offense canceling another."

Her lips twitched. "I rather like that." Though some might name the glint in her bright green eyes mischief, it was too sharp. Pressing her shoulders back, she winced and clasped her hands at her waist—the left fit with a wedding band. "Tell, Sir Durand, are you kin to the renowned William Marshal?"

"Distantly."

She nodded. "I assume you now have a name with which to credit the marks I bestowed."

That which she had earlier refused. "Unlike Sir Oliver, I have not had time to inquire after one who laughs too often and loud. I have been with the king these past hours."

She searched his face with the intensity of one in pursuit of a lie, dipped her chin. "Then I shall tell it. You may call me—"

"The queen," murmured the men and women in the hall.

Those who were not facing the stairs, including Durand, turned to receive Eleanor with bows and curtsies.

Trailed by two of her ladies, King Henry's wife smiled and waved to indicate the occupants of the hall should return to their conversations. When her gaze settled on Durand, she adjusted her course.

Those around him dispersing, though he yet felt the nameless woman at his back, he bowed again when Eleanor halted before him.

After a quiet word to her ladies, who quickly departed, she said, "We are pleased you are returned to us, Sir Durand, and wroth with our lord husband for not consulting us ere dispatching you to Rouen."

Henry had not? Though Durand had once numbered among the king's knights, longer he had numbered among the queen's personal guard, and when Henry called upon him to perform one service or another, it was with her knowledge and blessing.

"I am sorry if it proved an inconvenience, Your Majesty."

"It did, but we forgive the king and you." The glimmer in her eyes evidencing pleasure, he guessed she had not been surprised by his departure. She stepped forward and looked close upon the damage done his face. "This seems recent."

Certain she had been apprised of the incursion on her husband's lands and had already granted the one behind him an audience, he stepped aside to reveal the woman. "A small cost for delivering the lady out of Count Verielle's hands."

"Small?" Eleanor's eyebrows arched. "It is good you are not as vain as some, Sir Durand." She looked to the woman. "Ah, here is the one my ladies tell makes mischief among our men."

Durand frowned. The two had not spoken?

The lady slowly bowed, the depth of which Durand suspected was more a reflection of her aches than a lack of deference. "Your Majesty, I thank you for allowing Sir Norris to speak in my stead. Blessedly, I am mostly recovered."

Eleanor motioned for her to rise. "We understand your company is much sought after."

The woman smiled, this time not enough to show teeth. "I do like to laugh, Your Majesty."

"We remember your penchant for such, though you were ten and five when last we met and the habit was still fairly acceptable for one so young. That was…ten years ago."

Were the lady shamed by the rebuke, her color did not reflect it. However, her tone was all respect. "Henceforth I shall endeavor to temper such displays of joy, Your Majesty."

"Then you are welcome at court, Lady Beatrix."

Durand jerked. Over the years, he had encountered other ladies who bore the name that always moved him to memories of one of petite figure and golden tresses, but never had there been a poorer fit.

"I thank you, Your Majesty," said the woman of good height, curvaceous form, and dark tresses. "I do not mean to sound impertinent, but if you are agreeable, I prefer to be called Lady Beata."

It still did not sit well with Durand, but better that name.

The queen's quiet drew his regard, and he saw she had narrowed her eyes. Just when it seemed Eleanor's silence might grow into one of grave disapproval, she said, "We believe there is another name by which you are better known. One that speaks more to the devilry you cast about our hall."

"So there is, Your Majesty. But alas, that name was altered this past year."

The queen's face softened. "Our belated condolences."

"Gratefully accepted, Your Majesty."

Irritated by the riddle batted between the two, Durand ground his teeth.

"Lady Beata it shall be," the queen said. "It is as your husband called you, hmm?"

A widow, then.

"He did, Your Majesty."

"We shall speak further, Lady Beata, but now we must relieve you of Sir Durand."

The woman glanced at him, inclined her head.

As he fell into step with the queen, she said, "You are not in this moment, are you, my gallant monk?"

He did not like being called that, but he hid his aversion more easily than when she named him that before others. "I do feel as if elsewhere, Your Majesty—as though that lady and you seek to tangle me in confusion."

She did not speak again until he handed her into a chair before the hearth. Peering up at him where he stood with his back to the fire, near enough their conversation would not carry, she said, "Tell, Sir Durand, what do you think of Lady Beatrix?"

A pity she did not use the woman's preferred name outside of her company. "I know too little of her to think anything of her."

"Be it so, you know of her."

"I do not, Your Majesty. Until you spoke her name, I had none by which to call her."

Eleanor's eyebrows rose.

He inclined his head. "Her man, Sir Norris, would not divulge her identity when we aborted Count Verielle's attack. Neither would the lady speak it. Not until this eve did a word pass her lips in my hearing."

Laughter escaped Eleanor. "No word out of... What was it her husband called her? Ah, *she of many words.*" She shook her head. "Another curiosity to ponder alongside her flight and the count's attempt to abduct her."

"May I inquire into Sir Norris's account of their journey?"

"He told that, as the lady is widowed, he is charged with escorting her to England so she may aid her father's young wife in keeping his household. As for Count Verielle's men giving chase, Sir Norris suggested they may have been acting of their own accord to attain the lady's purse." She smiled thinly. "There is much more to it, we think."

"I agree, Your Majesty."

"Though Verielle has taken several mistresses, it is hard to believe he would be so desperate to resort to abduction. Unless, like many a man, he is enamored with the lady—"

"Enamored? Truly?" Durand was not in the habit of interrupting the queen, but this surprised. Fascinated was one thing, enamored quite another.

"Truly. Though her easy behavior repels men who believe a woman's worth is measured by how well she orders his household, fills his bed, and births his children, many are attracted to her." Eleanor gifted him a brilliant smile. "You are astonished. But then, we have yet to remedy your ignorance."

Reminded of her belief he knew *of* the lady, he waited.

"Though we wager much of France has heard of her, most know Lady Beatrix as The Vestal Wife—now The Vestal Widow."

Durand had heard of Conrad Fauvel's bride, and not only in France. Whilst serving the keeper of a castle upon the barony of Wiltford before entering the king's service, there had been talk of Baron Rodelle's daughter.

Said to be over forty years younger than her husband, it was rumored she served the old man in the capacity of daughter rather than bedmate. And yet this *daughter,* having no need to attract a husband, had been indulged, in some ways as if she were a son—ever at the count's side, regardless of the matter under discussion, and allowed to offer thoughts and opinions on things best left to men. Thus, the girl grew into a woman who others said was too comfortable in the company of men. And that she had demonstrated this day.

"As told," Eleanor said, "you know *of* her."

"I do."

"And so you know her father."

"Only by sight. I served the keeper of one of his lesser castles."

She nodded. "Tell, are you among those who approve or disapprove of the lady?"

"I have no cause to feel one way or the other." The only thing of which he was certain was she was not the sort to whom he was drawn.

Eleanor considered him. "So, my gallant monk, do you think it was for love the count sent his men to capture the lady?"

"I cannot guess, Your Majesty."

"You can. You just do not wish to."

Certes, he was uncomfortable with talk of love. Hoping to end his audience with her, he forced a smile.

She snorted. "Oh, be of use, Sir Durand."

Still, he waited her out as was best when she persisted past his ability to indulge her probing and teasing.

"Perhaps lust," she suggested. "After all, a man does not have to be in love to so desire a woman he risks much for her. What think you?"

That he was even less comfortable with talk of lust. Memories of his own, with which he continued to struggle, causing his center to coil, he maintained his silence.

Eleanor dropped her head back and considered the ceiling. "If not lust, then vengeance? Did she wrong the count? Ah, hold!" Her eyes flew back to Durand. "Count Verielle's sister is wed to the heir of Lady

Beatrix's departed husband. There could be ill feeling there, that lady having long played second lady to The Vestal Wife."

A possibility, Durand concurred, though not one he would long entertain.

"Even so, abduction is too extreme for so petty an offense, especially dealt by one with much to lose. But had Count Verielle something considerable to gain..." The queen's eyes widened. "Were Lady Beatrix an heiress, abduction would fit—that he hoped to force her to wed to gain her fortune."

To which Eleanor could relate. Following the annulment of her marriage to King Louis nine years past, she had once more become the most eligible woman in France. Thus, during the return to her vast lands in Poitou, she was forced to outrun the Count of Blois who sought to make her his wife. Knowing she required a protector, she had secured a husband of her own choosing, wedding Henry Plantagenet who later made good his claim to the English throne.

The queen expelled a sound of disgust. "Alas, Count Verielle is already wed, and Lady Beatrix is no heiress." Irritation pinching her face, she looked about the hall and narrowed her lids.

Durand followed her gaze to the one whose name better fit another woman. The lady walked alongside her man, Sir Norris, who bent near as if to catch whispered words. Moments later, the two entered an alcove where torchlight ventured only enough to reveal the place was occupied.

"At least, as far as we know, she is no heiress."

Durand looked back at the queen, and the gleam in her eyes made him pity The Vestal Wife—now Widow—who was likely unprepared for the depth of Eleanor's interest.

3

"Were you believed?" Beata asked.

Standing apart from her in the alcove, Sir Norris hesitated. "I do not think I gave her cause to disbelieve me."

But as Beata had realized the first time she met Eleanor whilst the great heiress was yet Queen of France, the lady was shrewd—so much that even in the absence of offense, she could leave the taste of wrongdoing in one's mouth, Conrad had said. Doubtless, Sir Norris was experiencing the same bitter patch that coated Beata's tongue.

Wishing she had not allowed him to persuade her to beg off standing before the queen upon their arrival, she asked, "Will we be allowed to depart on the morrow?"

"She did not agree nor disagree, said only 'tis a foul time of year to cross the channel."

"But we must."

"Aye, my lady. That which your father holds close will not likely remain so much longer, especially if—"

"This I know," Beata said sharply and regretted there was not enough light in which to offer an apologetic smile. "Forgive me. 'Tis just that I can hardly catch my breath."

It felt as if every bit of air lodged in her throat no matter how deeply she drew it in. Though heartsick over Conrad's passing a year ago, she had begun to rise above her loss and smile and laugh again as she settled into widowhood. If not for the news Sir Norris had delivered, within a month she would have departed the great castle where she had lived nearly a dozen years and gone to live on the dower property Conrad had provided her.

Now, just as when she had left her home in England to do her duty, she must leave her home in France. However, there was one good thing in this, but only if she could reach her father with King Henry and his queen unaware of her real purpose for answering his summons. And that one thing, in which she had a say, was all she had to hold to.

Sir Norris blew out a breath. "I wish this burden did not fall to you, my lady."

She believed him. Though genial enough, he was uncomfortable with her outspokenness and expressions of delight and humor. The day he had come for her—before revealing she must return to England—he had grimaced at her contributions to conversations led by Conrad's eldest son and heir, while his younger companions struggled against smiling and showing too much interest.

"But it does fall to me." She slid a hand inside her veil and rubbed her neck whose ache was more Sir Durand's fault than the angst that grew each day since learning what was required of her. "Do you think it possible to steal away from court?"

"You would be missed, my lady, and we would be overtaken. Even could we escape, 'twould be an offense your father would not wish visited on our sovereign."

Especially since what he planned would breed wrath enough, Beata conceded. "What should we do?"

"Wait, during which you give the king and queen no reason to doubt our tale. And play The Vestal Wife as is expected of you."

At the realization he granted her permission to engage in behavior he deemed unseemly, she longed to laugh. "Now The Vestal Widow, Sir Norris."

He inclined his head.

"What of the ship?" she asked. "If we are too long delayed, will it sail without us?"

"Not only did your father pay well for it to wait, but he withheld half the payment until you are on English soil. Providing another does not tempt the captain with better, the ship will not leave without you."

That was not much comfort. "Providing? The man lacks integrity?"

"Without question. But such a lack and a goodly amount of arrogant courage is needed in such dealings that could make one an enemy of the king."

"Then even if Henry and Eleanor permit me to leave, we have no guarantee of reaching England. Our ship may have sailed."

"Not likely. The weather has been too poor to risk the channel. But worry not, we shall get you home to your father."

Fatigued as much by her flight as a lack of adequate food, Beata smoothed her skirts with trembling hands and wished she had eaten more of the viands delivered to her abovestairs. "Is it acceptable for me to return to my chamber and rest ere supper? I am a bit out of sorts."

He turned his head, and she also looked to the hearth. Minutes earlier, Eleanor's audience was exclusive to Sir Durand. Now she was surrounded by a half dozen ladies. And the knight who had delivered The Vestal Widow from one captivity into another, stood behind the queen.

Beata groaned when she saw his gaze was on the alcove.

"You are watched, my lady."

"Aye, all the more reason I would go abovestairs."

"Then do so now whilst the queen is occupied."

As she stepped forward, he rasped, "Better you present as joyful rather than anxious."

Containing the height and breadth of the smile she summoned lest it appear false, she exited the shadows, blinked prettily at Sir Durand as if surprised to find herself beneath his regard, and turned toward the stairs.

As she traversed the hall, she was approached by one of the noblemen who had gathered around her before Sir Durand's appearance. No sooner did she extricate herself than Sir Oliver—he who could not imagine cursing her—moved toward her.

She quickened her step and ascended the stairs. At the first turning, she halted and set her back against the curved wall, splayed her palms against the cool stones, and lowered her lids.

"Almighty, I am pressed on all sides," she whispered. "Pray, make a path clear enough to set my feet upon." She exhaled, and hearing a scrape on stone, opened her eyes.

One moment her pursuer stood a step down, the next he did not. "Sir Oliver!" She started to push off the wall, but he drew so near she could not move without brushing against him.

"I am pleased to find you waiting for me." He showed teeth that lacked only sharp canines to make him appear the wolf to the lamb he wished her to be.

Courage, she counseled as she was moved toward a dark corner of her mind carved out of a terrible childhood dream that had resolved once she wed Conrad. Or mostly. When a man pressed attentions on her, the mold-blackened leaves heaped in that corner stirred.

Seeking to propel her thoughts opposite the place that had transformed the girl she had been into one so joyless she had not known herself, she gave a laugh that cracked straight down its center.

Get yourself in hand, she tried again. *You have been cornered before. This is no different.*

But it was. Ever she had been under Conrad's protection. Thus, when she proved unreceptive to the advances of her husband's guests, she had laughed and teased her way out of the corners into which they backed her. Here she was alone. But not defenseless.

She pushed her lips into a small, sad smile. "If only, Sir Oliver." She perused his pale face. "Alas, I but paused to ease my aching head."

He placed a hand on either side of her, lightly settled his body against hers, and on ale-scented breath said, "You need not play coy with me, my lady."

The leaves stirred. "Sir Oliver, you would do yourself a kindness to remove your person from mine."

Though outside of violence, she could make her feelings no clearer, he chuckled, tugged the veil from her hair, and lowered his mouth toward hers.

Granting herself the right to defend herself, she positioned her knee to haul it up between his legs.

"Sir Oliver!" a voice shot up the stairway. "I am certain I did not misunderstand the lady's request that you remove your person from hers."

The knight swung around to face the one who stood three steps below.

Though Sir Durand's stance was relaxed, there was threat in the hand he rested on his sword's pommel.

Sir Oliver gave a tight laugh. "The lady and I but discuss the details, Sir Durand."

The queen's man swept his gaze over Beata. "Which details?"

Sir Oliver shrugged. "As you know—rather, *ought* to know—timing is all."

What should Sir Durand know? Beata wondered.

"So it is. Hence, I recommend you think well on this timing and honor the lady's wishes. As you *ought* to know, the queen looks ill on any who think to molest one of her guests."

"You read too much into this." The knight looked across his shoulder. "There is naught amiss here. Is there, my lady?"

"Naught amiss." She smiled wide. "Were I a strumpet…a trollop…a whore."

Color rose up his neck and his eyes darkened, but she stared back as Conrad had advised she do during such encounters. And was not the first to look away.

"I shall leave you." Sir Oliver began his descent.

"Pray, forgive my lapse in neglecting to inquire after your wife," Sir Durand said. "I trust she has recovered from providing you another child?"

The knight looked around. "She is well." He shifted his gaze to Beata. "And most eager for my return."

Is that meant to tempt me? she wondered.

"Then best you not disappoint her," Sir Durand said.

The knight continued down the stairs and out of sight.

Though Beata's sigh came naturally, she let it linger in hopes of easing the awkwardness between Sir Durand and her. "I am grateful for your aid," she said. "At least, I think I am."

When he ascended but two of the three steps so their eyes were nearly level, she appreciated the consideration, and not only because his proximity lacked the threat of Sir Oliver's. Her husband had impressed on her the importance of keeping enough distance between one's self and another to avoid tipping the head back. A short though solidly built man, he had known the danger of relinquishing even a small measure of power.

"You *think* you are grateful?" Sir Durand said.

Previously, she had looked near upon him, but only now realized she had not truly seen him. She liked his frown. Not every man could express such confusion and still be pleasing to the eye. And yet this one, whom she had earlier dismissed as not to her taste, was attractive—even with the damage done his face.

She arched an eyebrow. "I believe the only reason you arrived in time to save that miscreant from being unmanned is that you were set upon me. Queen Eleanor, hmm?" She who had surely revealed that the one tossed from his horse was the near scandalous lady wed to Conrad Fauvel.

His frown easing, he bent and retrieved her veil. "I fear you are right, Lady."

"'Tis good you are honest."

He held out the veil, and when she plucked it from him, said, "Is it your habit to cause a furor wherever you go?"

The charge was not new. "It does seem that way."

Her words returned a frown to his face, and she wondered what it would take to summon a real smile rather than the studied one he had presented in the hall. She did not believe it was solely disapproval that made the turning of his lips less than sincere. What, then?

"Aye," he said, "methinks it is that way."

Then he thought her behavior had invited Sir Oliver's attention. Unfortunately, he was not entirely wrong. Some men interpreted her enjoyment of good company and talk as evidence she was not averse to a tryst. But as The Vestal Wife, she had only ever known such freedom. Freedom not extended to The Vestal Widow.

"I will see you to your chamber, Lady." He started up the stairs.

Beata followed, and when he paused at the landing to allow her to draw alongside, kept her eyes forward as she led the way down the corridor—and with each step became increasingly aware of him.

Durand Marshal was no giant of a man like Count Verielle's bearded Sir Renley, but he was built well and carried himself with strength and confidence that told luck played no part in him snatching her from his opponent. But there was something else that made her keenly aware of him. Whatever it was, it was so uncomfortable she knew it best she quickly shed his company.

She halted before her chamber. "I appreciate your escort, Sir Durand."

He dipped his chin and pivoted.

Beata was not displeased it was so easy to send him away—it should be thus for all men—but her behavior panged her. "Sir Durand!"

As if he had no wish to prolong their encounter, he slowly turned, and she caught the flash of jewels in the hilt of a dagger on his belt. "Lady?"

Am I so unpalatable? she wondered. "I thank you for all your help."

"I am glad to be of service."

"And I am sorry."

He raised his eyebrows.

"For the injuries done you in routing my pursuers."

His mouth curved. "Be assured, I do not fault you. And 'tis nothing that will not heal."

"Forsooth, I did not know your intent and feared…" Words failing her—most unusual—she jerked her shoulders.

The movement drew his gaze. Once more frowning, he stepped near, and awareness moved through her when he lifted her bodice off her collarbone. "What is this?"

Something breathless, she thought. But when she glanced down, she saw the abraded skin and bruising that had spread and deepened to dark purple and green. "Oh, it has worsened!"

"Worsened?"

He was almost as near as Sir Oliver had been, but she did not find herself drawn toward that dark corner. So far was she from it, her gaze was tempted to his mouth. But she resisted, knowing he might think she issued an invitation.

"Aye, 'tis not only discomfort I suffer at being tossed from a horse, but being wrenched between two knights. My bliaut and chemise cut into my shoulders."

"I apologize." His eyes rose to hers, and she saw flecks of brown amidst the gold. "But I hope you agree it was better I not allow the miscreant to carry you away."

"I do." Her voice that normally suffered no lack of volume was almost a whisper, but well enough heard it moved his eyes to her lips. And she sensed he had received the invitation she had not meant to send.

He dropped his hand and drew back. "Forgive me, I should not be so familiar."

Fearing he sensed her regret, she quipped, "Aye, first you ought to call me Lady Beata, which you have yet to do though twice you have saved me from men of ill intent."

His face closed up as if she rebuked him for being too familiar with her name. "I am oft lacking in the recall of given names." He dipped his chin. "I shall leave you to your rest."

Following his departure, she stared at the emptiness he left and tried to find a fit for him amongst those to whom she had been exposed during her marriage. Considering what had *not* transpired between them, he was not one who saw her as a challenge and sought firsthand knowledge of whether she was that rare creature, The Vestal Wife. Nor was he one of those comfortable and open-minded enough to gladly spend time in her company. That left those who disdained her for overstepping the bounds imposed on her sex, comprised of men who grudgingly tolerated her company and those who could not and made little effort to be discreet in distancing themselves.

Raking fingers through her braid she ought to have covered upon the return of her veil, she murmured, "Well, at least I need not worry about suffering your attentions, Sir Durand."

It was a lie—a pernicious failing that, goaded by dread of exposing one's self, sweeps over the tongue and off the lips just as one recognizes it as sin.

Queen Eleanor had not set him upon Count Fauvel's widow. He had done that when Sir Oliver followed her abovestairs.

With each stride that carried him across the hall, he had berated himself for interfering in something not of his concern, especially since the lady presented as one who might be agreeable to a tryst. Hence, he had hoped Eleanor would call him back. But though too perceptive not to notice his retreat, she had let him go.

Had she seen the unapologetic adulterer follow The Vestal Widow? Very possible. Thus, as often happened at her suggestion, since she had the luxury of watching over her ladies whilst he watched over her, he had accepted responsibility for protecting a woman's virtue—he, Durand Marshal, dishonorably discharged from service to the renowned Wulfriths. Ever the irony of that...

He would suffer Eleanor's amusement once he returned to her. But not just yet.

He stepped off the stairs. Avoiding looking directly at the queen lest she beckoned, he confirmed his men were not remiss in watching over her and continued to the iron-banded doors beyond which lay cold air that would allow him to feel every blessed breath.

"Sire," the porter said with a deferential nod, then swung open the right-hand door.

The heavily cloaked porter outside, this one tasked with granting entrance to the hall, also inclined his head to acknowledge the queen's man. "'Twill be a painfully chill eve." His breath clouded the air. "If yer of a mind to linger, ye'd do well to fetch a mantle."

Durand did not take offense at the advice which few commoners dared dispense to nobles. He knew the older man to be kindly, though that kindliness would vanish should an enemy seek to enter the donjon. Before an interloper could draw his next breath, the sword at the porter's side would come to hand, ready for gutting.

"A short walk only," Durand said and descended the steps.

Despite the nearing of night, the inner bailey teemed with castle folk. Thus, he headed for the wall-walk atop the inner wall that knew only the tread and murmurings of patrolling men-at-arms.

"Sir Durand!"

As ever, that voice stopped him, and he almost yielded to another of his failings. Setting his tongue against cursing, he looked to the gatehouse's open portal. Beneath it strode a warrior—of note as much for the color of hair that belonged on one older than his thirty and six years to Durand's thirty and two, as for the height and breadth made more imposing by a fur-lined mantle.

Durand settled into his heels and suppressed a grimace when a narrowing of eyes evidenced the man noticed the scratched and bruised face gained en route to Bayeux.

"Baron Wulfrith," Durand acknowledged his former liege as the warrior halted before him.

With enough of a smile to evidence the one he bestowed it upon was forgiven as much as possible, the baron said, "I had thought our paths would not cross."

"Neither did I expect it, my lord."

Wulfrith tilted his head, causing the light of torches that sought to ward off night's descent to course his silver hair. "Do you think they conspired?"

He referred to the queen and king. It had been convenient that with Wulfrith's impending arrival at court, the one who had betrayed the baron was given reprieve from once more facing the betrayed. But regardless of whether it was by God's hand, royal machinations, or mere coincidence Durand was absent, he had been grateful. His error had been in believing Wulfrith had returned to England by now.

So had Eleanor and Henry prevented a meeting between the two men, showing Durand mercy for the sin the Wulfriths had endeavored to ensure others could only guess at?

Durand raised his eyebrows. "With the king and queen, most things are possible."

"Quite, but my only regret in meeting you is my inability to sail for home though I have concluded the earl's business. Twice I have boarded ship to make the crossing and been forced to return to court. It is a treacherous time of year to put out upon the narrow sea."

So it was. The lady who had fled Count Verielle's men knew not the depth of gratitude she ought to feel for her rescue. "Then you shall spend Christmas in France, my lord."

"Not if my prayers are answered. I have just received tidings that if day dawns bright and clear as expected, the ships will sail."

Durand glanced heavenward. Clouds moved across the darkening blue, but there was more sky and awakening stars to be seen.

A good thing, not only for Wulfrith but the woman Durand had just left—providing Eleanor's cat to The Vestal Widow's mouse did not so entertain that the queen denied the lady permission to leave court.

"I shall add my prayers to yours, my lord."

"I thank you." Wulfrith glanced at the donjon. "You are content with serving the queen?"

There could be but one answer, and it was mostly true, providing he did not indulge in his longing for a life of greater challenge and meaning. "I am."

Though Wulfrith's eyes were only as readable as he allowed, disbelief flickered in their depths. Still, he let the matter be—just as he had not inquired into the injuries to Durand's face. "How fares your family?" he asked.

"Well." As Durand had confirmed during a brief visit before concluding King Henry's business in Rouen. As the last of three surviving sons, he was of little consequence to his sire, but his parents were always pleased to see him.

The baron waited, and Durand knew what was expected of him. He had learned the lesson at Wulfen Castle when he was a lowly page who revered this man's father as England's foremost warrior and trainer of knights—*Be of good courtesy with one's lessers, equals, and betters.*

Ache though Durand did for the restorative breaths denied him, he truly wished an answer to the question he ought to have asked sooner, "Your wife and children, my lord?"

"By God's grace, we are well. And by Christmas, we shall add to our numbers when Lady Annyn gifts me with another son or daughter. More reason to pray for good weather."

Durand grinned. "You are to be congratulated."

"I thank you."

"And your brothers and sisters, Lord Wulfrith?" he pushed himself further, though that last roused memories of she who embodied the name that was an ill fit for the much-too-spirited woman he had tossed from his horse—Lady Beatrix Wulfrith, now Beatrix D'Arci.

And not far behind the image of the one he had once loved was her sister, now Lady Gaenor Lavonne who had loved Durand as she should not have. Hence, his fall from grace.

A hand settled on his shoulder, and he was ashamed he had to bring the brother of the two women into focus—and more so that the feared warrior Durand had become had drifted away like the squire he no longer was.

"Also well," the baron said, "as are their children."

"I am glad to hear it."

Wulfrith stepped back, and as his gaze lowered, Durand became aware of what was too late to rectify.

"I am pleased you continue to wear it upon your person," the baron said.

Durand considered the pommel beneath his hand—that of the Wulfrith dagger, awarded to those worthy to receive knighthood at Wulfen Castle.

"It is a reminder of who I trained to be ere I forgot," he said before pride silenced the truth. "A reminder of what I aspire to be again."

"Were you not once more the warrior to whom I awarded that dagger, Sir Durand, you would not serve the Queen of England."

That still surprised. Though certain Henry and Eleanor knew the *gallant monk* had once been far from gallant and even farther from a monk—that they knew the extent of his sin even if only by way of conjecture—he was entrusted with safeguarding the queen amidst her ladies.

Almost pained with relief over Wulfrith's assurance he was once more worthy, Durand's mouth moved toward a smile. But then came pride, too quick to pass through the door thrown wide by relief. He too much wanted Wulfrith's acceptance and to congratulate himself on gaining it.

Do not hold tight to that which you long for, he silently recited what he aspired to live by. *Far less it aches to have it slip through your fingers than torn from your grasp.*

He let a shadow of a smile onto his lips. "I am grateful for your faith in my honor and ability, Baron Wulfrith. And now I shall take my leave. It has been a day without end, and before it becomes as long a night, I shall seek respite."

Wulfrith inclined his head. Torchlight once more coursing the silver hair bound back off his brow, he said, "Lesson sixteen, is it not?"

The first imparted by this man when Durand's squire's training with the father had passed to the Wulfrith heir, a lesson meant to tame the restless young man who had struggled to master impulsivity as required to gain his spurs.

Seek the still of prayer that you may know yourself and make order of what is required of you.

"Aye, sixteen. I shall see you at supper, my lord." Durand stepped around Wulfrith and, as he strode toward the wall-walk, was glad the baron and he had crossed paths. And for the reminder that made him seek prayer to aid in weathering the storm he sensed ahead.

4

Supper was tedious, though never had Beata seen such lavish presentation of what was typically a light and informal meal. It was even more impressive than the feast over which she had marveled the one time she accompanied Conrad to King Louis's court. That memory made her wince.

Her husband had advised her to temper her exuberance, but at ten and six, she was too foolish to heed his warning that Louis was of a prudish bent—more, the king had yet to recover from news that, following annulment of his marriage to Eleanor, the heiress to the largest of the French duchies had wed the young duke of Normandy without her former husband's consent. Thus, King Louis publicly admonished Conrad for Beata's expressions of joy, saying if she was not taken in hand, the count would suffer as Eleanor made him suffer. Conrad and Beata had left court the next morn.

Grateful to be seated at a lower table distant from King Henry and his queen, unconcerned it reflected her reduced status as a widow, Beata folded her hands atop the linen tablecloth, while below it her feet tapped out impatience. It was past time to end the meal, the ravaged viands having been removed and goblets and tankards upended time and again by those whose jovial mood almost suffocated.

Under normal circumstances, she loved to converse and laugh, and though it was not unusual for wine to be present when she indulged in lively conversation, her own joy did not depend on drink.

With a sigh, she once more picked out Sir Norris seated between her father's younger knights at a table below hers.

He acknowledged her with a nod and looked to the dais.

She did the same. The king and queen presided over the high table, flanked by high-ranking nobles, most of whom would likely remain in Bayeux several weeks to enjoy the festivities and favors for which the Christmas court was known. God willing, Beata would not be here that long.

Please Lord, she sent heavenward, *be willing. And may there soon be an end to this meal.*

She longed for further ease of her pained joints and bruised places. More, she ached for quiet. However, until she could slip from the hall with none the wiser, she must remain.

Leveling her gaze on Henry, who was too content perched above his audience to grant them leave to quit the tables, she saw his attention had returned to the one seated to his right. The powerfully built man could not be beyond thirty and five, yet he possessed more silver hair than Conrad at his passing.

The knight beside Beata had informed her this was the warrior known England over and much of France as Baron Wulfrith. For generations, his family had trained young men into the worthiest of knights. And like Beata's family, they had supported Stephen's claim to England's throne—until Baron Wulfrith wed a woman who stood on the side of Henry. Whatever that tale, which her dear friend, a troubadour knight, rued he knew little of, Beata would love to hear it. Just as she longed to hear what was now spoken between the baron and the one who had wrested the crown from Stephen.

Had the esteemed Wulfrith ever sat at table with Conrad, Beata would have been as present in the men's exchange as Henry's queen who oft inserted herself in her husband's conversations.

THE VEXING

"Tedious, this," Beata muttered and plucked at a shoulder of her bodice to ease the discomfort caused by Sir Renley's attempt to snatch her from...

She resisted, but her eyes moved to the high table's farthest end against which another table sat perpendicular to the one reserved for the noblest of nobles.

There sat Sir Durand, who had more than denied Count Verielle's men their prey. In the corridor outside her chamber, he had disturbed her as no man had done. Why? Because all others who drew so near did so not out of concern but to gain what she did not want to give?

Throughout the meal, their eyes had not met, though they would have had she looked long enough as he surveyed the hall—sometimes over the rim of a goblet, more often over bites of meat, which seemed his preferred viand.

Not that she ought to be familiar with his preferences. But then, she was nearly as acquainted with Sir Oliver's that ran to the rich and the sweet. That one's gaze she had not been able to avoid, but when she happened on it, he had ended it with a dismissive roll of the eyes.

Beata almost cried with relief when the king commanded the gathering to move to the great hearth. Rising with the knight seated on one side of her, whilst the priest seated on her other side continued to doze on an upturned hand, she heard, "I hope we shall meet again in days to come, my lady."

She looked to the knight. Though he spoke with the sincerity of one who seemed more the sort to enjoy her company than tolerate it, she lied in saying, "As do I." But only a lie because she hoped she would soon be gone from court.

Restrainedly, she made her way amongst the others and reached the stairs without hindrance.

"Lady Beata!"

With a low groan, she turned to a pleasantly plump young woman. "Aye?"

"The queen would have you attend her."

Propriety be cursed! Beata silently swore. *I should have run!*

"I feel unwell. Mayhap Her Majesty will grant me an audience on the morrow?"

A snort sounded from the lady, causing her to flush and clear her throat as if to explain away the sound with which Beata herself was more than familiar. "I fear she will not, my lady."

It was no easy thing to carry herself well, shoulders longing to bow and feet to trudge, but Beata did so with the reminder she remained a reflection of her beloved Conrad.

Upon reaching the hearth, she moved past Henry where he sat surrounded by men on one side of the fire, whilst his queen was thronged by women *and* men on the other side.

"Lady Beata," Eleanor said as her subject curtsied, "we hoped you would not slip away ere we could speak."

Once more an object of interest, Beata straightened. As she did so, she avoided looking at Sir Durand who stood to the right alongside Baron Wulfrith.

"You will be grateful we did not allow you to sleep night into day," the queen continued. "Had we, you would miss your ship."

Breath fled Beata.

"And now you may thank us," Eleanor said.

"Wh-what say you, Your Majesty?"

"Though we would be pleased to have you pass Christmas with us, it is selfish to keep you from answering your father's summons."

And foolish to risk a disrupted household, Beata mused. There was something good to be said about making a nuisance of one's self.

She stepped forward, bent, and kissed the proffered hand. "I thank you, Your Majesty. You are kind and generous and—"

"Considerate. Most considerate, Lady Beata."

Something in the queen's tone causing Beata's relief to waver, she straightened.

Returning her revered hand to the chair's arm, Eleanor said, "Sir Durand."

He stepped forward, and though his eyes brushed Beata as if to sweep her away like rubbish, she sensed wariness. Neither did he expect to like what the queen would say. "Your Majesty?"

Withholding her gaze from him, Eleanor said, "What think you of our gallant monk, Lady Beata?"

"Monk?" Beata slid her eyes down the tunic belted over a chain mail hauberk, recalled Sir Oliver's taunt that the queen's man ought to know timing was everything in gaining a woman's intimate favors. "I was unaware he is of the Church."

The queen laughed as a lady ought to. Were it not at Beata's expense, she would think it a pretty sound. "I assure you, my man is not of the Church, though he as good as could be."

Then he had also earned a name indicative of chastity. That surprised. He was of face, form, and carriage that provided opportunities aplenty to satisfy a man's need. What kept one not committed to the Church from answering those needs? A religious bent?

"As we understand," Queen Eleanor continued, "you could qualify for a life on your knees praying for England, Lady Beata."

Was that an idle comment? Or a portent of things to come? Would the ship of which the queen spoke deliver her to an English convent to live out her years in the quiet and still of the cloister? Had she so offended?

Dear Lord, she silently beseeched, *forgive me for not better keeping my tongue.*

"Well?" Eleanor prompted. "What think you of Sir Durand?"

Beata moistened her lips. "He seems honorable and courageous. Certes, I am indebted to him for the aid given this morn."

"The necessity of which is a curious thing." The queen raised an eyebrow. "We are most interested to learn the reason Count Verielle's men risked trespassing upon the King of England's lands." She clicked her tongue. "A pity you are also uninformed."

Beata tucked apology into her smile. "I am determined not to worry over it since Sir Durand made it unnecessary."

Eleanor considered her. "We are pleased you think well of him." She looked around. "You have heard of Baron Wulfrith."

Beata met the warrior's gaze. Whatever he felt beneath the regard of those who watched as if a play unfolded, it could not be known. "Aye, Your Majesty. His is a reputation above reproach."

"Thus, any concerns you have about the safety of your journey are settled."

No further explanation needed. Regardless of her fate upon reaching England, these two men would ensure she did so without falling victim to any who should have no good reason to stop her.

"You are kind, Your Majesty. And considerate. But——"

"Most considerate. Thus, should the morrow's weather permit a crossing, we give you leave to do so in the company of Sir Durand and Baron Wulfrith."

Were only that required of them, Beata would happily accept. "I am honored and grateful, but I would not take these men from matters far more pressing than delivering a widow of little import to her father, especially as I am not without escort." She glanced across her shoulder. "Sir Norris——"

"Failed you, Lady Beata. If not for Sir Durand, you would have been abducted for... Well, that we must needs discover."

Which she would though, hopefully, not until the one who had become a playing piece on her well-appointed board was out of reach. Providing the queen had no easy connection with Count Verielle, it was possible.

"Lady Beata"—Eleanor's tone was conciliatory—"we seek only to ensure a noblewoman born of England does not find herself at the mercy of men such as those who sought to capture and force us to wed following the annulment of our marriage to King Louis. Blessedly, as you are not an heiress..." She frowned. "Do we assume something we should not?"

Heart beating hard, Beata flew her eyes wide. "An heiress! Surely you received tidings my father's wife birthed a son?"

"We did, but..." Eleanor sighed. "...is it not the third child your stepmother has birthed?"

The first two stillborn. But the last had survived. Hopefully, he yet lived. "It is, Your Majesty."

"We pray your father's heir thrives, but should he not..."

Beata glanced at Sir Durand and found herself watched by eyes that proved he was not as adept at masking his thoughts as the baron. "As I also pray," she said, "but does God claim another of my father's children, still there is my brother, who could be released from his holy vows."

It was true, though Beata's father told that Emmerich was adamant about remaining of the Church.

"*Should* he wish to eschew his vows," Eleanor mused. "But does he not, you will wed again, hmm?"

Beata suppressed a groan. "I do not believe it will be required of me and pray it will not, Your Majesty."

Eleanor inclined her head. "Regardless, we shall ensure you reach your home unmolested." She looked around. "Sir Durand is acquainted with the barony of Wiltford, having served there several years past."

Beata blinked. "You know my father, Sir Durand?"

His smile was strained. "I do not, Lady. It was the keeper of Firth Castle who bought my sword arm, and for a short time only."

The queen waved an impatient hand. "As for Baron Wulfrith, he resides at Stern Castle." She looked to the large man. "Is it not two days' ride from Wiltford?"

"To reach the lady's home, one passes near my family's demesne, and 'tis possible to gain Wiltford in a day providing one begins the journey at dawn and rides hard."

She smiled. "You know Lady Beata's father, do you not, Baron?"

"Distantly, Your Majesty, and not much better than I knew his nephew."

Whom Beata's father had long served before Ralf's death by drowning. Her cousin having left no heirs, his widow was returned to her family when Beata's father inherited the rich, strategically situated lands four years past amid cruel speculation he was responsible for his nephew's death. Absent proof, he had soon wed a much younger woman in the hope of producing a surfeit of sons.

"As we are aware of your eagerness to return to your family, Baron," Eleanor said, "we shall not impose beyond asking you to accompany Lady Beata across the channel and only as far as Stern, aiding Sir Durand should he require it."

He dipped his chin. "I am pleased to do so, Your Majesty."

She looked to Beata. "Ere dawn, you shall depart for the docks and, weather permitting, set sail."

"I thank you." *Though I would rather curse you,* Beata silently added.

Eleanor motioned Beata away, moved her gaze to the gallery above, and called, "Music!"

As the musicians took up their instruments, Beata gained Sir Norris's side. "She suspects," she said low.

"And chose her words accordingly." He sighed. "She is to be admired."

"And feared, whether she plans to force me to enter the convent or give me no opportunity to wed a man of my choosing."

"The barony of Wiltford is a great prize, my lady. Our king and queen would see it bestowed upon one they favor."

Meaning a nobleman who had supported Henry's claim to the throne. Thus, she must escape her royal escort and reach Wiltford ahead of Sir Durand.

"Wulfrith comes," Sir Norris rasped, and she turned to follow the renowned warrior and Sir Durand's approach.

Though her family's lands were near those of the Wulfriths, she did not think she had ever met one. Too much her father resented his nephew being found so wanting by the current baron's father that his training at Wulfen Castle had been terminated after two weeks. The reason for Ralf's return to Wiltford was not revealed to her, but her cousin's penchant for quickly moving from pleasant to morose to raging was likely the cause. Eleven years older than she, he had mostly been kind to her, but on many an occasion he had given her and others cause to slink away.

When the two men halted before her, Beata said with as much cheer as she could summon, "Baron."

He inclined his head. "I am glad to be of service, my lady."

She glanced at the knight beside him whose mouth remained seamed, further evidence he did not share the other man's sentiment. "I am grateful, my lord."

A sparkle in gray-green eyes, Wulfrith said, "Are you?"

She blinked. He could at least feign ignorance of her opposition to his accompaniment. "Forgive me if I seem ungracious, Baron Wulfrith. 'Tis only that I see no cause to add to your burden."

"Since I have concluded my business with the king, I would be aboard ship regardless of your presence and, once in England, traveling north. Thus, no burden."

"A pity the same cannot be said of Sir Durand." A shiver coursing her upon meeting golden eyes she would not know were flecked with brown had she not been nearer him, she said, "I shall endeavor to make no nuisance of myself so you may all the sooner return to your queen."

"Much appreciated, Lady."

Though Beata longed to withdraw from the hall through which voices, laughter, and music once more sounded, she knew it best she play the part expected of her lest what was not expected raised more suspicion. So...conversation, and most easily accomplished by encouraging one's partner to speak of himself.

"Tell me of your family, Baron. Do all boast as imposing a presence as yours? Are they worthy of the Wulfrith name?"

"I have two brothers."

Everard and Abel, she knew from a tale spun by her friend, the troubadour knight. And quite the tale!

"And two sisters. Though all my siblings are worthy of our name, one's presence is much less imposing than the others."

"Naturally, a sister."

After a hesitation so fleeting it might be imagined—though the same could not be said of Sir Durand's stiffening—the baron said, "My youngest, with whom you share a name."

"Beatrix," Beata said, since those given her name were rarely called by its shortened form, and more rarely once they grew into women.

"Aye, her character can be imposing, but she is so slight as to be delicate."

Beata laughed. "Something not said of this Beatrix." Gaze once more drawn to Sir Durand, she saw his eyes were on her mouth. But he did not look at it with fascination as some did. Doubtless, in addition to her expression of joy, he regarded the slight gap between her front teeth as a flaw.

Telling herself she did not care what he thought of her, reminding herself she liked the space from which a sweet whistle oft sounded ahead of laughter, she returned her attention to Baron Wulfrith. "So now I am to imagine Lady Beatrix's older sister boasts a presence as imposing as her brothers."

"That would be exaggeration, my lady, though Gaenor is quite tall."

"As tall as Sir Durand?"

"A bit taller."

And he was a good height. "She is wed?"

The baron arched an eyebrow, and she guessed he understood the reason for her question. "Happily, as is my youngest sister."

Then Gaenor was matched to a good man who cared enough for her he did not mind that she stood above him—that or he feared the Wulfriths. "I am glad of it. But what of your brothers?"

"All of us have wed well."

"A rarity. One would think you had a say in whom you wed."

"All but one. We count ourselves blessed that the marriage ordered by King Henry to effect peace between our family and another is a good one."

As Beata had counted herself blessed that Conrad proved a man above other men. Sorrow causing tears to sting her eyes, she lowered her gaze. And found a change of topic in the dagger the baron wore, its pommel set with jewels.

"A Wulfrith dagger," she said, having once before laid eyes on one. Or was it twice?

"It is."

She looked to the dagger of his companion. "Why, Sir Durand, was it at Wulfen Castle you received your knight's training?" Without awaiting an answer he would not likely provide, she gave her tongue room to play. "But of course! Only one of England's mightiest defenders, worth two or more knights trained elsewhere and of immaculate courtesy and unbreakable honor would be entrusted with serving the queen." She laughed. "I am even more impressed."

Before her tongue further unwound, his expression darkened. And it piqued that he was offended by her good opinion.

Found wanting by a man she found less wanting than any heretofore encountered, she narrowed her eyes. "It seems you know not how to take a compliment, Sir Durand. I find that sad and—I am sorry to say—dull. Thus, since you have days ahead in which to suffer my company, I will grant you respite the remainder of this eve." She looked to Wulfrith. "Until the morrow, my lord."

He shifted his gaze between Sir Durand and her, dipped his head. "Lady Beata."

Accompanied by Sir Norris, she moved through the gathering, allowing herself to be drawn into conversations which twice brought her near Sir Durand, who seemed to have no difficulty recalling the given names of other ladies as claimed when she encouraged him to use her own.

At hour's end, she slipped abovestairs.

As best she could, she had played her part—smiles, laughter, and mild flirtation of a degree that should not offend the queen who watched. Oh, how she watched!

He was ashamed of his response to the lady's lively chatter that had not meant to offend. And mostly it had not.

Resentment too fresh over learning he was to deliver The Vestal Widow to England, he should not have accompanied Baron Wulfrith to her side, but what poured through him as he stood before her was anger at himself for so keenly feeling her words. Had the baron not been present, he might have better tolerated them. Unfortunately, the one betrayed was reminded of how far the Wulfen-trained knight entrusted with his sisters and mother had fallen from grace—so much he likely approved of accompanying Durand to ensure the lady reached England unmolested. Still, when she and Sir Norris had departed, Wulfrith simply said, "Lesson twenty, Sir Durand."

Learn from the past. Live in the present.

He was right. But though Durand continued to exhort the Lord to forgive him when mind and body sought to move him from temptation to sins of the flesh, as when ladies of the court made known their desire with longing looks and covert touches, his past clung like a second skin. A past he had allowed to spill onto a woman who could not know how much her words affected him—she who named him dull.

Though he aspired to be viewed as such by Eleanor's ladies, and for which the queen called him her gallant monk, it stung as it should not, especially with a woman like that. A woman for whom he had no cause to feel attraction.

"Dear Lord," he rasped, "I am in need of more prayer."

This time, the chapel.

5

The air—freezing but blessedly still.

The heavens—clouded but too thinly spread to present a threat. For now.

When the sun once more took to the sky, giving faces to those who rode upon the coast, Beata glanced at Baron Wulfrith to her left and Sir Durand to her right. Though grateful to part from Eleanor and Henry, the obstacles ahead were daunting.

Behind rode her father's knights, farther back two of Baron Wulfrith's, and ahead three of Sir Durand's, who set the pace that drew them toward the port town.

Once it came in sight, Sir Durand ordered his men to slow, and a quarter hour later they reached its walls.

While they waited for the captain of the guard to verify the papers granting them entrance at the early hour, Beata considered Sir Durand. Gloved hands resting atop his saddle's pommel, he watched the small door set in a much larger door through which they would enter.

When he looked around, eyes that had grown dark on the night past were once more golden. "Soon you shall be bound for England and returned to your father, Lady."

Hoping to disarm him to better her chance of slipping from his grasp, she urged her mount alongside. "I apologize for last eve. I do not understand how my compliment offended, but I wish you to know I was sincere."

"Think no more on it, Lady."

No hesitation. To sooner quiet her? "Now you, Sir Durand."

He frowned.

Fixing her gaze on his, she raised a hand, lifted the cuff of its glove, and blew breath down stiffly cold fingers. The warmth provided relief. And gave him time to decipher her meaning.

A corner of his mouth convulsed. "Pray, accept my apology, Lady."

She lowered her hands. "Now that we are all better, tell me about the gallant monk. Is all of it true?"

The ease with which he sat the saddle departed. "All?"

"I have experienced how gallant you are, though I yet question the necessity of tossing a lady from a moving horse." She did not truly, aware of the danger her struggle had placed them in, but there was fun to be had—more, a lightening of mood that might make him vulnerable. "However, the monk of you implies much. Are you deeply religious? Do you observe the hours of prayer when not defending king, queen, and country? And…well, you know what else it implies."

He looked as if he might smile. "I do, but were I to answer, you would have to accord me the same consideration by revealing whether the title of Vestal Wife—now Vestal Widow—is true."

Still he sought to quiet her. And this time he succeeded. "Argument well made, Sir Durand. Thus, you must content yourself with ignorance of my true nature as I must content myself with ignorance of yours."

Now he smiled, the bowing of his lips turning the man more handsome and the monk less believable. "Just as you must content yourself that though such amiable talk tempts me to lower my watch, I shall resist."

Found out, but she laughed. "I am glad you are not without humor, Sir Durand."

"You are saying I am not entirely dull?"

As she had suggested last eve. "I shall suspend final judgment until I have more time to gather further evidence."

"Then I need not fear your judgment."

She raised her eyebrows. "What say you?"

"I am as eager to deliver you to your father as you are to gain his side, Lady."

So he might quickly rid himself of The Vestal Widow. Determined not to take offense, especially as there was teasing in his tone she had not heard since he sought to converse with her after tossing her from his horse, she said, "Well and good, Sir Durand, but have we not days ahead in which I may render judgment?" She smiled.

His eyes lowered to her mouth. As he considered it, once more she was reduced to the breathlessness of the day past when he had been nearer yet. Then his gaze swept past her.

Following it, she saw Baron Wulfrith observed them. But before she could delve the warrior's expression, the large door groaned open.

Horses stabled, their riders seated in an inn near the docks, Durand studied the other patrons as he knew Baron Wulfrith did where he sat at the opposite end of the table—also with his back to a windowless wall.

Beyond having accorded nods and murmurs of respect, none of the inn's guests seemed interested in the knights and the lady with whom they broke fast. Thus, the weather seemed the greatest threat to the journey, the clouds having thickened and lowered.

Hoping the crossing would not be delayed, as The Vestal Widow surely hoped where she sat to his left, hands cupped above porridge whose steam caressed her palms before curving around her face, Durand dipped into his own bowl and spooned up a meatless bite. The only good of it was that it went down warm.

Bellies were filled and the chill chased from travel-worn bodies when Sir Jessup, the young knight Durand had sent to the ship to confirm it would sail, returned.

"The captain says an hour, providing the heavens do not birth rain and the air does not stir more than already it does."

Out of the corner of his eye, Durand saw the woman beside him lean toward Sir Norris. Unable to catch her whispered words, he said, "'Tis time to depart for the docks."

The breeze tossed and the sun lit the clouds as they exited the inn with Durand and his men at the fore, The Vestal Widow and her father's men center, and the baron and his knights at the rear.

It was well they did not go into that foul-smelling street with arrogant confidence. Though the inn was chosen for its wide, well-lit approach and proximity to the docks, those who converged on them front and back chanced what they should not despite outnumbering the ten tasked with protecting the lady bound for England.

Before Durand clearly saw the one rushing toward him past fleeing passers by, he knew their attackers were Count Verielle's men. He dropped his pack, thrust his mantle off his shoulders so it draped his back to provide his arms full range of movement, and drew his sword.

As the ring of chain mail and blades leaving scabbards were nearly muted amid Durand's and Wulfrith's shouted orders, The Vestal Widow's men moved her to the side, allowing her remaining escort space in which to defend her.

The bearded knight, whose face evidenced bruises and swellings dealt by the boots of the lady he had sought to abduct, ran forward.

The clash of their swords overhead jarred Durand, his opponent having the advantage of bulk. However, the man lacked the Wulfen training necessary to withstand the strain of nearly displaced bones and the burn of muscles. And when Durand swept his blade off the other's, it was his greater speed and agility that allowed him to draw first blood.

The knight raged, and with the sliced flesh of his collarbone staining his tunic, came again.

Durand deflected the swing, and as he spun around, saw Wulfrith deal a killing blow to his own opponent. The baron's men and Durand's quickly thinning the threat of harm to The Vestal Widow, a glance in her direction assuring him her men held off Count Verielle's, Durand evaded the blade seeking his neck.

Though his next swing connected, he had only the satisfaction of bleeding the knave's forearm, the man's chain mail a barrier to the heart of which so foul a being was undeserving.

Then Durand bled, causing his opponent to shout as the end of his swing and the beginning of his next flecked his face with crimson droplets.

Durand wasted no moment determining the severity of the injury to his lower leg. He lunged and retaliated with a slice that snapped the other man's head up and back, made him stumble and drop his sword, and clap a hand to his throat as if that might turn back the tide.

When the bearded knight crashed to his knees, Durand turned to the attacker who sought to engage one of The Vestal Widow's men. "Here!" he shouted and leapt over another fallen enemy.

His new opponent came around. And met his end on Durand's sword that so easily penetrated chain mail there was no doubt the armor was in poor repair.

But there were more who aspired to deliver the lady to Count Verielle though they should have retreated as they had on the day past. Either their reward for success was great or punishment for failure dire.

Confirming Wulfrith held his own, Durand moved to intercept two of the enemy who moved toward Sir Norris and glimpsed the lady where she pressed herself to a wall behind her father's knight.

Eyes wide, she clutched a dagger. Against sword-bearing men, it would be ineffectual, but he admired her attempt to protect herself rather than succumb to shrieking and weeping.

Moments later, he put down one of the two who sought her, and when Sir Norris toppled the other, turned back to assist his own men. They fought well, but though the contest would be over soon, he would not risk any suffering dire injury or death.

But just as he set himself at the soldier who drew blood from Sir Jessup's arm, Wulfrith bellowed, "The lady, Durand!"

He swung around. She and her men had abandoned their packs and were running toward the docks, retreating as if Count Verielle's men were winning the day. And he knew what Wulfrith knew. Here was their opportunity to resume the secretive journey that had set them across King Henry's lands, the same which could render impotent the missive the queen had entrusted Durand to deliver to the lady's father.

Feeling the presence of that sealed document in his purse, he looked back at his former liege and saw the baron had landed a blow that dropped his opponent onto his face.

"Go!" Wulfrith shouted and lunged forward to aid Sir Jessup.

As Durand dodged carts and cowering citizens, he felt the injury to his leg but did not let it slow him. Upon reaching the docks, he saw the lady's destination was its farthest end. Beyond the ship that was to have transported her across the channel, another sat at anchorage—a black-hulled thing of the sort that harried other ships, preferably French, and of which King Henry did not *openly* approve. Were stolen cargo in its hold, it was likely of less value than what was paid to wait upon The Vestal Widow. And if Durand did not reach her before she gained a rowboat to deliver her to a ship of thieves, he would fail his queen.

He ground his teeth, and as he stretched his legs longer, Sir Norris sounded the alarm that caused the knights on either side of him to turn back.

It mattered not whether they were a match for one trained at Wulfen. They need only slow Durand long enough to see the lady and Sir Norris into a boat headed for the ship whose deck had come alive in preparation to sail.

"Fool woman!" Durand growled. Did she not consider the danger of entrusting her person to men of ill repute, and more so now she had only one knight to protect her?

Dear Lord, a better name for her is The Vexing Widow.

Hoping he would not have to severely injure the young knights advancing on him, he pounded the boards beneath his feet.

Though his opponents maintained a united front, forcing him to fend off two swords and dealing him a cut across the forehead, neither were as fortunate with the injuries dealt them, and it but took the thrust of a shoulder to send the bloodiest into the water.

"The same end for you," Durand growled as the other knight danced back in search of space in which to wield his sword, while beyond him the lady and Sir Norris had reached a rowboat.

Ignoring his pained leg, Durand rushed forward, slammed his blade so hard against his opponent's that the knight's sword flew from his hand, then also sent him into the water.

But not soon enough. Sir Norris pushed the boat off the dock, and the oarsman set to traversing the distance to the ship.

Durand sped toward the nearest rowboat. "Make ready!" he shouted and, when the two oarsmen only stared, hauled one up by the neck of his tunic. "Get in and row!"

"B-but sire," the other stammered, "one does not approach that ship without permission."

"You have my permission." He thrust the younger one toward the boat and all three boarded.

With two rowing, it was possible to overtake The Vestal Widow. Had there been another set of oars, there would have been no question of doing so. However, did Durand fail to reach the ship ere the lady and her man boarded, he was not without hope.

Providing the weather continued to distance itself from the mild thing it had presented at dawn, the ship would not venture far from land. It would drop anchor farther out, giving Durand time to enlist the aid of those eager to aid Queen Eleanor's man—and drag the lady off the ship kicking and screaming, if need be.

As the first boat neared its destination, a rope ladder cascaded down the ship's side.

"Sir Norris!" Durand shouted, but the knight who stood before the lady did not look around.

"Faster!" Durand commanded the rowers, and readying himself to follow The Vestal Widow up the ladder, shoved his sword in its scabbard.

Despite the churning water, the boat ahead smoothly slid up against the ship's hull, and the lady rose and reached for the ladder.

"Lady!" Durand shouted.

As if she did not hear, she began her ascent.

"Lady Beata!"

She stilled, and her head came around so sharply her veil escaped its pins and began a slow, fluttering descent to the sea. Across the distance closing between them, their eyes met. Likely, she was as surprised as he that her name came off his lips. But if that was what it took to reach the ladder before it was pulled up...

"Go, my lady!" Sir Norris called as he climbed after her.

She did as bid, but as the second rowboat replaced the one starting back for the docks, Durand snatched hold of the ladder and, telling himself there would be time aplenty to feel the pain of his injury, hauled himself upward.

At the railing above, men lifted The Vestal Widow over the side, then reappeared to assist Sir Norris, whose lower foot was within Durand's reach.

Durand gripped a rung tight with one hand and turned his other around the man's ankle and yanked.

The knight cursed, kicked, and attempted to add to the damage The Vestal Widow had done Durand's face.

Seeing those above reach to Sir Norris, determined he would not play again the game by which he had wrested The Vestal Widow from the bearded knight, Durand yanked harder. But this time he lost as the seamen hauled the knight off the ladder.

He followed. Not because the boat that had delivered him had pushed away from the dreaded ship. Because having reclaimed much of his honor these past years, he could not bear to be found unworthy again. He had to try though he could bring no weapon to hand until he was aboard.

The Vexing

He reached the railing and butted his forehead into the nose of a narrow-faced seaman who believed he, alone, could prevent a knight from boarding. Pain shot through Durand's skull and blurred his vision, but as the man reeled backward, he swung himself over the railing and drew his sword.

He had only a moment to locate the lady who stood wide-eyed alongside Sir Norris before being forced to turn his attention to the half dozen coming for him wielding swords, daggers, and pikes.

Beware the odds, one of Baron Wulfrith's lessons resounded through him as he swept up his sword.

Hopeless odds. Regardless of his Wulfen training, he was outnumbered, not only by those drawing near, but the rest of the crew who seemed content to watch the slaughter of however many of their fellows it took to gut a knight.

But there was naught for it. Entrusted with delivering The Vestal Widow to her father, honor bade him retake ground the treacherous lady and Sir Norris had stolen, even if he let his life upon this deck.

He adjusted his stance, picked out the three who would die ahead of him, and started toward the nearest whose pike sought to put him through.

"Do not!" the lady cried, and Durand saw Sir Norris snatch her back so forcefully she dropped to her knees. Straining against his hold, she reached toward the murderous men. "Death need not be the end of this!"

Her words reminded Durand of another lesson. *Ofttimes, victory gained at the point of words rather than blades is more godly, Squire Durand.*

But before the knight he had become could determine how to apply it, the seaman wielding a pike lunged.

Durand sidestepped, clenched his jaws as pain shot up his leg, and landed his blade a foot back from the pike's point. The weapon spun out of the seaman's hands, forcing Durand to duck as it sailed over the railing into the sea.

Another attacked, but a slice to the forearm caused the man to lose his grip on a wickedly long dagger. The weapon landed near Durand, and after kicking it behind, he braced himself for a sword-wielding youth whose pink grin showed he possessed few teeth.

The rusted and nicked blade begging to be broken, Durand obliged. As the youth stared at the hilt left to him, Durand grabbed him and spun him to face his mates, pinning him with an arm against the neck and a sword to his belly.

"I would speak with your captain," Durand shouted. "I am King Henry and Queen Eleanor's man, tasked with delivering the lady to her father." He jutted his chin at The Vestal Widow whom Sir Norris continued to restrain. "She is in no danger from me."

"And yet she seeks to escape you," said one who leaned a shoulder against a mast. "Curious."

Durand assessed him. Not what one expected of a man who led others in the plunder of ships, often at the expense of lives. He was thick but short, face fleshy rather than hard-edged, and voice pitched somewhere between a boy's and a man's. But the teeth flashed in a grin were right, those still set in his jaw discolored.

He straightened from the mast and ambled forward. "It matters not to me who is in the right. What matters is the second half of the payment due upon delivery of the lady to England. Have you that amount upon your person and a means of preventing me from relieving you of it, you may take her. Otherwise, we set sail." He shifted his gaze to the docks. "And soon. Your men will not be long in coming to your aid."

Durand had no reason to chance verifying that, certain the baron and knights had put an end to Count Verielle's men and followed. But unlike Durand, no effort would be wasted on rowboats whose occupants would have no means of boarding since the rope ladder would be taken up before another boat could come alongside. Baron Wulfrith would give chase in the ship that was to return him to his family.

Shouting for the anchor to be raised, the captain halted ten feet from Durand. Letting the sword at his side hang, he said, "As much as I value the lad for keeping us off the rocks many a time"—he flicked his eyes to the youth—"I'm more partial to my neck. Thus, kill him if you must but, dead or alive, you shall go into the sea."

The threat had too much substance. Though most of the crew were dispersing, Durand remained outnumbered, the injury to his leg felt beyond the burn. Not only did the shifting deck threaten his balance, but the loss of blood clouded his vision and loosened his grip on his sword.

Were he tossed over the side and able to shed his chain mail, he swam well enough to reach the docks. But consciousness waned. It would be a dead man who went down into the dark, chill water.

Not alone, helplessness demanded what little revenge could be had while he yet breathed. But another of Wulfrith's lessons begged an audience—that which told death should be dealt only in the absence of choice. He had violated that lesson, most notably in slaying the man who had tried to murder the woman he loved, but he would not do so again.

He thrust the young seaman away and took a step back to gain the railing's support.

Dear Lord, my blade is heavy, he lamented as the enemy rushed forward and their captain smiled. Then a fist snapped back his head.

He heard a clatter he guessed was his sword, and as his arms were gripped to send him into the sea, he closed a hand over the Wulfrith dagger of which he ever aspired to be worthy. Just before taking another fist to the face, he saw The Vestal Widow break from Sir Norris, her mouth wide with a cry.

Then nothing, and his last thought was wonder over whether it was the black of unconsciousness embracing him or the sea.

6

His leg was all she had of him, and though the elbow of one of those lifting him over the railing struck her in the mouth and Sir Norris's arm pulled at her waist, she held on.

"I tell you, do not!" she screamed across the blood of a split lip. "He will die!"

"My lady, come away!" Sir Norris dragged harder, the pressure of his arm threatening the contents of her belly. "There is naught you—"

"Captain!" She snapped her chin around. "Twice what is owed you. Twice, I vow!"

He arched an eyebrow, and as Sir Durand was pulled out of her hold and she fell backward, commanded, "Halt!"

Having taken Sir Norris to the deck with her, she scrambled off and looked to the seamen who had only to open their hands to send the knight down into the sea.

"Twice?" the captain said.

"My father will pay it!" And with little argument, she suspected. Sir Durand being a favorite of the queen, if the Baron of Wiltford's plotting was responsible for his death, the entirety of what he hoped to pass to those of his blood would likely be lost.

The captain looked to his men. "There is profit in sparing the knight a watery grave. Deliver him to the lady's cabin and bind him."

Grumbling abounded, but Sir Durand came off the railing. As the men carried him past Beata with wide strides to compensate for the deck's movement, she looked closer at his blood-stained chausses that evidenced his clash with Count Verielle's men. The spilled blood surely as responsible for his loss of consciousness as the seamen's blows, his leg was in need of tending.

Then there was the slash across his forehead. When the whole of her name passing his lips brought her head around as she scaled the ladder, she had bemoaned the injury that might mar his countenance. Fortunately, it appeared only surface deep, similar to the scratches she had dealt him.

"Hold!" the captain ordered the men carrying Sir Durand, then stepped near and removed the knight's belt from which hung the Wulfrith dagger and a thick purse.

"Those belong to Sir Durand!" Beata protested.

"No longer, my lady." The captain motioned his men to continue and fastened the belt around his waist.

"Captain—"

"Speak no more!" Sir Norris gripped her arm as if for fear she would set upon the one who was to deliver them across the narrow sea.

Wiping the back of a hand across her bloodied lip, Beata watched the captain cross the deck, snatch up Sir Durand's sword, and slide it in its scabbard.

He turned back and raised an eyebrow. "I may be persuaded to return these—for a price." He chuckled, but his mirth dissolved as the ship heaved. "Sir Norris, the sea is less and less of a mind to be crossed. As we must stay ahead of your pursuers, see the lady below deck."

"Come." The knight pulled her around and guided her to a small, lantern-lit cabin that smelled of things she did not care to think on.

One of two who had carried Sir Durand from the deck was on his haunches behind the knight he secured to a post that supported one end of a swinging bed. He jerked a knot into the rope around Sir Durand's wrists, straightened, and as he stepped past Beata, ran his eyes down her with such familiarity she felt as if unclothed.

"As I am but one knight," Sir Norris said when the door closed, "you are to remain here throughout the crossing which, if God be with us, may see us delivered to England by nightfall. In my absence, unbolt the door only when I command it."

She inclined her head.

"As for him"—he looked to Sir Durand whose chin was on his chest where he sat against the post—"'tis an ill thing he accompanies us."

She gasped. "You do not say he should have been thrown into the sea—murdered?"

"I would not wish that on him, but neither would I have him tight on our heels as we make for Wiltford." He sighed. "I do not trust the captain and his men to return him to the queen. Thus, we will have to bring him ashore and enlist the aid of one who can ensure he remains bound until your father determines it is safe to release him."

Would it ever be safe? Would the man who had risked his life rather than disappoint the queen forget what he had suffered at the hands of The Vestal Widow? And what of Eleanor's wrath?

Pulling back from worry, which life with Conrad had mostly shielded her from, she said, "I require hot water, bandages, strong drink, and needle and thread to tend Sir Durand's leg."

"My lady, until we are under sail—"

"Do you not gain them, I shall."

He scowled, pivoted, and over his shoulder tossed, "I will return as soon as possible. Bolt the door."

She did as told, then lowered to her knees at Sir Durand's feet. Though the light of a hanging lantern barely parted the shadows around his downturned face, it seemed he remained senseless. But that was good. It was unseemly what she must do.

"So we begin," she whispered and unfastened her mantle, let it fall from her shoulders, and turned her attention to his injured leg. Blood not only stained his chausses but the hem of his tunic above and his boot below. She gripped the latter and tugged.

He groaned.

Eager to finish her ministrations before he awakened, she put more strength into the effort, causing the boot to release so suddenly she nearly toppled.

She dropped the boot beside her. Drawing a deep breath to calm her speeding heart, she turned back his tunic and chain mail and settled their weight atop his upper thighs.

Next, his chausses. But as she eased the material up his hosed calf and thigh, she saw him raise his head.

Feigning ignorance of his regard, she loosened the ties securing his hose to his braies. Though she avoided touching the short expanse of thigh between the two garments, twice her fingers grazed him as the knots resisted her efforts, but throughout he said naught—at least by way of words.

How I am hated, she bemoaned. *But then, one ill after another I have dealt him.*

Remembering the two knights Sir Norris had set upon the queen's man, she sent up a prayer they had been pulled from the water. Of course, their fate might be no better were they brought before the king and queen.

Beata released the last of Sir Durand's ties, took hold of the top of his hose, and slowly rolled it down lest his injury began to form a scab amid the woven cloth. It did not, and when she revealed the gash, she was so relieved it was not bone deep she looked up.

Sir Durand's eyes awaited hers. "You," he said with so little movement of the mouth it seemed imagined. "Are." No movement at all. "A curse."

She whom Conrad had oft named a blessing. "I vow, I seek only to honor my father's request as a daughter ought to."

"What of honoring one's sovereign?"

Though humor was not appropriate, the Beata who had long enjoyed the indulgences allowed The Vestal Wife quipped, "I did not know that was amongst God's commandments."

A growl tore from him, at the end of which he barked, "If you are truly vestal, Lady, 'tis because you vex! Now where are my sword and dagger?"

Beata felt as if sliced by those absent blades. He was not the first to suggest her virtue remained intact because of behavior and opinions deemed unseemly for a lady, but it hurt more for him to speak it.

She raised her chin. "The captain has claimed them, along with your belt and purse."

He cursed and bucked against the post, doubtless testing the rope binding his hands behind him. Though a kick could have relieved her of a few teeth, he did not take advantage of her vulnerability.

"Sir Durand, Sir Norris has gone for the items required to ensure you do not suffer to your end days the injury done you by Count Verielle's men. Hate me if you must, but allow me to tend you so I am not responsible for further ill."

So heavily he dropped his head back against the post it had to pain him, but his only response was a strident breath.

"I saw my father's knights go into the water," she ventured. "Do they live?"

Just when she thought he would not answer, he said, "Unless necessary, I do not kill men who labor under the orders of others. For that, I sent them into the water. But what the king will do with them..."

She set her teeth and returned her gaze to his leg. "Your injury is not as bad as feared, but you have let much blood." When he did not respond, she continued rolling down his hose and, discomfited by the feel of hair roughening the skin of his calf, bit the inside of her cheek.

Durand considered the slope of the lady's forehead, the rise of her nose, the cracked bow of her upper lip gained between his loss of consciousness and awakening. Refusing to pity her that last, he wondered when he had known anger such as this.

When the woman he had not loved became a pawn to the king Durand now served? Certes, he had been moved enough to further betray the Wulfriths, forcing him to turn outlaw. But he had been angrier.

When the woman he could have loved was nearly hunted to ground to be tried as a witch? He had been angrier.

When he had killed the man who sought to murder the woman he had loved? Aye, that was his angriest. Now, bested by miscreants and having borne the humiliation of lost consciousness, he once more approached that threshold.

"You will answer for this, Lady."

She sat back on her heels. "That I do not doubt, and though I would release you that I not be the cause of further harm, all I can do is better your chance of healing."

Anger aside, that was everything to a man of the sword. "Then better it!"

Minutes later, she admitted Sir Norris to the cabin. He handed her a sack, then positioned himself to one side of Durand and braced his legs apart to counter the inhospitable waters—hopefully, not so inhospitable Baron Wulfrith's ship could not give chase.

The lady threaded a needle, then put a wine skin to Durand's lips and encouraged him to drink it all to dull the pain of the stitches to come. He accepted half and took his time, not only to allow the wine to do its work but to savor her discomfort.

Next came the burn of strong alcohol and further ache when she pressed the edges of his flesh together for the stitching. The only thing for which he was grateful was her confidence.

"I can sew it, my lady," Sir Norris said as she retrieved the needle.

She considered his offer, then said, "Since it cannot differ greatly from joining cloth, albeit messier, methinks the queen's man would prefer the finer stitches of which I am capable."

Durand wanted to demand she pass the needle to Sir Norris, but her belief she was better qualified to more securely—hopefully, more quickly—seam the wound, was not without merit. Still, it surprised that The Vestal Widow was skilled in needlework.

She looked to Durand. "It will hurt."

He thrust his eyebrows high.

"It seemed the thing to say," she muttered.

"Be done with it!"

Ire flashed in her green eyes, but she said, "Bring the lantern near, Sir Norris."

When light fell full on Durand's leg, the lady much too slowly and intently taught herself how to sew a man's flesh.

Again, he held close his pain, allowing only grunts to escape. Once the misery was done, he breathed deep while she bandaged the wound.

"There." She sat back. "Methinks it will heal well."

Were she not responsible, he would be grateful. But he was grudgingly impressed by her willingness to stitch him. All other women known to him, except Helene the healer, would have balked.

Moments later, orders sounded overhead, cloth snapped, and iron fittings rang, further evidence the captain had committed his ship and crew to a crossing the boat's increasingly erratic movement told was better left for another day.

"God be with us," the lady gasped when the hull creaked loudly and listed hard to one side.

There being little chance it would be other than a rough passage, Durand revised his hope that the baron's ship put to sea. Regardless of the aid Wulfrith would provide, he would not have the warrior's wife and children lose a beloved husband and father, especially for such a woman as this.

If ever he required further proof women were more trouble than they were worth, here she was—The *Vexing* Widow who had dragged him into a mess not easily pieced by the edge of a sword.

"Please, Lord," she entreated.

"Pray harder," he bit, then looked to Sir Norris. "If you truly wish to deliver the lady to your liege, you will instruct the captain to turn back before this weather sees us all dead."

The man shook his head. "We shall have to trust God to deliver us."

"Is that who you believe commands this ship? 'Tis not. It is a foul being who would commit unspeakable acts against your lady if not for the promise of coin."

The lady rose and snatched at the swinging bed to keep her balance. "Sir Norris, though I know you would do your duty to my father, methinks Sir Durand is right. We should turn back."

"My lady, if you fall into the king's hands again, you will be given no room to…" He glanced at Durand. "…do *your* duty to your father."

"But if our lives are in danger—"

"More in danger they will be if the reward you doubled is denied the captain."

Durand jerked. This woman had persuaded the captain to ignore warnings against exploring the deadly curves and hollows of the sea?

"And for what?" Sir Norris continued. "That he and his crew find themselves at the mercy of King Henry rather than the sea? Nay, this is our course." He returned the lamp to its hook, said, "Secure the door," and departed.

Avoiding Durand's gaze, she assured her footing across the floor and struggled to fit the bolt.

"Is it worth your life, Lady?"

She peered across her shoulder. "You misinterpret what Sir Norris told. I did double the reward, but not to ensure we set sail. I did it to keep a senseless man weighted by chain mail from being dropped into the sea when my hold on him failed." She touched her cut lip.

One of the crew had struck her? Before the wrath Durand did not want to feel for that offense could displace his anger toward her, she hastily added, "It was not intentional. It was a lesson learned that a woman stands little chance in physically opposing men—that her efforts are best spent on bargaining. But you have only my word for the reason I doubled the reward, and I doubt it holds much value."

He did not want to believe her, but he was here with her rather than beneath the sea.

She turned away, resumed her struggle with the bolt, and forced it into its hole.

"It will not long keep out whatever wants in," he said.

She stumbled back against the door and slapped palms to it.

"Be it the sea," he continued, "or seamen too lusty to remember there is coin to be had in ensuring The Vestal Widow remains vestal, that lock can be rendered useless."

"You seek to frighten me!" Her words were nearly lost beneath a shout from the deck that called for the raising of the foresail.

"With good cause," he said, "and having succeeded, you shall release me."

She shook her head, and more of her hair abandoned its braid.

Patience, he counseled himself. "Ere this crossing is done, you will need me unbound, whether to keep you from ravishment, a watery grave, or both."

"I cannot."

Though tempted to curse, he resisted gaining the Lord's displeasure when what he and every soul aboard needed were His good graces. But that did not prevent him from using their breath against this woman. "Fool!"

She pushed off the door and crossed the floor that was less aslant than moments earlier. As she came alongside Durand, she gripped the post to which he was bound. "So you name me because I refuse to allow the queen to order a life that does not belong to her."

"Order? She but wishes your safe return to your father by one she trusts."

"As she would have me believe. But in your hearing, did she not imply a better future for me was one spent at prayer—a cloistered life?"

"Aye, and in your hearing she said the same of me, as she has many times. Yet 'tis far from a cloistered life I live."

Though not so far where chastity is concerned, he silently acceded, *Lady Gaenor being the last woman I—*

He pulled back from the memory that more dishonored him than it had the one whose life was almost ruined for what she had gifted to one unworthy of such.

"Then you were not to deliver me to a convent?" The Vexing Widow said and caught her breath when the sea once more asserted its superiority by knocking her against his shoulder.

"My word I give, Lady. My orders were to escort you to your father upon the barony of Wiltford."

Gripping the post, she looked so long at him he tired of tipping back his head and lowered his chin. In the silence, he tested the ropes binding his wrists. Only enough slack to allow blood to flow and evidence whoever had tied the knots had shown some consideration.

"Even do you speak true," the lady finally said, "'tis not all you were ordered to do. The queen would not so concern herself with one she finds as improper as me."

She was right, but he was not at liberty to divulge Eleanor's suspicions though the queen had alerted The Vestal Widow to them.

"You were to report upon my father, aye?"

He raised his head. "I was to deliver you to Wiltford. Only one disloyal to his sovereign need be concerned over my report to the queen." *Or any action I might take,* he did not say. "Your father and you are not disloyal, are you?"

"Though our family—the same as the Wulfriths—once supported King Stephen's claim to the throne, that is in the past."

Because Stephen and his heir were dead. Thus, it was not for fear of losing the crown Eleanor had set Durand upon The Vestal Widow. It was reluctance to part with a privilege that could benefit royal coffers.

"Then since you can have no objection to my accompaniment, unbind me so I may do my duty, ensuring you and yours are more easily forgiven."

She appeared to consider it, but more shouted orders sent her gaze to the ceiling. "I cannot," she said again and stepped away.

"Lady!"

She caught hold of the swinging bed and looked around.

Determined to be prepared for escape, he said, "My boot."

With the ship so loose beneath her, he thought she might refuse, but she retrieved it and sank to her knees.

Durand followed her gaze to the hose bunched around his ankle. Though not opposed to her unease, he knew it would be uncomfortable for him as well. But there was nothing for it. "Unless you release me, Lady, you must set it aright."

He heard the breath she drew through her nose, then she slid her fingers into the top of his hose and eased it up over his calf. Her touch was as infrequent and light as when she had lowered the hose, but this time he felt an awareness of her and was struck by exactly how many years had passed since soft fingertips had moved over his battle-toughened flesh.

She tugged the hose up over his knee, and again her fingers grazed his thigh as she fastened its ties to those of his braies. Though he searched her face for something sly and seductive that would allow him to blame her for his body's response, he found naught. She kept her eyes lowered and lips compressed, and once she finished her task, sat back and shoved his boot over his foot and up his calf.

"There." She stood and sought the opening in the cradle of material that would make the ship's movements more bearable.

Were Durand less disturbed and the drink less felt, he might have scorned her fumbling and tumbling into the bed that provided a glimpse of shapely calves.

He closed his eyes, but the memory of her touch and the curve of legs once more moved him as he had long struggled against being moved.

Only lust, he assured himself. *No other feeling.* Not sympathy, grief, or fondness that could move one toward love to which he had succumbed only once.

"Sir Durand?"

Not caring to look into eyes that required little light to dance with life he did not think he had ever felt as deeply as she did, nor look upon a mouth so expert in forming a smile that her imperfect teeth could make no ruin of it, he lowered his chin to his chest.

"Would that you had not followed me aboard," she said. "I am sorry. Truly."

"Not as sorry as you shall be."

7

SHE THOUGHT SHE would die. Almost did not care if she saw another sunrise. Almost wished the ship would go down and sooner end her misery.

During her first voyage across the narrow sea, when the girl she had been was to wed a man of an age he could have been her great grandfather, she had been ill despite fairly calm waters. Now, a dozen or more hours into this crossing, night had dropped its cloak, the shouts above deck were without end, and rain beat and slashed and squeezed through cracks that made it appear the walls of her cabin wept.

"I am in hell," she breathed.

Thrice Sir Norris had returned, each time bearing simple viands that she had not dared eat and Sir Durand had refused though she offered to feed him.

The queen's man spoke little more whilst awake than during rest. The few sounds that parted his lips were those of discomfort and pain when the ship heaved and the floor went out from under him, wrenching his shoulders and arms and distancing him from the pole before slamming him back against it.

Beata had attempted to ease his discomfort by belting him around the hips with her girdle, but his anger had sat her back on her heels. "More bindings I must escape to keep you alive?" he had barked. "Nay, Lady, I shall endure that I may sooner see you punished."

Once more huddled in her mantle and encased in the material of the swinging bed with her back to him, she trembled and perspired as she tried to keep bile from spilling.

"Dear Lord," she whispered since He did not heed prayers spoken over and over in her mind, "deliver us."

"Unbind me, Lady, and mayhap He will."

Sir Durand's voice made her startle. She had been certain he could not hear her above the din. Or mayhap it was not a whisper upon which she had spoken.

"Lady!"

Except for when he had called to her as she scaled the ship's ladder, *Lady*—not even *my lady*—was all she was to him, as if to ensure she remained so.

"Listen to me. Even if the captain does not try to make the coast, we will likely be broken on the rocks. He has no stars to guide him and too little visibility to see warning beacons."

She turned in the bed and gulped as bile scorched her throat.

"Do you understand, Lady?"

Moaning as the acid burned its way back down, she waited for him to continue.

He did not. As a shake of her head would not suffice, the lantern having extinguished long ago, she said, "We shall die."

"If you do not untie me."

"'Twill make no difference."

"If you believe that, you can have no objection to releasing me."

It was so true she nearly laughed. "Wh-what can you do?"

"As we will die trapped here, I shall deliver us to the deck."

"But up there is only the sea and the storm, and…" She gasped. "I am so tired. All of my insides—"

"Get up!"

His cruel tone offended, but she had no strength or stomach for anger.

"Do you wish to live, Lady?"

Not like this. Not with all her—

Enough, Beata Fauvel! The voice sounded so loudly through her, she almost rebuked the knight for it, but that was her, hating that the mere tossing of her body reduced her to apathy. The Vestal Wife who could almost always find something over which to smile or laugh was worse than dull. She was pitiful.

She opened her eyes and strained to see the one who shared the dark with her—he who had gone silent amid the clamor overhead and must think her the foulest, weakest being.

I am not, she told herself, and as she moved as she did not wish to move, he bellowed. Then she heard the kick of his boots over the floor and felt the slam of his back against the post supporting one end of her bed. Another slam followed—and the cracking of that post or some other part of the ship.

All of her shaking, she peeled herself out of the bed, but could make no sense of her feet and crashed to the heaving floor alongside Sir Durand—so near his breath moved the hair across her cheek.

"Do it!" he bit.

Lest she retch on him, she pressed her lips tight and dragged her legs beneath her. Though pained by splinters that slid into her palms as she crawled to the post at his back, they offered reprieve from the sickness felt from the roots of her hair to her toes.

She groped her way up the post in search of the rope that would require a blade, the knight's struggle having made the seaman's knots too tight to pick loose.

As she slid her hands up over Sir Durand's, his fingers gripped hers so hard she gasped.

"Cut it, Lady!" he demanded, then released her.

She took hold of the rope in the space between his wrists and reached for the meat dagger on her girdle. Before she pulled it from its scabbard, the ship listed hard, and she fell onto her side. As she slid across the floor, the queen's man called to her over the shouts above. And somehow she had the presence of mind to tuck and throw an arm around her head. Had she not, her meeting with the hull might have broken her neck. Forearm taking the brunt of the hit, she cried out and heard the knight call again.

Blessedly, the ship did not soon right itself, allowing her to return to her hands and knees. Then she retched, the force of a belly expelling contents it lacked causing her eyes to burn and head to pound.

"Forgive me," she gasped before once more bending to the cramping.

Then she was tumbling opposite, but one of her flailing hands caught the post to which the knight was bound, and when the ship found its center again, she made it to her knees and drew her dagger. She slid the blade between Sir Durand's wrists and, hooking her other arm around the post, choked, "Spread your hands wide," having too little control to keep the blade from slicing through his fingers once the rope fell away.

"I do not require your counsel," he growled. "Highly I value my hands."

His tone was so dangerous, she reconsidered releasing him, but she set her teeth and put her weight behind her blade's stroke. She had to pause often to accommodate the ship's roll, but finally the rope gave way.

A moment later, she slammed to the floor, carried there by the man who snatched hold of her hand that held the dagger aloft.

"Yield!"

There was no reason to fight him. Even if he decided his chance of survival was better with her dead, she would likely meet the same end without his aid.

Staring into the dark that denied him face and form, she opened her fingers. "'Tis yours."

His hand moved up over hers, took the dagger, and from the ease of weight on one side of her, she guessed he secured it in his boot. "I ought to leave you to your fate," he growled.

"You should."

He muttered something and pushed back.

The removal of his body from hers allowed her to draw a full breath. And lose it when he yanked her upright.

No sooner did she gain her balance than he pulled her close and her shoulder struck the post. She started to protest his violence against her person, but it proved consideration when the ship careened, stilled, and crashed down with such force that had he not anchored her, she would have been flung across the cabin.

"Come about!" The shouted order was louder than the others. More desperate.

"Hold to the post," Sir Durand commanded and set her arms around it.

"But—"

"Do it!"

Beside her, she felt his jerky movements, accompanied by the din of his mail until it rang more harshly upon hitting the floor, sliding across it, and striking the wall. There could be only one reason a warrior shed that valuable keeper of life—that it would prove a giver of death. They were going into the sea.

Of a sudden, his hands were at her neck, and for a moment she feared he meant to strangle her. But as she strained away, the weight of her coin-ladened mantle fell from her shoulders. "Nay! I need—"

"Not if you are dead," he snarled, and she knew he had guessed what she had sewn into the hem. Like his mail, it would more quickly deliver them to the bottom of the sea.

"We go now," he said and hauled her across the cabin.

She heard the scrape of the bolt and felt the gust of the door's opening.

The short passageway that led to the steps was nearly as dark as the cabin had been and more treacherous to traverse. Blessedly, Sir Durand was not unversed in the sea's temperament, ever bracing them before they were knocked off their feet.

When he tossed open the hatch following their ascent of the steps, the storm-beaten night that flung rain and wind in their faces and blinding light in their eyes was more fearsome than anything Beata had experienced on that canvas between heaven and earth.

How she hated thunderstorms!—and all the more when they stirred the leaves in that corner of her mind, threatening to reveal what lay beneath.

She shrank back, but as if she were a wisp of a thing, Sir Durand drew her onto a deck slick with rain and sea water whose frantic course was corrected by one backhand after another.

"Come about! Come about!" That same command, as if not heeded before, followed by a great tearing of cloth.

Sir Durand did not pause, keeping his footing as he traversed the sodden deck and pulled Beata with him.

Then she was backhanded, something whipping across her face and dropping her to her knees so suddenly the queen's man dragged her a space before hauling her up against his side.

"Pray," she gasped, "let me catch my breath—"

"It will be the last you draw," he shouted so near her ear, it felt bloodied. And as he propelled her forward and between seamen too beset to pay them heed, he shouted again, "We have reached England, Lady, and she is not pleased to see us."

"Sir Durand—"

"Rocks ahead!" he snarled.

Just as he had predicted.

"Lady!" This time it was not Sir Durand who afforded her so little a name.

She peered over her shoulder and saw the lightning-lit figure of Sir Norris run toward them from the opposite side of the deck. Then a wall of water snatched him away. Its reach toward Sir Durand and her exceeding its grasp, it drew back to recover the strength needed to reunite them with her father's knight. And came again.

A woman's scream, so loud it pained.

A man's shout, so mighty it struck like a blow.

A crack of wood, so thunderous it was as if a mighty oak fell.

A great cry, so desperate it proved even the ungodly could be moved to call upon the Lord.

Then iron bands clapped around her back and hips, her feet left the deck, and the sweetest air filled her before being replaced by water so vengeful its brine burned her mouth and throat.

And so I die, she allowed as the arms of the storm gripped her harder and the cold sea swallowed her.

The need to survive demanded he release the lady, but he held to her. It tried to convince him better one dead than two, but he kicked harder toward what he prayed was the surface, his senses so upended he might sooner deliver them to the deep.

Lungs aching for air, the voice once more urged him to abandon The Vestal Widow.

As once I abandoned Beatrix Wulfrith, believing her dead in the ravine? he countered.

Injured leg protesting, survival snarled, *She is no Beatrix Wulfrith. Let her go!*

As once I let Gaenor Wulfrith go, too soon ceding the chase when she fled to protect me from her family's wrath?

The cold clenching his body, survival taking him by the throat, he heard, *She is no Gaenor. She is a liar. A deceiver. Let her go!*

I am Wulfen-trained, he silently declared. *Wulfen-worthy. No more will I break my vows. Never again will I dishonor the name of Marshal!*

Then he broke the surface, but he managed only a gulp of air before he was knocked back down and the lady was nearly torn from him.

Merciful Lord, he implored, *give me the strength and sense to save us.*

He surfaced again, and though the water slapped at him, he kept his head above it and dragged his charge up. Her head dropped onto his shoulder. If her life was not yet forfeit, soon it would be.

Spitting out the sea, he turned and searched for something to support her while he cleared the water from her lungs.

As he swam toward the nearest section of hull torn from the ship, he saw the broken vessel list hard and heard the cries of men abandoning the coffin lowering its lid on them, past it saw rocks nearer the shore whose brethren had lain in wait for those who dared sail the sea. Those whose lives were lost for their arrogance.

A small loss, he thought as he took hold of the planks and moved The Vestal Widow onto them. Once he had them out of the water, he straddled the lady to keep his balance and empty the water from her.

The sea fought him, rocking the makeshift raft front to back and side to side in an attempt to return them to the depths, but finally the lady emptied her lungs, gasped, and collapsed.

Durand confirmed she yet breathed, then unfastened her girdle, wrapped it around her upper arm and his wrist, and forced its buckle between two planks. When the fastener unhinged against the underside, anchoring them to the raft, he hooked an arm around the lady and fell onto his side.

As he prayed for the sea to send them toward the shore, he pressed the woman against his heaving chest and watched across the top of her head as the ship slipped lower, affording a glimpse of something beyond whose shape seemed that of a vessel.

Was it possible they had not only struck rocks but another ship? Both? He squeezed his eyes closed and opened them, but the wave that swept over the raft blinded him and forced water down his throat.

Expelling water, he clamped a leg over the lady to keep her from being snatched away as the sea sought to do time and again. Unfortunately, it was only the beginning of a journey he prayed would move them toward land.

8

**Sussex, England
Early December, 1161**

I BREATHE.

Of that Beata was certain, her heart's movement so strong she felt its every beat. And though the back of her was cold and damp, her front was warm from cheek to thighs.

She lifted her lids, and as she brought the dawn-feathered, rock-strewn scene into focus, made sense of the sound that was like a mother shushing her child. Lazily, the tide crawled up the shore. Listlessly, it slid back. Half-heartedly, it washed down another mouthful of land.

On the night past, the sea had been murderous, and yet she had survived while others perished. And absent a miracle, among the dead would be the man swept away before her eyes.

Sliced by regret, she moved her thoughts from Sir Norris to the one who had saved her. And was cut again by the likelihood Sir Durand had died so she might live.

"Lord, not also him," she whispered across a raw throat, then turned her face into what should have been sand. But no rasp of grains across her face, and she lost the sound of her heart in her ear.

Realizing the beat had moved to the base of her throat, she questioned if it was hers and drew her fingers into her palms. Sand did not slide between them but moved over what seemed muscle. It had to be him. His body. Heart. Warmth. Arm holding her to him as if...

...we are lovers, she thought and immediately prayed for forgiveness. Then thanking the Lord for sparing their lives, she moved her hands to the sides, pressed them against something slightly more solid than the body she lay upon, and raised herself on trembling arms. Not surprisingly, Sir Durand had appropriated wreckage to deliver them ashore.

Though his hold on her was loose, she did not extricate herself but considered a face relaxed except for eyes moving behind heavily lashed lids.

Despite further scrapes, cuts, and bruises, the queen's man looked younger than his thirty or so years—enough of the youth about him to make the warrior appear vulnerable. But it was more than his state of repose. It was the absence of tolerant, dismissive, and judgmental expressions with which he mostly regarded her. And would again, and more severely when next he looked upon the one whose flight to England wrought such tragedy.

You would do well to distance yourself, urged the caution with which she had become familiar since her father's summons had upended her comfortably safe life. *You may have reached England, but the crossing is only one of several obstacles ere your journey's end.*

Amidst how many lost lives? her conscience tossed back. Regardless of the ilk of the ship's crew, many had died to deliver her across the narrow sea. And Sir Norris...

Her emotions shuddered, and she wished she had not run with him during the attack by Count Verielle's men.

But you did, caution spoke again, *and the lives lost will be for naught if you do not flee this one who will do as commanded no matter the right of it. If it is not the convent to which you are destined, then a husband of the queen's choosing. And what chance of another Conrad?*

She confirmed the rise and fall of Sir Durand's chest, told herself it was proof enough he did not need her aid, then eased his arm from around her and discovered something else held her to him. Peering between their bodies, she followed the girdle from around her wrist to where it wrapped his own to its end that disappeared between the planks.

It took little effort to free herself, but when she straightened, her legs were so unsteady she nearly fell. Finding her balance, loose hair dancing before her face where she stood with her back to the chill breeze coming off the water, she steeled herself for what awaited her. Then arms hugged over her chest, she turned to survey what the passing of night laid bare. And clasped herself more closely as she took in a scene that chilled her more than the air slipping through her garments.

Jagged teeth projecting far into the water beneath a sky clothed in enough clouds to stir up another storm, the shore's curved mouth stretched long from one end to the other. But not long enough that the bodies among the wreckage seemed a small number. Never would she have imagined so many would wash ashore nor that there would be so much wreckage. Whatever had settled to the bottom of the sea was surely too little to render tale of a ship gone asunder.

Teeth chattering and convulsing body tempting her to return to Sir Durand and curl against his side, she might have had she not glimpsed movement partway down the beach beside an overturned rowboat. Though possibly one of the crew who could prove dangerous, the hope it was her father's knight made her raise her damp skirts and run.

The sand was wet enough to offer firm footing, but twice her ankle bent to rocks, vegetation, and wreckage. Blessedly, she was sturdily built and suffered only mild discomfort as she continued forward.

"Be Sir Norris," she gasped. "Be alive."

She skirted a mast snapped to the height of a man, its lower end tangled in sailcloth, and averted her gaze from the blue-cast, open-mouthed young seaman whose life Sir Durand had spared only that he might meet a crueler end.

Avoiding the bodies of two others, a mere glimpse of whom proved they were as devoid of life with their frozen, discolored faces, she returned her regard to the one who moved.

Dawn's light too muted by clouds to reveal his identity, she called to Sir Norris, but he responded in no way to show he heard. Having made it to his hands and knees, he hung his head between his arms.

"Sir Norris!"

"Stay back!" he barked.

It did not sound like him, but seeing a knightly sword on his belt, she dropped beside him. As she set a hand on his shoulder, he fell onto his back and caught her wrist.

Her cry muffled by tight throat muscles, she looked from the teeth-baring grimace of the captain to his bloodied neck and chest to a belt hung with the purse and sword taken from Sir Durand. And coming up from his other side was the Wulfrith dagger.

"You think to scavenge from the dead?" He set the blade to her throat.

"Captain! 'Tis Lady Beata Fauvel."

Eyes spasming, he eased his grip, though not so much she could free herself. Then he lowered the dagger.

"Are my crew dead, Lady? All of them?"

Shivering as much from dread of how he would react as the chill, she said, "I know not."

"Look!"

She peered across the overturned boat and saw as she had before, that of all those strewn amid timber, sailcloth, and ropes, only the captain evidenced life.

"Are they dead?"

"It appears so." She swallowed. "But do you loose me, I shall go amongst them and give aid if any live." Not a lie. Though the search would delay her departure, shortening the distance between Sir Durand and her, it was the least owed the crew.

"Your word," the captain commanded.

"It is yours."

"And prayer."

"Prayer?"

He scowled. "Not all of us wanted this life…only until we could make a better one and right our sins."

Though part of Beata argued there were more godly ways to feed and clothe one's self—ways that did not steal the fruit of others' labor and their lives—she was in no position to judge him or his crew. Not she who was blessed to labor only as long and hard as she wished, and whose greatest desperation was experienced while fleeing Count Verielle's men.

"I shall pray for all, Captain."

He released her and let his arm fall atop his chest, then his mouth curved, but his smile was so misshapen it was ugly.

She set a cold hand over his, and though the dimming of his eyes told he required no prompting, whispered, "The Lord is merciful. Go to Him."

His lids dropped, but as if fearful of the darkness there, he sprang them open and looked to the heavens. Then he emptied his lungs.

Beata stared into eyes that saw only what lay beyond this world, and the finality of death made her press her lips against a sob. Only twice had she been so near the loss of life—that of her mother and Conrad—and as she had prayed for them, she would pray for this man.

She bowed her head and beseeched the Lord to forgive the ship's crew their trespasses and sins. And when she could beseech no more, she closed the captain's eyes and stood.

She started to turn away, but Sir Durand's sword caught her eye, next his Wulfrith dagger.

She looked across her shoulder at the wreckage to which the queen's man and she had been secured. It was angled such that she could not see him, but a sweep of her gaze across the shore confirmed she was the only one able to walk away. And impressed on her that no matter her duty to her father, it was wrong to risk the lives of others as Sir Norris had done for his liege.

She would not abandon the man who had saved her. At least, not until certain Sir Durand could also walk away. But first she must keep her word to the captain.

She started forward, but the possibility she would need protection made her turn back. It tossed her stomach to take from the dead, but she told herself she took only what the captain had stolen. "Forgive me," she said and uncurled his fingers from the Wulfrith dagger.

Wishing the sun beginning its ascent of the winter sky would burn away the clouds, she set off across the shore. Shortly, she heard a groan and followed it to a man so torn it was a struggle to keep her stomach from turning inside out. Though not unaware of the sorrows and ills of the world, Conrad had shielded her from what lay behind the talk of men.

She held the dying man's hand, prayed as life fled him, then searched for others. There were more than a score of bodies, several of whom stared at the lightening sky until she lowered their lids.

As she moved farther down the shore, she noted the garments of many over whom she prayed were finer than what the seamen had worn and realized her party could not have been the only noble passengers. Others had been as desperate to reach England that they sought passage aboard a pirate's ship rather than one with a legitimate reason for plying the seas.

More heavily feeling the deaths of those on this shore, none of whom proved Sir Norris, Beata looked and listened.

All was still but for clouds plodding across the sky, birds coming to earth, and the sea stirring itself into another frenzy.

Deciding it was time to face Sir Durand's wrath, she turned, but a glimpse of yellow cloth caught between large rocks near the shoreline gave her pause. Another body, and likely that of a woman, it being rare a man donned that soft, pale color.

With the hope of finding life there, Beata gathered her strength and moved toward rocks most easily reached by venturing into the tide. It was difficult to climb their slippery surface, and as reward for her effort, the only aid she could offer was prayer for another victim.

"I am sorry," she whispered as she knelt beside a lady of middling years whose woolen mantle was splayed beneath her like wings, face tranquil despite its horrible discoloration.

After beseeching the Lord for the woman's soul, Beata acceded it was time to return to Sir Durand, but her body would not obey. Despite the promise of warmth in movement, she was too cold to rise, her heart too heavy for all who would not know home and hearth again…whose absence would ever be felt by those who loved them…

She folded over herself, pressed her face to her bent knees, and finding warmth there, yielded to sobs as the day's horrors carved themselves into her memory.

9

The *Vexing Widow*—beyond any woman he knew—was more trouble than she was worth. Thrice he had dragged her out of a mess, first thwarting her abduction, next delivering her from a man's unwanted attentions, then keeping her from the great maw of the sea. For all that, she had stolen away whilst the exhaustion of ensuring they reached land held him in the depths of sleep.

Blessedly, he had not yet fallen prey to those quick to pick over the wreckage of ships. But they would come, ready to do to survivors what the sea had not lest witnesses threaten their claim on the wreckage.

Denying himself the comfort of cursing, Durand sat up and looked from the gray sky that portended another storm to the beach. The only surprise of the latter was the amount of wreckage and bodies.

"Too much," he rasped and recalled the dark of hours earlier when he had glimpsed another ship. Here was proof it was not imagined. Two ships *had* broken offshore.

His chest tightened. Had Wulfrith insisted on sailing to keep his vow to deliver The Vestal Widow to England? Had the other ship been his?

Nay, though he would keep his word at the cost of his own life, he would not risk the lives of innocents. But if the captain had been confident the crossing could be made...

Durand released his hand from the girdle looped around it and stood. Though his leg ached, it held, evidencing that woman was useful for one thing—sewing up a man's flesh.

Lest he required something with which to bind her, he freed her girdle. As he knotted it around his waist, he turned to study the land rising from the sea. On the left side of the cove to just past its center, a scrub-covered knoll sloped down to the beach. To the right, a chalk cliff rose.

But it was not of Dover. They had not been blown that far off course. Was it of Worthing whose settlement lay several leagues inland? Nay, farther east, likely near Brighthelmstone.

As he set off across the beach with a hitch in his stride, one moment he prayed that if Wulfrith had been on that other ship he lived, in the next he vowed if his former liege had died, The Vexing Widow would know no more joy.

Careful, Durand, his painstakingly restored honor warned. *Do you grind me in the dirt again, I might remain there and make of you a man like the one you killed so he could work no more ill on she who first owned the name Beatrix.*

Praying he would not return to that darkness, he followed footprints that showed the lady had searched body to body, including that of the captain from whom Durand retrieved his belt, sword, and purse. But though the miscreant was said to have also claimed the Wulfrith dagger, it was not to be found.

Lost to the sea? Or had the one forced to relinquish her own dagger taken it? Aye, just as she had taken coin and other items from the dead in preparation for her journey to Wiltford.

"I will find you Lady," he growled. After buckling his belt and adjusting his sword and purse on it, he opened the latter's drawstring that did not feel as it should. The stiffly rolled wax-sealed parchment was missing. Had the Vestal Widow taken it? More likely the captain. Whatever the missive's contents, only that miscreant and the queen knew what was expected of the lady's father should she prove an heiress. And now only the queen.

Once more tracking his charge, he noted an increasing number of the dead were not the sort to seek passage on the ship he had forced his way aboard. Here were honorable men of the sea, among them a handful of others whose garments told they were noble. But no Wulfrith, nor his knights, who might be at the bottom of the sea.

He lengthened his stride to sooner bring the lady to ground and learn the identity of the second ship, but discovered the rocks had wreaked as much devastation on the vessel as its passengers.

Damp garments increasingly uncomfortable in the brisk air coming off the water, teeth set to keep them from warring with one another, he silently beseeched forgiveness from the dead nobleman whose mantle he claimed. Though the garment was no drier than his own clothing, once it covered him shoulders to calves, it deflected enough of the chill to aid brisk movement in warming his body.

With further regret, he relieved the man of his wineskin and wet his salt-stung mouth with a long swallow before resuming the hunt.

When he lost the tracks at the tide's edge near the eastern end of the cove, he was tempted to leave the lady to a fate that could see her taken as booty, but faith and honor rejected that option.

Assuring himself there would be satisfaction in thwarting her, he considered the chalk cliff rising from rocks at its base, then the scrub-covered slope at the opposite end of the cove that provided the easiest and safest means of ascent.

Despite his injury, he must go the way of The Vestal Widow who appeared to have followed the chalk cliffs skirting the shore for what could be many leagues. Why had she gone that way? Was she addled? Did she hope to throw him off her scent?

The latter, he decided. But just as the disappearance of her footprints did not fool him, it would not deceive scavengers who might give chase lest a survivor carried away valuables or alerted others to the wreckage. Still, Durand also went into the cold tide in the hope pursuers were less likely to follow survivors who numbered two or more strong.

Resenting the soaking of boots that had begun to dry, he moved toward the rocks projecting into the sea and, as he began his ascent, caught the rumble of carts.

He looked around at the land above the shore. Assured the scavengers were not in sight, he turned forward again. And saw a piece of cloth between jagged rocks that stood like pillars near the point.

Though the material was not of a color worn by The Vestal Widow, and whoever wore it was likely dead, he altered his course. It was harder going. Worse, he would be seen more easily. But it proved worth the effort when he glimpsed in the space between the rocks the one who bent over her knees alongside a lifeless woman. She must have seen him coming and hidden.

As he moved around the side of the western-facing rock, he pressed down emotions that sought the surface as surely as he had done when the sea offered itself as a tomb.

Voices sounding above the turning of cart wheels, he peered over his shoulder. The scavengers visible now, he pushed his injured leg harder and sprang around the backside of the rock.

And there she was, shoulders convulsing and sobs muffled by her skirts. He would not have believed one who so readily indulged in laughter, teasing, and unsolicited opinions capable of such misery. But then, her sorrow was surely for her own circumstances.

When Durand closed a hand around her arm, she cried out and strained opposite. When he yanked her to her feet, she swept the Wulfrith dagger to his abdomen.

"Lady," he growled, "you do not want to do that. I vow, you do not."

Her tear-reddened eyes widened. "Durand!" she gasped and dropped the dagger and collapsed against him.

Though further angered by her disregard of his prized possession, her reaction and familiarity with his Christian name disarmed him.

As she intends, he told himself and set her away—only to drag her back when her knees would not hold.

"Save your games for when scavengers are not upon us!" he snarled.

She dropped her head back, and past damp tresses the wind slanted across her face, he saw what seemed confusion and fear. And noted her chattering teeth and chilled flesh beneath his hands.

As he pondered her reason for not securing a mantle, she mumbled, "They are lost. All are lost."

She wished him to believe her despair was for others. "Aye, and for no good cause. Now we are leaving."

He released her, and when her legs held, retrieved his dagger and thrust it in its sheath. Then he freed the hem of the dead woman's gown from the rocks so it would not draw the scavengers' attention and, as gently as possible, removed her mantle.

But when he opened it to The Vestal Widow, she stepped back. "I will not take from the dead."

That gave him pause, her movement body to body evidencing she had done exactly that to aid her journey to Wiltford. However, it appeared the Wulfrith dagger was the only thing she had taken, and though it was worth a fat purse, it was not conceivable she would be content with something for which she must secure a buyer.

Ponder it later, he counseled and whipped the mantle around her shoulders.

"Nay!" She jumped to the side, causing the garment to slide off her back.

With one hand he gripped her arm, with the other raised her chin. "Though I like it not, once more I shall risk my life to save yours, even if I must put you over my shoulder. Now behave!"

Her lashes fluttered, and the fearful woman shifted toward the one tossed from his destrier. Then she pulled free and reached to the mantle. And gingerly lifted it as if it were smeared with offal.

Durand snatched it from her. "God's patience, you vex, Lady!" He swept the damp wool over her shoulders, snatched it closed at her throat, and pulled her around and over rocks whose dark color he prayed was near enough that of their garments and hair that they would not be seen.

To the lady's credit, she was no fragile thing, and though she panted, she did not force him to slow.

Before leaving the cove, Durand looked back. A dozen men were halfway down the slope. Hoping the need to guide their carts carefully and quickly claim their treasures would prevent them from closely searching the area, he pulled the lady out of sight of the first cove and dropped back against a rock to rest his leg.

As he considered the new cove they must traverse—unscalable, being entirely rimmed by chalk cliff—he sensed the gaze of The Vestal Widow who kept the reach of his arm between them as if she feared brushing against his anger.

Feeling regret over alarming her, he thrust it away with the reminder Baron Wulfrith's wife might now be a widow and his children fatherless, then turned his attention to the beach. Only one body was visible amidst the wreckage that had come ashore here, and it was not of Wulfrith or one of his knights. The face down man was large, but in an extremely broad sense.

Durand pushed off the rock. Grateful the lady required no threat to set her moving again, he drew her along the cliff base, quickening their pace when the air stirred further and the darkening clouds began to spit.

In the same manner, they traversed two more stretches of beach almost devoid of wreckage before the knighthood training that had impressed on him the importance of being aware of his surroundings gained him a glimpse of men atop the cliff. They approached from the direction toward which the lady and he moved.

Durand yanked her back against the cliff, and when she looked wide-eyed at him, said, "At so early an hour, and with another storm in the making, likely more scavengers. A good thing, since warring over booty should prevent them from searching us out."

Shoulders shrugged up, she said, "S-searching us out?"

"Though our footprints disappeared beneath the tide, they will know we go this way."

"You believe they would harm us?"

Resolve once more tested, he said, "Do they decide 'tis worth their time to give chase, it will not be to assuage their consciences over our well-being."

She averted her gaze and asked low, "How fares your leg?"

Hitch apparent, patience stretched, he eyed the clouds that would not merely spot those caught out in the open.

"I am so dry," she said, and he heard her swallow. "May I have a drink?"

He passed her the wineskin and watched her put the spout to her lips. Before he could warn her to drink as little as possible lest the journey was long, she refit the stopper and returned the skin. At least she had some sense.

When the voices receded and rain fell with more enthusiasm, he accepted they could go no farther and searched for shelter among the caves pockmarking the cliff. Most were too shallow to offer much protection, but two were deep enough to shield them from the icy rain.

Durand chose the one whose opening was so low they had to enter hunched over and drew The Vestal Widow into the dim space. Ten feet in, they were able to straighten, and he released the lady to feel his way to the farthest corner that was wide enough to swing a sword if necessary.

He unsheathed his blade, lowered against the chalk wall, and inwardly groaned at taking weight off his injured leg.

"I can see naught," the lady whispered, the gray light behind her lower body revealing she remained where he had left her.

"Come, Lady."

Beata squinted at where she more imagined than saw Durand. She hardly knew him, but what she did know was that his anger at being bound aboard ship had swelled—so much that since putting the Wulfrith dagger to him, she had sensed his ire hovering about her throat. She would fare better to keep her distance.

"Sit, Lady!" he growled.

She startled and gasped, "I am afeared of you!" And not only did she hate herself for pleading that did not fit Conrad's wife and widow, she hurt over memories of when her husband had advised her against allowing crippling words to pass her lips.

Four and ten she had been the night her groom had gained their nuptial bed. Miraculously, her tearfully blurted declaration caused the aged warrior to draw back. But whereas Conrad had meant to loose lust on her, Durand Marshal might loose something more dangerous.

She heard him breathe deep as if to calm himself, then he said, "After what you have wrought, fear is the least owed you."

That should have quieted her, but she ached for him to understand she was without choice and know how deeply she felt the loss of those enlisted to deliver her to England. "I regret running with Sir Norris. Pray, believe me, I would not have—"

"You think *regret* is of comfort to the dead?"

She drew a quavering breath. "I am sorry for their terrible end, and that I could offer little more than prayer for their souls."

Silence, then he said, "I am to believe that as desperate as you were to escape me, you stopped to pray for them?"

She took a step forward. "When I left you, I meant to distance myself, but I realized I could not without being certain you were well. Thus, after keeping my word to the captain to pray for his men, I intended to return. And I would have had I not happened on the lady." She lowered her lids, and when she lifted them, found her eyes had adjusted enough to make him out where he sat against the rock wall. "I hurt for her and all the others—"

"All the others? Know you who *all* they are?"

She swallowed hard. "Except for Sir Norris, who is likely beneath the sea, I but know the others as the ship's crew."

"Not *only* except for Sir Norris!"

Realizing he could not see her confusion, she said, "Certes, I did not know the lady. I was unaware there were other nobles aboard—"

"There were no other nobles on *our* ship."

"You make no sense."

"But I do—providing you think beyond your narrow existence."

Beata would have taken offense were she not so unsettled by the puzzle cast before her. Groping at the pieces, she shivered harder as the wind stole into the cave and swept beneath her hem and up her legs.

"Our ship was not the only one claimed by the sea on the night past, Lady," Durand fit a piece.

"You are saying—"

"As I should not have to. Aye, the reason for so much wreckage and so many bodies—among them nobles—is that two ships broke on the rocks. And possibly each other."

It made sense, but as Durand had accused, she had not looked far enough beyond herself. "Dear Lord."

"Do not stop there, Lady. Tell, who besides the noblewoman, whose mantle warms you, do you think was aboard that other ship?"

She clasped herself close. "How can I know?"

"Think!"

It was difficult. Because the cold muddled her? Or did Sir Durand merely taunt her?

He made a sound of disgust. "You know the ship waiting to return you to England was not alone in hoping to cross the channel on the day past."

She did, but could it be? The wreck of a second ship was tragedy enough, but if it was the baron's...

"Aye, though I found no evidence to prove it was his, had its captain believed it safe to sail, Baron Wulfrith would have given chase."

Her knees quaked. She barely knew the warrior, but the possibility he was dead hurt as much as—nay, more than—the loss of Sir Norris. The baron had fewer years about him and was a husband and the father of young children.

"Why, Lady?" the queen's man demanded. "What about you is of such import so many have died?"

A question only her father could answer. And in light of the dead, a pitifully poor answer it would be.

"What about you?" he persisted.

She lowered her chin. "I cannot say."

She heard the rustle of his damp garments and boots over the chalk floor, stopped breathing when his shadowed figure halted before her. "I shall say it, then. As the queen suspected, Conrad Fauvel's widow is an heiress, aye?"

Though that suspicion was more the reason Eleanor had forced Beata to accept Durand's escort than concern over her subject's well-being, and it had angered that the queen sought to do unto another what she refused to have done unto her—bestowing power and wealth on a favorite through marriage to an heiress—Beata was almost numb over the offense.

Durand gripped her arms. "Are you?"

She should continue to deny it as her sire would have her do—laugh and feign astonishment—but her flight with Sir Norris during the attack outside the inn evidenced her deception. Still, she could straddle the line between truth and falsehood with what was true in this moment—rather, what she believed was true.

Lifting her face, feeling Durand's breath on her brow, catching the glitter of his eyes, she said, "I know not."

A growl rumbled from him. "The answer, Lady, is *aye or nay*."

"Or *mayhap*."

As if she were the foulest of beings, he released her and pivoted.

She had no intention of following him, but then came the roll of thunder and a crack of lightning that splashed blue light across the cave's walls—and scattered the leaves in that corner of her mind.

Having glimpsed the queen's man lowering to the right before the cave returned to darkness, she stretched out a hand and moved toward him. When her fingers met the wall against which he sat, she pressed her palm to its smooth, damp surface and turned her back to it.

As she began to slide down it, he said, "The other side of me, Lady."

She nearly asked the reason, but she realized here was the warrior. If any pursued them as far as the cave, he did not wish her between him and his opponent. He might not care to protect her, but he would do it for his queen.

If only he would do it for you, bemoaned a voice that did not belong in her head. Closing the door on it, she stepped forward. As she started around Durand, lightning once more lit the walls. She hated it, but it prevented her from stepping on the knight's injured leg and saw her seated beside him sooner—too near, her hip and arm brushing his.

He stiffened, and she expected him to shift away, but he left it to her to correct. She wanted to, but not as much as she longed for assurance of his presence when the storm once more made itself heard, felt, and seen and the rain gave rise to mist that billowed into the cave.

She tucked her chin into the neck of her mantle. "Forgive me, but for as long as I can remember, I have been afraid of thunderstorms."

"More than you are of me?" he said, not with threat but with what seemed accusation—as if her declaration was meant to lead him astray.

"Strange that, but aye. The wrath outside worries me more than that within."

As if to prove it, she jerked as the thunder of moments earlier birthed pulsing light of such duration that when she snapped her chin around, her gaze met his. And held long enough for her to note his concern.

In the ensuing darkness, she wrapped her arms around herself to keep from convulsing over imaginings that, as a child, had tormented her when ill weather threatened to blow away the rotting leaves and reveal what lay beneath.

Following marriage to Conrad, she had liked thunderstorms no better, but with each passing year, the dark corner had become more distant and blurred until only encounters with men like Sir Oliver drew her near enough to glimpse the leaves. Why did the storm so affect her now? Because she had returned to England where that childhood dream was dreamt?

"Lady?" The knight's hand touched her arm.

Struggling to keep from clapping her own over it to hold him to her, she gasped, "I wish you did not hate me so, but I understand and am all the more grateful you saved my life. 'Tis honorable."

Stranger yet, a moment later she was pressed to his side, the arm she had brushed against turned around her back and waist, her cheek on his collarbone, her head beneath his chin.

"Durand?"

"Silence, Lady Beata!" His breath wove through her tumbled hair and warmed her scalp. "Just...be silent."

She swallowed further words, mostly out of surprise at once more hearing her name pass his lips and the thought she would like to hear him speak it with more familiarity—absent her title.

"Let us rest while the storm is upon us," he said. "We are a long way from where we need to be."

Where was that? she wanted to ask, but she was too grateful for someone to hold to in a storm—even one who disliked her—to risk losing the comfort.

Compressing her lips so they would not betray her, keeping her eyes open lest she too soon drifted away from one more considerate than he had cause to be, she told herself to remember how it felt to be held by an honorable man.

10

*S*HE IS RESPONSIBLE, Durand reminded himself, having become increasingly aware of the woman he had been compelled to draw close an hour past. She must answer for the dead, especially if the second ship was Wulfrith's. And yet—

Yet? he demanded of the fool.

If what she told was true, she but remained loyal to her father as a daughter—

If! And what of loyalty to one's sovereign? The lady is a deceiver!

As once he had been. To that the Wulfriths could attest.

Aye, though perhaps no longer Baron Wulfrith. Because of her.

He lowered his gaze to The Vestal Widow. Though she slept, she continued to hold to him. As he tried to part the shadows across her face, he recalled how she had pleaded for him as he fought the ship's crew, declaring death need not be the end of their confrontation. He would have been tossed into the sea had she not promised a greater reward. And when he sought to convince her of the danger of setting sail, she had acquiesced. It was Sir Norris who would not be moved.

True, she had left him on the beach, but her claim she meant to return to him after praying for the dead was supported by footprints body to body and that she had possessed only his dagger, likely taken for protection.

Certes, she vexed, but she was not as senseless or self-centered as he wished to believe.

Aye, *wished*. His best defense against women who tempted him to abandon faith and honor to answer base needs was to exaggerate their ills, as it was also a defense against exposing a heart twice denied—first Lady Beatrix Wulfrith, then the healer, Helene. Or nearly so the latter, a half-noble whom Wulfrith's youngest brother, Abel, had taken to wife.

Durand had not felt as much for her, but he might have had he not learned from Lady Beatrix the folly of feeling much for a woman who felt little for him. Thus, he had pulled back from that disastrous edge when the kiss pressed on Helene had not moved her heart toward his. And he had further redeemed himself by aiding Abel Wulfrith and her in overcoming the obstacles keeping them apart.

Now here he was with The Vestal Widow, defending behavior earlier found indefensible, feeling the fit of her, and when lightning lit the cave, liking how well he wore her.

I have been long without a woman, he tried to excuse his softening toward one who should move neither mind nor body. Though at court, opportunities aplenty presented to be intimate with the fairer sex, it was years since—

He dragged his thoughts from Wulfrith's oldest sister back to this lady to whom he should not be attracted—she whose speech, mannerisms, and appearance were almost indelicate. And even if what drew him to a woman was so altered, there was the barrier of pursuing one he could not have. Were Conrad Fauvel's widow a great heiress, her wealth would not be wasted on a mere knight.

A distant crack of thunder made the lady startle. "Tell not," she breathed.

Did she dream?

"'Tis a secret." This time her words had voice, but she sounded more like a girl than a woman.

"Lady?"

Her fingers on his chest convulsed. "Ours alone."

Durand set a hand over hers. Feeling its tremble, he called again, "Lady?"

"Unto death." She whimpered, then hissed, "Shh!"

"Beata?" He grimaced over the ease with which he named her.

"Tell not!" she rasped and began to weep.

He knew better than to respond to a woman's tears, that having been the beginning of his downfall, but when her shoulders jerked and hand scrabbled at his mantle, he lifted her face. "Awaken, Beata!"

She stilled and rain-soaked light leapt into her eyes. "Durand?"

"It is I. You dream of dark things."

"Do I?"

He did not answer, and moments later she whispered, "Aye, the leaves."

"Leaves?"

"They rot away. I cannot allow that."

Clearly, she was not fully in this moment. "It is but a dream, Lady."

"Would that it were, but I do not think so."

"It is. *This* is real. Us. Here. Now."

Her chest expanded as she drew a deep breath, then she came up on her knees, slid her arms around his neck, and said near his mouth. "I would stay with you. Let us not go back."

"Beata—"

"Aye, Beata." Those words causing her lips to brush his, he wondered if he was the one dreaming and why he wanted the unseemly lady to fulfill the promise of a kiss.

She fulfilled it—tentatively and awkwardly giving proof of the name by which she was better known. And he responded, giving lie to the name the queen bestowed upon him. He drew her nearer, opened his mouth on hers, and tried what no man had tried. Just as he had done with—

He pulled his head back so sharply it struck the wall. Narrowing his eyes at the shadowed woman he had pulled onto his lap, he heard her soft panting and sensed her uncertainty.

This was a place ventured before. And he had been ruined for it. As then, now there was grieving over the dead. As then, now one he did not want tempted him. As then, now he had tasted what was freely given.

But not as then, he would not claim innocence that ought to be gifted to a husband, no matter that the lady invited his attention. When she was better of mind, she would be grateful.

Though he wanted to thrust her away, one other thing learned from the ruination of a lady was that it was cruel to be callous, even if only to discourage feelings he did not return. That he had done with Lady Gaenor who had looked at him with her heart in her eyes.

He did not believe this woman was enamored of him as the eldest of Wulfrith's sisters had been, but lest she moved in that direction, he must set her aright. For both their sakes.

"That should not have happened," he said and eased her off him.

He sensed her confusion, then its resolution. "Certes, it should not have." She scooted farther away as if she did not trust the one who had ended what she had begun.

Might she now accuse him of ravishment?

That riled him until hard-learned lessons forced him to take responsibility for his part that was possibly greater than that of one who lacked experience with the carnal. The first seed of intimacy had been cast by him when he drew her near to offer comfort, not unlike when he had soothed a grieving Lady Gaenor over the belief her sister had died.

"Pray, forgive one who knows it is ungodly to take advantage of a woman," he said. "I but meant to awaken you from a disturbing dream."

Her breath caught, but as if to cover something she had not meant to expose, she issued a sound between a laugh and a snort. "You need not be so honorable, Sir Durand. I was hardly myself, but not so unaware I do not recall *I* set myself at *you*."

She could not have surprised more.

"And now, methinks, we know the truth of the names by which we are called," she continued. "The Vestal Widow yet virtuous, though less than before this day. The gallant monk..."

She could surprise more, bold when coy was the way of most ladies. But then, she had chosen the lesser of evils to distract him from the greater, had she not? Strange that the dream she believed not a dream more disturbed her than discussing the intimacy they should not have shared.

She sighed. "As my experience is limited, I cannot know how much of a monk you are, but never have I been kissed and touched like that."

Further surprise. He had been certain her mouth was untried, but considering her penchant for flirtation, Sir Oliver was not the first to attempt to alter the name given her.

"The gallant monk has not always been that, aye?" she said.

Farther from *gallant* and *monk* than he would have her know.

"Regardless, I thank you, Sir Durand. Though my conduct is sometimes deemed unseemly, ere this day I could not be accused of behaving with wanton disregard for my reputation. And I can conceive of no means of explaining it away without sounding false."

He could, having grown accustomed to women who found him all the more desirable for his lack of interest.

"Forgive me," she said.

"As we find ourselves in dire circumstances, Lady, I believe we can be pardoned for behavior beyond our wishes and good sense."

"Beyond," she murmured, though he was not sure it was in agreement. "You are a rare man. Many of your sex would not concern themselves over compromising a willing lady, even one so undesirable."

Did she hope he would gainsay her? Assure her she was desirable? "I but aspire not to stand repentant before God more than already I shall."

Beata considered the figure of the queen's man. Hating that she felt the distance between them, she lightened her tone. "As I can attest, an aspiration well within your reach, Sir Knight."

"I thank you, Lady."

It bothered that he eschewed her given name—and more so after what had just happened. "Pray, Sir Durand, cease calling me *Lady*."

"It is done out of respect."

"I think not. Though at court you spoke the names of ladies alongside their titles, with rare exception, you deny me the same. For what I do not understand, but it is impersonal and dismissive, especially after..." She caught back what need not be spoken. "I am Lady Beata. As it seems we are to share company for a time, afford me that small measure of warmth."

After a long moment, he said, "Lady Beata. Now as you wish to be better known, tell me about the great heiress you may be."

She tensed. She had been appalled at betraying her father's confidence when faced with this man's anger over the loss of lives that might include Baron Wulfrith, but only until realizing it was already betrayed by the drastic measures taken to deliver her to England.

"Lady?" he prompted, then added, "Beata."

She liked even better her name spoken that way—liked being simply Beata to him. And wished she did not. She was not immune to attraction. Though faith, loyalty, and love of Conrad had prevented her from being tempted to act on it whilst wed, never had it so tightly wound through her. But it was folly to feel such for a man who felt only with the loins when he kissed her.

"You said *mayhap* you are an heiress," he pressed.

Grateful there was too little light for him to read her face, she said, "I did, but there is naught to tell, so slight is the possibility."

Feeling his disbelief move him toward anger, she longed to return to the relatively comfortable place they had landed following their intimacy...wished she could confide in him. But if what her father feared came to pass, she would further betray him, denying him time and space in which to free himself of the queen's plotting. And Beata a say in her future.

Tears pricking, she prayed that if the Lord once more denied her father an heir from his second wife, her clergyman brother could be persuaded to leave the Church. Did Emmerich relent, she would return to France and withdraw to her dower lands where she could laugh as much as she was moved to laugh, discuss whatever she wished to discuss, and determine the tasks and pleasures upon which to spend her life.

It was as Conrad had provided so she would not become chattel. True, she would grow old alone, but better hobbled by a heart with empty rooms than crushed beneath a man's heel.

"After all that has gone," Durand finally said, "I do not believe the possibility is slight. Certes, what you yielded to the queen is far different from what you yielded this day—that you do not know if you are an heiress but 'tis possible enough to merit *mayhap*. Thus, as eager as you are to answer your father's summons, it follows your infant brother has passed the same as the two birthed before him and your priest of a brother does not wish to leave the Church."

"My infant brother lives," she exclaimed. It was no lie, since she could not know if that truth had altered since Sir Norris had crossed the channel to bring her home.

"Perhaps he did, but does he still?"

She drew a deep breath. "Though I know not the babe, should ill befall him I shall grieve, and more deeply shall my father. Thus, I will speak no more on this."

In the long silence, she eased, then he said, "To make our wait on the storm's passing tolerable, let us speak of the dream you think not a dream."

She floundered, and happening on fading memories of what she had further revealed, almost wished to talk of her father's heir.

"You spoke of leaves and a secret to keep unto death."

And clinging to him, she had repeated the desperate words spoken to a little girl—*Tell not!* Not her nurse, not the children with whom she played, most certainly not the priest. Then glimpsing the leaves beneath the topmost layer, their curling spines and fingers speckled with crimson, she had begun to cry—softly, so none would hear and ask questions that might make her break the word given her mother.

"You feared the leaves would rot away."

And reveal what lay beneath. Beata drew her knees to her chest, wrapped her arms around them, and told herself she could comfort away her fears as well as Durand had done.

"You said you could not allow that. Why?"

She shrugged. "'Twas but a dream—one that has mostly flown away."

"You did not think it a dream."

"I must have been in that middle place between imaginings and reality." Again, not truly a lie. Though those imaginings were more real than any dream she could recall, far more resembling something carved from life than bits and pieces thrown against the walls inside her head, it had to be a dream just as her mother and father had assured their little girl.

"Only a dream," she said and determined that if they were going to speak, it would not be about her. "What of the gallant monk? I am certain that tale is more fascinating than a pile of leaves."

"It is not. The queen but enjoys raising questions more compelling than their answers."

She smiled against her knees. "But not without merit. Not without truths. So what is yours?"

"Only that I can be trusted with ladies of the court."

"And those not of the court. If ever you require a witness to vouch for restraint that extends even to women who seek your attentions, you have but to summon me."

"Lady!" he said sharply. "Too much your husband indulged you. Now that you are in the real world and no longer under his protection, you must temper your tongue and behavior. Do you not, men like Sir Oliver will happily teach you hard and painful lessons."

Beata set her teeth against argument. She resented the truth that made her long for her dower lands—and more determined to persuade her brother to stand as heir should that duty fall to one of them. But how she would do that, she did not know, it being many years since their tearful parting.

"Methinks it best time pass slowly, Sir Durand," she said and turned her back to him, lowered to the floor, and pillowed her head on the crook of her arm.

It was hours before he spoke again, and only then to rouse her from fitful dozing and inform her the storm had passed. It was time to make their way inland.

11

Death might await them there. Were he alone, he would not allow the threat to keep him from Brighthelmstone, where he could sooner discover the identity of the second ship and more easily secure what was needed to reach Wiltford. Unfortunately, the scavengers likely hailed from that town, and attention would fall on any who, disheveled and presenting injuries, possessed enough wealth to equip themselves with worthy mounts and supplies.

Thus, they must travel farther inland before starting for Wiltford, a journey made longer for the decision to go around London to sooner reach the renowned fortress where he had received his knighthood training.

Silently cursing the circuitous route that might not be necessary could he learn Baron Wulfrith's fate, Durand turned from the town that beckoned.

"Scavengers?" Lady Beata asked when he started past her.

Once again, he was grateful she was not delicate, especially since his injured leg would protest supporting her. "Aye, the town is too near the wreckage to risk entering it. Hence, we have many leagues to go if we are to find an inn ere nightfall." Hearing her stomach rumble, he added, "And food."

She gripped her mantle closed at her throat, doubtless to keep the cold air from slipping inside. "I worry for your leg."

"It does not bleed—merely aches."

"But—"

"My lady, the only thing with which you should concern yourself is giving me no more trouble so I may sooner discharge my duty to deliver you to Wiltford."

Her lids flickered. "I shall be as a lamb."

That was not possible. Wondering what she planned, he peered into her pale face and quickly moved past softly parted lips that showed the small gap between front teeth he had not found—*did* not find—appealing. Though her countenance was visible with her hair drawn back into a single braid, it revealed naught, but that did not mean she did not scheme.

"We keep to the wood as much as possible," he said and swept his hood over his head.

Rain that had earlier soaked the ground, turning dirt to mud and low places to small pools, made negotiation of the wood and occasional field troublesome.

Only twice was Durand moved to bring his sword to hand, and he was well enough aware of the advance of others that he and the lady had time to take cover.

At last, teeth aching over how hard he ground them to counter his leg's discomfort, he sighted a brown haze against the dusky sky. The small town beneath it boasted a tavern with lodging abovestairs. Though two rooms were available, he secured one, sacrificing propriety and comfort for keeping safe—and close—the lady he claimed was his wife.

Fortunately, The Vestal Widow's surprise over that was revealed only by her startle felt beneath the hand with which he guided her forward. Still, the tavern owner eyed his guests with interest, lingering longest on the husband's battered face.

Durand would sleep half-awake.

Though he preferred to secure horses and supplies ahead of the morrow to allow them to depart at dawn, his possession of the amount of coin required to do so would increase their chances of being set upon, especially while they were more vulnerable in an enclosed space. The morning was soon enough to risk it when he would have more room in which to wield his sword.

As he closed the door of the pitifully appointed but clean chamber, Lady Beata turned to him where she stood at the center of a room barely large enough to contain its small bed and thinly laid pallet.

"My lord husband." She fingered the tail of what remained of her braid. "It has not quite the sound it did with my first husband."

"As it should not," he clipped. "But do you suspect my intentions are no longer honorable, know I but keep you near to ensure your safety."

And that I cause you no more trouble, Beata silently added. Wishing her belly were less vocal so she might sooner huddle beneath the pallet's threadbare covers, she said, "Be assured, I do not suspect you of anything untoward. I know what you do."

He inclined his head. "The bed is yours."

"But your leg—"

"Do not grieve me, Lady…Beata. I shall take the pallet."

She sank onto the edge of the bed to await the arrival of brazier coals, water, hand towels, wine, and viands. The first three were delivered promptly, the last two much later. But the chill was chased from the room and filth cleaned from hands and faces when Durand bolted the door behind the retreating tavern owner.

"Eat." He nodded at the platter set on a stool between bed and pallet, then removed his mantle to reveal sword, dagger, bulging purse, and fine garments rendered tattered, bloodied, and begrimed. And that which he had used to secure them to the wreckage.

"You brought my girdle."

He glanced down. "Lest it prove necessary to bind you."

When he had believed she had fled him.

"I am pleased it has not been necessary," he said, *"thus far."*

Resenting his threat, she unfastened her mantle and let it fall to the straw-stuffed mattress. As she reached to the viands, Durand stepped alongside. He remained standing, picking over pulls of surprisingly succulent chicken, wedges of mold-speckled cheese, slices of shriveled apple, and slabs of brown bread—all of which seemed, in that moment, the finest of foods.

"You eat well," the queen's man said as he bent to the platter again.

She stilled. Did he mean *too well?* She looked up and found his golden eyes nearly level with hers. More disconcerting, he moved them to her mouth, and only then did she realize the pad of her thumb was on her tongue. It was coarse to lick the juices from one's fingers, behavior in which she did not normally indulge.

"I am thinking"—she lowered her hand to her lap—"you are a man who prefers ladies as small of figure as they are of speech and laughter."

He straightened. "I suppose I do."

Beata did not understand why his agreement bothered her so much. She was attracted to him, but that was all. Her heart was not a participant, and well it should not be since she was no fit for him. Though she did not carry excess weight, neither did she peck at her food like a bird.

Recalling an encounter with a visiting nobleman whose attentions she had spurned, and who sought to convince Conrad he only sported with the young lady of ten and six, she wondered if Durand thought her fat. It was as the nobleman implied when he assured his host he would not seriously pursue one so distant from slender.

Beata had been heavier then, having not entirely shed her girl's body nor attained her full height, but not fat. And Conrad had concurred, first with a fist that broke his guest's front teeth, then assurances to his young wife she was becomingly curvaceous as he would have her remain.

She raised her eyebrows. "Further proof that, where you are concerned, Sir Durand, I need not worry over my virtue?"

He frowned. "I did not mean to imply you are…"

"Nay, I am not *fat*. But I am quite curvaceous, hmm?"

His jaw shifted.

"Certes, I am not effortlessly flung over a man's shoulder." She wrinkled her nose. "Nor am I easily snatched from atop a moving horse and subdued. Now were I—"

Blessedly, her tongue did not keep pace with her thoughts, for she had almost compared herself to Baron Wulfrith's petite sister with whom she was to believe she had only a name in common. As the possible loss of the baron burdened Sir Durand, it would not do to make it more felt.

"Aye, not easily subdued," he murmured and raised the eyebrow above his bruised eye that showed the advantage of being of good build. Then he drained his cup of wine, stacked a piece of bread with other foodstuffs, and put as much distance between them as possible—the three feet separating bed from pallet.

Though Beata's appetite waned, she continued eating.

Afterward, with the black of night filling the cracks in the window's shutters, Durand moved to the flickering lantern hung on a hook alongside the door. Though she expected him to extinguish it, he removed his boots. Then with his back to her, he raised the hem of his tunic and rolled down the hose of his injured leg.

She rose. "Does it bleed?"

"No longer."

"It should be cleansed with wine and dressed with a fresh bandage. Will you allow me to tend you?"

Durand wanted to decline, further discouraging her interest in him as he had done in agreeing he preferred women of smaller stature and behavior—even more imperative than discouraging Eleanor's ladies, none of whom he had kissed. But if infection set in, healing would be prolonged, and despite her inexperience with stitching flesh, she had proven capable and strong of stomach.

"Aye, tend me." He crossed to the pallet and removed his sword belt, then lowered and put his back to the wall.

Beata retrieved her wine cup and a towel and sank to her knees before him. Though her touch was impersonal, it disturbed him more now that his mouth knew the fullness of her lower lip into which she pressed prettily gapped teeth as she unwound the bandage.

Prettily? Inwardly recoiling, he told himself he was too fatigued to think right.

"It looks worse than it is," she said, then poured wine on the towel and cleaned away the dried blood. "You pulled through two of the stitches, but the others hold and the swelling is slight." She glanced up. "Methinks you will suffer no lasting effects—providing horses are secured for the rest of our journey."

"On the morrow."

She lifted the skirt of her gown to show the chemise beneath. Its hem was stained by mud that had dragged at their feet as they made their way inland. "First I shall have to cut away the fouled cloth. May I use your dagger?"

He passed it to her.

"'Tis beautiful." She turned it around. "And well earned, I am sure."

Reminding himself he was once more worthy, he said, "Be of good care. It is sharp."

As she sliced through the linen whose color was distant from the white above, he glimpsed her knees and averted his gaze.

She dropped the soiled fabric beside her. "Almost done," she said, but a moment later gasped. Blood spotted the unsullied linen she had begun to cut. Durand snatched the dagger from her. "What have you done?"

She peered at the slice across the base of her thumb. "I forgot your warning of how sharp the blade. Blessedly, it does not go deep."

He caught up her hand. The cut would not require stitches, only bandaging. He cut a long strip of linen, poured the remains of her wine over the wound, and secured the bandage.

"Forgive me," she said. "I was to tend you."

"And so you shall. Stand and raise your gown."

She did so and slowly turned as he cut a swath of chemise that exposed shapely legs up to her lower thighs. Once more uncomfortably aware of her, he handed her the bandage, and she bound his leg.

"I thank you," he said and looked up to find her face near his.

Lord, he silently beseeched, *was it You who gave me so great an appetite for the carnal that I am attracted to a woman who should not appeal?*

The lady stood, moved to the lantern, and extinguished it. Moments later, the bed creaked with her settling. "Sleep well, Sir Durand."

Impossible. "Good eve, Lady Beata."

A single horse, meaning he shared a saddle with the lady. Worse, rather than have her cling to his back, he had placed her in front of him for the safety of his arm around her waist.

I have learned, he tried to talk down his discomfort over too much liking the feel of her. Curvaceous, indeed! And that was the third thing at which he had failed this day.

The first was securing two worthy mounts. The other horse offered for sale was so aged it would have slowed their journey more than having two astride one passably worthy horse.

The second thing at which he had failed was that of gaining tidings of the shipwreck. In the tavern where the lady and he broke their fast, then on the town's streets, naught was heard of it, and it would have been unwise to broach a subject that could see them pursued once word reached the town. And they might be pursued, regardless. Thus, Durand told the man from whom he purchased a horse that their mount had died on the way to London.

And now this third failure—his body's response to holding the lady.

It was time to take water. Having kept near the wood to sooner enter it when their path crossed others', he urged their mount amongst the trees.

"How much farther to London?" the lady asked when he lifted her down beside the stream.

"Though 'tis good any who seek to follow us believe London is our destination, we are going well around the city."

She took a step back. "But I…"

"What?"

After a long moment, she said, "My brother is there. As it is over ten years since we parted, I hoped to seek him out."

He suspected there was more to what she told, but he would not waste time questioning her. "I would think you more eager to answer your father's summons in advance of him receiving tidings of your ship."

Her eyes widened. "I am ashamed to say I did not consider that." She pushed a hand back through hair that was ever escaping its braids, the tresses so smooth and silken they did not fare well against wind and restless fingers. "Aye, we must go directly to Wiltford."

Though that was as he preferred so he might sooner shed himself of the lady—providing her father's infant son lived—it was not what he suggested nor intended. But it was best she believed it.

He gestured to the trees. "Relieve yourself."

She did not become flustered as many a lady would, but hurried opposite.

Durand did not expect her to try to escape—at least not here—but he heeded her movements.

A short while later, he once more suffered the discomfort of holding The Vestal Widow in the curve of his body.

And Beata wished that so honorable a man did not mind she was not petite.

12

Two days of riding. Another night in an inn. At last, Wulfen Castle.

As Durand reined in, Beata shifted beneath his mantle he had earlier drawn over her when the cold air stirred by their ride made her shiver. "Tis sad I do not recognize it," she said. "When I knew Heath Castle, it was formidable, but it ought to be less so through the eyes of one who is no longer a girl."

He considered the fortress last ridden upon to enlist the aid of the youngest Wulfrith brother in saving Helene the healer from being tried as a witch. Knowing it best the lady learn the truth of their destination from him rather than the patrol soon to appear, he said, "I would not be surprised if Heath Castle is less formidable."

She looked around. "What say you?"

He jutted his chin at the great edifice. "That is Wulfen Castle."

She caught her breath, in a smaller voice said, "Wulfen?"

"I thought it best we stop here first."

Lest he once more find himself struggling with her atop a horse—all the more likely since he had advanced the importance of reaching Wiltford ahead of word of her ship's fate—he tightened his hold.

But with an air of fatigue, she said, "The Wulfriths must be told. And I cannot be angry you did not tell me."

Was she ailing? *She of many words* had become increasingly quiet these past days, and this morn he had noted her pallor.

"Do you think they...?" She sighed. "Aye, the same as you, they shall hold me responsible if Baron Wulfrith is lost to them."

The same as I? Durand mulled, and not for the first time acknowledged he was less certain she bore the blame. But before he could further delve such thinking, he first felt—then heard—the patrol.

"Prepare yourself, Lady Beata. We are about to be overtaken."

"Overtaken?"

Though he longed to bring his sword to hand, it would be seen as an act of aggression. "Fear not. Providing we do not present a threat to those of Wulfen, no harm will befall you."

Moments later, he guessed three riders from the north, three from the south.

When the patrol appeared, it was with a show of might. These were not boys but young men soon to earn their spurs and a Wulfrith dagger. Mounted on destriers, swords drawn and teeth bared, they thundered out of the trees and drew a noose around the trespassers.

The slightest of them, who was slight only in height, reined in before Durand. "Who goes?" he demanded, the hitch of his upper lip revealing a birth defect his mustache did not entirely conceal.

Durand considered the other five—alert, eyes moving over the man and woman in their midst, blades reflecting the pale light of winter. "I am Sir Durand Marshal, also Wulfen trained, as evidenced by my dagger." He raised an eyebrow. "Would you have me show it?"

"Squire Gerard," the leader said, "confirm he speaks true."

That one urged his horse forward and captured Durand's gaze. It was a threat, but more importantly, an attempt to read the trespasser's eyes. Halting his mount several feet distant, he glanced at the lady, back at Durand, then moved the point of his sword to where Durand's mantle draped his shoulder. He pushed the material aside. "A Wulfrith dagger, Squire Rufus."

"One truth," the leader said with enough of a smile to cause his lip to reveal more of its deformity. "Your companion, Sir Durand?"

"Lady Beata Fauvel."

"Your business?"

"I would speak with the Wulfrith who is in residence."

It was not a request to be told whether it was Abel or Everard. These squires would not reveal that regardless of the possession of a Wulfrith dagger.

"Again, I ask your business, Sir Durand."

"I have answered as best I can, Squire Rufus. Do you deliver tidings to your lord that Sir Durand Marshal wishes to speak with him, he will grant me an audience."

"You perhaps, but as you must know, women are not permitted within our walls."

"I do know." Just as he knew there had been exceptions, and now the three brothers were wed, it was possible there had been more. Discreet, of course. "As I cannot leave the lady unattended, Lord Wulfrith will have to come out to me."

"If he deigns."

Durand inclined his head. "We thank you for your escort."

"First, your weapons."

As Durand reached to his belt, Beata snapped her head around. "You trust them?"

"I was once one of them, my lady. This is how 'tis done."

Doubt shone from her, but she leaned forward to allow him to unfasten his belt.

Shortly, Squire Gerard laid the steel-weighted leather across his saddle and looked to Durand's passenger. "Now you, my lady."

"I carry no weapons."

"Either you open your mantle to make truth of that, or we do it for you."

Durand thought he heard her growl, but she snatched open her mantle, causing the squires' armor to ring as they readied to strike.

"Lady!" Durand said. "They do their duty. Accord them respect and move slowly."

She sighed. "It is good there are men who do not underestimate the strength and resolve of a woman."

Remembering the one who had tested Baron Wulfrith on that front—Lady Annyn, now the man's wife and mother of his children—Durand almost smiled.

Lord, he silently entreated, *let him live.*

"Naught upon my girdle," Beata spoke of the belt returned to her this morn.

"Push your mantle back off your shoulders," Squire Gerard said, "and turn your girdle 'round."

This time certain she growled, Durand rasped, "Behave, Lady!"

She complied.

"I thank you," Squire Rufus said. "Now ride."

Squires all sides of them, Durand and the lady were escorted down the slope that granted a view of Wulfen.

When the fortress once more appeared, a thrill went through Durand—greater than when his family's home in France came into sight. His years upon Wulfen had been hard and demanding but more rewarding than anything before or since, having shaped him into a knight matched by few.

As expected even in winter, the daylight hours were spent on the training field outside the walls. Squires and pages met at swords and pikes, tilted at quintains, engaged in hand-to-hand combat, and mastered the skill of wielding weapons whilst astride.

Somewhere among them labored Everard or Abel, doubtless aware of visitors before they were seen. The three brothers were exceedingly tall, which allowed Durand to eliminate many of those who trained Wulfen's charges, but what decided him was the lazily confident stride of one who crossed from the farthest field toward the drawbridge.

Even before the limp became apparent, Durand knew it was the youngest brother alongside whom he had been knighted, and whose friendship he had betrayed. Though their bond could not be restored, that they were no longer enemies was better than once hoped.

Squire Rufus having spurred ahead to give his report, his lord beckoned the escort forward.

THE VEXING

Durand bent near Beata. "That is Sir Abel. Whilst Wulfen is in his charge, he is titled Lord Wulfrith."

She nodded, causing her ear to brush his mouth, Durand to pull back, and her to stiffen.

"Sir Durand!" Abel called as they neared the drawbridge. "Wulfen is pleased to receive one of its own."

Durand reined in, and Abel assessed the bruised and cut face of one he had once called *friend,* then that of the lady.

"I thank you, Lord Wulfrith. Though I am about the queen's business, I have something of import to discuss with you."

Perspiration darkening his tunic as if it were a summer day, Abel wiped a forearm across his brow and down the side of his face that bore a scar. It was not as unsightly as it had been after he and Durand nearly gave their lives to save his sister, but it surely drew Beata's regard.

"Squire Gerard," the Lord of Wulfen said, "return Sir Durand's weapons, then all make ready for the changing of the watch."

With murmurs of, "Aye, my lord," the young men did as bid.

When they departed, Abel said, "This thing of import, can it be discussed here, Sir Durand? As you know, women are not permitted inside Wulfen."

"It is best told inside."

The Lord of Wulfen stepped forward and patted the horse's jaw. "I am guessing what you have to tell accounts for so unworthy a mount."

"It does." Durand pushed back his mantle to fit his sword belt, and when it embraced his waist, once more felt fully clothed.

"It appears you are in need of a physician." Abel raised his eyes from the bloodied tear in Durand's chausses.

"I would welcome the attendance of yours." Durand looked to the lady. "Lord Wulfrith, this is—"

"Lady Beata Fauvel," she said. "The queen's business."

Abel's lids narrowed. "Beata—an affection for Beatrix, is it not?"

"Beatrix is my given name, but I prefer Beata."

He glanced at Durand. "My youngest sister's name is Beatrix."

"So I am told. According to your brother, she and I are quite different." The lady caught her breath.

Abel frowned. "You speak of Baron Wulfrith?"

Past the grinding of Durand's teeth, he heard her swallow. "Aye, we met at King Henry's court in Bayeux some days past."

"I thought him returned to Stern by now. Of course, it is an ill time of year to cross the channel."

"It is that which I would discuss with you," Durand said.

A muscle at Abel's right eye spasming, he nodded. "Cover your head, my lady. Though our young men will be aware I have let a woman inside, 'tis best your presence is unobtrusive."

She complied, and Abel led the way into the outer bailey where a dozen pages swung swords at posts set in the ground.

The lady peered over her shoulder. "I am sorry I did not first consider my words."

As was Durand though it hardly mattered she had sooner laid the ground for the tidings. "'Tis done."

Rather than order them to dismount at the stables, Abel continued to the inner bailey, surely the sooner to have the woman out of sight rather than over consideration of his old friend's injury. Still, Durand was grateful. His leg was much improved since they had obtained a horse, but it ached.

At the donjon steps, Durand dismounted, lifted his charge down, and led the lady up the steps.

"Sir Rowan!" Abel called as he entered the hall ahead of them.

An older knight seated at the high table looked up from a ledger. "My lord?"

"We have visitors. Take word to the cook we shall require drinks and viands in the solar."

"Aye, my lord."

"Also, send for the physician."

The knight pushed back his chair and stood.

Durand did not know him until they passed before the dais and he saw in the older man's eyes recognition. Here was the knight who had aided Lady Annyn Bretanne in seeking revenge against the oldest Wulfrith brother—so well, he had put an arrow through the baron. When the lady's revenge withered and in its place grew love, Sir Rowan had left her to redeem himself through service at Wulfen Castle. And here he remained, well enough trusted to have charge of the accounting.

It was a grave thing to make an enemy of the Wulfriths. Thus, all the more blessed to be gifted a chance to earn forgiveness.

Durand and Beata followed Abel onto the dais. At the curtained wall that accessed the solar, the Lord of Wulfen paused. "Sir Rowan!"

The knight halted at the entrance to the kitchen. "My lord?"

"Rather than the physician..." Abel nodded toward the stairway. "By way of the hall."

"Aye, my lord."

For the benefit of Beata, it was cryptic, but Durand was well enough acquainted with Wulfen to know whoever would tend him was abovestairs and was to traverse the hall to reach the solar rather than risk revelation of the castle's secret passages.

Was it possible she was here? That not one but two women were inside Wulfen?

Glad to be alerted ahead of the appearance of the lady whose gender prevented her from being titled a physician, Durand drew Beata past the curtain Abel held back.

The solar was as spacious and simply furnished as he recalled from when he had squired for the young Baron Wulfrith, nothing to indicate its purpose had changed since the brothers had taken wives.

He smiled. If the one he suspected was here, the tower room beyond the chapel where Lady Gaenor Wulfrith had hidden years past was likely the place from which Sir Rowan would collect her. Doubtless, that room was much changed to allow husband and wife to carry on as married couples were wont to do.

Determined not to envy Abel's happiness, he halted at the center of the solar and looked to the woman whose face remained beneath her hood. Like him, she had little chance of gaining a spouse so devoted that rules would be broken to keep the lovers close.

Very well, Lord, he acceded. *I envy Abel. And Everard. And...*

The baron, for whom he was here rather than bound for Wiltford.

"Make yourselves comfortable whilst I kindle the fire," Abel said.

Durand handed the lady into the chair nearest the hearth and lowered into the one beside hers.

"These tidings," Abel said as he added logs to small-tongued flames. "They are of Wulfrith?"

Even with one who knew the Christian name of the head of the family, respect was ever shown him in the presence of non-intimates by referring to him as *Wulfrith,* which told all one needed to know of his person.

"Possibly," Durand said.

"Possibly?" Abel retrieved a poker and prodded the logs. "That does not sound of great import."

"Still, it is something I believe your family should be made aware of."

Abel turned. "Speak."

"Four days past, my men and I were returning from Rouen when we happened upon the King of France's vassals trespassing on King Henry's lands. As they were in pursuit of Lady Beata and her escort, we set ourselves at them and—"

The curtain rustled, and he looked over his shoulder at a slight, hooded figure.

It *was* her, as confirmed by a dark red braid visible alongside her neck. Though her face was in shadow, he knew the moment her eyes lit on him. She gasped, dropped her bag, and ran forward.

"Durand!"

Such joy in her greeting. And her face when the hood fell to her shoulders.

He glanced at Abel and, receiving a nod, strode toward the man's wife.

A moment later, she landed against his chest and wrapped her arms around him. "Too long!" she exclaimed.

Keeping his arms at his sides lest the permission granted him did not extend to an embrace, he said, "Greetings, Lady Helene."

She put her head back. "Greetings? That is all, dear friend?" She scowled. "We mean more to each other than that."

He was both heartened and disheartened by her enthusiasm. It salved his soul to be so...

Was it loved? Aye, albeit chastely. But even were her husband not present, he would not be comfortable being familiar with her.

"You may embrace my wife," Abel said. "After all, you have been as a brother to her and are owed much for that."

Helene raised her eyebrows, and Durand hugged her—lightly. Then she clasped his face between her hands and considered his bruises and cuts. "What happened?"

"Nothing I will not survive," he said and momentarily wondered if he would survive The *Vexing* Widow.

"I would hear tale." She looped an arm through his and started toward the hearth. And halted. "You have injured your leg. I can feel it in your stride." She wrinkled her nose. "For this I am summoned to the lair of the Lord of Wulfen?"

"And to be reunited with our friend," Abel said.

Our friend. Those words so pained Durand he had to choke down emotion. Never had he expected this man to once more extend friendship.

Toleration. Grudging acceptance. Civility. Durand had been content with that depth of forgiveness. Or so he told himself. Despite's the tidings he must impart, something tight inside him loosened. And breathed.

"Durand?" Helene squeezed his arm.

Wondering how much of a fool he looked staring at Abel, he forced a smile. "Our journey to Wulfen has been long, dear lady."

Uncertainty flitted across her eyes, but the lovely Helene, who probably understood him more than any woman, said, "And your injury needs tending." She drew him forward. "Lord Husband, would you retrieve my bag?"

As Abel strode past, Helene's step once more faltered. "Who have you brought to Wulfen?"

Though Durand knew her to be observant, only upon reaching the hearth had she noticed the hooded figure.

"My charge," he said and returned to his chair.

"Not also in need of my ministrations, I pray. Are you injured, sir?"

Beata dropped her hood. "I am not, my lady."

"Pardon!" Helene looked to Abel, who approached with her healer's bag. "My, *two* women at Wulfen!" Now a glance at Durand, rife with questions he did not care to answer, then back to Lady Beata. "Hopefully, I can be forgiven."

"There is naught to forgive. I am Lady Beata Fauvel and, as Sir Durand tells, I am his charge."

"A story I hope you shall recount in full."

"Whilst you tend Sir Durand," Abel said.

Helene accepted the bag he extended and lowered to her knees before her patient.

As Durand tugged off his boot, Abel asked, "Did you set Sir Rowan an appropriate task to await your return, my lady?"

"I did, and as ever he is most capable."

Many a coin Durand would wager Sir Rowan tended the child born to the couple a year past. Was it a brother or sister they had given the son from Helene's first marriage?

Durand was ashamed he had not considered that one of those on the field was the boy of whom he had grown fond. Doubtless, John had learned enough self control during his page's training to allow him to keep his feet firm to the soil. But it was likely the boy had been clanging inside.

Once more, Durand asked the Lord for aid, this time to ease the ache of longing for the company of those more like family than the Marshals. It seemed unnatural, and yet more of his remembered life had been spent with the Wulfriths.

As Abel pulled a chair around to face his visitors, Helene exposed Durand's leg. "Fine stitches," she said. "More than I would have set."

More than needed, Durand silently begrudged.

Helene looked up. "Methinks the only reason some pulled through is because you did not stay off the leg."

He glanced at the lady beside him. "I fear 'twas not possible."

"Then it is good you suffered so many stitches. Whatever curses you cast upon the physician, the poor man was undeserving."

"Nay," Beata said, "the one who caused your friend's suffering is deserving. 'Twas I."

Helene looked around. "*You* placed these stitches?"

"I did."

"You are a healer?"

"Would that I were." The lady looked to Abel, then Durand. "Methinks it is time the queen's man finished his tale."

13

An interesting tale. At times, an amusing tale. But in the end, an ugly tale.

As Durand ended his recounting of how he had become acquainted with The Vestal Widow—excepting what had transpired on the stairs with Sir Oliver and in the cave when he made more of her kiss—Beata stared into the flames.

Clasping the mantle closed at her throat, though she was so warm she perspired, she wondered if the woman to whom it belonged had ever been as burdened by guilt as the one who now huddled beneath it.

She had not needed to look upon Abel Wulfrith to know his anguish at the possibility his brother was lost to him, nor hear it in the demanding questions put to Durand. But to gauge how much he held her responsible, she would have to rise above the sanctuary she made of her chair. And that she did not wish to do.

"Lady Beata." A hand touched her knee, and once more she found Lady Helene bending near. "I must insist you either remove your mantle or come away from the fire. You grow feverish."

Becoming aware of the moisture on the hand bunched beneath her chin, Beata released the mantle and drew her fingers up over her jaw and cheek. Her face was damp as if with tears, and her garments clung.

"Allow me." The healer peeled the mantle from Beata's shoulders and settled it over the back of the chair. "Now drink, my lady."

Beata blinked at the goblet held so near it was almost at her lips. As with the food delivered earlier, she had meant to partake of the wine, but her hunger and thirst had mostly fled when Durand's tale moved toward revelation about Baron Wulfrith.

"I will hold it for you." The healer smiled.

You are not weak, Conrad Fauvel's wife! Beata told herself and sat straighter, unfolded her fingers, and took the goblet. "I thank you, but I am only a bit tired and can see to my own needs."

"More than a bit tired, methinks," Lady Helene said, and as Beata sipped the watered wine, saw the woman look to her husband.

Beata could not know what passed between them, but whatever it was, it seemed to have no effect on the Lord of Wulfen, the eyes he settled on the stranger unblinking and chill. She lowered the goblet. "Forgive me, my lord. Had I known what honoring my father's instructions would wrought, I would have defied him."

"Then you accept responsibility?"

Hand trembling, fearing she would slosh wine on her skirts, Beata set the goblet on the table beside her and frowned over the viands she had barely touched.

"Are you responsible?" Abel Wulfrith asked again.

More blinking. Wonder over how numb her head felt. A grimace as ache moved hip to hip. And shame that *she of many words* was so bereft of them.

She pulled her tongue from her palate. "If ill has befallen your brother, I believe I am responsible."

"Nay," spoke the one whose presence had so dominated these past days she should not have forgotten he was here. She *was* more than a bit tired.

"Sir Durand?" said the Lord of Wulfen.

Beata looked to the queen's man, but his eyes were on Abel Wulfrith. "I also thought to blame Lady Beata, but if Baron Wulfrith's ship left port that day, I believe it is because the captain was confident of a successful crossing."

Perhaps what ailed her was more than fatigue, Beata thought. It sounded as if Durand defended her.

"As you know better than I," he continued, "regardless of a vow made his sovereign, your brother would not risk innocents by insisting on sailing. Thus, if the second ship was his, it would likely have met the same end had Lady Beata been aboard as planned."

Silence. Strained as if the din within wanted out. Then a harsh sigh and sudden movement that returned Beata's regard to Abel Wulfrith.

He dropped back in his chair, shifted his jaw as if to unbind it, then glanced from his wife where she stood alongside Beata to Durand. "I know my brother. As we must discover the identity of the second ship, this day I shall send knights to Brighthelmstone."

"You need to eat." It was Lady Helene again, this time handing Beata a wedge of cheese before turning to her husband. "The lady ought to rest."

Beata longed to lie down, but her stay within these walls was to be brief. And she must not forget the urgency of reaching Wiltford.

"I am certain Sir Rowan would not mind relinquishing his chamber to the lady," the Lord of Wulfen surprised, though with grudging. "But only a single night's lodging, and 'twill be discreet."

"Of course." Lady Helene swung back around, clicked her tongue. "Lady Beata, food is of no benefit to the body if it does not pass the lips."

Tempted to protest being treated like a child, Beata looked up. But only kindness shone from the lady. She popped the cheese in her mouth and was glad it was not tasteless. Still, one piece was enough, and she shook her head when offered another. "I wish to lie down."

The lady set a hand on her brow. "You have cooled, but we shall require assistance in seeing you to your chamber. 'Tis a good distance and the stairs are many. Sir Durand—"

"Nay!" Beata stood so quickly her head lost its bearings. Seeing the lady's hand on her arm, ignoring Durand and Lord Wulfrith who also rose, she said, "You make too much of me. I am but tired."

"My lady—"

"Merely tired," she said sharply and winced at how ungrateful she sounded.

Ah, she thought, *I know what this is.* The timing could not be worse. But as ever, it did not seek permission.

"Forgive me, Lady Helene. I appreciate your concern, but the only aid I require is to be shown to my bed."

"Then that I shall do."

Beata retrieved her mantle, bit back protest when she was aided in donning it, and nearly yelped when she saw the hands fastening it closed were not a woman's.

"Behave," Durand murmured.

She allowed him to settle the hood over her head. Silently welcomed his grip as he led her past the Lord of Wulfen. Eased into his support when the stairs proved more difficult than expected. Sighed when he released her as she lowered to the bed. Did not care what whispered words passed between the two who had escorted her to the chamber.

Slept.

He was not the boy he had been. Though three years older than when Durand had last seen him and far from the worthy man the Wulfriths would make of him, Durand knew that smile and the life teeming behind it.

"You have aged, Sir Durand!" Helene's nine-year-old son halted before the one who had thought he would like to be a father to the unruly boy.

Durand pushed off the gatehouse wall to which he had set a shoulder to watch Abel's knights depart for Brighthelmstone. "As have you, John Wulfrith."

There was pride in the boy's smile, and Durand knew it was not only for having grown in height and breadth but owning the esteemed name gifted him by his mother's marriage to Abel.

The shifting of John's shoulders evidencing the control he exercised, Durand recalled how the boy had flung himself at him each time Durand visited his mother and him to ensure their safety until Abel and Helene could find their way back to each other. Had John not an audience of peers who would ill judge him for yielding to a youthful show of affection, the boy might bend to his nature.

Durand clapped him hard on the shoulder, not only for benefit of those who watched for weakness that could be exploited, but to provide acceptable contact.

As John held beneath the blow, Durand said, "What happened to the boy I knew? I hardly recognize him."

"I am Wulfen-trained now."

"The pride of your sire, no doubt."

The boy looked to where Abel had hopped a fence to demonstrate the simultaneous wielding of sword and dagger, something he had been forced to relearn following the battle that had nearly killed Durand and him.

"My father is the greatest warrior," John said.

His only exaggeration was ignorance—or rejection—of Baron Wulfrith's claim to that title.

"He is formidable, John."

"And he will make me the greatest warrior after him. You are to remain at Wulfen, Sir Durand?"

"At most, until the morrow. I am about the queen's business."

He frowned. "That lady who came with you looked a mess, but I thought her pretty. Are you to wed her?"

Durand almost laughed. "Indeed not. What makes you think I might?"

He looked down, toed the ground. "I did not mean to listen in—a Wulfen-trained knight does not—but when father and mother and I were at Broehne Castle last summer, I heard a chambermaid tell another that the king had ordered Aunt Gaenor to wed Baron Lavonne—that they did not choose each other the same as my father chose my mother."

So they had not, and Durand had tried to prevent that marriage. But it was he who had been in the wrong, though King Henry could not have known it was a lifelong blessing he bestowed rather than a curse.

John shrugged. "It sounded business to me."

Perceptive. "You are right, but your aunt and her husband are happy, are they not?"

"They oft smile at each other and have made another baby, but my mother and father are happier."

Of course they were, just as Abel was the greatest warrior.

"So if you are not to wed the lady, what business have you with her, Sir Durand?"

"I must deliver her to her father."

John wrinkled his nose. "That is all?"

"Forsooth, where this lady is concerned, that is much." And he had said enough. "Tell me, John, did the Lord gift you with a brother or sister last year?"

"A brother!" he said as if there could be no other answer, then added, "Though he cries like a girl—or did. Not so much anymore."

Durand reached to ruffle his hair. Instead, appearing to have taken the long way around, he pushed his hand through his own hair.

"My water break is done," John said as his fellow pages, who had earlier surged into the outer bailey, reappeared. "I am glad to see you again, Sir Durand. I know my mother would be, too."

At first Durand thought the lad held close the secret his mother was in residence, but more likely he was unaware. All—including Wulfriths—left their mothers behind when they began their training.

"I have missed you both, John."

"Then come again and do not be so long next time." The boy turned and rejoined his peers whose breath clouded the air as they tramped to the field where next they would train at quarterstaffs.

As Durand crossed into the outer bailey, he was once more struck by John's perceptiveness. He was right in thinking the queen's business with Beata involved marriage—just not marriage to the one entrusted with delivering her to Wiltford. And only if the lady proved an heiress.

For her sake, he hoped she was not that. From what he had seen of marriages made for alliance, it was rare what Lady Gaenor had with Christian Lavonne.

Aye, better The Vestal Widow remain vestal. And vexing.

14

This time Helene had come by way of the secret passage. Now from where she sat opposite Durand at the table in the lord's solar, she eyed him over her goblet.

"Aye, my lady?" Abel prompted, as Durand had not lest what caused her eyebrows to draw close led to talk best avoided.

"I am thinking," she said, "Lady Beata must be of some import for the queen to concern herself over a widow's return to her father. And as evidenced by her resistance to Sir Durand's escort, Eleanor's concern is unwelcome."

Durand pushed away the sodden trencher that remained of the supper shared with her husband and her in the solar. "In that you are right, but I cannot elaborate."

She inclined her head. "Then I shall not press."

Abel lowered his tankard. "Sir Durand, you said the father of The Vestal Widow is—"

"Pray, do not name her that," his wife said. "It is disrespectful."

Abel, whose struggle against condemnation of his unwanted guest was surely felt by Helene, said, "The lady's father is Baron Rodelle?"

This being one of the few times the Lord of Wulfen had conversed throughout the meal, his brooding evidencing worry over his brother, Durand allowed himself to be pulled deeper into what should not become a discussion.

"Aye, Baron Rodelle of Wiltford, the barony upon which I served before Lady Helene and you wed."

Abel raised an eyebrow. "He who has thrice nearly killed his very young wife in a bid to make sons on her."

Clever Abel. "'Tis so."

"Ah." Helene shook her head. "Methinks yours is a difficult task, Sir Durand."

"Certes, Lady Beata is a trial."

"That too."

"Too?"

She shrugged.

She thought too much of his earlier inquiry into the woman's well-being. As Beata remained abed, he had but sought confirmation she required only rest to ensure their departure on the morrow. To Abel's displeasure, Helene had expressed doubt but said it was possible.

Not wishing to offend her, Durand forced a light tone. "If you believe I have too much a care for the one given into my charge, you are mistaken. My interest lies in fulfilling my duty so I may all the sooner give the lady my back."

"Of course," Helene said, but he was certain she thought she knew him better than he knew himself. And in that moment, she annoyed him as he would have sworn she could not.

She pushed back her chair. "Methinks I have asked much of Sir Rowan this day. Thus, I shall leave my lord husband and his friend to converse on matters of *their* choosing."

Both men rose with her, Durand wished her a good eve, and her husband led her toward the tapestry from behind which she had earlier emerged.

There, she paused. "Your garments, Sir Durand. I am sure my husband will provide others until yours are laundered and mended that you may be more presentable when you depart Wulfen."

He knew his appearance offended, but just like Beata, what he wore was all he possessed. "I thank you, my lady."

She smiled and Abel followed her around the tapestry.

Durand heard their whispered voices, a long silence, then a murmur of contentment.

When Abel reappeared, his face was serious, but his mouth less grim. He crossed the chamber and swept aside the curtain wall, more fully admitting the din of boys and young men relaxing after the meal. He commanded all to prepare for bed, and his first and second squires returned to the solar with him.

"A walk?" he asked as the young men cleared the table.

Durand inclined his head. "I shall retrieve my mantle and meet you outside."

A quarter hour later, they stood on the gatehouse roof and looked out across the land lit by a moon so full it appeared it might soon give birth. And Durand recalled other times he had been here with Abel—first as pages, then squires, lastly knights who more keenly felt the Wulfrith daggers on their belts than their swords.

Regardless that during training toward knighthood the two had gained the majority of their scrapes, cuts, and bruises from each other whilst putting into practice all they were taught, Abel had been so close with Durand that only his brothers were better known to him.

It was he who rent the silence. "I am grieved by your tidings, Durand, and tempted to anger at The Vestal..." His brief smile was white against the night. "...Lady Beata. But as best I can, I shall keep my face to God and prayers to His ears in the hope He will return my brother to us."

"I am sorry to have borne such tidings, but I thought you ought to be prepared."

"I am grateful." Silence slid back between them, then Abel sighed. "I would not have said it did I not mean it."

Our friend, he had named Durand who, since his great failing, had sought no friendships lest he disappointed—worse, betrayed. "This I know, as I would have you know I am aware of how great your generosity. I did not expect it, did not even hope."

Abel lifted a hand from the embrasure, turned it up, and closed his fingers toward the heel. "All is breakable," he said, demonstrating that truth when the gap between fingertips and palm would not be bridged. Then he lifted his other hand which, following injury to the right, had been trained to the sword. The exercises required to effect such facility had been rigorous, subjecting his entire body to learning a different way to wield a lengthy blade.

"However," he continued, "if the pieces of the vessel are not too far scattered, not too small, not too jagged, and if God is present—as my wife and brother would remind—what is broken can be fit back together."

As Durand had aspired to do these past years, seeking restoration of his good name and the unlaming of his faith.

Using the hand that could have left him forever broken, his soul discarded, Abel drew the Wulfrith dagger from its scabbard and wrapped his fingers around a hilt thickened to accommodate his altered grip. "Made whole enough," he said and turned his face to Durand. "Better, it knows the hand of my wife. And those of our sons."

John and the babe who no longer cried like a girl. Mostly.

Abel returned the dagger to his belt. "Where I am concerned, you are whole enough, Durand."

Those words—and the familiar use of his name caused the tightness in Durand to loosen further. "I thank you, Abel."

His old friend nodded and clapped him on the shoulder. "Do not tell my mother, hmm?"

Lady Isobel, who would never forgive the knight who had been entrusted to protect her and her daughters. "Not even had I the opportunity to do so."

Abel grunted low. "I have a boon to ask of you."

Durand narrowed his eyes. "If it is in my power, I shall grant it."

"It means your journey to Wiltford will be delayed another day—mayhap two should Lady Beata require further rest as I believe my wife will insist upon."

"Tell."

"With the impending arrival of those who come to collect their sons for the Christmas celebration, I cannot leave Wulfen, nor thereafter, there being a good number who will pass the season here."

Most years Durand had himself remained, the crossing to France ever uncertain in winter.

"Thus, if word of the identity of the second ship does not come ere your departure, and I think it unlikely, I wish you to pause at Stern Castle."

Hence, the opportunity to reveal to Lady Isobel that her son believed Durand was whole enough. What had loosened began to tighten. It was not only Abel's mother Durand wished to avoid, though she was reason enough to keep his distance. Her daughters and their families might also be at Stern to celebrate the Lord's birth. Though Durand had made his peace with both sisters—more importantly, they had made their peace with him—it was best not to stir up the past.

"Hopefully," Abel continued, "Wulfrith will be there, having arrived safely in England and gone directly to Stern for the birth of his child. If he is not..." Abel slowly nodded. "I would have you deliver your tidings to Everard, who has journeyed there for the celebration. If our eldest brother is lost to us, Everard will administer the barony until Wulfrith's heir is of an age to assume his title. Will you grant me this?"

At Durand's hesitation, Abel said, "Methinks Beatrix and her family are there now, but as involved as Christian Lavonne is with administering his lands, 'twill likely be nearer Christmas Day before he and Gaenor arrive—a sennight or more."

So easily read, an unpleasant side-effect of friendship. "I do not believe my telling of events would be of greater benefit than words on parchment," Durand said.

"I shall compose a missive, but methinks if the tale must be told, Everard would hear it from you so you might answer his questions."

It would be awkward, and more so in the company of Beata, but it was a small favor, especially after what had been gifted him. "I grant it, Abel."

"I am glad. Now, I have matters that need tending before I can gain my bed." He turned from the embrasure toward the steps to the outer bailey. "And I am sure you would appreciate a good night's rest."

He would, having slept lightly at the inns. "Aye, but I also have a missive that needs writing, and which I will entrust to you to arrange for its delivery to the queen." Not only must he inform Eleanor that The Vestal Widow and her gallant monk had survived the shipwreck, but that the missive to the lady's father was lost. Another would have to be sent to the Baron of Wiltford.

"Of course," Abel said.

Beneath the regard of the squires who manned the walls, keeping watch for things that should not move in the night, Durand and Abel did not speak again until they ascended the donjon's steps.

"I do not seek to learn the exact nature of the charge given you by the queen, Durand, but your defense of Lady Beata makes me question if you are once more in danger of being tempted to save a woman whose sacrifice appears to be of far less benefit to her than others."

Like Helene, he suspected enough that he had good cause to ask. "Be assured, I will not betray my liege again nor subject your family to further dishonor for having trained up one unworthy of a Wulfrith dagger."

Abel halted before the doors. "'Tis good your mind is turned that way, but that does not absolve you of doing harm."

"Harm?"

The torch to the left of the doors showed Abel's struggle. "Rosamund," he finally said.

His first wife, whom he had not wished to wed, and having done his duty, nearly paid with his life. Were there any doubt he had guessed the queen's interest in Beata, it was no more.

"As I know you would not have me be disloyal to the queen, what do you advise, Abel?"

"Certes, not that you act as you did with Gaenor. That served none well—for a time was the ruin of both of you."

"I need no reminder," Durand said sharply.

Abel drew a deep breath. "If ever you find yourself in a similar situation, think it front to back and back to front. Find another way."

Had there been another way? Durand almost laughed at asking himself so foolish a question. With Gaenor, there *had* been another way—to not allow resentment to guide him...to leave her be...better, to confess his sin and face the Wulfrith wrath far sooner than he had.

He nodded. "I do not foresee making use of your advice where Lady Beata is concerned, but I appreciate it."

Abel considered him. "One more thing, Durand. No matter what you are moved to do, if you believe your are in the right, ask for help—and not only from God."

15

She did not wish to know what lay beneath the leaves. Still, she should not have yanked herself up out of the dream. She should have braved the crimson-splattered layers—swept them aside and looked long enough to know what they hid. Perhaps then her frightening night travels and disturbing day flashes would once more recede.

"'Tis good to see you are no longer abed," the increasingly familiar voice of Lady Helene heralded her entrance.

Beata took a step back from the window whose shutters she had cracked open only enough to permit her to look out upon this place forbidden women. She turned. "I am much recovered and grateful your husband agreed I may stay another night."

"He respects my judgment." The lady set a bundle on the bed. "Besides the cloths you requested"—she turned back a corner of homespun fabric—"I brought a gown, chemise, and hose."

When the folded garments beneath the strips of linen were revealed, Beata said, "I appreciate your kindness, my lady, but I am a hand taller than you and at least a hand wider in the waist." And then there were her breasts. Though Lady Helene was fairly endowed, not as much as Beata.

"Certes, you possess more of a figure than I, but the gown and chemise can be adjusted."

Unfortunately, only so much would laces cinch and loose a garment. "I fear you are too hopeful."

When the Lord of Wulfen's wife shook out the blue gown, further protest ran to the back of Beata's mouth and she smiled. "You have birthed a babe, my lady."

"A year past, though I continue to wear these gowns since the bodices better fit a nursing mother."

Beata blinked. "Your child is here with you?"

"Aye, though not as forbidden as I."

"A boy, then."

"'Tis so. And too soon, rather than visit he will come to live at Wulfen and train the same as our older son. It will be no easy thing to let him go, but Lord willing, I shall have a daughter to occupy me—or more boy babes as the Wulfriths are prone to bring into the world." She held out the gown. "Hold it against you so we may see how much length is needed."

When the lady determined just under a hand's width of material would suffice, she said, "Has your menses begun?"

"Nay, but soon."

"You are certain you do not wish me to prepare a draught?"

"My flux does not overly trouble me. At worst, it makes me uncomfortable and less inclined to talk and laughter." She raised her eyebrows. "For that, many a man—and woman—is grateful."

"I am intrigued."

"And I am sure Sir Durand can be persuaded to satisfy your curiosity." Beata lifted a rolled strip from the bed and started toward the garderobe. "He is among those who do not approve of me."

When she stepped back inside the chamber, Lady Helene beckoned from the window. "Come see our John."

Beata halted alongside her, and the lady opened the shutter wider, letting in more cold air. "There he is, just come out from beneath the portcullis."

Easily noted since the boy who appeared to be near ten years aged was one of only a few youths in the inner bailey, unlike a quarter hour past when those trained at Wulfen had streamed to the donjon for the nooning meal.

The lady sighed. "It does not bode well he is late to meal, and from the drag of his feet, he was made to run the land before the castle."

"Punishment?"

The lady glanced at Beata. "At Wulfen, it is called a lesson—correction meant to guide a boy during his training, then a man so he remains worthy of every year gifted him."

Hence, the reputation for which this place was esteemed, Beata reflected and leaned nearer to follow the progress of the lady's son toward the donjon.

"He is a good boy," Lady Helene continued, "but sometimes he forgets all that is expected of him."

"I wager more is asked of a Wulfrith."

"Aye, and more often than not, John makes his father proud. Oh, there is Sir Durand!"

With eagerness that would shame her were she closely observed, Beata swept her regard to the knight who strode beneath the portcullis into the inner bailey and called to the boy.

"Certes, John longs to hasten to him," Lady Helene said, "and the temptation is greater with few to bear witness, but he controls himself."

Beata recalled the permission Abel had granted Durand to embrace his wife and his acknowledgement the knight was as a brother to the lady. "Your son is fond of Sir Durand," she said as the queen's man came alongside the boy, set a hand on his shoulder, and bent near.

"So fond that had not difficulties between my husband and me resolved, John could have been content with Durand as a father."

Beata startled. "Lord Wulfrith is not John's father in truth?"

The lady laughed. "He is, though not in blood. Like you, I was widowed young."

But unlike Beata, she had not been vestal, had given her first husband a child. "You have been blessed, Lady Helene."

"That I will not argue, nor that it was with Sir Durand's aid the Lord made it possible. Now, since I do not think you will ask it, I will give answer. Had it not been possible for me to wed Abel Wulfrith, and had

Sir Durand offered to take me to wife, methinks eventually I would have accepted."

Then there was much to their tale. But how much? And what had—or did—Durand feel for her?

"He has his failings—do not all men and women?—but he is honorable, Lady Beata."

Her heart swelled as she watched Durand and the boy mount the steps. When they went from sight, she said, "This I know."

The lady reached to shut out the cold. "Just do not…" Her smile was strained. "No matter what tales are told of him, do not forget what I first told."

Curious. "Though I doubt I shall have occasion to hear any speak against him, I will not forget."

Lady Helene averted her gaze and closed the shutters. Much she had revealed, but there was something she did not. And Beata thought she might have occasion to hear others speak ill of Durand.

16

She made him uncomfortable—rather, more uncomfortable. He had been in a heightened state of awareness since she had first dragged him into her mess.

This morn, after two nights' stay at Wulfen, during which he had not seen Beata, he noted her improved appearance. Were she the sort to whom he was attracted, he would think her becoming in a blue gown altered and laced to fit a figure far different from Helene's. Too, though surely by basin rather than tub, much of the ill befallen her since the day of their first meeting had been washed and brushed away. Her skin glowed and hair was so admired by the sun that its light lingered amid dark braids whose crossings had, unsurprisingly, loosened during the ride.

But the appeal of the one who should not appeal did not make him as uncomfortable as the way she had looked at him whilst they broke their fast in the solar before departing Wulfen. And he had become more discomfited when Helene leaned near and whispered that she very much liked Lady Beata.

What had she told The Vestal Widow? More importantly, how was he to undo whatever had been done? Were he at court, he would avoid the lady. If that did not suffice, the queen would discourage her attentions—once Eleanor had her fill of amusement. But there was no avoiding the lady and no queen. And now with Stern Castle before them, his unease increased.

He glanced around at Beata where she was mounted on one of two horses Abel had provided to speed their journey. Her gaze was forward as it had mostly been since he had informed her they would not ride directly to Wiltford.

She had not seemed surprised, but the return of vibrancy that had seen her more conversant than since their arrival at Wulfen had dimmed. Just as the prospect of facing a gathering of Wulfriths held no appeal for him, it held none for her.

Though his defense of her caused Abel to concede the difficulty of holding her responsible for any ill that might have befallen his brother, once more she would face judgment.

"Sir Durand!"

He turned in the saddle, causing the armor Abel had given him to sound its song of metal on metal. "Judas?" he prompted the boy who, a few years older than John—though of a size he seemed twice as many years removed—also trained at Wulfen.

"May I ride ahead?"

Doubtless, to sooner reunite with his aunt, who had wed Everard Wulfrith a year and a half past.

Durand surveyed the winter-bitten land again. Seeing and sensing no threat, he moved his regard to the castle with its lowered drawbridge that accommodated villagers whose business at Stern had begun to conclude with the passing of day. "'Tis well with me, providing your escort does not object."

"Sir Rowan does not. He but told I should also seek your permission."

"Then ride and deliver word to your uncle that Sir Durand Marshal requests a private audience." Hopefully, rather than Everard, Baron Wulfrith would receive him, having arrived in England and ridden directly to Stern.

Judas inclined his head, and his friend and he put heels to their mounts.

Fine horsemanship, Durand noted and approved of how the mature and confident boy had grown more so since Durand had accompanied the queen to Stern to settle disputes in her husband's name—one of those disputes being whether Judas de Balliol was his father's heir. Eleanor had determined he was.

Now here Durand was again, the bearer of tidings that would make him even less welcome were it Everard who received him. Regardless, afterward Beata and he would take refreshment and depart for the nearest inn from which they would set out for Wiltford on the morrow. God willing, he would soon discharge his duty and...

What?

As discontented as he was serving the queen, his lot was cast. Or mostly. He could seek release from her service and, were it granted, turn to knight errantry or become a household knight to his brother or another landed noble.

Regardless, his restored friendship with Abel would likely remain distant. And more distant was the possibility of gaining what Abel had with Helene.

Do not hold tight to that which you long for, he told himself as he slowed his mount near the drawbridge. *Far less it aches to have it slip through your fingers than torn from your grasp.*

"Sir Durand?"

He looked to the lady who drew nearer and raised an eyebrow.

"I am sorry this falls to you, but I would have you know I think you honorable. And worthy."

He did not want to linger over a face flushed from the cold, nor be moved by how feminine it appeared with wisps of hair caressing her brow, cheeks, and jaw. But once more she appealed as she should not.

Rather, her words, he corrected, and guessed that whatever Helene had revealed to her had not included his sin and betrayal.

"I thank you, Lady Beata, and I pray never shall I give you cause to amend your opinion."

"As do I." Interest in her eyes. Far too much interest.

He started to look away, but there was a better means of discouraging her, and if it did not, it might gain him insight thus far denied him.

"Now I have proven myself, might so esteemed a knight know the truth about your father's heir?"

It was she who averted her gaze. "Forgive me, but I have told all there is to tell."

"Mayhap an heiress," he said with an edge of sarcasm.

She tucked her chin into the mantle's collar and said almost too low to catch, "Mayhap."

Everard was Everard, still as pensive, observant, and slow to rise to emotion. But the latter was present if one knew where to look.

Though Durand had not been close with him, he had grown up alongside Everard the same as Abel. Thus, from the flicker of lids, set of teeth, and folding of fingers into palms, Everard revealed that beneath hair too golden and fine to be gifted a man, his concern for his older brother twisted him as tight as it had Abel.

"That is all there is to tell," Durand said, "and I regret being the one to speak it."

Still Everard said naught, having gone silent after closing the three of them in the chamber shared with his wife.

"There is hope, is there not?" Beata said with apology.

Everard moved his gaze to her. No anger. No condemnation. And Durand was grateful the second born was not as disposed as Abel and he to place blame on another.

"Aye, Lady Beata. As Sir Durand concluded, Wulfrith would not have pressed to set sail that day. Thus, we may hope his captain was better versed in the weather than yours, and 'twas another ship that met yours on the rocks." He drew a deep breath. "Sir Durand, as we have shifting to do to accommodate your charge for the night, I think it best she shares this chamber with my wife and sister."

The latter being Lady Beatrix D'Arci. "I thank you, Sir Everard, but now that our mounts have been provided for, we shall further impose only to take food and drink."

A frown narrowed the space between Everard's eyebrows, and he crossed to the window and laid back the shutters. Though oilcloth covered the opening, it was clear the sun would soon depart. "It is winter, Sir Durand, nearing nightfall, and the closest inn is an hour's ride. Though I understand your reluctance to pass the night with us, for the lady's sake, reconsider."

Everard did understand his reluctance, every bit as much as his brothers. This place that had become Durand's home following his attainment of knighthood, when the baron had trusted him to serve the women of his family, was no longer and would never again be that—and most obvious Everard's mother would make it given a chance. But he was right. It was nearing night, and Durand must think first of Beata.

"It seems we shall leave on the morrow."

"Then either you may share a chamber with me and my sister's husband or bed down in the hall."

Though Durand had become easier in Michael D'Arci's company whilst recovering at the man's home following the attack that had nearly seen Lady Beatrix murdered, he said, "The hall suits me well."

Everard closed the shutters and strode to the chair where Beata perched. When she looked up, he said, "I would not alarm the ladies, especially Baron Wulfrith's wife, who will give my brother another child ere Christmas Day, nor my mother, who is of an age when hearts are easily broken. Thus, until those sent to learn the identity of the second ship return, we shall hold this close, including tale of the downing of your own ship."

"I shall speak naught of it, Sir Everard, and continue to pray if your brother yet remains in France, his crossing is uneventful."

He looked to Durand. "Since you serve the queen, it will be expected you had occasion to speak with Wulfrith, and the ladies will ask after him. Thus, a measure of deception is required."

Durand's mind already moved in that direction. "I shall be truthful as to our meeting and the charge given me by the queen that required

I depart France before Baron Wulfrith concluded his business at court." Hopefully, he would be forgiven the lie.

Everard started forward, halted, and turned back to Beata. "I trust The Vestal Widow, of whom I heard tale when she was yet The Vestal Wife, will temper her behavior."

Something that did not bode well flickered across her countenance.

"'Tis a season of celebration, my lady," Everard prompted, "and let us pray it remains so, but my mother insists on order in her household."

Durand tensed in anticipation the lady would offend though Everard but prepared her to meet the mother of the formidable Wulfriths.

"As Sir Durand is fond of reminding me to do, I shall behave," she said and forced a smile. "I thank you for the comfort of this chamber."

He dipped his head. "Supper is served in an hour. We shall leave you to freshen yourself."

Durand followed Everard, and before exiting the chamber did what too much encouraged. He looked back.

In the midst of loosed braids, Beata's gaze awaited his, and something he did not feel for her made itself felt. And more when her lids widened and the smile that made light flicker in her eyes drew his attention to lips more softly curved and parted than when she had smiled at Everard.

Stiffly, he inclined his head. Tightly, he gripped the door's handle. Firmly, he closed the door. Desperately, he beseeched the Lord, *Not again. Not any woman. Not her.*

17

"Elias!" The moment his name fled Beata, she wished it back. Then there was the impulse to run across the hall to the one whose grin invited her to do so. *That* she would not have had to wish back, but having unsettled those gathered—thus, failing Everard Wulfrith—and being in need of joy, she reasoned it was too late to keep from making a spectacle of herself.

Worth all the displeasure cast upon me, she told herself as the knight enfolded her and took a quick step back to keep his balance.

"Lady Beata, my eyes do not deceive me!"

Amidst the murmurings of those too proper to express true pleasure, she lifted her face to his. "Elias de Morville," she sang his name. "What do you here?"

He looked left and right, and though she felt his hesitation over the audience for which he was given no time to prepare, the grin that became a smile was genuine. "I would ask the same of you, dear lady."

Certain the eyes boring into her belonged to Sir Everard and Durand, who alone knew she was at Stern Castle not as a guest with cause to be light of heart, but as one whose journey to England could bode ill for them, she released her friend and dropped back on her heels.

"I pass through," she said, and out of the corner of her eye saw the woman with whom he had been conversing reposition the babe on her hip and tilt her head questioningly. "Now you, Elias. What brings you across the channel?"

He traveled his gaze back up her blue gown and nodded at the woman. "By invitation of my friends, Lady Susanna and her husband, Sir Everard, I am to spend Christmas at Stern. A generous offer, and welcome considering…" He raised his eyebrows.

Though she knew it was past time to rectify behavior that disrespected the Wulfriths' mother, she leaned near. "I look forward to learning how you escaped your sire."

"Less and less a feat." He winked and turned her toward the one beside him. "Lady Susanna Wulfrith, meet my dear friend, Lady Beata Fauvel."

"Ah!" the woman exclaimed as if with recognition.

Here was how her husband knew of The Vestal Widow, Beata realized. A good tale was a good tale, and Elias too much enjoyed lighting up eyes and hearts not to have shared that of a most unusual wife.

"It is a pleasure to meet you, Lady Beata." There was no falsity in her tone or amber eyes. "Any friend of Sir Elias is welcome."

Now recognition struck Beata, and she caught her breath. She was privy to how Elias had become acquainted with the Wulfriths though he had given some of the characters imagined names.

Lady Susanna set a hand on Beata's arm. "Are you well, my lady?"

"I am." She peered sidelong at Elias, and he smiled sheepishly. Next, she glanced at the Wulfrith dagger he wore—awarded only to young men who had received their squire's training at Wulfen. For Elias, an exception had been made.

The blonde babe Lady Susanna held gurgled, and Beata touched the dimpled hand gripping his mother's bodice. "Your son is handsome and a good size. Already he is walking?"

"He tries, but he has only turned eight months. Soon, though, methinks."

Further evidence of the blood coursing his veins.

"Allow me to introduce you to the ladies of my family ere we are called to meal." Everard Wulfrith's wife moved toward the hearth.

As Beata had not looked near upon the others scattered here, her eyes having first found Elias, she considered them now where they stood and sat amidst the finery of the season that saw the hall hung with greenery, lit by dozens of candles, and scented with fragrant herbs.

Lady Susanna's nephew and his friend, who had accompanied them from Wulfen, were seated at a small table before an alcove. They acknowledged her with nods and resumed their game of chess.

Before the high table were the men. Beata allowed herself a moment to appreciate how handsome Durand looked in a tunic surely provided by one of the Wulfrith brothers. Of a color between gold and tan, its sleeves were gathered at the wrists, its belt emphasizing his trim waist and broad shoulders.

Averting her gaze before making eye contact with him, she was grateful for the smile Sir Rowan bestowed where he stood alongside a handsome, dark-haired nobleman. Though that one was of good height and build, he had not the proportions of the Wulfrith men. Since Beata knew their youngest sister was here, she guessed this was Lady Beatrix's husband, Michael D'Arci.

To the right of the hearth, children had gathered. More Wulfriths, Beata guessed. The girl of seven or eight was only slightly taller than the oldest of two boys, but the authority she exuded in reprimanding both told they were large for their ages. And before the hearth sat three ladies.

Certes, Baron Wulfrith's youngest sister was the petite one whose thick, golden hair was worked into braids that looked in no danger of losing their crossings.

Aye, Beatrix D'Arci was far different from Beatrix Fauvel. And in another way. Standing alongside the former's skirts was a girl child of an age to have just begun walking—if her size and surety of foot were true. And providing the small bulge beneath her mother's breasts did not lie, she would have a sibling four or five months hence.

Here be babes, Beata mused with a twinge of yearning for what she had expected would not be hers once she settled on her dower property. And still might not be if her father's fears were unfounded.

She looked to the woman whose age and bearing identified her as the mother of the Wulfrith siblings, next the one whose red and gold bliaut was stretched to its seams' limits. Baron Wulfrith's wife, soon to be a mother again.

Ache shot through Beata at the possibility Lady Annyn was a widow and her unborn babe fatherless.

"Sit with us," Lady Susanna said.

Blessedly, no matter how much the Wulfrith women disapproved of Beata's entrance, they were gracious—even Lady Isobel, who was said to like an ordered household.

For a quarter hour, during which scores of knights and men-at-arms assembled in the hall to join the Wulfriths at supper, Beata answered questions put to her and did her best to make light of those which sought news of Baron Wulfrith.

Aye, Queen Eleanor had introduced him, and he had been of good health and temperament. He had even accompanied Durand and her to the docks, but that was the last she had seen of him. It was the truth, providing one did not believe omission a lie.

Most grateful Beata had been when the Wulfrith children were summoned and introductions made—until Lady Annyn's oldest spoke quite seriously of the necessity of her father returning from France before her mother birthed what *must be* a sister. Then there were Issie's brothers, the oldest of whom might gain his inheritance far sooner than expected.

Lord, do not take Baron Wulfrith from them, Beata sent heavenward as the meal was called.

When all but the oldest children were passed into the care of women servants to be taken abovestairs, fed, and put to bed, the ladies moved to the high table.

Beata was seated between Lady Isobel and Elias. Though the former mostly conversed with Lady Annyn on her other side, from time to time she addressed Beata in the softly lilting voice that evidenced her Scottish birth.

As Beata scooped up another spoonful of meat-ladened stew she shared with Elias, not for the first time she saw Lady Isobel peer past her daughter-in-law at those on the other side.

Before, Beata had wondered if it was Durand she so intently looked upon—he who made the lady stiffen and lids narrow—but here was proof. The queen's man met the woman's gaze, and the smile about his mouth dropped. Then he gave Lady Isobel a curt nod and returned his attention to Sir Rowan.

Beata knew it was not her business to take offense over the other woman's dislike of Durand, but whatever ill she thought of him, it must be a misunderstanding.

Lady Isobel looked around. "I still cannot conceive of the queen providing you but one knight for an escort, Lady Beata. It is almost unseemly."

More than almost, but she was being kind. As Beata could not own to the sizable escort that had included Baron Wulfrith and his men, she said, "It is obvious the queen holds Sir Durand in high regard. Fondly, she calls him her *gallant monk*—"

A *harrumph* sounded so loud Beata nearly looked past the lady in search of its source. But it was the Wulfriths' mother who caused heads to turn. Then of a sudden, she laughed and looked to Lady Annyn. "I believe our Issie and Jonas shall enjoy the tales Sir Elias weaves this eve."

Only when Beata moved her gaze to Durand, who looked between Lady Isobel and her, did she realize her mouth so gaped it must appear she suffered a lack of air.

What went between these two? Why did Lady Isobel dislike and distrust the queen's man though Abel regarded him as a friend and Everard seemed to like him well enough?

Not your concern, she heard Conrad advise. *Stir not the pot.*

But the misunderstanding that surely caused Durand to feel unwelcome ought to be set aright.

"As your husband would advise," Elias warmed her ear, "stir not the pot."

She laughed as loud as Lady Isobel had, though with sincerity. Deciding not to worry over what others thought of her expression of joy, she swung her head around. "I was thinking the same."

He grinned. "Many stories here, but where the Wulfriths are concerned, some are best left untold, hmm?"

This was the wiser Elias who had returned to France eight years after vanishing so completely his father had to accept his youngest son had met a foul end. Before his disappearance, the foolhardy youth had several times visited Conrad and regaled the count's young wife with tales and songs, for which Elias's father had berated him.

Conrad had been amused but grateful such a son was not his. But when Elias returned six months before Conrad's passing, boasting knighthood earned at Wulfen, Beata's husband had been impressed—mostly, for still Elias was given to storytelling and song. Once Conrad had even mused that when his old bones were interred, Beata might find a good second husband in one as compatible as Elias.

She had refused to think there, not only because she wished her life with Conrad never to end, but as much as she enjoyed Elias's company, her feelings for him were brotherly. Too, such was not possible now the second son had become the heir. Elias must wed well. And even if his controlling father could be thwarted in that, Elias's feelings for her were as comfortably benign.

"Of course," he said, "I concur with Lady Isobel it is peculiar Queen Eleanor provided you only one escort."

Were they alone, she might tell him that story. She shrugged. "Of greater interest is what goes between Sir Durand and the lady."

He clicked his tongue. "You are stirring, Beata. Put down the spoon."

She blew a breath up her face. "Injustice chafes me, as well you know, but I shall try to keep my tongue."

He glanced past her. "Whatever *your* tale"—he held up a hand to stay her protest—"the gallant monk is bothered over our friendship." As she looked around, he rasped, "'Tis too late. He now feigns interest in whatever Sir Everard and his wife tell."

Beata sighed, and as she reached to the trencher, caught movement on Elias's other side and saw Lady Beatrix lean toward her husband, who smiled and moved toward her.

"Lady Beatrix is beautiful," Beata whispered. "Forsooth—" She closed her mouth, having almost revealed it was Baron Wulfrith who had prepared her for the differences between his sister and The Vestal Widow.

"Forsooth?" Elias drawled.

She cleared her throat. "I understand she hardly resembles her older sister."

"I have not met Lady Gaenor, though she is soon to arrive with her husband and son, but I also understand the sisters are different in looks and disposition." He leaned in. "This afternoon, I heard two chambermaids twittering over Sir Durand. One claimed that were she as blond, fine of face, and small of figure as Lady Beatrix, she too could catch his eye. And his heart."

In that moment, Beata feared she understood the reaction of the queen's man when Eleanor had revealed Beata's name, as well as the encounter with Baron Wulfrith when Durand had become visibly discomfited over talk of Lady Beatrix.

Nay, I do not fear, she told herself. *I have naught to lose. And Durand has naught to gain with a happily married woman.*

"I am thinking *your* tale might be worth stirring the pot," Elias murmured. At her forced smile, he clicked his tongue again. "You will have to do better than that to fool me."

"What?" She opened her eyes wide.

He rolled his. "If Sir Durand feels the same for you, methinks it possible you may shed the *vestal* and the *widow*." At her gasp, he added, "Preferably not in that order."

She pressed her knuckles hard into his upper arm that, before the youth had fled France, had not been as muscled. "Ever the teller of *imagined* tales!"

He frowned. "Just invite me to the wedding. As my father cannot object to me accepting an invitation from the Wulfriths, one from Conrad Fauvel's widow ought to go down easily."

Knowing further protest would only goad him, she said, "You forget he does not approve of me."

"His loss." He wiggled his eyebrows. "Mayhap Sir Durand's gain."

"Do stop, Elias!"

He raised his goblet and winked. "I shall require another pour, mayhap two, before the night is done."

At her frown, he said, "Sir Rowan and I are to entertain those of Stern. The children—young and old—demand it."

So they did, the most outspoken being Lady Annyn's daughter, who might one day find herself as maligned as The Vestal Widow. But as a Wulfrith, perhaps *she* would be granted grace.

18

She had watched wide-eyed, gasped, laughed, and clapped. Though she might have been too loud and generous with her encouragement, she had not felt as constrained as she had at court.

At Stern, the presence of children loosened propriety's laces, granting even men of the sword permission to enjoy themselves as if they were of an age it was acceptable to appreciate the sweet things in life.

For the sake of the children, they would surely excuse their behavior were they called to account. Just as likely, some of the blame would fall on the example set by The Vestal Widow.

Fortunately, Lady Isobel delighted in her grandchildren's response to the tales of Elias and Sir Rowan, as evidenced by smiles and soft laughter. Of added benefit, she seemed to have forgotten Durand. Of course, that was more easily accomplished since he hung so far back that the few times Beata searched him out, he could have no doubt he was the reason for the disruption of her attention. But each time their eyes met, he had given a semblance of a smile that seemed acceptance of her enthusiasm—perhaps even amusement.

Though she normally stayed for a second round of tales, she was weary, and what better time to slip abovestairs than whilst Elias and Sir Rowan's audience clamored over the refreshments?

It seemed she was the only one of that mind. Though she had thought Lady Isobel and Lady Annyn, who walked well ahead of her, might also make for the stairs, they continued past toward the high table. But a moment later, the younger woman said something that made Lady Isobel pull her daughter-in-law into an alcove.

"Gallant monk!" the hissed words halted Beata just short of her destination. "Oh, such fun Eleanor has with that, though well she knows—"

"Do not do this to yourself," Lady Annyn said, only her skirts visible where she faced Lady Isobel whose back was turned to Beata. "'Tis in the past where the Lord would have it be, just as you would remind me did I not let go of what ought not be held."

Do not listen, Beata counseled. But they spoke of her escort and of things that would account for the reason the lady looked ill upon Durand.

A strident breath was drawn, and in a calmer voice that played Lady Isobel's accent as if it were music, she said, "You are right. 'Tis just made all the worse with Garr's delay and the feeling Everard knows something he will not tell. For what else would Abel have Sir Durand deliver a missive that could more easily have been carried by Sir Rowan? And what of Sir Durand's injuries? Something is afoot, Annyn."

"I also worry, Mother. But for all, especially your grandchildren, we must carry on in the belief the Lord will return your son to us ere this babe blesses my straining seams."

A weight pressing on the soul Elias and Sir Rowan had lightened, Beata would have braced a hand to the wall were she near enough to do so.

Lady Isobel sighed. "I just pray Sir Durand is well gone before Gaenor's arrival."

"My lady, it is unlikely Gaenor will arrive ere the sennight. More, she and her husband have made their peace with him."

Peace. What so terrible had happened that Lady Isobel's daughter and her husband needed to make peace with the queen's man?

"This I know, just as I know we are much in Sir Durand's debt, but—"

"It is only for the night, my lady. On the morrow, he departs to deliver his charge to Wiltford."

Silence, then, "Ah, that lady!"

Now I am to be disparaged, Beata brooded. But such was the price of listening in on others. Turning toward the stairs, she caught movement across her shoulder.

Durand remained just inside the corridor that led to the kitchens. A shoulder to the wall, one leg crossed over the other, his attention was on the girl before him—she who was named for Lady Isobel.

Head tilting this way and that, one hand gesturing then the other, Issie Wulfrith might one day rival Elias in the telling of tales.

"Dear Lord, what was the queen thinking to trust *him* alone with her?" Lady Isobel continued. "If she *is* vestal, the longer she keeps company with him, the less likely she will remain so."

It took Beata a long moment to make sense of that, there being no fit for the man with whom she had spent several nights without fear of being reduced to a mere widow. No fit for the one who had ended her kiss, receptive though he had seemed.

"I do not believe that of Sir Durand," Lady Annyn said. "He is changed."

Changed? Beata mulled and startled when the queen's man looked to her and frowned. Not an expression of displeasure—rather, concern.

"'Tis as he would have us believe," Lady Isobel scorned, causing Beata to break eye contact with Durand and look around, "but to think changed one given to preying on young women—"

"Cease!" The word sprang from Beata.

Lady Isobel swung around, then she and her daughter-in-law stepped from the alcove. Eyes wide, they stared at her—as, doubtless, did others in the hall.

Stir not the pot, Beata told herself. *Do as Lady Isobel and conceal your blunder beneath laughter.*

She could have, but the lady looked past her and gasped, "Issie is with him!"

"Mother!" Lady Annyn was the first to voice disapproval of what was implied.

Beata was the second—and not as proper. "You are mistaken, Lady. Horribly mistaken! Why, it is unimaginable you raised honorable sons."

Boots across the rushes. The silence of voices no longer lit with merriment. Movement before and to the sides of her. Tears brightening Lady Isobel's eyes.

Dear Lord, what have I wrought? Beata sent heavenward.

"Lady Beata!"

Did that voice belong to Durand coming behind her? Or Sir Everard approaching opposite? Both? Regardless, she was at the center of their wrath. And soon to be cornered. Though it was not the same as when men sought to press their attentions on her, the leaves stirred so much she felt them rise on the wind of her imagination and brush her fingers, throat, and cheeks.

She looked from Lady Isobel to Lady Annyn who—was it possible?—regarded her with concern. "Forgive me," she gasped and took a single step forward before arresting her flight.

There were too many corners abovestairs. Certain she would soon find herself backed into one, she turned. Glimpsing Sir Everard advancing on one side, Durand the other, she snatched up her skirts and ran toward the doors that gave unto the inner bailey.

It is dark there, protested the little girl within.

It was. But this night no thunder. No lightning. No rain.

Hearing Durand call to her, she pushed past the porter and opened the door herself.

It was cold outside, but not as frigid as that shore across which death had scattered itself. Though she had been damp and weak following the shipwreck, for a long while she had weathered the elements without a mantle. This was naught, and she welcomed the brisk air gulped down as she descended the steps.

Ignoring the sharp regard of those manning the inner bailey, she looked around and confirmed she was not followed.

Where? she wondered as she passed beneath the portcullis into the outer bailey.

Anywhere absent disapproving eyes. Anywhere without a corner. Anywhere.

Stern's guard pointed the way as Durand had known they would when Elias de Morville stepped in his path and insisted he be the one to bring Beata back. He had not insisted long, Durand surprising him as much as himself when he slammed a fist in the eye of one who was a knight only because the grateful Everard Wulfrith had bestowed the title. It would be days before the troubadour once more used that eye to wink at a lady.

Before the stables, Durand halted and drew a calming breath before opening the door and stepping into the building that housed dozens of horses, their feed, and equipment.

Lanterns burned at both ends, placed where their flames were in no danger of being tempted beyond their wicks. Though they provided little light, it was enough to see one's way between the stalls.

He glanced at the loft, dismissed it for the difficulty of ascending its ladder in skirts, and strode forward. Nearly all the stalls were occupied by destriers, palfreys, and workhorses, and those empty of beasts were also empty of the lady. As he neared the far wall, remembrance struck of what had happened there eight years past.

Lady Annyn would have died had her husband not gone looking for his missing bride. With bestial wrath, Baron Wulfrith had laid down the miscreant who tried to hang his wife, and Sir Rowan had dealt the killing blow.

That was during Durand's early days of service at Stern, before Beatrix Wulfrith had reached an age to capture his heart. In later days—and years—she had entranced. But now...

If only one good came of him pausing at Stern, it would be the discovery she no longer made him ache. Though his love for her had eased considerably when his acquaintance with Helene made him realize the Lord could not have created only one woman capable of claiming his affections, this day nearly all that remained of that love had blown away with Beatrix D'Arci's kind greeting.

The answer to prayer. The lifting of a great weight.

Seeing the door of the farthest stall was open, Durand increased his stride.

Beata was inside, but not tucked in a corner. She sat at the center of the stall where enough light shone to reveal she rested her chin on knees drawn to her chest.

When he halted before her, she lifted her face, and he caught a sparkle amid the shadow he cast over her. Tears?

"They would not let me out," she said with more calm than when she had defended him to Lady Isobel.

"Out?"

"The drawbridge is raised for the night."

Of course the castle guard would not allow her to depart without escort—be it night or day. "You meant to leave?"

"In a temper, I grow foolish, as can attest Lady Isobel, Lady Annyn, Sir Everard—" She gave a huff of laughter. "As can all who but wished a night of merriment. Blessedly, I soon come right once I have space and air aplenty to breathe."

Knowing it best they converse where they were visible enough to keep tongues from wagging more than already they did, he said, "Come," and raised her to standing.

When he released her, he saw the hair braided off her brow had worked free on both sides, causing dark tresses to curve about her cheeks and their ends to perch on her shoulders.

"Certes, Sir Everard will wish the guard let me out," she said. "And now you must be all the more eager to give me over to my father."

He ought to be, but—

What? he silently demanded. *She is trouble you do not need. Trouble you do not want. And likely soon to be another man's trouble.*

"Are you not angry?"

He was, though not as much as when he had found himself bound aboard her ship.

Take her from here now, reason commanded, but he asked, "Why did you defend me over something you cannot speak to?"

"You know what Lady Isobel suggested?"

"I heard enough." And even that little had been unnecessary. Though a good and godly woman, the Wulfriths' mother could not forgive him.

"If you heard, how can you question my defense? Surely better than many a woman, I can vouch for the high regard in which the queen holds you—tell 'tis not foolery that causes her to name you her gallant monk."

He longed for that to be the truth of him, not merely a truth amended, but he could not undo what he had done. Nor did he wish to explain Lady Isobel's disdain. Revelation of his past would tear off the scab that grew smaller with his every triumph over sins of the flesh, causing this lady, who thought too well of him, to think ill of him. Too, his great failing could be of no consequence to her. Soon he would leave her behind, whether as a widow caring for her aged father or an heiress wed to the nobleman who proved most grateful for the king and queen's generosity.

"Aye, I can vouch for you," Beata said, and when still he did not respond, took a step nearer. "I know not what misunderstanding caused Lady Isobel to speak as she did, but she is wrong."

Durand wanted her to believe the lie that she knew his character well, but he could not. "Lady Beata, even were we of better acquaintance, 'twould be impossible for you to vouch for my honor."

Silence, as if she doubted herself, then she said, "I can."

The light reaching across his shoulder revealing the dance of dust between their faces, he reminded himself of the importance of not delaying their return to the donjon. But her eyes were luminous...lips soft... voice honey...

"I know you, Durand." She slid a hand over his right arm and shoulder, then moved the other up his chest and set it on his bearded jaw.

He could not move. Or was it he dared not lest he move in the wrong direction? The only thing of which he was certain was of being too aware of every place their bodies touched.

"I know you," she breathed and pushed her fingers into the hair at his nape and urged his head down.

He did not set her back, but neither did he yield to a taste of her mouth. Feeling the absence of breath between them, he set his forehead against hers and a hand on her waist.

"Durand," she whispered.

Heart beating faster, he explored the reach of her lower back, and when he curved his hand around her other side and gripped the soft place between ribs and hip, she arched toward him.

"Beata," he groaned.

"At last, I am that to you."

It *was* as he had come to think of her. Why? More, why did he revel in the feel of one so different from the women to whom he was attracted? That question needed an answer before—

Before what? he wondered. *The only* before *with this woman is before you were given charge of her. The only* after *shall be remembrance of the trouble she caused.*

"This time, I would have *you* kiss *me,*" she said.

Do not, Durand. You will only make this moment more regrettable.

"Durand?"

The Durand of now, who knew the folly of uncoupling mind from body, stepped back from the Durand of old, who moved his forehead off hers and touched his mouth to her nose...cheek...corner of her lips...

Then he angled his head, pressed his mouth to hers, and coaxed the exquisite response that would grant him permission to proceed. When she sighed into him, he deepened the kiss. When she murmured encouragement, he gathered her nearer.

These things he did that he should not. Things that could be the ruin of her.

And the ruin of him—ashes from which he would not rise again.

19

Durand Marshal, Wulfen-trained and Wulfen-proud, had just begun to believe himself more redeemed than not—that should he fall again, it would not be far. Certainly not as far as he had fallen with the Wulfriths. Now this.

Other than Beata's hands straining where he gripped them between their chests to keep her fingers from convincing him this night was all that mattered, she was still.

Cheek pressed between his neck and shoulder, it was she who rent the silence. "You stopped," she said. Not with sorrow. Not with accusation. What?

Telling himself it did not matter, he breathed deeply for the dozenth time since heeding the Durand of now who protested caresses and the undoing of hair so undone it caped the lady's shoulders and back.

"I did, and you ought to be glad, my lady."

She drew her head back. As the dust resumed its dance between them, she said in a voice so small it was difficult to believe she had caused all of Stern's hall to seem a stage, "Unless you feel naught of what I do—and I am not so innocent to believe it—I am right about you. You *are* gallant. Though certainly no monk, you are enough in control that were I to wed again, as on that day no more could I be named a widow, only on that night could I no longer be named vestal."

Thus, now each knew what the other had refused to reveal about the names by which they were known. But it was her faith in him that most unsettled, making him more vulnerable to a woman than he had been since Helene—nay, Beatrix Wulfrith. Some part of him, so weak it turned him from his purpose and good sense, longed for a woman to believe in him. *This* woman of questionable behavior and much too short acquaintance.

She tried again to free her hands, but he would not risk her once more loosing them on him as he had loosed his upon her, too much familiarity having impelled him to move her back against the wall.

"Durand Marshal," she said on a sigh, "I do not understand how 'tis so, but I feel much for you."

He stiffened. She did not speak of what moved the body but what moved the heart. The same as Gaenor had done. And so here he was again—

Nay. He had cared for Beatrix's older sister and, for a broken moment in time, desired her. But though what had happened this eve was far different, there could still be terrible breakage.

"Never have I felt what I do with you, Durand—"

"Enough! You may think you know where such talk leads, but you cannot conceive of the consequences."

She fell silent, then said, "Feel the beat of my heart," and tried to draw his hands downward.

"Behave, Beata!" He pressed her hands more firmly beneath his collarbone. "Already I know the beat of your heart—and yet know mine. And there is no good in it."

"Why?"

"Lust moves them. That is all."

Beata was surprised by how much she hurt over words meant to convince her that all he felt for her resided in a place distant from the breast. But the hurt was deserved. In her quest to prove she knew him—that Lady Isobel could not be more wrong—she had turned wanton.

"For this, lust being a great failing of mine," he said, "the queen has her fun in naming me a monk."

"Surely you do not say she allows you to sport with her ladies?"

"She does not, and I do not."

Beata almost laughed. "Is not lust a fairly common sin? And not only for men?"

"Aye, but what makes it among the greatest of failings is acting upon it, as Lady Isobel knows well." He released her and strode from the stall.

Did he mean...? He could not.

He turned to her, and she wished the bit of light on her face shone more on his. "My lady, each minute that passes disposes us to more talk of what goes between *The Vestal Widow* and the *gallant monk*. For your sake, more than mine, let us return to the donjon."

She did not move.

"Come, Lady Beata."

"You wish me to believe you prey on young women? Nay, I have frightened you, is all. Lest I am so silly in love I become more of a nuisance, you seek to discourage me."

She seamed her lips to allow him space in which to respond, but he did not. Because the man she had tempted in order to prove she knew him *had* taken advantage of Gaenor Wulfrith? If so, surely he had not lain with the lady...

She slid a hand up her throat and pressed fingertips to lips fervently explored by his. Had he not stopped, they might now be upon the straw.

She lowered her hand and gripped it with the other at her waist. "Either I have proven what I set out to prove—that I can vouch for your honor. Or I have proven what I did not set out to prove—though you find me desirable, you are insufficiently moved to divest me of the vestal."

He drew a sharp breath. "'Twas a test? For this, you approached me?"

"'Tis where I started, though I did not intend it to progress as far as it did." She pushed off the wall. "It seems I am no better than Queen Eleanor's ladies whose attentions you must ever be—"

"Almighty!" His bark halted her advance. "What fool are you to play such games, Beata? Were I many a man, I would have—"

"That is what I say! You are not *many a man.*"

"Certes, not with you."

She blinked. *That* was what she had proved? She was not desirable enough? She swallowed hard. "So be it, but though you would not risk your reputation with one such as me, still I will not believe you prey on young women."

"No longer," he said gruffly. "It was ere I served the king that I dishonored my name and knight's training."

Alarm shot through her, but she muffled it.

No longer, he said, and had he not served Henry for years? Had not the queen entrusted him to deliver Beata to her father? And what of the reassurance Lady Annyn had given her mother-in-law that Durand was not the same as he had been?

"Were I to believe you were ever so dishonorable," she said, "I could also believe you changed."

"All you must believe is that my great failing went well beyond my failing with you this eve. Hence, its price may never be paid in full."

"Then Lady Isobel's daughter... You say you ravished—"

"Not ravishment!" His silhouette gained height and breadth. *"That* I would not do!"

She took a step back. "Of course you would not. Pray, forgive me. I but try to make sense of what you say and yet do not."

When he spoke again, it was with strained calm, "Ravishment is not the only road to ruin, Lady Beata."

"I understand." She did. And prayed he *was* changed, that it was not a lack of desire for her that caused him to end what they would both regret. "If you would give me a few minutes, I shall compose myself and put my hair in order." She swept the mess back off her face and shoulders. "As I spent too little effort on it this eve, I should be able to make it appear as it did ere I upset Elias and Sir Rowan's audience."

He turned and strode from sight.

It took more time to locate the ribbon to secure her braid than to rework the crossings, and further time to accept little could be done to make her mouth appear as if it had not been intimate with another's. Thus, one good thing came of her disruption of the hall. Upon her return, contrition would provide a good reason to keep her face lowered.

Durand awaited her outside the stables, doubtless to give Stern's guard less cause to believe something untoward had happened within.

He did not offer his arm, but she took it. "Had I not tested you," she said when he stiffened, "would you not have ensured my footing over unseen ground?"

Silence.

"Aye, you would have."

He drew her forward, and only when they entered a hall much changed from the one she had fled did she release him. She murmured her thanks, then made her way amongst those who, preparing to bed down earlier than expected, made their curiosity felt.

A hand settled on her arm as she ascended the first step that would deliver her to the chamber she was to share with Lady Susanna and Lady Beatrix. "Beata."

She stared at the toe of her slipper. "I am sorry I ruined everyone's fun, Elias."

"Ah well, they had their fill."

She was so grateful for his kindness she nearly lifted her face. "Nay, they had not."

"Look at me, Beata."

"I am ashamed and tired and long to gain my rest." She leaned into the stairs, but he gripped her more firmly.

"Look at me."

"Elias—"

She was unprepared for his finger beneath her chin—more, the blackening of his eye. "Dear Lord, what happened to you?"

"I would ask the same of you." His eyes—one wide, the other narrow—considered her mouth. "But though my answer would prove the same as yours—Sir Durand—methinks you were more receptive to your encounter than I who pushed too hard to be the one to return you to the donjon."

She sucked a breath, told herself she was a fool to think too much of Durand's behavior. "It was all my doing—but an attempt to prove something I had no cause to prove. Be assured, Sir Durand takes his duty to the queen seriously."

He snorted. "No assurance of that do I require."

"Cease, Elias!"

He released her. "We will speak more on the morrow."

Unlikely. Did he arise to see Durand and her away, there would be little time to converse. "On the morrow," she said and climbed the stairs.

Her entry into the chamber was uneventful. As revealed by a single candle on the bedside table that would soon be but a puddle, the other women were abed—Lady Beatrix on the left, her daughter asleep in a cradle alongside, and Lady Susanna in the center, her infant son curled against her chest.

Amid the dim, Beata crossed to the right side of the bed, removed her gown, and slid beneath the covers. It was a snug fit, but more comfortable once she turned onto her side and hugged the bed's edge.

She would not think on Durand—dare not, lest he appear to her in sleep.

Accursed reality! Ever pushing its way into dreams. Ever causing one to question what was imagined and what was not. Ever making ruin of rest.

She drew a deep breath, slowly released it.

A hand touched her back. "You may not believe it, Lady Beata," Lady Susanna whispered, "but there are better days ahead. The past is not your future."

That last was certain, her past having been spent as Conrad's indulged wife. But better days ahead? Days and years in which to forget the man whose kisses and embraces seemed a place she could call home?

"I thank you," she whispered.

The lady left her hand on Beata's back, and it was not long before her breathing revealed she slept the sleep of one who loved and was loved in return.

Back to the wall where he sat on the pallet he had claimed for the night, Durand stared across the shadowed hall.

On the other side slept Elias de Morville, who was nearly as responsible as Beata for making the queen's man aware of the lie it was not merely lust which drew him to yet another woman he could not have. Had the troubadour not guessed from the fist taken to the eye that Durand overstepped his duty to The Vestal Widow, he knew it from those few minutes with the lady before the stairs.

Certes, it was safer for Beata to pass the night at Stern, but not her escort. Far safer it would have been for him to resume their journey to Wiltford. After what had happened in the stables, he could no longer deny he was drawn to one too tall, dark of hair, indelicate, opinionated, loud, and…compassionate toward one such as he.

He ground his teeth. He hated it had been necessary to reveal his past, hated he had hurt her by implying she was not desirable enough to tempt him beyond kisses and caresses. Still, it was better she did not spend more of her heart on one who had rejected Gaenor's heart. And better for him. More difficult it would be to lose a woman who did not wish to be lost.

Thus, he was grateful to Lady Isobel. Whatever was required of him to fulfill his duty to the queen would be less difficult now.

He dropped his head back against the wall. *Pray, Lord, let the Baron of Wiltford's infant son be of good health that I may quickly depart and not be tempted to hold tight to Beata. Above all, let her not number among my losses.*

20

"I hoped to find you here."

The spoon slipped from Beata's fingers, clattered against the side of the bowl. Looking up from the porridge she had mostly stirred since the cook seated her at the rear of the kitchen, she dropped her feet from the stool's rungs and stood. "Lady Isobel, I…"

What was she to say? Having slipped out of bed well before dawn, she had not expected to see any Wulfriths. And hoped that expectation would be met.

The woman halted, glanced at the porridge. "I apologize for interrupting your meal, but I would speak with you."

"Of course."

Lady Isobel crossed to the door, beyond which lay a winter garden. Upon Beata's entrance into the kitchen a quarter hour past, Durand had exited through that door after informing her he would see to the horses.

Knowing the dark yet lurked there, she faltered. "Can we not speak here?"

The lady moved her gaze down Beata's mantle that provided little excuse for remaining indoors. "What I would discuss with you is best done in private."

Heart sinking further, Beata followed. As guessed, day had not dawned. The torches on the walls beyond the garden provided the only light by which to know this place that was dead but for the occasional evergreen bush and tree.

Beata closed the door, and avoiding peering into the darkened corners ahead, clasped her arms over her chest and braved the shadowed face of the woman before her.

"Lady Beata, I—"

"Pray, forgive me, my lady. I did not mean to listen in last eve, but when I heard…" She replenished her breath. "Grievously, I trespassed on you and Lady Annyn. I am ashamed of what I said, and more so now I know 'twas I who erred."

The lady's lids narrowed. "How do you know you erred?"

"Sir Durand assured me he could not give you more cause to dislike him."

Lady Isobel's head rocked back. "Did he?"

"Aye, but do not think he revealed anything I had not guessed. Indeed, he was reluctant to speak of what he calls his great failing."

"I see." She nodded. "Then I suppose *I* might be more easily forgiven."

"You?"

"For my own words and behavior. I aspire to be godly, but where Sir Durand is concerned, I oft fail. And my only excuse…" Her sigh clouded the air. "There is no *only* about one's beloved daughter."

Beata touched her arm. "Of course there is not."

Lady Isobel's gaze flicked to the hand upon her, but she let it be and gave a sorrowful grunt. "Love makes women fierce, especially mothers. One day you will know it yourself."

Would she?

"That is, do you not already."

That last was no thoughtless aside. Considering their unfortunate encounter, it begged examination. In defending Durand, she *had* been fierce, but that did not mean she loved him. Still, she would be a liar did she not accept she was—*had been*—moving toward something so wondrous.

"I believe it can be said, Lady Beata, you were most fierce last eve."

"Again, I apologize, especially for saying it was unimaginable you raised honorable sons."

"'Tis mostly truth. All were very young when their father took them from me to begin their training at Wulfen. Though never would I have admitted it to my husband, he is more responsible for the men they became than I."

Such sorrow in that honesty.

"Regardless, I reflected poorly on our family and could not sleep for the need to right my wrong. Even were we not to be neighbors, I would not wish harsh words to define your stay at Stern."

"They will not, my lady, and I pray that should the aid I give my father become permanent, we shall have more occasions to be kinder to each other."

The lady considered her. "Though I was wrong in speaking against Sir Durand, who does seem changed, 'tis my hope that when his duty to the queen is done, your fierce heart will be blessed by a heart more fierce than your own."

Had her daughter been so blessed? Did Lady Gaenor's husband feel fiercely for his bride who had not come to him chaste?

She lowered her hand from Lady Isobel's arm. "Once Sir Durand returns to France, I am certain all will come right." *That* was a lie, further evidencing her feelings for him.

Dear Lord, she sent heavenward, *let this be infatuation only. To my end days, I would not suffer love denied.*

"Forgive me," a voice tight with anger spun Lady Isobel around. "I did not expect to once more find myself the subject of idle conversation." Durand strode the winding path from the garden's gate toward the kitchen.

As Beata searched through her conversation with Lady Isobel to recall what he might have heard, she noted he brought the dawn with him. It gilded the ends of his dark hair, burnished armored shoulders, absented black pupils from golden eyes.

If avenging angels existed, they could not present as more formidable—nor appealing.

He halted a stride from them. "Lady Isobel." His nod was so slight it was almost disrespectful.

"Sir Durand, I am glad you are here."

His jaw convulsed. "Are you?"

"Just as I owed Lady Beata an apology, one is due you."

His lids narrowed.

"Be assured, Sir Durand, I do not seek to work further ill upon your character. I wish to make amends for behavior unbecoming a Wulfrith. Pray, forgive me."

Beata heard him draw breath through his nostrils. "It is done," he said, though still his anger was felt, "and I hope one day you may come as near as possible to completely forgiving me so we may be easy in each other's company as we were when my first offense was gifting Abel a pair of dice."

Curt laughter escaped her. "Mayhap in time, Sir Durand. The Lord does delight in surprising us." She turned to Beata. "Now I wish you Godspeed."

Beata thanked her, and when the lady returned to the kitchen, said, "She was gracious."

"'Twould seem."

"Then why are you still angry? You believe *I* spoke ill of you?"

"Elias," he growled. "He intends to accompany us to Wiltford, and Sir Everard agrees. Your friend did not tell you?"

She recalled their parting last eve. Elias had assured her they would further discuss Durand. "I believe he tried, but I would not listen. I shall speak to him—"

"Nay, it is decided and the horses are ready. Do we leave now and set a good pace, you should be reunited with your father by nightfall."

Though her belly was almost empty, were she given further opportunity to fill it, she would only push her spoon around. And since Durand had earlier taken her small pack with him, there was no reason to return to the donjon. "Deliver me to my sire, Sir Durand."

Eleven years much changed a man. At least they had this one whom she had not seen since he had lifted his frightened daughter of ten and four into the saddle and wished her away from Heath Castle with a sorrowful smile.

Though Beata had known his first duty was to his nephew who too slowly grew into his title, she had so resented that he would not accompany her on the journey—over land, over sea, into the bed of an old man—she had not returned his smile. Instead, she had held so tight to her saddle's pommel she would have strangled it were it a living thing.

"Beata!" her aged sire finally responded to the lowering of her hood. Then there on the drawbridge to which he had been summoned at the setting of the sun, he dropped to his knees and gripped his head in his hands.

She so quickly dismounted it surprised she kept her balance long enough to reach his side. "Father!" She flung her arms around him.

All of him shaking, he wept. Though not so hard a man he had been difficult to love, never had she seen such an outpouring of emotion—not even upon her mother's death.

She looked around. Her escort had dismounted and stood a stride back. Hands on sword hilts, their eyes were fixed on the knights who had accompanied the baron outside the castle. Throughout the ride, the air between Durand and Elias had been strained, but in this they were united.

She put her mouth to her father's ear. "I have come home. Now speak to me."

"My Beata," he choked. "My only hope."

She caught her breath. Then what she had prayed would not happen had? And if Durand heard, did he also suspect?

Lowering her voice further, she said, "My escort—"

He lifted his head so suddenly, he nearly clipped her nose. Grasping her arms, he pulled her close and searched her face with eyes so red and swollen she did not think these his first tears of the day.

Though his loss tempted her to cry, foremost for the poor babe and its parents, no self-pitying tears would she shed over what was now expected of her. Still, she would seek to convince her brother, Emmerich, he was the better choice of heir.

"You live," her father gasped, confirmation he had received word of the shipwreck. "Mere hours ago, you were dead to me, just as—"

"All that matters is I am here and well. For that, we owe all to the queen's man." She nodded over her shoulder. "Sir Durand Marshal."

Realization slid into his eyes, and he drew a breath that put his shoulders back. "How will I ever thank the queen?"

He knew as well as she how Eleanor wished to be shown gratitude.

"Welcome home, Daughter." He kissed her cheek, then raised her with him and turned to her escort. "Sir Durand."

Of course Durand suspected her father's infant son had died. It was in his eyes. Might even be certainty.

"Marshal, hmm?" her father said. "Kin to William Marshal?"

"So distant, my lord, you could be forgiven for naming it a lie."

"Well, since you have safely delivered my daughter, methinks you are to be as highly regarded."

Durand smiled tightly.

Beata's father frowned. "Have we met?"

"In passing, Baron Rodelle. Years ago, and only for a short time, I served the keeper of Firth Castle."

"Ah, and now you serve the queen. Impressive."

When Durand did not respond, Beata looked to Elias, winced over his bruised eye, and said, "Sir Elias de Morville, Father—a friend of mine and my departed husband. When Sir Durand and I paused at Stern Castle, I was surprised to find he was the Wulfriths' guest. Generously, he offered to—"

"The Wulfriths," her father said with an edge of the old resentment over his nephew being dishonorably returned to Wiltford. "Long it has been since I had occasion to sit at table with that family—"

"Baron, what tidings did you receive of the wreck of your daughter's ship?" Durand asked what she was also eager to know.

"Tidings most distressing. But look, my Beata is here! Answered prayer I did not pray for the futility of begging what could not be given."

"Baron Rodelle—"

"Come, 'tis too cold to converse outside, and your bellies surely ache with hunger, your throats with thirst."

"Father, about the shipwreck—"

"It can wait." He patted her hand and led her past the gatehouse into the outer bailey.

While Durand and Elias gave their mounts into the care of stable boys, Beata's father rasped, "Not for nothing did I warn you to be discreet in departing France and guard well your purpose in returning to England." He glanced at her escort. "This bodes ill."

For what was required of her. "As told by the tears you shed ere our arrival, I assume your infant son has passed."

She heard him swallow. "Three days gone. A terrible enough loss, but when word came of your shipwreck this morn..." He shook his head. "I feared for my heart."

"I am sorry. How fares your wife?"

"Once more, she grieves—will not move from our bed." He sighed. "Our babe died in her arms. Poor lass."

Lass, indeed, Beata disdained. Three babes in less than three years, and if the girl was ten and six, it would be of recent attainment. Beata had wed nearly as young, and if not for Conrad's honor, her fate could be the same as her father's wife. In that moment, she resented him more than when he had made chattel of her.

He returned his attention to Durand and Elias. "Most unfortunate this."

"More unfortunate 'twould be had I not Sir Durand's escort. Though you might have no body to bury, I would be as dead as Sir Norris."

"Such a loyal man," he said as if he did not catch her tone. "I am sorry to lose him. To the sea, aye?"

"He was swept away before my eyes—is as dead as the captain you paid to deliver me across the channel."

"What of the two knights who accompanied him?"

"I will speak later on what transpired, but I believe they are well despite being detained by the king and queen."

He heaved a sigh. "At least the ship's captain did not fail me."

"Did he not?" she exclaimed and saw Durand look around. She leaned nearer, hissed, "He should not have put to sea." Though still pained over doubling the man's reward, that had been necessary to save Durand, and she had tried to persuade Sir Norris to delay the crossing. "'Twas the queen's man who did not fail you, Father."

"Then I owe him gratitude alongside God."

She moistened her lips. "Tell me what you learned of my ship's wreck."

"What would I know that you—?" His eyes darted toward the stables. "They come! Be silent and speak not of my son's death. I may have a solution."

"Solution?"

"Aye, one that will see your escort all the sooner depart, leaving the business of Wiltford to its lord, not Henry and Eleanor."

Though she longed for an explanation, Durand was nearly upon them, his suspicion striding well ahead of him.

Beata almost pitied her father who would soon learn that ridding himself of the queen's man was no easy thing.

21

Upon the Baron of Wiltford's return to the hall after excusing himself to see to his wife, who suffered what he called a *passing illness,* he found his steward had seated his guests before the hearth and provided them food and drink.

While mulling his *solution,* Beata had spoken little with Durand and Elias in the half hour since their entrance into a hall that, though as fine as remembered, was somewhat disarrayed. But the Lady of Heath Castle was young, and when not occupied with giving her husband an heir, was surely too beset with recovering from the attempts to keep the household in order.

Might she yet birth a healthy babe? If she succeeded, it would free Beata and Emmerich, though only of inheriting Wiltford. Either Beata would be bound to a man for life, or Emmerich's commitment to the Church would be dissolved. However, providing her brother did not quickly wed, his sacrifice would not be lifelong. He could return to the Church.

"Baron Rodelle," Durand said as the other man lowered into the chair beside his daughter, "What tidings of the shipwreck?"

Beata's father plucked an apple from the platter of viands. "Surely I am less informed than you."

Durand lowered a twice-filled goblet. "Your daughter and I escaped ahead of the scavengers and traveled well inland lest they followed. Thus, we heard no tale of the wreck."

The baron cut away the soft of the apple and tossed it on the fire. "The men I sent to meet my daughter and Sir Norris told it was not only their ship that sank."

"The name of the other?"

"I know not—only that it also struck the rocks and went under not far from Brighthelmstone."

Durand dragged a hand over his head, tousling hair his hood had flattened during the ride.

Beata looked away, ran into Elias's gaze, and averted again. Though she should be grateful it could not be confirmed Baron Wulfrith was lost to his family, she wearied of the unknown. Were he dead, better she grieve now for her part in his demise than allow hope to breed more hope, an abundance of which could be more detrimental than a surfeit of its opposite.

"Such tragedy, though far worse 'twould be were my daughter lost to me," her father said. "As word spreads, English and French alike shall mourn the loss of family and friends aboard those ships."

Durand sat forward so suddenly the baron sat back. "The second ship was of French origin?"

Understanding made Beata lean in as well.

Annoyance unsettled her father's eyebrows. "Aye, that much is known."

"What else?"

He shrugged. "'Twas bound for France—departed Dover ere the storm struck and was blown down the coast."

Durand's face swam before Beata, then the bread she had nibbled tumbled from her fingers and she folded over herself.

She heard her father call to her, but when she lifted her face from her skirts, it was Durand she sought. And he was before her, a hand gripping her shoulder.

"Not Baron Wulfrith," she said past a smile that trembled so much it could be no pretty thing. Yielding to impulse, she set a hand on his jaw. "He shall return to his family, Durand."

Though he looked discomfited, his mouth softened. "Answered prayer, Beata."

She longed to go into his arms—to kiss him no matter how improper it would appear.

"I am glad to have lightened the mood," the Baron of Wiltford drawled.

As Durand straightened, Beata swung her head around.

Disapproval lined her father's face.

"Certes, you have lightened our mood, Baron Rodelle," Durand said. "It was feared the second ship carried Baron Wulfrith and his men who were to depart court shortly after Lady Beata."

"A terrible loss that would have been," her father said, "not only for his family but all of England."

Durand inclined his head. "If your steward will lend me parchment and ink, I shall compose a missive to each of the baron's brothers so their minds are eased."

"Certainly. Now——"

"Beata?"

Though it was a voice somewhat deeper and of greater volume than she remembered, she knew it. She jumped up and swung toward the young man who stood just off the stairs. At twenty-one years to her twenty-five, he had grown square-jawed and taller, but his face and slight figure were familiar.

"Emmerich!" As she ran to him, his eyes moved to their father. There had never been ease between the two male Rodelles, but she had hoped in her absence they would become comfortable in each other's company. It did not feel that way, the tension in the hall increasing. Because Emmerich would not give up the Church?

Only when she neared her brother did he step farther into the hall, and it was she who wrapped her arms around him. "My little brother, who is little no more."

As if unaccustomed to displays of affection, awkwardly he put his arms around her. "My big sister, who is big no more," he said, and when she dropped back her head, she saw him glance toward their father again.

"What do you here, Emmerich? I thought you were in London."

Though his smile was tight, it revealed enough of his teeth to evidence the front two had not closed as hers had not done. It was their mother in them.

"I am on Church business," he raised his voice as if to be heard beyond her, "but since I was passing near Wiltford, I paused to meet my new little brother."

With the speaking of that last, a dark space appeared in his eyes that sent a chill through her, but she warmed it away with the reminder he must know their sibling was lost to them. And godly though he was, just as she must bend her faith to do her duty to their father, so must he.

Emmerich set her back, adjusted his priest's robes, and nodded at those before the hearth. "I would meet your escort."

Their father made the introductions, calling his son *Brother Emmerich*. As Beata observed the latter, it struck her he was too lean, as befitting one who sets an example of sacrifice by not yielding to gluttony. Just as he lacked the training of a warrior, he had not the build or presence.

"Tell us, Brother Emmerich," Durand said, "how fares your brother?"

"The babe is——"

"Ah, here he is now." Her father nodded toward the stairs. "Come, Petronilla. My daughter would meet the brother who shall one day lord Wiltford."

The pretty woman cradling a bundle against the bodice of a homespun gown glanced amongst those gathered, paused on Durand, then lowered her face and crossed the hall with what seemed reluctance.

Beata's stomach heaved. Here was her father's solution—claiming another's child as his own the sooner to see Durand and Elias away. And like Emmerich, she must participate in the deception.

Resentment once more roused, she wished Durand's suspicions strong enough to see through the ruse. And recanted. If she must wed a man, better one of her choosing than the queen's.

"My lady." The woman halted before Beata, glanced at the dozing infant. "You would like to hold yer brother?"

Beata reached, and as the babe was passed to her, it blinked sleepy eyes, and its sweet mouth formed a smile. "Oh," Beata breathed, "such a beautiful child."

"So handsome, he is near beautiful," her father said before she realized her poor choice of words.

"Indeed," Petronilla said with thinly disguised pride.

Beata glanced at Durand and was not surprised by his sharp gaze and firm mouth. Then her wish was granted that he not be taken in by the ruse?

"Return the babe to his mother, Petronilla," her father said. "My lady wife will not sleep until he is settled beside her."

"Aye, my lord." The woman eased the babe from Beata, and when the child cooed, twittered back. As she started past Durand, he stepped into her path. "May I, Petronilla?"

She nodded, and Beata saw her father stiffen as Durand peered at the child.

"The babe *is* beautiful," he said.

The woman thanked him and continued across the hall.

After she disappeared up the stairs, Beata's father looked to Durand. "It has been a long day, and Sir Elias and you will wish to leave early on the morrow. I will have you shown to your chamber."

No offer of supper, Beata noted. They had been fed, but it was impolite not to include them among the castle folk who would gather to share the day's last meal. But what choice had her father? Though he had surely held close the death of his son three days past in anticipation of Beata's arrival, enough must know of it that it could prove impossible to control their tongues.

"Certes, we are travel won and in need of a good night's rest," Durand said. "As requested, you will send up parchment and ink?"

"It shall be done."

Beata was fairly certain her escort would not leave on the morrow. Not only was her father a poor liar, but no missive need be written if Elias and Durand were to quit Wiltford at dawn. Even if Durand returned to

France by a route different from the one Beata and he had taken, Elias could deliver tidings of Baron Wulfrith to those of Stern Castle and send them on to Wulfen.

"I would also like to see my chamber," she said.

Emmerich stepped forward. "I will take you."

"If my wife is agreeable, Brother Emmerich," their father said, "first introduce your sister to your stepmother."

Beata's inside jumped. Though it was true her father's wife was a stepmother to the children of his first wife, it was beyond peculiar that one ten years younger than she was accorded that title.

Her father summoned his steward, and as he instructed the man to escort Durand and Elias to their chamber, Beata followed Emmerich up the stairs.

"'Tis good to see you," she said when they reached the landing.

He glanced across his shoulder, allowing a glimpse of fire in cool gray eyes. "From you, I believe that."

She halted.

He turned to her. "Forgive me. Despite the circumstances we are made to suffer, I am also pleased to see you, Beata."

She inclined her head. "I am sorry father and you remain distant. He wants what is best for Wiltford and surely believes the best is you. Though I know you are devoted to the Church, would you not—?"

"I would not. Nor would our sire who does not believe I am best for Wiltford."

She blinked. "What say you?"

He glanced past her, and as she also caught the sound of boots ascending the stairs, he took her arm and drew her to the solar. After a single knock to alert its occupants to visitors, he opened the door and pulled her inside.

Nursing the babe at the hearth, Petronilla looked up and quickly away. If Beata guessed right, she had served as wet nurse to the Baron of Wiltford's infant son before his death, and the one she cradled was her daughter or very pretty son. Woe to her that she had yet to return to the village from which she, a new mother capable of nursing a babe besides her own, had come. Of course, it was likely she had not been allowed to depart Heath, since to do so would cause some to question the health of the babe whose last two siblings were long buried.

As Emmerich secured the door, Beata looked to the figure curled beneath the bedclothes, no hair of the lady's head visible.

"Go to her," Emmerich said. "Lady Winifred is eager to know you."

Beata crossed the chamber she had only glimpsed in passing when she was the niece of the Baron of Wiltford and her father little more than a servant who aided in administering lands denied him as the second son.

She halted alongside the bed. "Lady Winifred?"

Slowly, the coverlet drawn over the lady's head was gathered down. Wide eyes set in a round face met Beata's, lingered, then lowered over her. "'Tis not right you are my daughter," she whispered.

"The world of men." Beata forced a smile and brushed a lock of blond, unwashed hair out of the lady's eyes. "Aye, unseemly this."

"I thank you."

"For?"

"Where the Lord has failed me, you will not."

"You will have to explain that, Lady Winifred, but perhaps later when you feel better."

"You are here to do what I cannot, aye? What thrice I failed to do for your father?"

Beata looked across her shoulder at her brother who stood alongside the wet nurse. Hands clasped behind his back, he raised an eyebrow.

Beata breathed deep. "Mayhap, Lady Winifred."

"Mayhap?" The lady shoved aside the covers and sat up. "But you are alive, and it is why you are here. My lord husband promised! You would make a liar of him?"

She was so young, this mother of three lost babes. "I would not, my lady. 'Tis just that I believe my brother, Emmerich, would serve our father better."

The lady's head fell forward. "It must be you. Your father will not have him."

"But——" Beata caught back her questioning, examined the words exchanged with Emmerich on the landing. Her father had led her to believe her brother did not wish to succeed as baron. Another ruse?

The young woman raised her head and snatched hold of Beata's hand. "Tell me you will do it. I would rather die than try again." She leaned to the side. "Have I not said it, Petronilla. Do I not mean it?"

"I fear my lady can give no more," the wet nurse agreed. "And the physician concurs." She sighed. "Too young. Her body is done."

Weeping eyes and running nose making a mess of a face that must have been lovely when first she was wed to one old enough to be her grandfather, Lady Winifred said, "To the convent I would go. No man's hands upon me. No babe in my belly tearing me apart. Days, weeks, months on my face before the Lord I would trade for this life, even though the stones be hard and wicked cold!"

Fearing she might be sick, Beata wished she had not eaten.

"You will do it, Lady Beata?" It was more command than question.

"I will speak to my father and try to make him see the sense of my brother being his heir."

As a note of scorn sounded from the hearth, Lady Winifred said, "And if he will not?"

"I——"

"I would have your word you will wed whoever is required so I may leave."

Blessedly, if an heir must be got from Beata, she would have a choice of husband unlike her stepmother. "I will do my duty, Lady Winifred, that you may find your peace among the good sisters and, from time to time, spare a prayer for our family."

"Blessed be!" The lady drew Beata's hand to her mouth, kissed her knuckles, and fell back on the pillow. "I must sleep. It is a long journey to the convent."

Doubtless, one as far from Wiltford as possible. "We shall speak more later," Beata said.

Winifred's only response was a small sob.

After thanking Petronilla for aiding her lady, Beata accompanied her brother to the chamber beside the solar.

"May we speak?" she asked as he motioned her to enter.

"There is naught to discuss," he said as he stepped over the threshold and closed the door. "But I will tell it again if you must needs hear it. I am of the Church and would remain of the Church."

She frowned. "'Tis truly your calling?"

"Nay, but it was for this life I was raised. Had our father known one day he would need an heir, mayhap he could have changed that, but his efforts were spent upon our cousin. Thus, as I was educated for the Church, it is too late for me."

"You are still young. You could—"

"Nay, Beata. I would only disappoint myself—worse, our father—more than already I have done. I am where I ought to be and, given more time in which to believe as is required of me, methinks this life will become more agreeable."

"To believe as is required of you? I do not understand."

"I have some faith in the Lord, but it is the Church I clasp close, that which can be seen, heard, and felt. That which causes men to behave with civility—at least, appear to."

She took a step back. "You jest!"

His face darkened. "'Tis not something over which one jests if they truly believe—and fear." He drew a deep breath. "Now I shall leave you to your fervent prayers for my soul. Good eve."

Once the door closed, Beata fell across the bed. And wished herself in a cave, even if the rain slashed and the wind howled—providing her face was pressed to Durand's chest and his arms held her.

"I assume we shall not depart on the morrow."

Durand secured the shutter, turned from the window, and regretted—somewhat—the damage done the other man's face.

"We shall not. Hence, I have missives to compose." He crossed to the desk and dropped onto the stool.

"His infant son is dead."

Durand recalled the look he had exchanged with Petronilla, each warning the other to keep their previous acquaintance secret, then peered across his shoulder at the troubadour knight who sat on the side of the bed. "I fear 'tis so."

Disgust curled Sir Elias's lips. "Many an old man is guilty of sacrificing a woman's youth, if not her life, to gain an heir. My father, believing me dead..." He held up a hand. "Do we further our acquaintance, I may be persuaded to tell that story. Regardless, my sire attempted the same as Baron Rodelle. And also failed. But whereas this prodigal returned home to take his place, it seems either Brother Emmerich eschews his place or his father eschews him. If so, that leaves only Lady Beata, which begs the question of what you intend."

Durand turned back to the parchment. "Does she prove the heir, I shall do my duty to the queen—as shall you in aiding me."

The knight grunted. "Let us hope Brother Emmerich is made heir."

"That would be best. Unfortunately, I cannot take Baron Rodelle's word for it. He is a liar."

"As is many a desperate man."

Durand hesitated over the ink pot to which he reached the quill, looked around. "I know the lady is your friend, but she is not to wed without the queen's permission. I tell you this only because you have guessed that delivering her safely to her father is not my sole purpose. Too, I am certain you would not want Baron Rodelle to press her into a marriage she does not wish."

"Indeed," the knight drawled. "Something so important as her happiness ought to be left to the queen, who surely knows what is best for a lady whose first arranged marriage was to one who could have been her great-grandfather—blessedly, a man well enough supplied with sons he did not risk her life in pursuit of an heir, honorable enough to leave her vestal, and old enough not to steal all her youth."

Durand stared.

Sir Elias raised his eyebrows, dropped back on the bed, and clasped his hands behind his head. "Alas, the quandary you face. Did we weave in a chase, a murder, give our lovers no hope of reuniting..." He heaved a sigh. "Quite the tale we would have, one to make our audience hold their breath. Will our heroine suffer love in vain? Or will our gallant hero weather every storm to claim her for himself?"

This was not cruel mockery, but it was mockery, and it tempted Durand to balance out the state of the man's face. "You have much imagination, Sir Elias."

"So I am told, but every story is a story because it can happen, even if 'tis rare."

Durand dipped the quill. "I require only your sword arm, Sir Elias—assuming you have one."

He chuckled. "I am Wulfen trained the same as you."

The quill jerked, marking the parchment with a splotch of ink. "Not the same."

The man grunted softly. "I suppose not, but near enough I also wear a Wulfrith dagger."

"The cost of gratitude."

Another chuckle. "I am not one to hug the side of a bed, Sir Durand. You will have to make do with the pallet."

Setting his teeth against further words, Durand turned his thoughts to what would actually be three missives—one each to Abel, Everard, and the queen. The last would inform Eleanor that what she suspected of The Vestal Widow was true and her man would remain near the lady until he received further instruction.

22

He looked as though he might have an attack of apoplexy, and considering what was being thwarted by Durand's tidings that he would remain a time at Heath Castle, it was possible.

The Baron of Rodelle cleared his throat, glanced across the drawbridge at the receding rider he had provided the queen's man to deliver his missives. "I do not understand, Sir Durand. Not that you are not welcome after what you braved to deliver my daughter, but surely your liege is anxious for you to return to her service?"

"'Tis for Eleanor I must impose on your hospitality for several weeks."

"Weeks?"

"At this time of year, perhaps months." Durand nodded at the rider. "One of my missives is for the queen, informing her your daughter is returned to Wiltford and assuring her that until she replaces the missive lost at sea which I was to deliver to you, I shall remain."

A loud swallow. "Tell me, what did the queen wish to impart by way of the missive?"

"'Twas sealed, Baron. Surely you do not think I would trespass on our sovereign's privacy?" What he did not reveal was that he was to have read it before giving it into this man's hands so he would know the one Beata would wed.

"Curiosity makes me speak ere thinking," the baron said. "Forgive me."

Durand inclined his head.

The baron moved his regard to Elias, who seemed content to observe Rodelle's wiggling. Likely the troubadour knight studied it for how best to convey that behavior when next he had an audience. Such a curious man he was, but possibly likable—if not for his penchant of winking at Beata.

"What of you, Sir Elias?" the baron asked.

"As I am not in service to the queen, my stay will not be as long as Sir Durand's. However, I shall remain a few days to better acquaint myself with your daughter before I return to Stern to celebrate the birth of our Lord and the impending arrival of Baron Wulfrith."

The baron's smile was taut. "I have business to attend. I hope you will avail yourself of all Wiltford has to offer." He jutted his chin at the wood beyond the walls. "Good hunting there."

And the possibility of shutting out unwelcome guests.

"Another day," Durand said. "As it is weeks since I had occasion to practice at arms, my time is better spent on the training field—and you, Sir Elias?"

He expected the man to excuse himself so he might compose verse or some such, but he said, "I can think of naught I would rather do than hone my skill with another Wulfen-trained knight."

Then hone it they would. Hopefully, Baron Rodelle would not be so fool as to test it. And Beata would not long play the game her father sought to draw her into.

Women. If only they *were* more trouble than they were worth.

"Daughter!"

Beata looked around. "Father?"

He shot his gaze to Emmerich. "I would speak with your sister in private."

"In private?" her brother drawled.

"Already I have asked much of one whose first duty is to the Church. I do not wish to sully you further, Brother Emmerich."

"Of course not." His son rose from the chess table over which Beata and he had settled. "I pray you well, Sister." He inclined his head and strode to the stairs.

As the baron lowered into the chair Beata preferred filled by her brother she said, "That is your son. 'Tis wrong for you to be dismissive of him."

He stilled. "You take your father to task?"

"If I think it necessary, aye."

His brow lowered. "The tales of The Vestal Wife are not all exaggeration. Too much license you had in expressing yourself on the matters of men. Perhaps I did not choose a good husband for you after all."

The anger pricking her skin began crawling across it. "You did not. But a good father? Aye, *that* Conrad Fauvel was. *That* you chose well."

He blinked, and what seemed regret replaced displeasure. "When I heard what they were calling you, I guessed he was unable to do his husband's duty. Much it aggrieved me."

"He was not unable!" She loosed her frustration over the common assumption Conrad had been too old for relations. "Honorable is what he was. Though he wished to consummate the marriage, when he saw how afeared was the *girl* in his bed, he determined to seek the favors of women. By the time I was a woman myself, I was too much a daughter for him to think there."

"Only because he already had an heir," her father said, defensively.

That she would not argue. Though she did not wish to believe it of Conrad, he might not have waited had he lacked a son. Certes, when she had come of age, he would have exercised his husband's rights and rectified what others viewed as a deficiency.

"Regardless," she said, "I could not have loved a father more than I loved him."

The Baron of Wiltford caught his breath. "Beata!"

She stood. "I am sorry you are so changed. I may have been a girl when you sent me to play a woman, but this I know—in the absence of power, a better man you were."

He grasped her arm as she started past. "You cannot know what these years have wrought for me."

"I know what they have wrought for Lady Winifred and Emmerich, and if not that I might set aright what is wrong, I would regret answering your summons."

Tears wetting his eyes, he released her and lowered his face. "Forgive me, but I am desperate to do what is right and best for our family."

Though Beata longed to distance herself, compassion rose as she stared at his bent head.

"Only that, Daughter," he rasped, "without interference from those who call themselves our king and queen, yet reside on the continent."

"Their French lands are vast and oft suffer more turmoil than these," she surprised herself in defending Henry and Eleanor.

Her father looked up. "England will ever be second to them—a spare heir. For that, our family supported Stephen's reign."

"A disastrous reign that is long over."

He nodded. "It can never be again, but England's noblemen ought to have the greater say in how they administer their lands and live their lives."

Noble*men*. Sympathy dwindling, she said, "What about me? What about your wife? Should we not have a say?"

"Beata, we have no time for this—"

"And your son? He for whom neither had you time?"

He stiffened. "Emmerich is where he ought to be."

"Where he had no choice but to be!"

"Beata! Once this day is done, we will speak more on it."

She stepped back. "Once it is done?"

"Pray, sit."

With greater foreboding, she dropped into the chair.

Her father swept his gaze around a hall empty but for the two of them and a servant humming as she strew herbs across the rushes at the far end. "Since Sir Durand and Sir Elias have determined they shall remain guests well beyond their welcome," he said, resuming his seat, "we must needs get you away from Heath Castle."

Of course the two would remain. And Beata was not sorrowful. "Why must I leave?"

"So you may wed without interference from Eleanor and Henry."

Nor was she surprised. "Then I must go into hiding for weeks? A month?"

"Nay, this day you shall wed, and once 'tis done, there is naught Sir Durand can do."

"This day?"

"Accursed tidings!" He grunted. "'Twould already be done had news of your death at sea not caused your betrothed to depart believing he must look elsewhere for a wife."

Frantically, Beata searched for an explanation less distasteful than what he implied.

"Following your arrival, I sent a rider after the baron to inform him you had come, and he turned back. Now he awaits you in yon wood so you may speak vows in the nearest village."

As he drew breath to continue, she said, "You told I was to have a choice in whom I wed."

He hesitated, then ordered the servant from the hall. When the woman departed, he said, "I wish I could give you a choice, but this is most urgent. You shall have to trust I chose well."

Either he was something of a fool, or he thought her one. "Alas, if only I could be the dutiful daughter," sarcasm frolicked across her tongue, "but as you seem to have forgotten—certes, a result of what these years have wrought—the banns must be read three Sundays, one after another."

"They have been read, and with utmost discretion."

She folded her hands into fists, gained her feet, and strode toward the stairs.

"Aye, make ready," he called. "I shall come for you a half hour hence."

She swung around. "I will not be a party to this."

He stood. "You shall. It is why you came."

She lunged in front of him and was glad he was not of a height she had to strain her neck to see to the top of him. "You lied! Never was I to have a say in the one upon whom you would have me sacrifice myself."

"Nay, Daughter. I—"

"The banns! That took planning. And your choice of a husband was waiting for me here." She tried to draw a deep breath, but more words tumbled forth. "Was I so slight of mind as a child that you thought I would not see your deception? Were I, then I am all the more grateful my husband saw to my education, especially in the *matters of men*."

He set a hand on her arm. "This time a better husband I have chosen. He is but a few years older, of good appearance and of a size your sons will be all the better warriors. Though his lands are not as extensive as ours, nor as fertile, they are bettered by an abundance of sheep and good grazing."

"I say *nay*."

He ground his teeth so hard she heard their protest. "Beata, there is no other. Though I wished to give you a choice, he is the only one worthy of Wiltford *and* willing."

"Willing!"

"First you were The Vestal Wife, now The Vestal Widow."

"Why is he willing when others are not?"

"He is in need of a wife with funds to aid in setting aright his own demesne that was ill-managed by his mother until he took control."

Then she was the price he must suffer to save his lands.

"Too, your marriage will resolve the differences between our families—"

"Differences? Of which family do you speak?"

"That of Soames."

She knew the name. As a girl, she had not been oblivious to her father's grumblings over the strain between their families, it being believed the Rodelles were complicit in the disappearance of Baron Soames. No body was found, and there was naught to do but conclude the man met his end by foul means, leaving his young son to grow into his title much the same as Beata's departed cousin had done.

"*That* is who you would have me wed? One who believes ill of our family? *That* is the better marriage I am to make?"

"Lothaire Soames is more reasonable than his mother and desirous of better relations between our families. Though his lands do not border ours, they are not so distant Wiltford will be difficult to administer when I pass. And I do not doubt this barony will prosper beneath Soames's guidance. Though a fairly young man, he is shrewd. Too, he and I are of a mind about Henry and Eleanor."

Meaning he had also supported King Stephen's reign over Henry's. "A good marriage that may make for you, Father, but not for me."

"Beata, you cannot think only of yourself. What of Wiltford's people? 'Tis our duty to ensure they prosper."

There was that, but... She tried to blink away remembrance of Durand.

As if it were tears she sought to clear from her eyes, her father patted her arm. "It must be done, and all the more imperative it is now I have learned Sir Durand was to deliver me a missive from the queen. Since it surely directed me to wed you to a man of her choosing, that it was lost at sea is God's blessing upon your marriage to Soames."

Beata should not be surprised by the existence of a missive, nor hurt that Durand had not told her of it. Both were to be expected, and yet her throat tightened.

"This day the queen's man sent word to Eleanor informing her of your arrival at Wiltford," her father continued. "As I have yet to lay eyes on her missive, I do not act against her wishes by wedding you to one I would have father my grandchildren."

Resolve weakening, Beata said, "Still, she will not like it."

"Not liking what I do and exacting retribution for what is done is very different. Now are we of a mind?"

She shook her head.

"Beata, if you do not secure Wiltford's future, I will have to try for another babe with Winifred, and the poor lass—"

"Aye, lass!" she snapped. "And what of Emmerich? He could—"

"Not Emmerich! Never Emmerich!"

"Why?"

For some moments, he looked everywhere but at her, then he said, "Always he was destined for the Church, and as his mother would wish him to remain there, so he shall."

"There is more to it. Long you have had your heir. Instead, you choose one who does not want that burden, who speaks too much on the matters of men, who is twenty and five to Emmerich's twenty and one."

Whatever he held close was visible just beneath the surface of his eyes, and so she dragged harder. "You are ashamed of him. Ever you have been. That is the ill between you. Do you even love him?"

"I do! 'Tis just…" He sighed. "God knows Emmerich is not to blame, but he was born too early—ever too slight and prone to illness, fearful of weapons and violence, and better at wielding the edge of a quill than a blade. A worthy lord will administer Wiltford when I am gone, not one whose place is within the Church."

Beata wanted to slap him.

"There is naught more to discuss, Daughter. Now will you do the duty owed me as blood of my blood?"

She made him wait on her answer, then feeling leaden, said, "I have no choice."

He nodded. "As we have wasted much time and can only pray Sir Durand and Sir Elias continue to practice at arms, you must gain your mantle quickly."

And as her father's only heir, this day wed a man unlike the one who had lovingly shaped her into The Vestal Wife. She would become a possession, never again see Durand, never again feel the only hands she wished to feel, nevermore know his kiss.

"Daughter?"

Oh Conrad, you did not want this for me. But what am I to do? Right or wrong, he believes he has only me. And am I not to honor my father?

Listen well, Beata, Conrad spoke to her from the past as he had many times spoken to her in the present. *Know all that can be known ere you give answer. Not in haste. Never in haste.*

She looked to her father. "Send word to Lothaire Soames I will not wed one who skulks outside the walls. If he wishes to proceed, first I shall make his acquaintance here." Where she was not without recourse should he be unsuitable, but that she did not say.

"Nonsense, Beata! That will leave no time for vows to be spoken this day. Worse, it will alert Sir Durand—"

"He need not know of my betrothal. It can be said Baron Soames but visits."

"You think the castle folk will not speak on the peculiarity he is so soon returned?"

It was true, but on this she would not move. "I am sure your steward can instruct them to be cautious in the hearing of Sir Durand and Sir Elias." Seeing his face redden further, she said, "I am sorry it inconveniences you, but if I am to wed a man not of my choosing, I shall myself determine he will not make my life miserable."

"As told you, he is—"

She held up a hand. "I yield this and no more. If you do not like it, leave Baron Soames in the wood. And now"—she turned away—"I shall visit with your wife and give succor as I can."

Though it took little time to reach the solar, she stood outside a long while, praying for strength to enter, certain the more time she spent with Winifred, the more difficult it would be to refuse her sire, even if she found Baron Soames repellent.

23

He was charming. Not utterly charming. Reservedly so.

Handsome. Not staggeringly handsome. Reasonably so.

Polite. Not stiffly polite. Languidly so.

Observant. Not offensively observant. Mysteriously so.

And familiar. Not distinctly familiar. Strangely so.

And not at all what she expected of a man who hid in the wood.

But for her fortune, he would wed a woman he did not want, and of whom his family believed ill. For that, Beata did not like Baron Lothaire Soames. Nor, it seemed, did Durand and Elias, who had earlier accompanied her father's *guest* from the outer bailey to the donjon.

Of note when Beata had departed the solar, hurting anew over the lady who was grateful another was to bear her burden, was that neither man had been eager to shed his sweat and filth though the nooning meal was soon to be served. They had remained belowstairs, watching Beata and Baron Soames as introductions were made, and allowing her father to carry most of the conversation while servants moved tables and benches into place for the main meal of the day. And when they had withdrawn to make themselves presentable, they did so singly.

Now as the meal neared its end, with Durand and Elias on one side of Baron Rodelle, she and Lord Soames on the other, Emmerich absent, Beata bemoaned her future.

Other than dislike of her deceptively agreeable betrothed, thus far she had little cause to object to their marriage. However, if she could move his attention from her father to her, perhaps she would find something significant over which to object.

She touched his sleeve, and when he looked around, strands of hair the color of wheat escaped the leather thong holding them captive at his nape.

Telling herself it was irrelevant she did not like long hair on a man—especially of a length that, unbound, would skim the lower reaches of his shoulder blades—refusing to allow her gaze to stray to Durand, she said, "Speak to me of your family, Baron Soames."

A harmless question, she assured herself, one any new acquaintance might ask. And yet something flickered in his eyes that made her wonder if his first thought was of his missing father. Did he still suspect the Rodelles were involved?

An instant later, a smile curved his mouth.

And here another thing it did not matter whether she liked—a face so clean-shaven. She much preferred the dark and rough of Durand's short beard.

"'Tis kind of you to ask, Lady Beata."

She arched an eyebrow. "Curious me."

He leaned so close she almost pulled back. "And curious me. Do I pass inspection, my lady?"

She nearly protested, but that *was* what she did. "I have yet to decide, but I am pleased you ceased lurking in the wood."

"Your sire is not. Nor Sir Durand and Sir Elias. I do not believe they like me." His smile rose, and she thought him more handsome. "Tell me, Lady Beata, are you yet vestal?"

She startled and had to snap her teeth closed to keep from rebuking him for all to hear.

He grimaced, but the expression seemed a lie. "Forgive me for being so bold, but your escort, Sir Durand, is overly interested in your well-being."

He was, his gaze often felt throughout the meal. She swallowed down offense. "Interested only in how it affects his duty to his liege. He would not want you or any man laying claim to lands of which our sovereign wishes to dispose."

"Henry and Eleanor," he slid their names across his tongue. "I suppose I ought to better explain my interest in the vestal since you have, on several points, passed *my* inspection."

More anger. "Have I? Since until now you have spoken little to me and only of niceties, the only requirement of which I am aware is the funds needed to set aright your mismanaged lands."

A muscle in his jaw convulsed. "That is of great import, but there is something more important, which seems unattainable where many a lady is concerned."

"That is?"

"What has been asked of you and remains unanswered."

She lowered her frown. "The vestal."

He set a forearm on the table and leaned into it, blocking Durand's view of their faces. And making her feel like prey as he awaited the answer she was not inclined to give.

"Do we marry," she said, "and that remains to be decided, an answer you will have on our wedding night."

"Nay, among my requirements is that you are vestal. Hence, why I care not for the depth of Sir Durand's interest, which is all the more concerning for your determination not to look near upon him. Guilt? I ask myself. Or a valiant battle against yearning? If the latter, it is admirable, though still of concern."

Dear Lord, he is far too observant—and abominable to question my virtue!

She opened her mouth to correct him, but he held up a hand, and she was reminded it would not do to draw Durand's attention more than already they did.

"I have cause to question the vestal, and I do it at this time and place only that we not prolong the game, if that is all this is to your father and you."

She leaned closer. "The longer we converse, Sir Lothaire," she eschewed his greater title, "the more tempted I am to make this but a game. And one in my favor that I never suffer your attentions."

He drew a breath between mostly straight teeth. "Bear with me, and all the sooner we will be done, whether we decide against spending our lives together or steal away from Sir Durand and speak vows on the morrow."

"I am bearing, but not much longer."

"So, vestal or nay?"

She imagined fire leapt in her eyes, for he raised a hand again.

"More and more I see what is said of you, Lady—so much it may not matter whether you are a maiden."

"I believe we are done, Sir Lothaire. You must look elsewhere for a sweet, do-with-as-you-please virgin bride who happily packs up her own wishes and desires to fulfill yours. Why, such valuable chattel she will prove that you will have to put locks on her!"

The tolerant teasing about his face slipped, and in its place rose anger that startled her for how much more familiar he seemed in that moment. But a blink snatched tolerance back into place. He considered her, but just when she thought she might yield to impropriety and take herself from the hall he said, "You repel, Lady Beata, and yet you intrigue. Thus, as methinks I need not temper my words any more than you do, let me explain myself better. The woman I take to wife will have known no lover's hands before mine. Not unreasonable, and less so for one who has been twice cuckolded."

She caught her breath and he laughed—strategically, as if to make those curious about their conversation believe it was of little things.

"Aye, my first betrothed, with whom I thought myself in love, proved to be with child—blessedly ere I wed her. With my second betrothed, I was not as fortunate. Only after consummation was it discovered she had lain with another, deny it though she did." He tilted his head as if to ask if that sufficed.

"I am sorry," she said and wished she had not spoken of putting locks on one's wife. He must think it entirely humorless—though perhaps a serious consideration.

"Twice humiliated, something over which a man does not boast," he said. "Now then, a reasonable person would understand why I ask after your state and suspect the attraction between Sir Durand and you—an attraction all the more worrisome in light of the days and nights spent alone but for the other's company."

She did understand, his explanation making it easier to accept what her father asked of her and what Lady Winifred needed from her. "I understand as much as I can."

"Good. Then you will submit to an examination?"

She was glad he blocked her from Durand's sight. "What say you?"

"After all I have told, it cannot be unexpected. Too, as it must be obvious I am in good health, for what else would I travel with my physician?" He glanced past her to where the man was seated at the end of the table.

Her father had known about this, then. Beata longed to spit.

"You are angry," Soames said. "Again."

That did not help. At all. "Strange that, but you and my father give me good cause to be so affected."

"I advised him to prepare you."

"Had he, I do not think you would be here, Sir Lothaire. As well he is aware."

"So I have wasted my time seeking to wed a Rodelle?"

If only. Though she ached to bid him farewell this day, if she must wed one not of her choosing, he seemed not a bad choice considering the unknown. Easily, Queen Eleanor could wed her to another old man, this time one who did not eschew the nuptial bed. Or a lecher like Sir Oliver whom Durand had sent scuttling into the shadows.

Of a sudden, she wanted to cry. Just as suddenly, the baron's hand covered hers upon the table's edge.

"I am no monster, Lady Beata," he said and, for the first time, she noted the silken brown of eyes and heaviness of lids that made him appear almost like a young boy awakening from a nap. "I would wed you, make children on you, and waste no worry over you remaining faithful to our vows. An easy arrangement."

A loveless arrangement. As she stared at him, she wished it was Durand's face before her. *That* would be no loveless arrangement—at least not on her part.

Dear Lord, she silently entreated. *At last I love, but I did not choose well. I chose one denied me, a landless knight who shall spend his life in service to the queen and never know wife and children.*

"What say you, Beata?" Soames said with more familiarity than was permissible.

Certain no offer would be forthcoming that would be of better benefit to her or her family, she said, "I shall submit to the examination."

Truly, he had a wonderful smile, especially this one which was more genuine than the other that seemed almost sly. "I am glad, Lady Beata."

Lady Beata. No longer Rodelle. Soon no longer Fauvel. Then to be Soames. Never to be Marshal.

Making no attempt to smile for how false it would appear, she said, "After meal, I shall be in my chamber. When my father determines 'tis safe, send your physician and a woman servant." If she was to be humiliated, all the worse it would be were she alone with the man.

"'Twill be done, my lady."

Beata did not intend to leave the table before meal's end. To do so would draw attention, but dread anticipation offered a powerful incentive. "Forgive me," she said when her father looked up, "but I must lie down a while."

"You are ill?"

She wanted to pinch him for the disbelief and accusation in his tone that would draw as much attention as her departure. "I am weary. As you know, these past days have been difficult."

Grudgingly, he inclined his head. "Rest well."

All the way to the stairs, she felt the eyes of Durand and Elias. Thus, she was grateful her hands obeyed, remaining loose at her sides until she was out of sight. And tenfold more grateful her belly obeyed until she had her head bent over a basin and hair out of the way.

"I do not like this."

Elias grunted. "Nor I."

As Durand looked sidelong at him, he thought how strange that the one whose eye he had blackened and whom he had not much liked previous to that should present as a possible ally. Also unexpected was the troubadour knight's facility with weapons. Though he lacked the years of discipline and training required to be knighted at Wulfen Castle and awarded the coveted dagger, he did not sully the Wulfriths' reputation.

Granted, many a knight alongside whom Durand had trained was more fierce and deadlier, but Sir Elias was so unpredictable—one moment crisp in the execution of a swing or thrust, the next lazy—that his opponent could either find no pattern or acted too late upon it. Too, he lacked the indelible, well-earned pride of a Wulfen-trained warrior, expressing his joy with laughter and shouts of triumph, his disappointment with groans and mutterings. Much too often it broke his opponent's concentration. And he knew it.

Near the end of their practice on Heath Castle's training field, the knight had been close to yielding when, past their crossed blades, he chided Durand for being so forceful when it was but an exercise in which they engaged. When that gained no concessions, with great exaggeration he had assured his opponent his only interest in Beata was in the capacity of a friend.

Durand had ignored the implication his aggression had anything to do with feelings for the lady—outwardly. Inwardly, he had recalled how emotion gripped him at Stern when Beata and Sir Elias stood close, easily conversed, comfortably flirted, and the troubadour knight winked and she brightened.

But his undoing was remembrance of himself being nearer her and bypassing flirtation. When it should have been his blade alone at his opponent's throat, it was also Sir Elias's at the throat of one worthier of the Wulfrith dagger—providing Durand had not allowed a woman to come between his blade and him. A truce then, proving women ought to be more trouble than they were worth.

"Ought to be," he muttered.

"What ought to be what?" Sir Elias returned him to the present.

Durand ground his teeth, looked from the other man's quizzical brow to the two they observed from atop the wall-walk between the inner and outer baileys. "We ought to be vigilant," he said, and it was true. Baron Soames had not paused at Heath Castle only to take meal and gain a night's lodging.

As evidenced by surreptitious murmurings between host and guest and how closely Baron Rodelle attended to the other man, including an obvious attempt to listen in on his daughter's conversation with Soames, he had no good purpose.

"I agree," Sir Elias said. "'Twas not fatigue that caused Lady Beata to leave the table. Those two plot."

In opposition to what the queen required of the Rodelles, Durand mused. Even had he not overheard an exchange between stable boys into whose care the mounts of Soames's party had been given upon their arrival at Heath, he would have been on the alert. But the grumbling of one lad over the baron's inability to decide whether to stay or go had well-seeded the field of suspicion that, God willing, could soon be harvested. Or burned.

"What know you of Baron Soames?" Sir Elias asked.

The answer was at hand, Durand having dug it up the moment Baron Rodelle introduced his *guest*. "He came into his title young following the disappearance of his father by what is believed to be ill means, and with possible involvement by the Rodelles—"

"Ah, sounds quite the tale!"

"He received knighthood training at home rather than through fostering," Durand continued. "His first betrothal was broken when he learned the lady was with child—a lady I met years ago while I…"

He paused. His infiltration of Castle Soaring to free Beatrix Wulfrith from the man who was now her husband need not be told, especially not the name of the one Soames had rejected—the sorrowful Lady Laura who, with her misbegotten daughter, had been Michael D'Arci's guest.

"While, Sir Durand?"

"It matters not. After some years, Soames wed, and that lady soon made him a widower."

"Intriguing."

The lack of exertion this past half hour having allowed the winter air to make itself too comfortable across his skin, Durand shrugged his mantle closer around him, leaned deeper into the embrasure, and considered the barons who stood at the training yard's fence where the din of men at practice permitted conversation to which no others were privy.

"Aye, they plot," he said, "with your friend and my charge at the center of their machinations."

"Your charge," Sir Elias murmured. "Often you must remind yourself of that, hmm?"

Durand refused to rise to the bait though the troubadour knight and he no longer swung deadly blades at each other.

Sir Elias grunted. "Ah well, it must needs suffice we both want what is best for Lady Beata. And since we are fair certain that is not Baron Soames, the only question you alone must answer is if what the queen thinks best for her shall gift Lady Beata with a life across which she dances to its good end, or a life through which she trudges to its ill end."

How does one speak to that? Durand wondered.

One did not. They did their duty to their liege and did not look back, even if in doing so it sentenced one to trudge through life. Alone.

Sir Elias slapped Durand's back. "Think on it, Friend."

Durand looked around. "Friend?"

The knight shrugged his mouth. "I speak loosely. Much depends on how you answer that question."

Already it was answered. Never again would he dishonor his training nor his name. Returning his regard to the barons, he said, "Vigilance, Sir Elias. Vigilance."

24

T REMBLING. TEETH CHATTERING. Face burning. Belly threatening to expel what it had not. Hand gripping that of Lady Winifred's wet nurse.

Then it was done.

"Intact," Baron Soames's physician pronounced.

Feeling as if her head broke the surface of the ocean, Beata sucked air, whipped her skirts down, and scrambled backward to the head of the bed.

"Lady," Petronilla soothed, "'tis over, and all is well."

"All is not well! I have...never have I been...he..." Moisture burning her eyes, she shook her head.

The physician heaved a sigh. "Calm thyself, my lady. 'Tis for you to rejoice."

"Rejoice?" she screeched.

He waved Petronilla aside, and the woman withdrew to where her babe watched the other occupants of the chamber from a chair before the hearth.

"Lady Beata"—the physician set a hand on her shoulder—"be assured—"

She shoved his fingers off. "Do not touch me!"

"You make too much of this, Lady."

"Do I? You would not object to such humiliation—nay, degradation!—were it done you?"

"As I am not in the business of bearing children—"

"Business? Business!"

Dear Lord, she silently beseeched, *I do not want to cry. But I shall, and soon do You not smite this creature!*

He crossed his arms atop his abdomen. "For the sin women brought into this world, such is their burden. But as you have shown yourself to be more redeemable than many, I will be pleased to inform Baron Soames his bride shall come to him pure. Providing he guides her with a firm hand, he need never question if the children of her body are also of his."

Was it Conrad's joyous wife who sprang to her knees? She who named the physician a vile son of a sow? She whose palm was set afire? She who *did* rejoice, albeit over the snap of his head and the livid mark upon his cheek?

It was, and she was not as appalled as she should be.

Not appalled at all! It was not she who so unashamedly trespassed on another. And yet, she was going to cry, perhaps as loudly as the babe whose contentment was lost in the midst of a lady's raging.

Beata lurched off the bed alongside the physician who remained too stunned to offer further counsel and started across the chamber.

"My lady!" Petronilla called. Beata threw out a staying hand, flung open the door, and ran down the corridor.

She wanted out—did not care that a wise woman would first gain a mantle. She was not wise. Had she been, she would not have believed her father's assurance she would have a choice in whom she wed. She would not have answered his summons. She would have stayed in France and retired to her dower lands.

"If only, if only," she chanted down the stairs, quieting herself only when she saw servants about the hall and two of her father's knights conversing before the great doors.

Fearing the sobs in her chest would burst from her, she veered opposite. With lowered face, she traversed the open path to the kitchen that was populated by those who would bring to table the final meal of the day.

Beata hesitated on the threshold, knowing to go forward would see her in a garden that had ever spooked her, but to go back...

Distantly hearing the cook's polite query, making no attempt to order his words into something meaningful, she skirted him. Moments later, she slammed the door, collapsed back against it, and slid down it.

The first sob was more hiccough than misery, but the next...

She dragged her knees up, pressed her mouth against them, and as she yielded to all that had scraped and clawed at her during the physician's examination, sent her gaze around the garden. Then she squeezed her eyes shut lest tears soak the skirt of her gown.

"Since she is your *charge*, I suppose I should allow you to go to her. Again."

Allow? That was no consideration. The slam of the door having turned Durand and Elias toward the donjon's garden that hugged the edifice's southern wall, they had watched Beata drop back against the door and sink to sitting. Though they could not hear the noise of her weeping, both knew the sound was muffled by her knees.

"We have been fooled," Durand growled and set off along the wall-walk as the curses confined to the space between his ears searched for a way out.

If he had to place a bet, it would be that Baron Rodelle and Baron Soames had served as a distraction to prevent Beata's escort from interfering with whatever had been done to her within the donjon.

Though tempted to seek the garden's exterior entrance, the likelihood it was secured sent him up the steps to the hall.

The knights just inside the door he thrust open parted to allow him past, and he felt the regard of servants as he strode toward the kitchen.

"Sir Durand!"

He had no intention of answering whoever called to him, but when the woman drew alongside at a run, he realized the voice belonged to the steadfast Petronilla and the soft snuffling was that of the babe whom Rodelle would have him believe was his son.

He halted, demanded, "Lady Beata?"

"Aye, she..." The woman's eyes flicked past him, and he took her arm and pulled her into the corridor that led to the kitchen.

"Tell me."

"Forgive me, Sir Durand, but 'tis not for me to do."

"Then for what do you keep me from the lady?"

"I vow she is not hurt, only much distressed." She patted her babe's head onto her shoulder. "Still, I must tell you that as Helene once needed you, so does Baron Rodelle's daughter."

"She is in danger?"

"Of a different sort."

Spilling a curse for which he would later repent, he started past the woman.

"No matter her father's plans, do not allow her to wed Baron Soames," Petronilla entreated.

He looked across his shoulder. "I have no intention of permitting that union. But I thank you, and if I do not have a chance to speak with you again, I would have you know Helene is happily wed and has another son."

"Aye." She smiled. "When she writes, our preacher reads her words to me."

Of course Helene had not forgotten her friend. He continued down the corridor, tossed open the kitchen door, and might have knocked aside those preparing food had they not jumped away.

Knowing Beata likely remained on the other side of the garden door, he slowly opened it.

She was there, so steeped in misery she seemed not to notice she slid further down the door. But when he spoke her name, she snapped forward and stumbled to her feet.

He stepped outside, closed the door as she scrubbed a forearm across her eyes, and nodded at Sir Elias upon the wall-walk. When the knight answered in kind, Durand closed the distance between Beata and him.

He had seen her more sorrowful when they were shipwrecked, but some*one,* not some*thing* had done this to her.

"I shall beat them bloody," he growled.

Her moist, reddened eyes widened. "W-what say you?"

He was also surprised by his choice of words, but he meant them. "What was done you and by whom, Beata?"

Relief swept her beautiful green eyes, then she looked away. And lied. "Naught. No one."

He lifted her chin. "Tell me."

She searched his face. "Had anything been done I did not like, still your first duty would be to your queen, aye?"

"I cannot change that I serve Eleanor, but I can stop whatever happened from happening again."

"By beating the perpetrator bloody?" Her laughter was bitter. "I assure you what happened will not happen again."

He breathed in patience. "What will not happen again?"

She stepped back, turned and walked the stone-laid path to a bench at the center of what hardly resembled a garden this time of year, and eased onto it.

Durand glanced at Sir Elias who had positioned himself so he could easily look between garden and outer bailey, then he followed. As he lowered beside Beata, she wrapped her arms around herself and sank into her shoulders. Ashamed he had not considered her comfort, he straightened, removed his mantle, and draped it over her.

"I thank you." She tucked her chin into the wool. "I did not realize I was cold."

He took a seat on the bench, keeping a respectable distance between them.

"Oh, it smells of you," she breathed.

Her observation disturbing him, he leaned forward and clasped his hands between his knees to keep from pulling her against his side as he had done in the cave.

She burrowed her nose into his mantle, and a section of hair escaped its braid and swept across her face like a raven's wing. "Not so long ago, still it smelled of the one from whom you gained it. That poor, lost soul."

He angled toward her and gripped his hands tighter to ensure they were where they belonged, rather than plowing silken strands. "Beata, I can better aid you if you tell me how."

She sighed, raised her chin. "Conrad spoiled me, and now I struggle to keep my head above real life. It almost makes me wish he had not been so good to me, that this were just another day, as would be the morrow and every morrow thereafter."

"To lessen the drudgery and pain, you would know no joy?"

A sorrowful laugh. "You sound like Conrad. And I sound self pitying—not at all The Vestal Wife of whom I have been so fond though more disapprove of her than approve, including Eleanor's gallant monk."

He had disapproved of her, but now...

He wanted that Beatrix back, even if she opened her mouth without benefit of a smile, expressed joy with laughter not befitting a lady, caused others to keep their distance and speak behind their hands, and if what was perceived as flirtation caused him to rescue her from knaves needing lessons from a well-placed fist.

But it would not do to admit it. It would only encourage her in a direction neither could go.

A soft sound slipping from her, a flash of green between dark strands telling she watched him, expectant silence evidencing she awaited a response, she shifted on the bench. Then she cleared her throat, sat taller, and turned her face forward. "I do not like this garden, though now I sit here, I do not think 'twas ever so."

Wondering if the weight on her chest was as heavy as the one on his, he said, "I am sure it is lovely in its time."

"To the eye, but..." Once more she shrank into the mantle. "Do you not think it has too many dark corners?"

He ran his gaze around the large, walled area. "As many as any enclosed space."

"Nay, it has more, especially come autumn when leaves gather deep."

It was no flung comment. It called to mind the cave and her dream murmurings of a secret she could not share and leaves she must not allow to rot away. And when he had awakened her with assurances she but dreamed, she had told she did not think it only that. Then their first kiss...

"Too many," she whispered.

Deciding this was worth pursuing until he could move her to reveal what Petronilla would not tell, he said, "What made you so fearful of a place of beauty and peace?"

Her chin whipped around, lifting the hair off her face and revealing skin washed of color. "I did not say anything bad happened here. I think I just... I may have seen something here when I was a small girl."

"May have?"

"More likely, 'twas a dream."

"Of?"

"My mother. She was here. And there was a man. He was angry."

"Your father?"

Her hand shot up from between the mantle's edges, slid into her hair past her temple.

"What is it, Beata?"

She lowered her arm. "Not my father. Certes, a dream."

"Then tell me of it."

She shook her head. "Conrad said it best I not speak of it. 'Tis of the past and ought to stay there."

"Not if you dream it still."

She leaned toward him with the urgency of one who must convince another of the impossible. "For years I did not dream it—only remembered pieces when cornered as I was by Sir Oliver at court. And sometimes during thunderstorms. But of late..."

"When did the dream return?"

She moistened her lips. "The night after I received my father's summons, the one night at court, and after the shipwreck."

"In the cave. I remember. You spoke of a secret that must be kept unto death and worried over the leaves—feared they would rot away. For that, I awakened you."

He had not thought she could go paler, but she did, and her eyes moved to the garden's left corner where the back wall cast deep shadows.

Beata stared, and as she recalled what she wished was only a dream, heard a small voice say, "There."

"There?" Durand reminded her she was not alone.

Nor had she been alone that day. Her mother had been here. And that man. Nay, two men, and they had not known she watched. But it was not a game of *seek me* she played, for which she was proud her stockinged feet made pretty whispers of her footsteps. No game at all. There had been an argument. And blood.

She caught her breath, told herself naught had happened here, and returned her regard to Durand. "Forgive me for needlessly worrying you."

His lids narrowed. "Do not do this, Beata. I cannot help if —"

"I thank you, but I am of a mood, that is all."

"That is not all."

She lowered her chin, drew another breath of him from the mantle, and stood. "I would think you, so often in the company of the queen and her ladies," she said as he rose beside her, "are accustomed to the peculiarities of women during their monthly time."

That last she spoke in the hope it would make him so uncomfortable he would seek their parting. Instead, he blocked the walkway.

"So be it," he said, golden eyes gone dark. "If you will not speak of what happened this day, nor what happened years ago, let us speak of your purpose at Heath Castle, which I do not doubt is the reason Count Verielle's men sought to capture you—a forced marriage to gain your lands the same as was attempted with Queen Eleanor."

"Pray, Durand, I am tired and—"

"You are your father's heir, not the babe presented to me who belongs to the wet nurse."

Beata closed her mouth against further lies. Considering the suspicion sown by Eleanor and fertilized by her father's behavior, there was no benefit in lying. And all the more ill she would appear to Durand.

"To speak to that would betray my sire. That I cannot do."

"He has already betrayed himself, Beata—more, you."

She unfastened the mantle and handed it to him. "So he has, but no more than Eleanor betrays in denying me what she herself sought when she ran from those who wished to gain her fortune. A worse betrayal that." She stepped around him, and with smaller than usual steps to counter the discomfort of the examination, walked to the kitchen door.

"Beata."

She looked around and was struck by such longing to bury her face against his chest that she had to clench her toes to keep from returning to him. "Durand?"

"I know you believe it your duty to do your father's bidding, but I cannot allow you to wed Soames. Do not fight me on this."

Of course he knew. "It is my sire you ought to warn. Good day."

She entered the kitchen and, ignoring the curious regard of the workers, traversed the sweltering room. Blessedly, none crossed her path in the hall nor upon the stairs.

But sympathy crossed *her* when she passed the solar and heard Lady Winifred weeping and Petronilla soothing her.

Oh, to be Queen Eleanor, possessing the strength and power to prove the equal of men in this man's world!

25

"I CAN GUESS what was done her." This from the troubadour knight, who had said little throughout the supper meal from which Beata had been absent.

Durand looked from the barons where they bent over a chessboard on the opposite side of the hearth to the one cradling a goblet in the chair angled toward his. "Then guess, Sir Elias."

"Forsooth, 'tis more than a guess."

Since the knight's return to the donjon, Durand had sensed there was something he wished to say. And that it might be the cause of Beata's distress once more gave rise to the temptation to balance out his bruised face. "The sooner you speak, the less likely you shall add missing teeth to your grievances against me."

Sir Elias glanced at the barons, leaned forward, and further lowered his voice. "First your word."

"For what?"

"You will not like what I tell, and it will be of no help to Lady Beata do you forget whichever lessons of restraint you learned at Wulfen Castle."

I will more than not like this, Durand silently prepared himself. *Lord, help me think first, then attack.*

"I have that particular lesson in mind, Sir Elias. Now my patience thins."

He set his goblet on the table between them. "Whilst you were with Lady Beata in the garden, Soames's physician left the donjon in a stir—absent a mantle, arms flying, and stride so long for one short of legs it was quite the show."

"Elias," Durand warned when the knight paused as if to provide an opportunity to show appreciation for his tale.

"He made for his liege in the training yard, and though of what he spoke I could make no sense, he was more expressive than I in telling a tale—stomping his feet, pointing at the donjon, and flapping a hand at his face, one side of which was the color of an enraged woman's slap."

Durand's hand went to the Wulfrith dagger, his eyes around the hall.

Elias leaned forward. "You gave your word," he began, then grunted. "You did not. Regardless, stay your hand lest you disappoint Baron Wulfrith."

He was right. And Durand was ashamed this one had to counsel him. He released the hilt, all the easier done in the absence of the physician.

"Good. And for the sake of our own plotting, put the murder in your eyes to the farthest reaches of your mind."

As Durand returned his regard to the knight, his eyes glanced across those of Baron Soames and Beata's father. With effort, he eased his jaw.

Sir Elias chuckled, and past a smile murmured, "Acting. A neglected area of your training. I may have to see to it myself."

Durand narrowed his lids.

The troubadour knight bent nearer as if to share a joke. "Aye, neglected. At least where your lady is concerned."

Durand put his face nearer the other man's. "She is not my lady."

Elias arched an eyebrow.

Durand glared.

A heavy sigh. "Be assured, no attempt was made to ravish her, only to ascertain if, following your unchaperoned journey across sea and land, she remains worthy of wedding a baron in want of a virtuous woman and in need of an heir."

Durand's hands convulsed, but with effort that made his innards quake, he denied his fingers the hilt.

Of course that was what had been done her. Of course she could not speak of it. Of course she could not bear to sit at meal with the perpetrator—nor those whose orders the physician but followed.

He looked to where Rodelle's hand hovered above a chess piece, then Soames.

The latter watched Durand. And continued to watch. Then he inclined his head and returned to the game.

"You are not very convincing," Elias muttered. "Were he not already wary of you, he is now."

Silently conceding perhaps he could benefit from acting instruction, Durand said, "I shall take first watch."

Sir Elias nodded. "I will linger awhile, perhaps play the weary, sodden knight and doze. Who knows what might drop into my ears?"

Durand stood and nodded at Baron Rodelle, who wished him a good rest. Anticipating hours beside the door to his chamber, listening for those who would try to take Beata from Heath Castle to wed her to Soames, he ascended the stairs.

He passed the silent solar that was not always so. Twice he had heard weeping there. Though muffled, it differed greatly from that of a babe. Also heard had been Petronilla's attempt to soothe the bereft lady. Regrettably, until the threat of Durand was removed, the village woman could not return to her husband and other child.

As Durand neared Beata's chamber, he guessed from the light shining beneath the door she was not yet abed—might even be dressed for night travel to do her father's bidding. Which would not happen while Durand watched over her. Before his duty to the queen was done, Baron Rodelle would like him even less.

He meant to continue past that chamber, but something made him halt—that something at the center of him he had locked away as was best for one given to betrayal and the sacrifice of honor.

As he stood unmoving, knowing he would look the fool should any find him there, he realized he would not appear just any fool. Quite possibly, a besotted fool.

He closed his eyes. How had this happened? Never should The Vestal Widow have been a danger to him. Not one who, upon first acquaintance, had at best amused him. Indeed, over and again Beatrix Fauvel had given him cause to be annoyed, offended, and angered. Not besotted. Not enamored. Not...

He opened his eyes, stared at the door that stood between him and the woman who, though she would not belong to Soames, would belong to another.

He loved. Again. And would be denied. Again. But there was a difference between Michael D'Arci's Beatrix and his Bea—

Not mine, he berated thinking which would more cruelly test him. And therein lay the difference. *This* Beatrix felt for him. *This* Beatrix would also know loss.

"God help us," he breathed. And caught the creak of a floorboard. Not from behind or either side of him.

Her footsteps. Then a shift in the light across the floor.

He looked down, and his heart convulsed when her shadow slipped through the seam and covered his feet.

Though when she opened the door he should not be standing here, her shadow upon him was almost as intoxicating as the absence of breath ere the touch of lips.

What did she on the other side? he wondered when she remained as unmoving as he. Did she think him her father? Soames? Was she afeared?

He stepped nearer. "If you have not locked the door, do so and open it for no one this eve."

Beata caught her breath, pressed a hand to the door to brace herself, the other to her chest to feel the thud of a heart that had leapt when footsteps paused outside her door.

She had feared it was her father come to deliver her to the man who had required that vile thing of her. But it was the one she wished it to be.

"I know you are there, Beata. You will do as I say?"

She reached to the bolt.

Do not, warned the dutiful, the inevitable, the unavoidable. *It will only make what you are called to do more difficult.*

But if this night they came for her and stole her away... If never again she saw Durand...

She slid the bolt, wrenched the handle, and stared at all that was everything to her woman's heart.

Durand held her gaze, then slowly moved it from her hair down around her shoulders, to her throat, to her chemise whose ties hung loose upon her breasts, to her waist, hips, and hands at her side.

His lids narrowed, and she knew he noted the absence of Conrad's ring she had removed, certain she would soon wear another's.

His gaze resumed its journey, moving down her legs to her bare feet peeking from beneath her chemise's hem, and when it returned to her face, emotion shone from eyes that seemed as raw and vulnerable as hers felt.

Gripping the edge of the door to hold herself inside, she said, "I hoped it was you."

His jaw tightened.

"I felt 'twas you."

His nostrils flared.

"I am—" A sob slipped from her. "I am so glad 'tis you."

"Beata," he rasped, and it seemed he would come to her, but he drew back. "Do as I say. Lock your—"

She collided with him, and as he stepped a foot behind to keep his balance, she threw her arms around his neck and from her lips spilled what she had promised herself she would not speak. "I love you. If you feel the same...and if I could and you could..."

He drew his hands up her arms and gently unlaced her fingers. "I but paused to—"

A door opened, and as their hearts bounded as if to cross from one chest into the other, they snapped their heads around.

Petronilla appeared in the solar's doorway. As Durand extricated himself and Beata stumbled back, the woman gasped, "Pardon!" and started to close the door. A moment later, she reappeared. Eyes wider, she pointed to the stairs.

Hardly did Beata catch the sound of boots ascending than Durand spun her around and pushed her into the chamber. And followed.

She turned at the center of the room and watched him quietly seat the door and restrainedly push the bolt.

"Snuff the candle," he hissed.

She moved more quickly than she would have believed possible and blew the flame into smoke.

"I am sorry," she whispered across the darkness. Had she not opened the door and flung herself into his arms, he would not be trapped with her.

"Quiet," he rasped as footsteps bypassed the solar. Moments later, they stopped where, minutes earlier, he had stood.

The door was tried, causing the bolt to rattle in its loop, then came muttering—likely a curse—and silence.

Her sire? A moment later, he called low, "Beata!"

Finding a thumbnail between her teeth, she clamped down on it.

He spoke her name again with more urgency, but no louder, obviously believing Durand was near. Entirely ignorant he was closer than thought.

Would Petronilla tell what she had seen? Beata did not think so. The woman had warned they were soon to be discovered.

Her father tried the door again, cursed without question, and retreated. Not to the solar but the stairs. To inform Baron Soames it would not be this night they stole away his bride?

Though the words he exchanged with someone on the stairs could not be understood, he had not gone far enough to allow Durand to slip from her chamber.

A moment later, she nearly yelped when a hand curled around her arm.

"Get some rest," Durand said. "When it is safe, I will leave you."

Selfishly…foolishly…she hoped it would never be safe. "Petronilla?"

"Fear not. From my service upon Wiltford, I know the mother of the babe your father wished me to believe is his son. She is a friend."

Relief fluttered through her, but dismay scattered it, and she stepped back into the bedside table, toppling a cup that silenced the voices on the stairs.

"She told you!"

"Hush!" He pulled her close and pressed her face to his chest. And though shame made her long to distance herself, there she remained as footsteps once more traversed the corridor, the bolt rattled, and her name was spoken through the door's seam.

When her father retreated, it was to his solar, as told by the slam of its door.

Then Durand's breath was in her hair, sowing shivers across her scalp and down her spine. "She did not tell me," he whispered.

"But you know."

"Sir Elias is most observant."

More shame.

His arms tightened around her. "Forgive me for pressing you to speak of it, and if not for your sake, for mine put it from you."

"Your sake?"

"Once was enough to dishonor my Wulfen training and my family's name."

Then for her he might again? She closed her eyes, and tears wet her cheeks and his neck. "I love you."

His chest expanded, then he scooped her into his arms. But before she could savor being cradled like a lover, he stepped alongside the mattress and lowered her to it.

She reached to him, but he swept the covers over her, then his lips were on her brow. "Were you mine…" He sighed. "But you are not and can never be."

Such hopelessness, and all the more painful knowing he felt at least some of what she felt, wanted what she wanted, would be denied as she was denied, would know longing she would ever know.

He straightened. "I shall be at the door."

And I shall ever wish you here holding me, lamented her heart as she pressed her mouth into the coverlet lest a sob escaped.

Durand stood there, wishing there were no temptation or danger in holding her, then turned away.

By the dim moonlight penetrating the window's oilcloth, once more he negotiated the chamber by memory. At the door he removed his sword from his belt and lowered to sitting.

As he listened for the donjon to quiet, two sets of footsteps minutes apart sounded. The first belonged to Soames, as told by the length of corridor he traversed, the second to Sir Elias, who would be curious over Durand's absence from their shared chamber.

Time creeped by and silence descended outside Beata's chamber. And within. When he stilled his breathing, he barely heard hers, and hers seemed not of sleep. Thus, he was not surprised when the bed squeaked and her feet padded across the floor.

He lifted his head from against the wall. "Go back to bed," he whispered as her dark figure approached.

When she continued forward, he shifted nearer the door to ensure she did not stumble over him. Then she was at his shoulder.

"Do not," he said as she sank against his side.

She reached behind, curled her fingers over his, and drew his hand around her.

"Beata..."

She wiggled closer and settled her head on his upper chest. "Durand."

"You should not be here."

"'Tis no different from when we were in the cave," she said softly, then added, "where we began." She threaded her fingers through his. "Or did we begin sooner? Upon the ship? Upon the stairs when you stopped Sir Oliver? Upon that frozen field when first you saved me?"

"It is far different, Beata."

"Only because now we know what it is." She released his hand and set hers on his cheek. "Kiss me again."

"What you ask could be the ruin of us." His voice was so tight it did not sound like his. "Now return to bed."

He felt her hurt, but in his state, it could prove too much temptation to kiss her.

"I will not." She leaned up and pressed her lips to his jaw.

Something between a sigh and a growl sprang from him. "Then sleep."

"I cannot whilst you are here. Talk to me."

"Of what?"

"Who came before me."

He tensed.

"Tell me of Lady Beatrix, whom you loved. And her sister, whom…"

He had not loved. "I will not speak of them."

"Then I shall tell you of Conrad."

He nearly silenced her, but he did wish to understand that peculiar arrangement. "Very well, but keep your voice low."

"Ten and four. Those are all the years I had when I crossed the channel to wed a man with granddaughters my age."

As ever, Durand found repellent the practice of marrying little more than a girl to one of great age.

"When he came to me on our wedding night, I was determined I would not dishonor my family. But when he set himself over me, I cried. And louder when…"

"When?"

"That dream—the same I had in the cave. It returned as it had not for years. I heard raised voices, glimpsed angry faces, my mother afeared, rain falling harder, blood upon leaves."

She fell silent, but after a time drew breath that made her quake. "And Conrad stopped. Just stopped. I lay there hardly able to breathe for fear of his wrath, but he did not rage or strike me. He was quiet a long time, then he said he was a perverse old man and rolled off. Still I feared, still I sobbed. Then he drew me against his side and said, *We will not do this, Beata. Perhaps when you are older. Not now.*"

Having already accepted she was vestal, Durand was surprised by his depth of relief.

"He was not impotent as many believed was the reason I remained vestal. Indeed, on occasion he sought other women. But even when I attained the age of ten and eight and knew he had been patient long enough and thought I would like a child, he turned aside—said I had become too much a daughter to him. For that, I loved him all the more."

For that, Durand thought he would have liked Count Fauvel.

When she spoke again, fatigue thickened her voice. "He was good to me, as were his children, though…"

"Though?"

"His heir's wife tolerated me well in spite of disapproving of my influence upon her daughters."

Durand recalled Queen Eleanor's revelation that Conrad Fauvel's heir was wed to the sister of Count Verielle, the same whose men had tried to bring The Vestal Widow to ground.

"But then," she said with less volume, "with Conrad's consent, I refused her family's offer of her youngest brother to administer my dower lands until widowhood moved me onto them."

"You did not like him?"

"He was troublesome, and I feared once Conrad was gone I would not easily rid myself of him as his family sought to be rid of him." She yawned. "Relations with my stepson's wife became strained. Then Conrad passed, and she did not disguise how much she wished me gone from *her* home."

As Durand waited for the rest of the tale, he worked at piecing together what was known with what was not. But she spoke no more.

"Beata?"

"Hmm?"

He knew he took advantage of her being between sleep and wakefulness, but he asked, "Verielle's sister knew the reason for your father's summons?"

"Aye. Sir Norris heard something. When he opened the door, she was in the corridor. I do not doubt she heard us and sent word to…" Another yawn. "…her eldest brother, Count Verielle."

"Her family thought to throw off the troublesome one by throwing you to him."

"Fools," she breathed. "No matter how miserable they made me, no matter their threats, I would not have wed him. Such a sacrifice should only be made for those we love."

"Then if I let you out of my sight, for your family you will offer yourself up to Soames."

She stiffened slightly but sighed back into him. "How can I not? Duty…" A sorrowful laugh. "More, Lady Winifred. She can bear no more. I am her only hope."

Over the next several hours, Durand held her while she slept, and each time he found his fingers in her silken hair or his mouth against her smooth brow, he reminded himself, *Do not hold tight to that which you long for. Far less it aches to have it slip through your fingers than torn from your grasp.*

But he was only fooling himself. Beata would be torn from his grasp.

When he conceded that the longer he held her the greater the damage to them both, he carried her to bed.

So complete was her rest, she did not stir. So complete was his ache, he vowed to never again suffer as the two named Beatrix made him suffer. And acknowledging this vexing woman's marks upon his emotions went deeper yet, he longed for the jolt of falling hard upon his knees.

The last time he had so thirsted for prayer was months after Gaenor gifted him her innocence when he realized how far he had dragged her down with him—betraying her and her family, his friendships, training, name, and honor.

Were a chapel near and had he the leisure, he would spend the remainder of the night on his face.

He turned from the bed. Though he loathed being unable to bolt Beata in her chamber, he assured himself the danger was mostly past and he would sleep light and in snatches.

Then there was Elias, who did not have to speak a word for his wakefulness to be known. Surprisingly, this eve he had not taken the bed, as Durand had seen before closing the door on the light cast by the corridor's exhausted torch.

He approached the bed opposite the pallet on which the troubadour knight lay, and as he eased onto the mattress, that one said, "Dare I ask?"

"Naught untoward happened, Sir Elias. Were Soames to succeed—and he will not—his accursed examination would yet be valid."

The other man clicked his tongue. "I have dozed. Now you. I vow I shall listen well."

More and more, Durand had cause to like him. Given time, he might.

He bunched the pillow beneath his head, fixed his gaze on the dark ceiling, and silently beseeched the Lord to strengthen him so he remain honorable for what lay ahead.

26

"It seems you must be reminded this is practice!" Soames barked as he danced away from the blade that sought to bloody the right sleeve of his tunic to match the left.

Durand followed. Like any true warrior, he was best satisfied when the offensive was his—as it was in this moment and most moments ere this one despite little sleep on the night past.

Not that Soames was unskilled. Unlike Sir Elias, his moves were too easily anticipated, lacking spontaneity capable of catching an opponent unawares. Thus, his left sleeve was soon a close match.

"Almighty!" Soames spewed a cloud across chill morning air that was trying hard to make flakes of the occasional drizzle. "'Tis practice!"

Durand grunted. "As I am not unfamiliar with your complaint, Sir Lothaire, I shall give answer as ever I do." He lunged, knocked his opponent's blade aside, and recovering with a backhanded swing, nicked the man's jaw—and bettered his answer by severing the hank of hair that had come loose from the thong at his nape.

"This is *Wulfen* practice," he said as the baron hurtled backward with bared teeth, "not *boys* at practice. If too much I test an ability gained at your mother's knee, I am sure one of Baron Rodelle's squires can better serve as your playmate."

Soames's color had been high before, but now it approached scarlet. But not near enough the color of humiliation donned by

Beata following the examination required of her. For this, Durand had accepted the baron's invitation to practice at swords, leaving Elias with Beata whilst the castle folk broke their fast as Durand had no appetite to do—as was best, the longing between her and him felt before he set eyes on her this morn.

But there was more to this than retribution. It benefitted both opponents—the one who kept watch over Soames whilst seeking a measure of recompense, and the one given a lesson in swordsmanship whilst paying in blood what was owed Beata.

As the baron continued to seethe where he had regained his balance a stride from the training field's fence, Durand examined the point of his sword. "The color one's blade ought to be," he said, "even at practice."

"Knave!"

"Name calling, Sir Lothaire. A most powerful weapon." Once more, Durand assumed the proper stance. "But given years of proper instruction, methinks your blade will serve better. Now try again—harder—else I shall engage another."

Soames bellowed, and this time as they met over blades across the training field, he proved worthy—insomuch as one not trained at Wulfen could prove.

Anger, Durand named that which could make of the man a formidable warrior. To excel, some required lessons in discipline, others stealth, others distraction and underestimation. But anger seemed this man's elixir, turning the edges of his blade the color they ought to be—even at practice.

Durand avoided her. As he should, she supposed.

Beata stared at her left hand clasped over the right and wished Conrad's ring yet covered that pale band of flesh. Too soon, Soames's ring would hide it.

Eyes stinging, nose prickling, she wished that were the Lord to answer but one prayer in accordance with her desires, it be that Durand Marshal's ring was the one fit around her finger.

Upon awakening this morn, she had lain unmoving, refusing to open her eyes and confirm what she knew—that he was gone from her. And not even remembrance of what she had sleepily revealed when he probed Count Verielle's reason for sending men to intercept her flight across Henry's lands made her regret seeking Durand alongside her chamber door.

But why should it? She had revealed nothing of which he was unaware. All she had done was provide details of what had first placed her in his path. The one whom Count Verielle intended her to wed was of no consequence now there was Soames. Soames who she imagined was this moment struggling against Durand's blade.

"At last, a smile!"

Beata looked to the hearth. Elias stood there, a shoulder against the immense wall of stone. She had not realized he had followed her from the table, having assumed he would seek the training field to observe the contest between Durand and her betrothed. But of course, in Durand's absence, he was to watch over her.

So how would her sire separate her from those who set themselves against him without being so obvious he incurred the queen's wrath?

"And now 'tis gone," Elias bemoaned.

She forced the smile back onto her lips.

He shook his head. "Like Sir Durand, you require lessons in acting." He took a long draught off his tankard.

"Alas, we are both helpless," Beata said and silently added, *not only in the inability to conceal our emotions.*

"Helpless, Beata? I would not say that. Indeed, I—" He grimaced, groaned.

She sat forward. "What is it?"

"Something does not agree with me." He patted his flat belly. "Likely the apple I swallowed down with cheese ere realizing it was past eating." He returned the tankard to his lips. And dropped it.

Beata sprang out of the chair. Gripping his arm as he doubled over, she bent near. Had she stepped closer, the contents of his belly would have soiled her skirts.

"Una!" she called to the servant who had paused in wiping the high table. "Summon the physician." Then she beckoned to a man-at-arms. "Aid me in getting this knight to his chamber."

"Nay, Beata," Elias gasped. "I am to watch—" His belly let loose again, and not one but two men-at-arms began moving him toward the stairs.

Beata hastened after them, but hardly had she taken a step up than one of her sire's knights pulled her back. "The time is now, my lady," he said low.

She strained to follow Elias, stilled at the realization the apple was not responsible for his illness. "He has been poisoned?"

"Of course not. He will merely be indisposed for a while."

Long enough to steal her away, and she did not doubt had Durand also broken his fast, he would suffer what could be named a passing illness. Thus, Baron Soames had invited the queen's man to practice at swords.

"Come, my lady." The knight drew her toward the kitchen.

"Where?"

"The postern gate by way of the garden, and from there to the wood where your father and brother await."

Here the reason neither had been present at meal.

"Baron Soames shall join you there once his practice with Sir Durand is concluded."

"But I—"

"My lady, pray do not put me in the difficult position of securing your silence and cooperation as my lord ordered should you refuse your duty."

Then he would gag and bind her?

Once more, he urged her toward the kitchen, and she achingly accepted she had no choice. If ever she saw Durand again, she would be wed to another, wanting a man whose life was no more his own than was hers. Better she had remained in France—mistress of her dower lands, husbandless, childless, thinking herself content to remain The Vestal Widow to her end days.

But for the Rodelles, and especially Lady Winifred, this she would do.

Dear Lord, she beseeched as she passed through the kitchen, *help me set Durand to the farthest reach of my mind that I might grow into a good wife and prove a good mother to the children made with Soames.*

Tunic streaked with blood wiped away between sword strokes and wet with perspiration diluted by drizzle, vengeance content to digest its morning meal before looking to the nooning, Durand determined it was time to end the contest.

He lunged back as Soames lunged forward, causing that one's descending blade to unbalance him. Next, he spun to the side, and as the baron stumbled past, landed the flat of his blade across the man's back.

Soames's sword flew from his grasp. As those watching gasped, murmured, and hooted, he went down, and Durand pinned him to the cold, moist ground with a foot at the center of his back.

"Not all bad, Sir Lothaire. We may make a warrior of you yet."

The man lay so still, the only movement about him his long hair playing in the cold breeze, Durand thought him knocked senseless. But as he eased the weight from his foot, Soames thrust onto his back, gripped the victor's calf, and yanked.

Durand dropped with enough forethought to roll out of the fall, regain his feet, and set his sword's point at Soames's neck before the man could get his own legs beneath him.

To Durand's surprise, the baron grinned. "That was worth every cut, bruise, and humiliation," he said, angry color receding into the collar of his tunic, then he laughed so deeply Durand shifted his blade aside to ensure he did not further bleed him. "Oh, what I would give to have been Wulfen-trained!"

Durand dropped back a step and angled his sword nearer the ground.

Soames straightened. Smacking the legs of his dirtied chausses, he strode to his sword. "If ever you tire of serving the queen"—he came around—"your sword arm I will buy."

Durand raised his eyebrows. "Unless you wed well, Baron, I do not know you could afford me."

Soames laughed again. "There is that. Puts us much at odds, does it not?"

As thought, he understood Durand's purpose as well as Durand understood his. "At odds, but *much*? For that you would, indeed, require Wulfen training."

Still the man's anger remained in check, and almost good-humoredly, he said, "Something I must needs remedy. I thank you for revealing my weaknesses."

Durand jerked his chin. "We are done here." He pivoted and strode opposite. But though he intended to relieve Elias, the chapel in the inner bailey called to him, and he altered his course.

A quarter hour only, he told himself, and following the quiet example set by Baron Wulfrith, prostrated himself before the altar. And once more prayed for aid in honorably doing his duty and accepting what could not be changed no matter how much Beata and he wished it. Last, he asked for healing of heart and soul and contentment in pleasing the Lord.

When he stepped outside into lightly falling rain and ascended the donjon steps, he did not feel much easier, but neither did he feel alone as often he did when he worked outside the Lord's will. Whatever came, he would not lose hard-won ground.

The hall was quiet upon his entrance, but there was an air of tension and expectation about the servants who made themselves busier and the men-at-arms who paused in filling their tankards at a sideboard.

Was Beata in the kitchen? The garden? Abovestairs? Providing the troubadour knight was near her, it mattered not. Providing…

"Where is Sir Elias?" Durand called to the men-at-arms.

The rotund one, much in need of daily exercise that would be required of him were it Durand under whom he served, jutted his chin toward the stairs.

His answer should not bother, but it did. And more it bothered since Durand would have sooner discovered what was behind it had he not gone to the chapel.

Trying not to begrudge what had stretched to a half hour, he called on the Lord to not let their time together breed ill and took the stairs two at a time. And heard groaning and the cry of a babe before he reached the landing.

That misery did not sound from the solar. It came from the chamber he shared with Elias.

Durand ran and flung open the door.

The unhappy babe on her hip, Petronilla knelt alongside the troubadour knight who bent over a basin, body convulsing. Then the woman was on her feet. "Sir Durand!"

"What has happened?" he demanded as he strode forward.

"Since Sir Elias shared viands with Lady Beata, he believes something was put in his drink. And I heard the men-at-arms say a basin and a few hours of retching would serve him far better than any physician."

"Almighty!" Durand nearly turned his anger on Elias, but talked himself down, reasoning the knight could not have known his drink was tainted. "What of Lady Beata?"

Gently jostling her babe, Petronilla said, "Though Sir Elias told she started to follow him from the hall where he fell ill, I have seen naught of her. He believes she has been taken from the castle."

Durand set a hand on the troubadour knight's back. "How long ago, Elias?"

"Feels like hours," he choked, then retched up spit.

"How long?" Durand repeated.

The knight lifted his pale, perspiring face. "An hour, Petronilla?"

"Not all of that, but near."

Before Durand had gone to the chapel, whilst he sought recompense for Beata's humiliation rather than yield vengeance to the Lord, she had gone from Heath by way of a postern gate, else slipped out through the main gate disguised as a commoner. Doubtless, as soon as Durand had left the training field, Soames had as well. But the miscreant's destination was opposite—to the wood where Beata and her father waited.

"Is not the nearest village Uppit, Petronilla?"

"'Tis."

"Has it a church?"

"Aye, but no priest. He fell into sin last fall and was removed."

"Then the village of Epswich."

"Certes, they have a priest."

Durand swung away, snatched up the mantle he had eschewed this morn, and started for the door. He halted when he recalled who, besides Baron Rodelle, had been absent from the morning meal. "Where is Brother Emmerich?"

Petronilla gave a helpless shrug. "Though every morn he comes to the solar and prays with Lady Winifred, not this day."

"Uppit, then. It is the nearest and will suffice since Rodelle has his own priest." He continued to the doorway.

"Durand!" Elias called and, struggling to right himself, said, "I shall come with—" His face contorted, and he dropped back to his knees and resumed retching.

"Stay with him, Petronilla." Durand ran from the chamber.

He was watched, but none tried to stop his progress to the stables, and the lad there quickly aided in saddling his mount. Just as Rodelle knew better than to make obvious the ill worked on Sir Elias, he did not openly obstruct the queen's man.

Grateful to be familiar with the barony of Wiltford, Durand rode hard toward Uppit, and with every reach of his horse's legs kicking up moist earth, prayed he would overtake Beata before she spoke vows.

But the one who languidly guided his horse through the sullen rain opposite Uppit boded so ill Durand nearly cursed.

He reined in before Beata's brother. "It is done?" he demanded, thoughts flying ahead to the only remedy left to him—thwarting consummation.

From beneath a thick woolen hood, Brother Emmerich considered Durand so long that he came close to finding himself unhorsed. "Nay, Sir Durand, 'tis far from done."

"Meaning?"

His smile was grim, shrug weary. "I agreed to perform the service, but when we reached the church, I could not—much to my sire's disgust. Fortunately, that made it easier not to be moved."

Was this a means of delaying their pursuer, giving Soames time to undo his bride? "I am to believe you?"

"The Lord knows I speak true and, methinks, approves that I refused to take part in ruining my sister's life."

Durand would himself have to discover the truth of that. "Where are they?"

"I would think gone on to Epswich seeking its priest."

The truth or a lie? Durand mulled.

Beata's brother crossed himself. "May God bear witness to what I have told." He set his hands on his saddle's pommel. "Do you wish to prevent this marriage, with all speed ride on Epswich."

27

More than the falling rain, fear of being unable to accept her loss made Beata shake as she urged her mount to keep pace with the men on either side of her.

Not for the first time, she silently thanked her brother for refusing to wed her to Soames. A futile gesture, but as Emmerich had not wished to take part in their father's scheme, she would not have that burden upon his narrow shoulders.

While her father had cursed and her betrothed watched, she had embraced her brother, kissed his cheek, and wished him Godspeed in resuming his travels in service to the Church.

"If possible, one of us ought to be happy," he had whispered then extricated himself.

As he mounted, she had smothered bitter laughter against the back of a hand. Even if Durand overtook them, and he would try, it would end the same for The Vestal Widow, whether she wed Soames or one of Eleanor's choosing.

"Epswich is beyond those hills," her father shouted. "Do we go through the wood, we will have to slow but shall sooner reach it."

Beata glanced at Soames, noted a section of rain-dampened hair, which had been long enough to be secured at his nape this morn, adhered to the side of his face.

He nodded at her father, and they veered off the increasingly muddy road and entered trees that offered slightly more protection from the rain.

For a while, it seemed they made good progress, but then thunder sounded, and Beata knew it was that which made her shake harder, and more when the dream stirred the leaves in that corner of her mind.

"Let us return to the road!" she cried.

"Not much longer!" her sire shouted.

She hunkered low in the saddle and prayed for the leaves to settle. Perhaps they would have, but lightning pierced the ground ahead.

Her horse reared, and her seat was too precarious for her to stay astride. She fell back and to the side, hit soft earth, and ended face down in a place that smelled warmly of loam and sharply of mold.

As she lifted her head, she heard her father call to her and felt the vibrations of hooves, but before she could offer assurance of her well-being, she saw what had cushioned her fall—an abundance of rotting leaves.

She shook her head to send her imaginings back to their corner, and they moved in that direction until she was pulled upright and found Lothaire Soames before her.

Nay, not Lothaire. This man was older by a half dozen years, hair close cropped, and it was not concern on his face but anger.

Beata threw up an arm to shield her head from his blow. It did not land. Peering between her fingers, she saw it *was* her betrothed, and rather than anger, he wore concern.

In that moment, she understood why he was familiar. And knew the one he resembled and the bloodied leaves were not of a dream.

She looked beyond the man she was to wed. "You lied," she said between chattering teeth. "You and mother lied."

Her father's brow grooved. "Beata?"

"You said 'twas only a dream."

Alarm leapt in his eyes. "Daughter—"

"It was not!"

"Quiet! Sir Durand is surely fast upon us, and we have no time for hysterics." He looked to the son of the one who...

Beata shivered. She was right about this.

"Baron Soames, aid my daughter in regaining her mount. We have a wedding to see to its good end."

Past rain dripping between her betrothed and her, Beata peered into Soames's face and was glad for his confusion. But that did not make what was wrong right. If she correctly fit the pieces of the dream alongside the things her father had revealed about this man's family, it would make what was wrong worse.

Though his confusion gave way to suspicion, he said, "Whatever lies your parents told, they must needs wait." He led her to his destrier and, despite her father's protest, lifted her atop and swung up behind.

She understood her sire's fear she might speak of what had come clear, but even were there an opportunity for her betrothed to question her, she was recovered enough from the shock of what had happened in the garden all those years ago to know she must hold close the answer Lothaire Soames lacked. And persuade her father to accommodate the queen, allowing Durand to do his duty to Eleanor and Lady Winifred to enter the convent.

When they reached the church on the outskirts of Epswich, the rain had eased. And the greater blessing was the priest's absence—gone to give last rites to a woman of four score years, told the youth who paused in mopping up rain that leaked through the church's aged roof.

"Take me to him," Baron Soames said as he set Beata on her feet alongside the church steps. Shortly, he spurred away with the boy clinging to his back.

Grateful he had gone, rather than one of her sire's knights, Beata said, "I would speak with you, Father."

He gestured for her to enter the church. "After I set my men to watch for Sir Durand, I shall join you inside."

It was a quarter hour before he lowered to the bench where she huddled to warm those places the press of Baron Soames's body had not reached.

"The dream bothers you still, Daughter?"

So he intended to cling to the lie. "Only because it was never a dream." She raised her chin. "As well you know."

"Beata—"

"Cease! I am no longer four years young. I know what I saw. And Lothaire Soames is proof. Though he is not the image of his missing father, he near enough resembles him to confirm the man in the garden was real."

Her father lowered his gaze. "Tell me what you remember."

The rest of it was there beneath leaves that awaited the invitation to shift and rise and scatter. And so Beata reached into them.

"Mother and I were in the garden, on our backs watching the clouds lose their pretty shapes and darken. She said rain was coming and we ought to go inside, but I begged a few more minutes—just until the babe stopped moving."

Beata could almost feel those kicks and flutters beneath the palm she had pressed to that round belly.

"She said Emmerich, if a boy…Emma, if a girl…wanted out but must be patient a month longer, that soon the little one would be in our arms and you would be a father again." Beata frowned. "Methinks you were gone from home. Aye, Mother said you would return the following day and was glad because my cousin was doing something he should not."

She touched her father's hand. "What was Ralf doing?"

"Foolishly falling in love with your nurse," he rasped, "a commoner twenty and five years to Ralf's fifteen. What else do you recall?"

"The rain. It began to kiss our faces and mother said we must go inside. But the kitchen door slammed, and we heard angry voices." She saw her small self jump up and peer around a tree as her mother raised her bulk from the ground. "Ralf was there and…the one I am certain was Lothaire Soames's sire."

Her father nodded. "He paused at Heath to pass the night ere continuing on to his home."

"Ralf was angry."

"Over your nurse. They were having relations, and after he saw Baron Soames flirting with her, he demanded satisfaction. Soames humored him by taking their argument to the garden, thinking it was a pup he had on a leash."

Had Ralf ever been a pup? Beata wondered, recalling her cousin's moods and how quick he had been to strike at those who offended.

"Your mother told you to go inside, aye?" her father prompted.

"She did and hurried forward, calling to Ralf to calm himself. But he did not even look her way." She swallowed hard. "I wish I had gone, but I could not move though the rain no longer felt like kisses and I began to chill. Then Ralf pushed the man, and the man nearly knocked him to the ground. Ralf came at him again, but this time he had a dagger. Mother jumped in front of him and begged him to put it away."

More leaves shifted, revealing how hideous it had turned. "The man shoved mother aside, and she stumbled. I was so afraid he would hurt her and the babe I ran forward and hit at his legs, and he struck me." She touched her head. "As I fell, Ralf—"

She gasped, and her father gripped her clasped hands. "You need tell no more."

She shook her head. "I was on the ground and my head ached, but I could see and...'twas like poking at logs upon a fire, but when Ralf let go of the handle, the blade stayed where he stuck it. And the man stood there and stared at his middle. When he started to fall, mother grabbed him, but he was too big and hit his knees, then his face. As he lay there, a terrible sound rose from him, then his eyes came to mine, and... They were so sad I was almost glad when they emptied."

Beata felt the wet on her face and thought it memory of the rain, but the moisture slid to her lips and she touched her tongue to its saltiness.

Her father squeezed her hands. "Enough is told."

But not remembered...

Another layer of leaves scattered. "Mother ordered Ralf to help her turn the man onto his back, but my cousin just stood there. I wanted to tell her it did not matter, that the man was empty, but neither could I move or speak. She became furious, told Ralf to help me, and herself turned the man. When I saw the dagger's handle was bloody and bent to the side, I began to cry hard and Ralf dropped beside me and pulled me into his arms. As the rain soaked us, mother dragged the man to the corner and dug beside the wall. After what seemed forever, she rolled him into the hole and pushed dirt over him. Then leaves. So many leaves."

"Dear Beata," her father choked.

She drew a shuddering breath. "I wish the tale were imagined."

"I wish it, too, but that is the mess Ralf left me to set aright. If only I had taken him to court, but..." He dragged a hand down his face. "Following his father's death a year earlier, the behavior that ended his training at Wulfen Castle worsened, and I did not dare expose him to King Stephen who might question Wiltford's stability." He growled low. "Curse the Wulfriths! 'Twould not have happened had they made good their reputation and trained him into one worthy of his title."

Beata pressed her lips against the impulse to defend that family lest her father close up, denying her what else he knew. When he continued to brood, she said, "There were no witnesses?"

He shook his head. "Blessedly, the foul weather turned the watch on the walls lax, so none saw what went in the garden. Of greater blessing, Soames traveled alone, as he was wont to do when visiting one of his mistresses. Hence, I disposed of the body, released Soames's horse in the wood, made much of the baron's disregard of our hospitality in departing without a word, and sent your nurse to serve at one of our lesser castles."

"And you and mother convinced me it was only a dream."

He sat back and dropped his head against the wall. "At the time, you were our greatest obstacle—too young to know better than to speak of what you had seen, too stubborn to be easily persuaded it was not real."

She recalled screaming at them and clapping her hands over her ears, all the angrier for her confinement in their bedchamber for an illness she did not feel. They had not dared allow her amongst others until she accepted it was only a dream.

"How long did it take to persuade me?"

"Several days, though it may have taken longer had your mother not gone into labor early, trading one horror for another. And giving me more reason to curse Ralf."

Beata started to ask him to explain, but the answer came to her—her mother's bulky figure soaked through, grunting and groaning as she dragged the man, digging in the dirt on her hands and knees, rolling him in, shoving wet earth into place, piling leaves atop.

"Because of Ralf, Emmerich was born too soon," her father said. "He was so small and weak that every sickness come unto Heath came unto him. Even in later years when his health improved, his build and disposition were so opposite mine one would not know he was my son. And how he abhorred violence! Like a woman, he closed his eyes against it, flinched and quivered when a blade was put in his hand. Perhaps had I more time with him..." He heaved a sigh. "Ever there was Ralf, determined to be our downfall. Though after what he did to Soames, much time he spent in prayer, his moods worsened. You remember what he was like, aye?"

She recalled the dread of his absence from supper that portended he was at prayer, where he would remain the night through, reappearing the morning after. None the better for his time with the Lord, it had taken little to send him into a rage that, until her father intervened, could see servants, men-at-arms, even knights struck down.

"I remember."

"It was guilt that made him so, Beata. Guilt that, once he wed, too often kept him from the nuptial bed, preventing him from siring children. Guilt that killed him at thirty and one years."

"Guilt? But he drowned."

"With his full consent."

She startled.

Eyes moist, her father nodded. "There was speculation I was responsible, but just as it was no crime, it was no accident. Ralf saw to his own end. Though only my eyes beheld the missive found the day after we pulled him from the river, in it he confessed to the murder of Lothaire Soames's father. He told that as the baron's six-year-old had lost his sire, who was but thirty and one, it seemed right the Rodelles should lose their baron at that age. He said though his ruined and sacrificed life ought to be payment enough, if ever Soames's son required aid, as the new Baron of Wiltford, I should give it."

"For this, you would wed me to him?"

"Nay, 'tis but a benefit of joining our families. I spoke true when I told there were no others worthy and willing to take you to wife. But not even that I would have risked had I known you would make sense of what should have remained a dream."

"Then now you accept I cannot wed Soames?"

He clasped and unclasped his hands. "Still, he will make a better husband than one chosen by Eleanor. Thus, if you can put from you what you have learned this day, I would have you exchange vows."

She drew back. "A marriage erected on the murder of his father by his wife's kin?" She pushed to her feet. "Even if Eleanor weds me to one older than Count Fauvel, I will not do this—will not birth children whose grandfather's life was severed by their mother's cousin. That is every shade of wrong."

Her father rose. "Beata, never will your children know."

An angry breath whistled through the space between her teeth. "*I will know*, and 'twill eat at me—so much I might confess the same as Ralf. I will not marry Lothaire Soames!"

"Aye, you will," a voice red with anger sounded across the chapel. "Like it or nay, you shall be my wife, Beata Rodelle…Fauvel…Soames."

28

Twenty-one years.

A long time to learn what had become of Ricard Soames—so long Lothaire had abandoned wonder, accepting that just as a father was lost to him and his sister, a husband lost to their mother, and a lord lost to the people of Lexeter, never would he know the reason for that loss.

It did not surprise it was murder, certain as his mother was Ricard had been a victim of foul play. What surprised was she had also been right in believing the Rodelles were involved.

Involved. A gross understatement.

Holding his gaze to those whose faces reflected horror, Lothaire stepped from the corridor that led to the priest's living quarters and into the light provided by a score of candles upon the altar.

"I think you must agree 'tis even more imperative we wed," he said as he continued forward. "For me, because the heiress of Wiltford is the least owed my family for our loss, for the Rodelles, because your family would not wish it known the blood of a murderer courses your veins—nor suffer punishment for being a party to that crime, Baron Rodelle."

Lothaire's betrothed, whom he had not previously found so disagreeable, stepped toward him. "Baron Soames, whatever you heard—"

"All of it. Of that I made certain by sending the boy for the priest so I might sooner return to learn the lie told by your parents. So I have. And shall use it well."

His betrothed's wet eyes brightened further, but he hardened himself against pitying her, the same as he had done his wife, who would have used such weakness against him. Beata Rodelle Fauvel was not to blame for his father's death—she was also a victim—but her family was, and the price of Ricard Soames's life was restoration of his family's wealth that would not have declined had he lived to administer Lexeter.

"Baron Soames," her father found his voice as Lothaire halted before him, "I cannot say how sorry I am."

"By your silence you can. Pray, keep it, for all is decided. Though your daughter's fortune will not make right my father's death, it will soothe the financial pain. And that is something." He looked to the church doors. "Now where is that priest?"

Too late, Durand's heart pronounced, and as its ache burned through him, the voice he should have heeded as if it were God's rebuked, *Did I not say not to hold tight to that which you long for? Have you not learned far less it aches to have it slip through your fingers than be torn from your grasp?*

Anger, so keen that were it given form it would prove deadly, shot up from his depths. "Not too late!" he shouted and pushed his destrier harder, putting more distance between him and the knights who had given chase moments earlier.

Those before the church turned—the priest who had been about to enter the sanctuary, Rodelle where he stood behind the one who had this day become his son-in-law, Soames who had just lifted his bride onto his mount, and Beata who sat sidesaddle.

Having known he might find this, he was prepared. Until her marriage was consummated, Beata belonged to no man.

You least of all, that voice reminded.

Soames had drawn his sword. The hank of hair cut from its tail lifting in the cool air, he strode forward to meet his opponent.

Though he was fairly easy to put down, no time would Durand afford him with the knights of the two barons seeking to aid their lords.

He veered wide as if to go around the church, then jerked the reins, guiding his mount left again and setting his sights on Beata.

So here we are again, he thought as she snapped her head around.

Hair slipping free of what remained of her braid, she raised a hand and shook her head. But as then upon Henry's French lands, now upon Henry's English lands, Durand answered to another. Thus, he slowed his horse just enough to keep control as he came alongside her and, as he had done once before, hooked an arm around her and dragged her in front of him.

"Nay!"

"Behave, Beata!"

Still she strained away, and he did not need to look around to know her added weight and struggle were allowing their pursuers to gain on them. The first he could do naught about, but the second...

Since their only chance of escape lay in subduing her, he growled, "Do you continue to fight me, this time when you go to ground, I go with you. And do not think the barons' men will not use the opportunity to ensure my *accident* is permanent."

He was not sure that was true, but he needed her to believe it.

She stilled. "Oh, Durand, you know not what you do."

"I do the queen's bidding, and that is all that matters."

She slumped against him.

Now to escape their pursuers.

He was not holding her to him, but neither was he letting her out of his sight.

Staring at Durand across the distance she had put between them after they entered the wood and took cover in a hollow to see their pursuers past, Beata hurt so much she wanted to cry and pound her fists at being made to pay for another's sins.

Though aware of her writhing depths, she had mostly been numb throughout the exchange of vows with Lothaire Soames. And for a long while she might have remained thus, but Durand had come for her as she should not have wished him to do for how hopeless—now dangerous—her family's circumstances.

Far better it would have been had she not seen him again, nor felt his touch or the strong movement of his heart that matched hers during the ride. Better numb than this which, no matter how many times she turned the ring on her finger, would not wear away.

Durand stepped from alongside his destrier, and as he strode toward where she sat on a fallen tree, unstoppered his wineskin. "Drink, Beata. Please."

She wanted to insist she was not thirsty as twice she had done in the hour since their dismount, but her mouth was parched.

She reached and was not careful enough to avoid exchanging touches. Berating herself for the shiver of awareness now forbidden her, she held his gaze as she put the spout to her lips and drank deeply.

She lowered the skin, fit the stopper. "You must take me back to Soames—" She drew a sharp breath, corrected, "You must return me to my husband."

He set the skin on his belt and dropped to his haunches. "I must not. What I must do is that with which I am tasked—prevent your abhorrent father from giving you to a man without the queen's consent."

Her laughter was brittle. "If my sire is abhorrent for asking me to wed a man of benefit to our family, what does that make Queen Eleanor who would wed me to one of benefit to her? What does that make you?"

Regret shone from his eyes. "One who keeps his word and his honor."

"Even though he ought not give his word when what is required of him is without honor?"

"I like it no better than you—"

"Do you not? You are not the one who, for the queen's pleasure, may once more be matched with an old man who will not eschew his rights and will make of me—"

"Beata," he groaned.

She swallowed hard. "At least Soames is of a good age, younger even than you, well mannered, and pleasant to look upon. I could be happy with him." *That* she did not believe, but if it persuaded Durand...

He cupped her cheek, tempting her to clap a hand over his to hold him to her. "As happy as you believe you could be with me?"

A sob hurtled forth, but she tightened her throat, and when that grief sank down, said, "Never has Eleanor's gallant monk been a choice. And even were he, 'tis too late. You may have stolen me from Soames, but we are wed."

He lowered his hand. "Not irreparably. Lacking consummation, a marriage can be annulled."

Were hers, Soames would reveal his father's murder. "I do not want it annulled. I vow I do not!"

His lids flickered.

Finding hope in what seemed hesitation, she said, "Eleanor need never know you reached me ere the marriage was consummated. Thus, it is upon my family and husband the blame will fall, not you."

"Do you truly think you could be happy with Soames, Beata?"

Then he cared enough for her he might yield?

It was hard not to swallow the lump in her throat, but fearing it would go down so loudly he would not believe her, she said around it, "Methinks I will grow to love him."

Nostrils flaring, he searched her face, then his lids narrowed. "As you love me?"

Once more, the sob rose. Once more, she pushed it down. And lied. "Surely you cannot think you are the only man I have loved?"

He smiled sorrowfully. "I believe I can. That is not to say you could not love another, but as I will not soon forget you, nor easily turn my affections elsewhere, I do not think you shall, Beata."

Her heart leapt, stumbled over its landing, fell on its face. If he but returned her feelings in half measure, being denied him made her sacrifice all the more tragic.

"Nor do I believe you will feel as deeply for Soames as you feel for me," he continued, "even if it is only because I do not wish to believe it."

The sob broke free, parted her lips.

"Beata." Drawing her onto her knees before him, he lowered his face to the tearful one she turned up. He touched his mouth to her brow, kissed her nose, brushed his lips across hers.

Though she could not forget all that had happened this day that made this wrong, she did not pull away. But neither did she respond as her heart and body longed to do. Not with Lothaire Soames's ring on her hand.

Durand ached. He was certain Beata wanted this as much as he, could feel the tension in her that held her from kissing him as she had wanted to do on the night past. But if he pressed her, that tension would snap and she would be his. Never would she belong to Soames, who had humiliated her to ensure her purity. That marriage need not be undone by lack of consummation. By this it could be undone.

Drawing her nearer, he opened his mouth on hers. An instant later, her breath rushed into him and she wound her arms around his neck and partnered in deepening the kiss.

How it could be so sweet and yet insatiable he did not understand, but soon he would lie her down and—

Ruin her, the same as you ruined Lady Gaenor when she fled marriage to a man she did not believe she wanted, rebuked the voice penance had refined these past years. *Once more you make mutual grieving into a dangerous embrace, turn an innocent's feelings into kisses and caresses, and now you move this intimacy toward something of greater sin.*

Next came Abel's words—*No matter what you are moved to do, if you truly believe yourself in the right, ask for help. And not only from God.*

But still he wanted what he wanted. With a last, desperate effort to pull back from the edge upon which he held so fast to Beata he would take her down with him, he reminded himself, *Do not hold tight to that which you long—*

Struck by the realization there was something that would serve him better in doing what was right and best for this woman, he reshaped his oft-repeated beseeching into a prayer.

Lord, let us not hold tight to those earthly things we long for lest You *be torn from our grasp.*

He lifted his head, pressed Beata's beneath his chin. "All is wrong," he said, "but this more so."

"I know." She trembled. "How I know! Thus, you must return me to Soames."

He almost wished he could so he might sooner seek healing for what was bleeding inside him, but that was not best for her. Nor him, for also in that direction lay betrayal of his liege.

Though Eleanor more grievously trespassed against Beata than did her father, the Rodelles and Lothaire Soames did not take seriously the queen's wrath that would be all the greater once she learned of the trickery worked on Elias and her man. Royalty needed no definite proof to dispense punishment. It was their prerogative to determine guilt based on their own needs and desires.

Thus, he must send word to the queen of what had transpired and allow her to decide whether to permit Beata's marriage or seek dissolution on grounds of coercion and non-consummation. And he would include a plea that Beata be provided the greatest chance at happiness.

He eased her arms from around his neck and, as he drew her to standing, said, "We should go."

"To Soames?"

"Nay."

She gripped his tunic. Eyes large with what seemed fear, she said, "If you truly care for me—for my future and that of my family—you will return me to my husband."

"Beata—"

"Do you care for me or nay?"

His harsh sigh warmed the air between them. "You know I do."

"Then do this for me."

She seemed more desperate than when she had confided her sacrifice would spare her father's wife another attempt at conceiving an heir that could see the woman into a grave. And he did not think it only because she had exchanged vows with Soames.

"You will do it?" she pressed.

Certain lulling her was the only means of learning what she held close, and regretting his deception, he said, "I understand your wish to do your duty, just as I know it is wrong our sovereign wields such power over our lives, but I am well enough acquainted with that power to know defiance will cause you and your family more misery than acquiescence."

Her upper lip trembling, drawing his gaze to the slight gap between her teeth that had once lacked appeal, she said, "What will it take to move you?"

He wanted to say *naught,* but whatever she hid would not see light if he trampled her hope. "A *very* good reason, Beata."

She released him, turned away. For some minutes she remained with her head down, then she came around. "This day the leaves proved not a dream." Her voice was tight with tears. "It happened."

As thought. He motioned her to the fallen tree and lowered himself several feet distant.

With stops and starts, suppressed sobs and winding tears that made him long to comfort her, she told of Soames's murder that brought to mind Sir Elias's comment their first night at Heath that were they to weave in a chase, a murder, and no hope of lovers reuniting, quite the tale they would have. And so they did, but at its end, it had the opposite effect Beata sought.

More than before, Durand was determined to keep her from Soames. Though he had sensed the man was not without honor, revenge could warp the good out of a person—so much it seemed likely the baron would ill treat Beata. Thus, Durand would have to place his trust in the queen.

Beata looked up, and as her tear-streaked face more deeply pained him, said, "Though I thought myself without choice before, 'tis now absolute. To protect my family from reprisal and scandal, I must return to Soa—" Her lids fluttered. "I must return to my husband."

He inclined his head. Though she might hate him for what that gesture led her to believe, better he forestall as long as possible the fight she would give him when she discovered her revelation had not moved him.

"I thank you," she said with more sorrow than gratitude and stood.

Blessedly, they were not long into the ride before all of her relaxed. In the hope she would remain oblivious to their destination, allowing him to keep a good watch for pursuers, Durand slowed their pace, tucked her more securely against his chest, and drew his mantle around her. And with regret, he accepted that even were they able to maintain a brisk pace, it would be impossible to reach Wulfen Castle before midnight.

However, there was sanctuary between here and the Wulfriths' stronghold. Long before they had taken cover in the wood, they had traversed that baron's lands.

But had Lady Gaenor and her husband departed the barony of Abingdale to join the Wulfriths' Christmas celebration?

"God willing," he breathed and set their course.

29

"THIS IS NOT Heath Castle. I know not this place."

Though Durand's hope Beata would not awaken before they reached their destination was granted, not so his prayer that the baron and his wife were absent, as evidenced by the one summoned to the outer walls as Beata had stirred.

The giant of a man who strode alongside Durand's destrier into the torch-lit inner bailey looked up. "Well come to Broehne Castle upon the barony of Abingdale, Lady Beata."

She stiffened further, swung her face to Durand's. "You lied!"

"I beg your forgiveness."

Her hand shot up, but though he thought she meant to slap him—and he would have allowed it—she thrust off his mantle he had pulled around her. "To be forgiven, one must truly regret their deception," she snapped, "and as this is not the first time you have delivered me *elsewhere*, you cannot possibly regret it."

"Then I regret there was naught for it."

"Naught for it because you are so blindly loyal to Eleanor you do not do what is right." Her nostrils dilated. "I should hate you."

Durand glanced at Christian Lavonne, who had graciously shifted his attention to the donjon. "Yet one more thing I regret," he said.

She turned forward, and when he lifted her down before the donjon, she strained against his grip.

He pulled her near. "Behave, Beata. We are guests——"

"Behave! 'Tis your solution to my every annoyance. *Not* mine!" She jerked free, whipped up her skirts, and ascended the steps.

"Almighty," Baron Lavonne said. "I need know no more about your charge to pity you the handful—or should I say armful?"

The bit of a smile gifted by one who had been wronged nearly as much as his wife, was a balm to Durand. Though years since they had seen each other, the last time being when Lavonne himself delivered tidings that Henry and Eleanor had absolved Durand of his offenses, it seemed he had not lost ground. His prolonged absence might even have gained him more.

Above, the porter opened the door for Beata and quickly closed it to keep out the winter.

"Give your destrier into my squire's care." Lavonne motioned to a young man. "I fear my wife will not know what to do with your lady."

Not my lady, Durand silently corrected as he passed the reins to the squire and mounted the steps. "Again, I apologize for pausing at Broehne, Baron. Were the weather not foul, we would have continued to Wulfen."

"I assume you are being pursued."

"We are. By the lady's father and…husband."

Lavonne halted, and the face he turned to the queen's man was stone.

Durand held his gaze. "I am on royal business, Baron. Though there is much more to that tale than when I was tasked with escorting Lady Beata from France to England, I vow the circumstances in which I find myself are far different from…"

Lavonne narrowed his lids. "I will be more comfortable once I know the tale in full."

Suppressing resentment with the reminder distrust was the man's due, Durand said, "Then over a tankard of ale and viands, you shall know it."

Without comment, Lavonne resumed his ascent.

The woman was tall, taller than any Beata had seen, but not ungainly as she strode from the hearth with hands folded at her waist. Elegant. And her questioning smile turned an unremarkable face lovely. Were she wed to the even taller man who had welcomed Beata to...

Which castle was it? Upon which barony?

She could not recall what he said, having been so unsettled at the realization it was not to her father's men Durand had given his name and hers in requesting permission to enter.

Regardless, if this woman who was nearly upon Beata was wed to the one who had walked alongside Durand's horse, and were that man kind, the lady would be blessed to have been matched with a husband over whom she did not stand. Rather like Baron Wulfrith had told of his—

She stuttered back a step, causing concern to line the woman's brow as she halted before her guest.

"Lady Beata?"

Beata snatched a breath of air. "I know who you are."

The woman's smile gave way to dismay, but it slipped out as quickly as it slid in. "Aye, I am Lady Gaenor, wife of Baron Lavonne, mother of Lyulf and soon to be blessed again"—she touched her abdomen that evidenced she was perhaps halfway through her term—"sister to Baron Wulfrith, Sir Everard, Sir Abel, and Lady Beatrix, and daughter to Lady Isobel." She drew a long breath. "Now that is done, I am pleased to receive you in our home."

Beata knew she should observe the niceties as she had done whilst Conrad's wife, but they fled her, and all she could say was, "I should not be here."

The lady stepped nearer. "You should. 'Tis cold out, dark, and the hour will grow old ere it grows young again. Now whilst your chamber is being prepared, come warm yourself at the hearth."

Though Beata longed to give herself into the lady's hands—she who should want naught to do with Durand and his charge—she hesitated.

In the next instant, the door behind opened, first granting entrance to chill air, then the men whose booted feet caused the floorboards to creak—one set of which made Beata close her fingers into fists.

"Well come, Sir Durand," Lady Gaenor said. "I have invited Lady Beata to rest at hearth whilst your chambers are prepared and refreshments assembled."

As Durand came alongside Beata, she dug nails into her palms to control the hurt and anger that tempted her to slap him.

Behave, she told herself and nearly gasped at her own counseling.

"Lady Gaenor," he said, "I am pleased to see you again, and I thank you for your hospitality. I would not have imposed were—"

"I am glad you paused at Broehne, Sir Knight." She gestured at the great fireplace whose warmth barely reached across the hall. "Pray, join my husband and me."

Durand took Beata's arm, and as he drew her across the beautifully appointed hall, she ached over not wanting his hand upon her for how much she did want it. This in spite of his profession of feelings—surely exaggerated—that had made her believe he would return her to Soames if she provided a very good reason.

Forgive me Father, Emmerich, Lady Winifred, she silently beseeched. *Had I not been so vain to believe he felt much for me, I would not have revealed our secret.*

When he handed her toward a bench, she slipped past and claimed one of two chairs, certain he meant to share that seat with her.

After an awkward pause, Lady Gaenor gestured Durand into the other chair, and her husband and she took the bench. Moments later, the baron clasped his wife's hand between his.

Regardless of what had happened between Lady Gaenor and Durand, the love between this man and woman had seen them past it—so far past, they could welcome the queen's man into their home. How?

Faith in one's spouse, Beata decided, perhaps as much as in the Lord. Surely only then could true forgiveness be attained.

Certes, Baron Wulfrith had spoken true. He and his siblings had made good marriages, even Lady Gaenor, who had been given no choice in a husband.

Beata was happy for them, but honesty bade her admit she was also envious. And promise herself that if she must pack away what remained of Conrad's beloved wife and widow when the vestal was no more, she would make peace with Lothaire Soames and carve out of their relationship whatever happiness could be had—even if only by way of children.

Lord, she prayed, *bless me with many that I may be so occupied I do not long for one other than my husband.*

"As told you, Sir Durand," Christian Lavonne said, "our journey to Stern was delayed. Unfortunately, due to our son taking ill."

"I am sorry," Beata found her voice. "Is it serious?"

"Nay, he is a strong lad, and so much improved we considered departing this day. However, with the weather so chill and changeable, we determined it best we remain here—mayhap altogether this Christmas."

Beata forced a smile, and when she glanced at Durand, found his eyes upon her. Glimpsing there what seemed yearning, she shot to her feet. "Forgive me, but I am weary. Even if my chamber is not ready, I beseech you to allow me to gain it."

Lady Gaenor reached her ahead of Durand. "I shall take you," she said and guided her abovestairs.

Beyond being assisted in the removal of her gloves and mantle and lowering to the edge of a wonderfully soft mattress, Beata was aware of little. But as covers were arranged over her and she drifted away, she heard again what Lady Gaenor had said when she peeled off her guest's gloves.

I see you are wed, Lady Beata. Happily, I pray.

It was not the goblet of wine nor the tankard of ale that made him confide. It was their seeming acceptance of Durand Marshal. Though they had given him cause to think himself forgiven, he had not fully believed it. And yet long they had sat with him in their solar as he told of the rescue of The Vestal Widow from Count Verielle's men and all the events that followed.

Nearly all. He saw no reason to reveal the murder of Lothaire Soames's father, and though he had confessed to his growing attraction for his charge, he barely touched on his feelings. But he saw that question in Gaenor's eyes before she gave herself permission to speak it.

More disconcerting, it was not quite a question. "You love her."

This lady, perhaps more than any, knew how love for a woman hung upon him. Sitting forward in the chair angled toward husband and wife, he dug his elbows into his thighs and clasped his hands between his knees. "Love," he murmured, pride causing him to make it more a question than confirmation.

She smiled softly. "The same as you felt for the first Beatrix."

Not the same, he could not say for how much it would gut him. "Another Beatrix." He shook his head. "Such irony, eh?"

She shrugged. "'Tis but a name in a world of too few names for how many we are. Blessed be the Lord who sees to it we are all different on the outside and more so on the inside." Her smile turned apologetic. "Meaning I chose my words poorly. I should not have compared what you feel for Lady Beata with what you once felt for my sister."

Once...

As Durand had done often to assure himself the conversation mostly carried by Gaenor and himself did not trespass, he moved his regard to Christian Lavonne.

The baron looked to his wife. "It is not my place to speak on what Sir Durand feels for the lady, but methinks he is as miserable as I was ere I had hope of a blessed future with you."

She blushed prettily, and Durand understood why he had never realized how lovely she was. True beauty lay not only in loving but in being loved. And that his actions had nearly denied her this made his throat tighten and eyes moisten.

He looked away. Though Baron Wulfrith had assured the young men who trained beneath him that even the greatest warrior was not above tears, they unsettled him, especially in the presence of others. And more greatly as they continued to gather.

He lowered his chin, set his teeth, and breathed deep. But his chest ached so much he drove his hands into his hair and clasped them at the back of his neck. "I have made a mess of it. All that was required of me was to deliver her to her father and, if she proved an heiress, ensure she did not wed without Eleanor's consent."

Gaenor laughed. Under different circumstances, he would have thought it a beautiful sound. "That is *all* that was required of you? No provisions made for a resistant charge, being injured, beaten, robbed, shipwrecked, and a victim of such devious design Sir Elias's drink was tainted?" She harrumphed. "*You* made a mess of it?"

Her outrage lightening his angst, he unclasped his hands and lifted his head.

"What do you intend, Sir Durand?" This from her husband, who surely wearied of their guest.

"I will write to Eleanor of all that has gone and, until I have word from her, prevent Lady Beata from falling into her father's and Soames's hands." He looked to Gaenor. "Providing Abel allows me to secure the lady at Wulfen, that should be easily accomplished."

"I am sure he will, but..." She turned to her husband.

He nodded. "Lady Beata and you are welcome to remain our guests. Though a chamber here is not as secure as locking your charge in one of Wulfen's towers, I will alert the garrison to be more vigilant in ensuring those who enter our walls are welcome, as well as offer a man to aid in watching the lady lest she attempt to escape."

Durand started to decline, but Gaenor said, "It could be weeks, even months ere you receive tidings of how to proceed. Having myself passed much time at Wulfen out of sight of all but my brothers—or nearly all"—she glanced at her husband—"I assure you, 'tis a less than agreeable stay. True, Helene is with Abel at Wulfen, but here Lady Beata will be more comfortable and able to move about with ease."

Still he longed to object, but the offer was generous. Though Beata would not like it, less she would like imprisonment at Wulfen. "You are certain it is no great imposition?"

"We are," her husband said and raised his wife beside him. "Think on it, and let us know come the morrow."

"Good eve, my lord…my lady." Durand crossed to the door. Shortly, he entered the chamber alongside Beata's he had been shown prior to joining the Lavonnes in the solar.

He shed his garments, slid beneath the bedclothes, and snuffed the candle on the table. "I praise You for aiding me with the Wulfriths and Lavonnes," he told the Lord as he stared into darkness from which his adjusting eyes gleaned light. "Now help us not hold tight to those earthly things we long for lest *You* be torn from our grasp."

30

The maid wore bells. Somewhere on her person. Softly tinkling like dainty rain upon steel.

"You are awake, my lady?"

Now she was. But she did not regret it. Sleeping through the day would not sooner see her returned to Soames to secure her family's secret.

She almost laughed at that last. Durand had betrayed her—no matter her revelation had never intended to choose her over Eleanor. Thus, if he shared with the queen the secret entrusted to him, Beata would be as guilty of betrayal.

Truly, I should hate you, Durand, she thought as she peered past the hair tossed across her face at the maid who halted alongside the mattress.

The young woman dropped to her haunches, and her eyes found Beata's amidst dark tresses. "Aye, awake—and hungry, I wager." She smiled brightly, reminding Beata of better times when she had been as free with that expression. "I be Aimee, Lady Gaenor's maid, and you must be esteemed for my mistress to sacrifice my service so I may assist you."

Beata was surprised by the stretching of her own lips. Flushed with guilt at finding pleasure in this sprite's company, she eased from her belly onto her side and looked more closely at the woman.

The maid's mouth so quickly puckered, it was as if its drawstring had been cinched tight. "Oh my lady, a sorry sight you are! Tell Aimee what so saddens you should cry the night through."

Beata fingered her puffed eyes. She did not recall crying or dreams so disturbed she would have wept through them, but she remembered words that had scraped her soul as she went down into sleep—*I see you are wed, Lady Beata. Happily, I pray.*

"'Twas only a bad dream," she said. And that was not truly a lie.

Aimee straightened. "Worry not. We shall apply cold cloths to your eyes and none need know your distress. Now let me tend you lest you present late for the nooning meal."

"The nooning meal?" Beata sat up.

"Aye." The maid crossed the room and banged back the shutters. Though the window was fit with oilcloth to deflect the chill air, unclouded sunlight filtered into the chamber. "See now, we must make haste."

Beata scooted back against the headboard. "Is it possible for viands to be delivered here?"

"'Tis, and I will see it done if you insist, but my mistress told that should you request it, I ought to assure you that the most comely knight—Sir Durand, is it not?—shall not take his meal at table."

Then he was elsewhere? Within the castle? Beyond the walls? Though first dismayed that he was gone from her and next dismayed he had left her with strangers, she remembered her duty to her family and told herself it was for the best. She had only to play well with the Lavonnes and, before long, they would ease their watch, allowing her to find a way back to Soames.

Not Soames, she once more corrected. *Your husband, not only in word but soon in deed.*

That stirred her bile, the thought of being intimate with one other than Durand—

Cease! she silently rebuked. *He can never be!*

"Well, my lady? What say you?"

Beata returned Aimee to focus. Though she preferred to remain abovestairs, the sooner Lady Gaenor believed her guest was easily in hand, the sooner she could be fooled. Too, barring illness it would be rude for Beata to keep to her chamber, especially since she had not appeared this morn to break her fast.

She looked down her rumpled gown. "Providing your mistress does not mind her guest wearing tired garments, I will join her belowstairs."

Aimee made a face. "Though stitchin' crosses my eyes something terrible, my lady made certain I did not lounge away the company I kept with you." As she strode back toward the bed, she gestured at a chair over which a pale green gown was draped. "'Twould not do for her loyal servant to enjoy a much-deserved rest. Humph! Know you how much hem I had to stitch up to be sure my lady's gown would not catch 'neath your feet?"

More than a hand's width, Beata was certain—providing the maid had correctly reckoned the height of the one who had slept through the alteration. Recalling the last garment altered for her, Beata wanted to smile. Unlike Lady Gaenor's gown, Lady Helene's had required the addition of material to its hem.

Aimee clicked her tongue, reminding Beata of Elias, worrying her over his recovery, and shaming her for being so taken with her own troubles she had hardly considered him since stealing to the wood with her father.

Had his belly settled sufficiently to allow him to return to Wulfen? *Would* he return? Though he was not vengeful, he was no longer the young man who preferred songs, plays, and the telling of tales to weaponry and strategy. He had become a warrior, and with that distinction came greater pride, which her father had trampled in reducing him to the helplessness of a boy retching up his porridge.

"My lady?"

Beata swung her feet to the floor and gave over to the chatty maid in whom she would have delighted if not for the misery of her circumstances.

The Vexing

The embroidered gown proved a good length and an acceptable fit. Granted, more of Beata's borrowed chemise showed past the lacings than she would have liked, but little of her modesty was compromised.

"I knew Aimee would set you right," Lady Gaenor said when she met her guest coming off the stairs. "You look lovely." She swept her gaze back up and lingered over Beata's face. "And fairly well rested."

Confirmation the cool cloths had reduced the swelling caused by tears.

"I thank you for the gown and loan of your maid," Beata said, and though tempted to ask after Durand, did not. "You are most kind."

The lady inclined her head and led Beata among the castle folk who gathered in the hall to enjoy the day's heartiest meal.

As Aimee had revealed, Durand was not present. Also absent was Baron Lavonne though the lord's high seat was not empty. A boy of four—perhaps five—perched there on his knees, raising himself well enough to reach the viands soon to be served.

"Ah, son," Lady Gaenor said as she strode the backside of the dais upon which the high table was erected, "you must earn that place ere you may even think there."

The boy whose plump, lightly flushed face made him appear younger than his height and breadth suggested, swept up long lashes and said in a voice also less mature than expected, "Only 'til you come back, momma." Then he ducked beneath the table and popped up beside the chair into which Lady Gaenor lowered.

"Who that?" He frowned at the one who took the seat her hostess indicated.

"Lady Beata." She ruffled his blond hair, then lingeringly swept it out of his eyes as if to test the heat of his brow. "Lady Beata, this is our son, Lyulf."

"Greetings, Lyulf. I am guessing you are four? Five?"

He snorted, rolled his eyes. "Fooled another, momma!"

She chuckled. "How many is it this month?"

Lyulf held up a hand and tucked his thumb beneath his fingers. "One...two...three...four!"

"You are right."

Looking pleased, he lifted his chin. "I am three, Lady. And big. Like papa."

Beata glanced at Lady Gaenor, who said, "Not even near four," then pecked a kiss atop his head and motioned forward a woman who stood to the right of the dais. "Go with Josephine, Lyulf."

His lower lip jutted. "Wanna eat with you."

"Not this day."

He sighed, took the hand Josephine extended, and tugged the woman toward the kitchen.

"Three years old," Beata said. "By the time he is five..."

"Aye. And when he leaves me to begin his page's training at Wulfen..." She touched her belly. "At least I shall have one great distraction. God willing, several."

Would all her children be of such build? Beata wondered, then mused, "I have never considered the benefit of a man wedding a woman of great height. It seems ever their sex seek to be matched with one easily tucked beneath an arm."

"My husband teases that—" Lady Gaenor gasped and deferred to the priest who had risen farther down the table to bless the meal.

Not until all were served drinks and viands did the lady resume their talk. "I ought not boast, but Lyulf is a fine lad—in temperament, looks, *and* size. My husband teases that all men in pursuit of heirs ought to first seek a wife of good height and solid build and assures me that if our daughters benefit the same as our sons, all the better." She wrinkled her nose. "I agree about sons, but as I have experienced the vanity of men afeared of appearing slight alongside a wife, I cannot wish the same on daughters."

"Your husband must love you very much."

"He does. In spite of all."

All being Durand for whom this lady had first felt, Beata guessed.

"I pray my lord husband is as loved by me," Lady Gaenor said and frowned. "A pity love is not more often the true measure by which one chooses a spouse."

"But you..."

She inclined her head. "The only choice I had was that of refusal and, in the end, it carried little weight since I could not bear for my family to suffer for my unwillingness. But see"—she held up her ringed hand—"the Lord made all right. There is no other man's ring I would have on this hand. Not that I believed it when Baron Lavonne placed it there. I quite feared him." She moved her gaze to Beata's hand. "Do I trespass in asking if you fear your husband?"

Though Beata's chest felt as if it were being pushed up her throat, she nearly denied it. Instead, wishing she did not so heavily feel the weight of her own ring, she nodded.

Sympathy lined Lady Gaenor's face. "I am sorry, but given time, mayhap you will be as blessed as I."

"Mayhap," she agreed, though it would be a miracle if Soames came near to replacing Durand in her affections. She drew a deep breath. "Let us not indulge in games, my lady. I know you must know, as I am aware once it was for you, Sir Durand possesses my heart."

Her smile was sorrowful. "I do. And as you feel never will you love again, I believed the same. Though for you it may prove true, I encourage you to set your mind to making the best of your marriage if it cannot be undone."

Durand had told her much. "I am determined, especially for the sake of any children we have."

"I shall keep you in my prayers, Lady Beata."

They fell more seriously to eating—rather, Lady Gaenor. A necessity, Beata thought, the woman's greatest bulge that of her growing babe.

Though Beata carried little excess weight, she was certain she would not fair as well had she the lady's appetite. Her lacings would not require loosening merely to accommodate naturally generous hips and bosom. But it was not that which discouraged her from eating well now. It was

Soames and her father somewhere outside these walls, Durand's whereabouts, and the older knight who came to her notice partway through the meal.

At a lower table where one of his rank would not normally pause, he sat with only a tankard of ale. He watched her, though one would not know it to look upon him, his gaze ever elsewhere. But she felt it when her own was distant.

"Lady Gaenor"—she leaned toward the woman—"who is that knight at the farthest table?"

The woman looked. And flushed.

"Ah," Beata murmured. "You cannot say, but that tells all. In Sir Durand's absence, yon knight is to suppress my will."

The lady moistened her lips. "Sir Durand would fulfill his duty to the queen, would not break honor..." That last was mostly breath.

"Again," Beata finished.

"Aye. I know not all your tale, my lady, but enough to assure you he also seeks to do what is best for you."

Beata pushed her goblet away. "So sweetly you defend him when I would have believed you..."

This time it was Lady Gaenor who finished the thought. "Uncomfortable. I am, though not so much I will not speak on behalf of one who cannot—or will not—speak for himself. Believe me or nay, even at the cost of his own heart, Sir Durand is determined not to repeat past mistakes and sins."

His own heart. That made Beata hurt and grasp at distraction found in that other disturbing word. "What sins?"

Lady Gaenor was a long while in answering. "I will not tell much of it, but I would have you know that sin was as much mine as his. Perhaps more mine. I knew he felt no great emotion for me, and it was my sister he loved. But it was I who first sought to salve our mutual grief by turning an embrace but meant to comfort into comfort of the wrong sort."

Beata pulled a breath so deep its release slumped her shoulders. "I appreciate your honesty." Then seeking to move the talk elsewhere, she said, "Sir Durand has gone to the queen?"

"Across the sea?" the lady exclaimed and visibly relaxed at leaving her sins behind. "Nay, he is here."

Now Beata's frame yielded to relief. "With Baron Lavonne? At sword practice?"

"He avails himself of our steward's chamber, though methinks he will not be there much longer."

Privacy in which to compose a missive to Eleanor, Beata guessed. "Then this knight"—she glanced at Baron Lavonne's man—"shall soon be relieved of his watch over me."

"He is Sir Hector, most trusted and capable of my husband's men despite his advanced years."

"Is that a warning against vexing him?"

Lady Gaenor smiled. "More a plea. He can and will do what is necessary to fulfill his duty, but he is slow to recover from great exertion, and I am as fond of him as is my husband."

Though Beata sensed Lady Gaenor sought reassurance her guest would not trouble her man, and she wished to give it, she could not. Were some small gap provided, she would slip through it if it meant saving her family.

She turned her attention to the platter between the lady and her, chose a slice of bread, and bit into its flour-dusted crust.

By meal's end, Durand had not emerged from the corridor down which the steward's quarters likely lay.

"You will join me in the solar for needlework?" Lady Gaenor asked as they rose from the table.

"Mayhap later. Now I would speak to Sir Durand."

"But he is still—"

"Do you have no objections, I shall seek him there."

Lady Gaenor glanced at Sir Hector. "As you will."

They descended the dais. As the mistress of Abingdale moved toward the stairs, Beata crossed opposite and felt the knight's eyes follow her.

Three doors were upon the corridor into which she stepped, but it was the one with a ribbon of light at its lower seam she opened.

Durand sat in profile on a tall stool at a writing desk, an arm stretched across its surface, a quill in hand alongside a parchment curled at its corners.

Beata lingered in the space between door and frame. As told by his posture—shoulders bent, head down, other hand gripping the top of his head—he could not have heard the sigh of well-oiled hinges.

Anger and frustration receding, she stared at the man she loved no matter his deception—and all the more for seeing him like this that made her believe it was no easy thing to put the queen ahead of the woman he felt for, even if not of such depth as he had felt for Beatrix Wulfrith.

The floorboards groaned softly as she stepped inside, and this he heard, lowering his hand from his head and straightening his shoulders.

"Forgive me, Cotter." He kept his profile toward the one he must believe was Lavonne's steward. "I shall not be much longer."

She closed the door, but it was the rustle of her skirts that turned him toward her. "What do you here, Beata?"

"I wish to speak with you."

He sighed. "To gain from me what I cannot give. Thus, I must be—I am—resolved to ill between us, meaning you waste your breath seeking to turn me from my course."

She halted alongside the desk, glanced at the parchment across which his bold writing marched. "To Eleanor?"

"To Eleanor."

"May I?" She reached, but he dropped the quill and caught her wrist.

Anger spurted through her, but it was a small thing compared to the awareness shivering across every hair upon every limb.

Staring at his broad fingers that made her wrist appear delicate and skin beautifully pale, she felt tears at the backs of her eyes. And they gathered when the ring on her finger caught light.

She swallowed hard. "Does not your missive concern me?"

"You know it does."

She looked to it, but before she could read past the greeting to his *most sovereign queen,* his other hand swept it to the opposite side of the desk. "You have revealed the secret I entrusted to you."

"Not yet. 'Tis that over which I struggle. Since it was your cousin who committed that heinous act and he is dead, it ought to have no bearing on the duty given me. But it does."

"Because it coerced me into wedding Soames."

"Which you would not have done once you knew the truth of his father's death, aye?"

It was true. At least, she had sought to persuade her father to yield to her wedding whomever Eleanor chose. "Had he not overheard and wielded our family's sin against us. But now…"

"That is my dilemma, Beata. I would not betray your trust, and yet I see no benefit in keeping it. Eleanor will undertake to see your marriage annulled, even if her only recourse is lack of consummation. Thus, I believe Soames will reveal the murder, hoping to persuade the queen to accept your marriage as compensation for the father and husband stolen by your cousin."

Dear Lord, she entreated. *He is right. Soames will not let my fortune slip away without a fight.*

"So it is as good as told. However, do I keep faith by first informing the queen, she is more likely to stand firm in wedding you to one of her choosing."

Beata would have pulled free were his thumb not so heavy on her pulse. "You think that a better thing?"

"I do, though mostly because of Soames's knowledge of your secret. Lest revenge cause him to ill use you, it is more imperative I keep you from him."

"You would have relented did he not know of my cousin's sin?"

He hesitated. "Even then I would not have returned you to him. As for Eleanor's choice of a husband, she may first set her sights on furthering her own interests, but she employs wisdom in doing so. I believe no matter whom she would have you wed, he will prove a better husband than one bent on revenge."

He made so much sense she felt almost weak, but her argument was not done. "You are probably right, Durand, but what you do not consider that I would have you think well upon is that if I cannot wed the one I want, it matters little whether I wed Soames or Eleanor's man. What matters is that my heart be less heavy knowing my father and brother do not suffer our secret being spilled across England."

"I am sorry. Ask me for a thousand and one things, and a thousand I will give you—just not that one."

She lowered her chin so he would not see tears sprung more from his words than his refusal to yield.

"Now do you hate me, Beata?"

A sob of laughter jumped from her. "I love you more."

He sighed. "And so I am further tested."

She looked up, and the tears that had begun to dot the floor at her feet slipped to her cheeks. "Tested?"

As he frowned over eyes that would soon look no better than before Aimee had applied cold cloths, she thought he might pull her to him, but the only intimacy he allowed was that of his thumb caressing the flesh of her inner wrist.

"Aye, tested. In every way since first we met—my patience, resolve, carnal nature, honor, faith, heart."

"Tell me of your struggle," she whispered, and when he did not speak, said, "I know more than you think, not only from observing you, but from others. And just as I am aware of your great sin, I know it has naught to do with who you are now."

He raised his eyebrows. "If you are that certain, you cannot know how near I came to committing that same sin with you."

"Can I not? I was there, and many a time I would have fallen had you let me. But despite your *carnal nature,* ever you caught me back up."

His thumb stilled. "You think you know all of it—all of me—but you do not."

"Then tell me the bad of you, even if only to make it easier to lose you."

He momentarily closed his eyes. "Do I, will you not fight me these weeks—perhaps months—while we await the queen's determination?"

She opened her mouth. And that was all.

"You hesitate, Beata."

"I am thinking I could reassure you as you did me when you sought a very good reason to return me to Soames."

A muscle in his jaw moved. "No better can I explain or excuse that. All I can do is believe you as you did me and hope you will not fail me as I failed you."

Would she fail him? She imagined an opportunity to escape, next the disgrace that would be his for not better guarding one who must be closely watched.

Nay, she would not fail him. She would also place her trust in the queen and seek comfort in knowing Ralf's sin was his alone and her parents might be forgiven for aiding in its concealment—even if only by the Lord.

Only, she silently scorned. Should He not be *all*? Aye, even if others could not accept the Lord's mercy toward another, she would strive to be content in pleasing only Him.

"Beata?"

"My word I give I will not fight you, Durand. But I would not know the bad of you in exchange for agreeing to wait on the queen. I would but know you better because you wish it."

He looked down, turned her hand in his, and frowned over the ink that had transferred from his thumb and fingers to her wrist. "I have marked you."

He knew not how deeply—more than she would ever be marked by Soames's ring.

When he reached for a cup of water, she said, "In its time it will wash away," and slipped free and crossed to a stool before a brazier whose glowing coals heated the room.

He followed and stood unmoving as if searching for where to begin, then he said, "Being a third son, after I earned my spurs and a Wulfrith dagger, my lot was to make my living by selling my sword arm. As I was Wulfen-trained, I had good prospects, but none as esteemed as that which Baron Wulfrith offered—a position at Stern Castle protecting his mother and sisters. But it proved tedious, the ladies requiring little protection since only fools set themselves against the Wulfriths. Still I remained, and when Lady Beatrix grew from a girl into a woman, I came to love her though such feelings were forbidden a landless knight who longed for a woman destined for the Church."

Beata tried to imagine that beautiful creature growing old beneath a habit, no husband at her side or children at her skirts. Though many a lady committed her life to the Church, it seemed no fit for the Beatrix D'Arci she had met at Stern.

"Then four years past, King Henry determined he would end the enmity between the Wulfriths and Lavonnes by uniting their families through marriage. During Baron Wulfrith's absence from Stern, Henry sent his men for one of the sisters, who was to be delivered to Baron Lavonne. Under order of Lady Isobel, I and another knight stole her daughters from Stern and made our way toward Wulfen where the ladies were to stay until her son returned to make a way past Henry. Well into our flight, the king's men overtook us. While I went one direction with Lady Gaenor, my fellow knight and Lady Beatrix went the other. Lady Gaenor and I evaded capture, and when we returned to search out her sister, we saw Lady Beatrix broken and bloodied in a ravine. Certain she was dead and knowing the king's men would circle back, we continued on to Wulfen to ensure Lady Gaenor did not fall into Henry's hands. And when later we paused... We grieved our loss, and here begins the bad of me."

He stepped past her, and when he opened his hands before the brazier, she glimpsed the stains on his fingers. "I would have been blind had I not known Lady Gaenor was too fond of me. Oft she gazed at me the way I looked upon her sister." He drew breath, slowly expelled it. "I knew that in her grieving she was more vulnerable, but... It was only an embrace, then only a kiss, then only this and only that, until it was too late." He lowered his hands. "I stole her innocence, quite possibly her future, and handed her off to Everard and Abel. And prayed—how I prayed!—I had not gotten her with child."

He turned before Beata could mask the distress she would not have him see.

"That prayer was answered, as was one not asked. When word came Beatrix lived and was held by Lord D'Arci, selfish Durand Marshal rose above guilt over his trespass against her sister and exalted that the woman he loved was not lost to him. But she was. She had given her heart to D'Arci. And here is more the bad of me. I begrudged them a love seemingly more impossible than mine for her. At their wedding, I transferred my anger to Christian Lavonne, to whom Baron Wulfrith had agreed to give Gaenor as his bride. Though I did not love Gaenor, I believed Lavonne would make her life misery once he discovered her loss of chastity."

Durand paused, met Beata's gaze. "I feared for her as I fear for you with Soames, albeit for a different reason."

"'Tis understandable."

"Were that all, but as told, I was angry—at Beatrix, D'Arci, Lavonne, Baron Wulfrith, even Gaenor. And so I offered to steal Gaenor away from a marriage she did not want. And thoroughly betrayed my liege."

Thus, for his regret, pain, and loss of honor, he strove to stay loyal to Eleanor.

He kneaded his neck, making Beata so long to go to him, she had to hook her toes beneath a rung to remain seated.

"For fear of King Henry's wrath upon her family, as I fear shall fall upon yours, Gaenor decided against accompanying me to France and slipped away. She wed Lavonne, and I do not doubt what they have now is far different from what they had when the truth was learned what had happened between her and me. But the Lord is merciful. Though I had intended to leave behind all I had laid ruin to, I was presented with the possibility of redemption and took it. Afterward, I found service with the king."

"Nay!" Beata shot to her feet. "You give me the bad with too little of the good. I would know more of your redemption."

He stared at her, wished her braid would sooner lose its crossings and a smile show the space between her teeth.

"It has to do with Lady Helene, aye?" she pressed.

"Some of it, but I will take the short way around the tale. After Gaenor left me in the wood, I happened on brigands wreaking havoc across Baron Lavonne's lands. They had stolen his sickly father from Broehne Castle and Helene the healer from her village to care for him. For weeks, I followed them hoping to end their terror, but ever there were too many." He sighed. "When I learned Beatrix was in danger from the brigands, I found a way though it meant I would have to face the wrath of Wulfrith *and* Lavonne. I revealed myself to Gaenor. Risking the happiness she was finding with her husband, she gained me an audience with him, as well as Abel, whose friendship my betrayal had ground to dust. Together, we saved Lady Beatrix, but not without sustaining life-threatening injuries. You noticed Abel's limp?"

"I did."

He touched his side. "'Twas feared we would both die, and though I slowly recovered, Abel's injuries were so severe he did not wish to live—until Baron Wulfrith brought Helene to tend him. Beneath her ministrations, he discovered an altered life was worth living. And he fell in love with her as I might have had she not returned his love."

"I am sorry."

"I am not. I am happy for them. The only thing I regret is what she made me think possible." He moved his gaze over *this* Beatrix, who was not at all like Beatrix Wulfrith, told himself this was his last chance to pull back. But it was too late to hide what he felt for her.

"Tell me what Helene made you think possible," she prompted.

"That God could not have made only one woman capable of laying claim to my affections."

A soft breath rushed from her. "You regret that?"

"It occurs that had I continued to believe I would love no other but Beatrix Wulfrith, I would have far less proof of that other thing Helene impressed upon me—that love seen mostly with the eyes may be love, but 'tis a shallow thing. Had I remained unaware that true love moves through one's entire being, I might have been more resistant to you."

Her lids flickered, tears pooled. "Durand!"

He stepped forward and set his hands on her shoulders so they would not venture around her. "I will speak this only once that ever you know what you are capable of doing to a man. I love you, Beata."

"Me? *This* Beatrix?"

"*This* Beatrix. No other. But though never shall that change, neither can it grow beyond this day. Thus, I shall do all in my power to make sure whoever you wed offers you the greatest chance of happiness."

"*You* are my best—my only—chance."

"As once you said, never have I been a choice, and I will not ruin us or any for whom we care."

Her lashes fluttered and tears spilled. "I understand. Rather, I shall try."

He released her and retreated a step.

As she wiped at her face, he saw the ink stains on her fair skin where he had caressed her racing pulse, next the wedding ring that did not belong on her hand.

"There is a knight," he said. "Baron Lavonne has given him to aid in watching—"

"Sir Hector." She nodded. "I saw him, and Lady Gaenor told me his name when asked."

"I will take him off your person."

Breath shuddered out of her. "I thank you. Be assured, I shall keep my word to await the queen's missive."

He returned to the writing desk. Moments later, she left him to the missive he prayed would not be long without an answer.

"Weeks, Lord," he rasped and took up the quill and, staring at the stains on his fingers and thumbs, said, "Pray, not months."

31

Four weeks. That was all Eleanor gave Beata to reconcile that the man she loved and who loved her in return would never be hers. It was not nearly enough time.

Though Durand and she mostly kept their distance and, when near, exchanged few words, that did not keep her from watching him and him from avoiding her gaze.

Of all those days, the best was Christmas. Lyulf had thought himself sly in coaxing Beata to the mistletoe she was not to know hung above, making her promise to wait while he searched for his new leather ball to toss with her. Instead, he had found Durand and tugged him toward the mistletoe.

Beata had not moved though she knew she ought to rather than stand there looking as if she wished to be kissed as Baron Lavonne had kissed his wife beneath that sprig. But she *had* longed to be kissed, and to her surprise, Durand had not disappointed her or the lad.

Though his smile had been taut as he lowered his head, his lips had briefly fit hers. And as he had drawn back, he had rasped, "Forgive me, but never will I have a better excuse for one last kiss."

That was certain now. What was uncertain was her understanding of Queen Eleanor's intentions.

The three knights who emerged from the corridor that gave unto the steward's chamber where they had met with Durand and Baron Lavonne, followed the latter across the hall to where Beata sat beside Lady Gaenor.

"Be of good courage, my friend," the Lady of Abingdale whispered, but her choice of words almost set Beata to weeping.

The woman had become nearer a friend than she had heretofore enjoyed. Though rather quiet, Lady Gaenor delighted in Beata's joy over the games Lyulf persuaded their guest to participate in. Never did she cause Beata to fear she laughed too loud and long those times when she set aside her heartache to feed her soul with the distraction offered by the sweet lad. Indeed, her laughter and cries of excitement had caused the boy's mother to be more expressive herself.

But that was in the past, as told by Durand's grim face where he had not progressed beyond the corridor. He met Beata's gaze, held it long as if for the last time, then turned and went from sight.

"What has the queen done?" Beata whispered.

Lady Gaenor's hand found Beata's in her lap. "Be The Vestal Wife," she said low. "Let us see her."

At the lady's prompting, Beata had shared tales of her life as Conrad's wife, and now she was asked to behave as she feared she could never again.

Forcing herself to sit taller, she moved her eyes from the emptiness left by Durand to the queen's knights.

As Baron Lavonne came around the table to stand alongside his wife, the visitors halted before the dais, and the stoutest inclined his head. "Lady Beata Fauvel, the queen sends her greetings. As told in her missive to Sir Durand, she directs you to accompany us to France."

She would have fallen out of her chair were she not well seated, would have cried out had she not halfway slipped into The Vestal Wife.

Pinning up her lips in as near a smile as she could stab into place, she commanded her breath to voice her words. "France! But I have hardly arrived in England. And the channel..." She did not have to feign distress, memories of her last crossing darkening her light tone. "Such crossings this time of year can see one shipwrecked. Pray, tell me I misunderstand."

"I cannot, my lady. Queen Eleanor is adamant. You are to come to court."

She swallowed. "When do we leave?"

"Now."

She sat back hard, whilst beside her Lady Gaenor drew a sharp breath that had her husband leaning near and whispering to her.

"But it is nearly midday," Beata choked, "and surely you ought to seek refreshment and rest."

"Food and drink we had whilst meeting with Sir Durand and Baron Lavonne. Rest can wait. Your ship cannot."

Pain in her hands, she looked to where she gripped the table's edge and averted her gaze as she did each time she looked upon Soames's ring. Pressing to her feet, she said, "I have but to gather my mantle and few possessions."

"We shall await you here."

When Lady Gaenor rose awkwardly—her belly having grown much this last month—Beata touched her arm. "Our parting will be easier if Aimee assists me."

"But—"

"Truly, my lady." She meant it. Alone with her sympathetic friend, Beata feared she would entirely misplace The Vestal Wife. For this, she was glad Durand had retreated and hoped he would not come out until she was gone. Otherwise, she might so completely lose that part of her, she would not find her again.

A quarter hour later, she thanked Baron Lavonne for lifting her astride, smiled as best she could at Lady Gaenor, and followed her escort across the drawbridge.

Away from Broehne Castle. Away from a friend she prayed she would see again. Away from Durand who had done as hoped. At least, as far as she could tell.

Though tempted to peer over her shoulder and search the walls, all the harder it would be were he there. And it was enough to cry on the inside.

Cloaked in the embrasure's shadow, Durand watched her go. It would not be their last parting, but when he saw her next, she would belong to Soames or, should Eleanor prevail as seemed likely, to another.

When Beata and her escort disappeared over a rise, he stepped into sunlight and pulled the queen's missive from beneath his belt. He knew what it said, having twice read it.

And now thrice, he allowed. Angling it toward the sun, all the more needed for how much his eyes burned, he stared at the greeting, then began again.

Sir Durand, your most sovereign liege is in receipt of your missives. It was with great relief we learned your charge and you survived the shipwreck, but of great disappointment your efforts to prevent the lady from wedding without our consent failed. Fear not, we do not hold you and Sir Elias entirely responsible, and we are grateful you arrived in time to prevent consummation that would give us no hope of seeing the lady properly wed.

"Properly wed," Durand scorned.

We found most disturbing your explanation of the events that led to the marriage. However, after consulting our advisors, we have determined Baron Rodelle has suffered enough for the crime committed by his nephew, providing he and his daughter cause us no more difficulties. Hence, by order of this missive, you are to give Lady Beata Fauvel—we shall not name her Soames—into the care of Sir Julien and his men, who will return her to our court where she shall remain whilst we remedy her marriage. It will not be without difficulty, but with your explanation and other documents attained, we believe the Church will grant our wish.

As when first he had read the missive, Durand questioned those *other documents*. Possibly from Sir Elias, but who else?

Until we have a determination, you are to take command of the half dozen knights Sir Julien delivers you at Broehne. Also accompanying him are Baron Rodelle's knights who sought to prevent you from following Lady Beata aboard ship. They have learned the folly of defying their king and queen and will prove useful in holding the barony of Wiltford until this tiresome business is done.

Durand gripped the back of his neck. Tested. Again. But he would do as commanded and, despite his anger toward Beata's father, be as civil as possible.

A missive to Baron Rodelle goes before this one, advising him of the consequences should you meet resistance upon your arrival and ordering his lady wife removed to a convent per her wishes. Once we are content, our great heiress shall return to Wiltford, and you will ensure she makes a good marriage. We pray this missive finds you well and as loyal as ever, our gallant monk.

With control that made his hands quake, he rolled the missive, then looked across the land for one last glimpse of Beata. It could not be had.

32

Normandy, France
Late January, 1162

THE CROSSING HAD been cold but uneventful. And rife with memories of when last she was upon the narrow sea. Never would she wish that tragic journey repeated, but she had longed for the hours...days...weeks with Durand. And like a girl, she imagined how she would do things differently.

A useless exercise. Only in her dreams would her ending and his play the same sweet note. The best she might have managed was not to love him so well she could find no contentment with another. Even were she destined for Soames, her father's choice of husband would likely have been acceptable. Despite that foul examination, the baron had seemed honorable, especially compared to many who had passed in and out of her years with Conrad. Providing her family's terrible trespass against his had remained beneath the leaves, it might have been a decent life.

Leaving behind what could have been, returning to what was, Beata guessed an hour had passed while she waited for admittance to the queen's private apartments. With a sigh, she thrust up off the bench and strode opposite.

She was not going anywhere. At court and under close watch, there was nowhere to go. She simply could not sit still any longer.

The door opened, and she swung around.

The lady there frowned Beata up and down and, likely believing The Vestal Widow thought to flee, scowled. "Lady Beata, a command you were given, a command you were to keep."

Smoothing the skirts of another gown Aimee had altered, Beata hastened forward. "I have. I but needed to ease the ache in my back."

Looking doubtful, the woman said, "The queen will receive you," and motioned her to enter.

The central room was large, lavish, and well attended. Though Beata fastened her eyes on the woman who sat at its center on a modestly proportioned chair that made her appear of greater stature, she counted four ladies to the right, two knights to the left, a woman of middle years before the great hearth, and a wizened clerk at a writing desk.

She had known she would not like her audience with Eleanor, but all the worse it would be in the presence of so many.

She halted just inside the chamber, and the queen made her steely regard felt before turning up a hand and sweeping her fingers toward her palm. "Come, Lady Beata. We would see how genuine your remorse for the deception and ill use of a most favored knight."

Beata continued forward. Ten feet from the queen, she bowed. And there she remained, growing increasingly uncomfortable.

"Rise, Lady Beata."

Hoping her hurting heart presented as remorse, she met the queen's gaze.

"It shall suffice," Eleanor pronounced, "though by the time we are done, methinks your regret will be more deeply felt."

Beata clasped her hands at her waist, and seeing the queen's eyes narrow on them, guessed Soames's ring offended. "May I ask what is to happen, Your Majesty? How we are to proceed?"

Eleanor eased back in her chair and sent her gaze around the chamber. "We would speak with Lady Beata in private. Lady Yola, Sir Calais, and Edwin, you may remain."

Though it was yet an audience, Beata was grateful it was no longer a crowd. As the door closed at her back, she glanced at the lady at the hearth, the clerk at his desk, and the knight alongside the queen.

"For a time," Eleanor said, "we shall not know with certainty your fate, though not as long a time had Baron Soames not made this matter easier for us."

Beata stiffened. What did she mean? That in hopes of a great concession, he had informed her of his father's murder as Durand believed he would do?

She took a step forward, took it back when the knight shifted as if in preparation to defend his liege. "Then Baron Soames has also informed you of…" She moistened her lips. "…his father's passing?"

The queen raised an eyebrow.

Belly taking up its increasingly familiar ache, Beata pressed a hand to it. "You have decided to permit our marriage as compensation—"

"Nay, Lady Beata, we have not. Nor shall we. Such a decision would encourage others to defy their sovereign in the belief they know better than we. Not that Baron Soames is not in need of a wife. Indeed, he is more in need than thought, as evidenced by his inability to control his mother."

"I do not understand."

"'Twas not he who informed us of your family's sin but the Lady of Lexeter. Her missive arrived before her son's, but whereas Baron Soames expressed a wish to see your marriage annulled—"

"He did?" Beata exclaimed.

Annoyance flashed across Eleanor's face, but there was a glimmer of pleasure in her eyes. She liked her subjects less informed. "He told he was not thinking clearly, that he had no wish to offend his king and queen—*unlike others*—and assured us your marriage had not been and would not be consummated. Hence, easier it is to undo your vows and see the heiress of Wiltford wed to one more fitting."

Though Soames was not to be her husband, there was comfort in knowing she had not judged his character too harshly. What did not comfort was the realization his lack of opposition to the annulment would more quickly see her wed to another. But she supposed the sooner the smallest crumb of hope for Durand was devoured, the sooner she could truly accept life without him.

"Once more, we shall have to aid Baron Soames," Eleanor said.

Once more? Beata pondered.

"Certes, he has been too long at his mother's skirts."

Then though he would escape marriage to The Vestal Widow, he would find himself provided with another lady. "What of his mother, Your Majesty? What did she hope to gain by revealing her husband's fate?"

The queen smiled. "Our answer will make you all the more grateful for our guidance, since we do not believe you would have liked her—nor she you. Baron Soames's mother wished your marriage consummated for the fortune needed to set aright the barony. Their due, she insists."

The same as her son had first determined, forcing Beata to speak vows with him.

"Did we grant her *demand,* a most unhappy daughter-in-law you would be."

"I am grateful, Your Majesty."

"As we know. And providing you remain grateful, your stay at court will be pleasant."

Sensing her audience with Eleanor was nearing its end, Beata asked, "What of my father, Your Majesty?"

Her eyes narrowed. "He has greatly offended—more than you, since it can be argued you acted out of duty to him." She looked to the knight, then the goblet on the table alongside.

The warrior lifted its bowl in his broad hand and passed the vessel to his liege.

The pretty ribbons adorning its stem cascading over the queen's elegant fingers, it was lifted to royal lips. Only a sip, and yet it was some time before she spoke again.

"We expect such behavior from your family, who do not well enough conceal that still you would have the long-buried Stephen upon

England's throne, but that does not forgive Baron Rodelle. Hence, he is taken in hand."

"Your Majesty?"

"By Sir Durand and the knights we sent to him at Broehne."

Beata gasped. Durand upon Wiltford? Would he be there when she returned?

"He shall make sure Baron Rodelle delivers his wife to a convent, if still the poor lady wishes it," the queen continued, "and hold Wiltford until you return and gratefully wed."

And if I do not? Beata longed to ask. But The Vestal Widow had no place here. Though her refusal to marry could at worst see her confined at court, at best allow her to take up occupancy of her dower lands, either would bode ill for her father. Henry and Eleanor had cause to strip him of his title and lands, and that Beata could not bear. Whoever she wed would assume his title, but he would have a home, and his honor would be mostly intact.

"You are in agreement, Lady Beata?"

She lifted her gaze from the floor. "I shall do as Your Majesty bids."

"We are pleased and shall continue to keep a close eye on your comfort."

She spoke of the guard who was out of sight on the stairs but would resume following Beata once she left the queen's apartments.

"I understand, Your Majesty."

"Have you anything else to say, Lady Beata?"

"I am deeply sorry, especially for the trouble caused Sir Durand, and I would have you know he was honorable and ever loyal to Your Majesty."

Once more the queen moved to silence and observation that made it impossible to draw a full breath. "Quite the trial your father and you were to Sir Durand," she said. "When this dreadful matter is done, we shall reward our gallant monk well." She put her head to the side. "How think you we might do that?"

"I do not know."

"Edwin"—Eleanor beckoned to her clerk—"give unto Lady Beata the most recent missive from Sir Durand."

It was at hand. Moments later, it was in Beata's.

"As it is not of great length, and I am at my leisure," the queen said, "you may read it."

Beata nearly questioned the handwriting that was not the same as when she had looked upon it in the steward's chamber. But the missive was surely a copy inked by the clerk, the original submitted to the Church to support the annulment.

As Eleanor sipped wine, Beata read Durand's account of what had transpired since informing his liege they had survived the shipwreck and he had delivered his charge to Wiltford. He told of Lothaire Soames's arrival at Heath, but not of the humiliating examination, then of what had been done Elias that would less dispose the queen toward her sire.

Beata winced, but she knew that were that trickery not exposed, her friend and Durand would suffer disgrace. She continued reading.

Durand was brief in relating how she was spirited away and had spoken vows with Soames before he could overtake them and convey her to Broehne to await Eleanor's instructions. Kindly, he defended Beata's defiance of the queen by telling she wed only to prevent Soames from revealing what the baron overheard of her recall of his father's murder.

Beata glanced up, found Eleanor watching her, and returned her regard to Durand's words.

My queen, I trust your wisdom in determining whether to permit Lady Beata's marriage or seek an annulment on grounds of coercion, the latter more easily granted due to lack of consummation. Whatever your decision, I pray it gives Lady Beata the greatest chance of happiness with one who is of few years, warrior enough to protect her, man enough to provide her the joy of children, and heart enough to love and be loved.

Beata's hands shook.

The parchment rustled.

Her eyes burned.

The writing blurred.

Blinking to clear her vision, she finished what remained of the missive.

Regardless, once I have done all you would have me do to remedy my failings, I shall seek permission to leave your service. It has been a great honor serving the King and Queen of England, but it is time I seek a life elsewhere.

As expected, nowhere in the missive did he mention their intimacies and feelings for each other. And yet there they were, pressed into his beseeching for her happiness. And here she was, chest constricted, fingers longing to trace every word though another's hand had written them upon this parchment.

"Why, Lady Beata, are you crying?"

She looked up. "Nay, I…" She was crying. Dropping her chin, she rolled the parchment, more to keep her tears from marring the beautiful words than to hide what was already seen. "Forgive me, Your Majesty, I know not what is wrong with me."

"You fear your sovereign's wrath."

"I do not."

"You do not fear our wrath? What are we to make of that?"

She lifted her chin. Tears tracking her face, she said, "I do fear displeasing you, but my emotions are ill for other reasons."

"As thought, there is more to the tale than our gallant monk has shared."

"Naught of consequence, Your Majesty."

"You do know it is for us to determine the importance of all that goes in our kingdom?"

"I do." Beata touched a hand to her breast. "But so much has happened I can make little sense of it myself. Thus, I would not waste your time on speculation that will likely prove of no benefit."

Looking smugly doubtful, Eleanor said, "Most considerate."

Beata stepped forward and extended the missive.

"You may keep it."

"Your Majesty?"

"It is but a copy of an accounting of events." Eleanor frowned. "Though did we not know our gallant monk well, we might think the last of it a letter of love."

More tears, but these Beata breathed down.

Eleanor gave a little laugh. "Fanciful us." She flicked a hand. "It is yours. Do with it what you will, though we advise it serve as a reminder of the great debt owed Sir Durand."

A reminder she did not need, and one that would make the years ahead more difficult, but she would set it aside later. "I shall, Your Majesty." She tucked it in her purse. "I thank you for your audience, and now I will leave you to your—"

"I am not done with you, Lady Beata."

"Your Majesty?"

The queen inclined her head. "Now for proof of your gratitude." She swept a hand toward the woman before the hearth. "The brother of our dear friend, Lady Yola, has arrived at court. At supper, you will be seated beside Sir George Pichard. Though he has yet to come into his title, his sire being of blessedly good health, and he nears his middling years, he is of good form and a pleasant conversationalist. We believe you will like him, and providing you conduct yourself as befitting a lady of our court, it is possible he will find you suitable."

Her stomach cramped. Already Eleanor set to matching her heiress to one of her choosing.

Dear Lord, she may see me wed the day my annulment is received.

"I shall not offend him, Your Majesty."

"We are glad, but we expect more of you than docility. Charm him, Lady Beata. We know you are capable."

"I will, Your Majesty."

"And remove Baron Soames's ring that we may see it returned to him."

Of course it must be removed—for Sir George. Still, Beata felt much lightened when it was off her finger and in the palm of Eleanor's clerk.

The queen passed her goblet to the knight and draped her hands over the chair arms. "You may take your leave, Lady Beata."

So relieved was she to exit the queen's apartments, she hardly minded the guard awaiting her belowstairs, nor the hours among ladies as resistant as ever to spending time in the company of The Vestal Widow.

As usual, she was approached by noblemen who found her of interest regardless of whether they approved of her. Not as usual, they did not linger. She had no patience for them, and even Sir Oliver let her be. But the distance that knave kept might have more to do with Durand's warning.

Finding respite in an alcove abandoned by a knight wearing a broad smile and a lady whose braids did not appear to normally have trouble keeping their crossings, Beata pressed herself into a corner and gripped Durand's missive through her purse.

A letter of love. It was, and she would put it from her. Not this day, mayhap not this week. But certainly before she returned to England.

33

Barony of Wiltford, England
Early May, 1162

I SHALL BEHAVE.

It was not the first time Beata reminded herself what was expected of her, and with Heath Castle ahead, it would not be the last. Durand was there and would soon be in receipt of the queen's instructions.

Beata considered her escort where Sir Julien rode ahead, eyed the large pouch at his waist. Within lay her future, one not unknown to her, as evidenced by the man who had also accompanied her to England.

She glanced sidelong at Sir George. He found her suitable enough. Or so she assumed by all the meals they had shared these past months and how often he sought her out in the hours between.

Per Durand's specifications, he was of few years—relative to Conrad—intimate with weaponry as proven when she accepted invitations to watch him at practice, presented as vigorous enough to father children, and...

Pain shot through her. He seemed to have heart enough to love her in his way, but she could only ever feel for him as a friend—and not likely of the depth felt for Conrad.

Once more, she looked to the pouch. Queen Eleanor had not disclosed the missive's contents, but it was unnecessary. It was obvious she was pleased with matching Beata with Lady Yola's brother, bestowing smiles of approval and commenting on how well Sir George tempered The Vestal Widow and The Vestal Widow animated the reserved knight. Sometimes, Beata lost herself enough to tease him, but if her tempering had anything to do with Sir George, it was that he was not Durand.

She looked to the castle that was prepared to receive its heiress, a messenger having heralded their nooning arrival. Was Durand among those mounted on the drawbridge?

He must be. All these months he had held Wiltford, acting as its lord while her father prepared himself to pass his title to the man his daughter would wed once the banns were read.

When her escort slowed further, she looked nearer at the three waiting upon the drawbridge. And recognized all. Avoiding staring at the one she most longed to drink in, she sent up thanks her father was afforded the respect of sitting front and center, and further thanks at finding Elias here.

Sir George urged his mount nearer hers. "Your home is impressive, my lady."

Soon your home, she forced herself to acknowledge this day's truth. "I thank you, Sir Knight."

"Quite the well come you are given." He nodded at the gathering. "One might think the queen herself arrived."

She almost smiled. She liked him, which was far better than hoped when she had departed the queen's apartments the day of her return to court. Theirs would not be a bad life. And what good could be had she would not taint by subjecting him to the heartache she would more keenly feel in Durand's presence.

She returned her regard to the drawbridge, put curve in her lips, and moved the false smile between her father and Elias. Both gave the smile back, though only the latter's was genuine.

Sir Julien reined in before the drawbridge, acknowledged the Baron of Wiltford, and addressed the one from whom Beata struggled to withhold her gaze. "Greetings, Sir Durand. King Henry and Queen Eleanor have tasked me with returning Lady Beata Fauvel to her home and giving unto you their wishes regarding the heiress of Wiltford."

"We are prepared to receive both, Sir Julien."

Durand's voice was no less dear to Beata for how emotionless it was. No anger, no bitterness, no sorrow. Just of one resolved to do his duty as was she.

"Well come to Heath Castle," he said and turned his destrier.

Did he look near upon me? Beata wondered. *Or could he not bear to anymore than I could bear to look upon him?* She drew a shuddering breath, told herself, *Do not think there. It will only add to your misery.*

"Lady Beata."

She looked around into the eyes of one she should not be surprised to find at her side. "'Tis wonderful to see you again, Elias," she said low. "I thank you for sending word of your recovery and willingness to forgive my family for the wrong done you."

He glanced at the Baron of Rodelle's back. "He has suffered enough."

Following his gaze, her eyes first settled on Durand.

Look away, she silently commanded. But none would know it was not her sire who held her captive, who made her mouth tremble and throat tighten as she surveyed his profile.

As noted peripherally, his short beard had lengthened—so much she imagined his kiss would be more thoroughly felt beyond her lips.

"Beata?"

She swept her gaze back to Elias. "Forgive me. The journey was long, and I am in need of rest."

He leaned near. "You have been missed."

Seeing the fullness of his meaning in the eyes that once more flicked to Durand, she looked down. "As have you."

"Will you not introduce me to your friend, Lady Beata?" Sir George asked.

She had forgotten he rode on her other side. As they passed from the outer bailey into the inner, she said, "Sir George, this is Sir Elias de Morville, whom I have known since I wed Count Fauvel. Sir Elias, here is Sir George Pichard. He has provided good company since we met at court."

The men acknowledged each other, and she was grateful Sir George did not exhibit the behavior of one who sensed a threat against something he believed belonged to him. If she had never met Durand, she might have been pleased with the queen's choice of husband.

If...

He did not need to look upon Beata to feel her to the heart of him, but he bore that added torment rather than appear the coward by going directly to the hall to receive the queen's missive.

Having passed his mount to a squire, Durand positioned himself before the donjon steps alongside Baron Rodelle, whose defiance had persisted only as long as he believed there was a chance the Church would accept his daughter's marriage and the unfortunate Winifred remained at Heath. Since learning Soames also wished an annulment, he had begun to bow to the inevitable, and all the more following his wife's departure for the convent. Beata was his heir, and he must accept whomever the queen chose to displace him.

Durand looked to the nobleman who swung out of the saddle and strode to Beata's mount to lift her down.

He was of greater age than wished, perhaps ten years beyond Durand, but he was not old, nor had he gone to fat. He was attractive, and when he had given his gaze outside the walls, Durand had read naught harsh there, just as he had not on the other occasion he had met Sir George Pichard.

God willing, he would prove a good husband. And that, more than anything, would make it easier to accept what the queen's missive would confirm. After the three successive Sundays set aside for the reading of the banns, Beata would wed and he would quietly remove himself from her life.

As the knight drew her forward, Durand continued to avoid looking directly at her. Hopefully, if she still felt strongly for him, she did the same lest too much was revealed to the one with whom she would spend her life. No man wished his wife to long for another.

"Baron Rodelle." The man halted before the one whose title he would soon take as his own. "I am Sir George Pichard, and I have had the honor of accompanying your daughter to England."

"I thank you for returning her." The baron turned his face to Beata. "I am pleased you are home."

"As am I." Her voice was tight, and Durand could no longer resist setting eyes upon her. Had she avoided looking at him, in that moment she also failed.

It was like staring into a great storm, knowing it so swiftly approached that no matter how well and often the Lord answered prayers, this one He would not.

It swept over them, the ache of the months behind and the years ahead bolting through him and causing her to catch her breath and eyes to overflow.

They would have been discovered had she not stumbled forward and given that emotion to her father.

"There now," he said gruffly and enfolded her, "I am here, Daughter. And well, I vow."

Forehead pressed to his shoulder, hands gripping his tunic, tresses of her beautifully failing braid brushing her cheek, she choked, "I have missed you. How I have missed you!"

"Truly?" It was said with surprise.

Standing in the shadow of her proclamation, Durand noted her left hand with its pale band of flesh at the base of that finger. Soon another's ring would cover it.

Feeling the gaze of the man he now called friend, only for that friendship did he respond to its beckoning.

Elias smiled sorrowfully.

These past months, Durand had not spoken of his feelings for Beata, but the troubadour knight had, though not cruelly and with only enough teasing to distract his friend during his darkest moments.

Durand looked to Sir George, and seeing the man watched him, turned on his heel. "Come, the Baron of Wiltford has ordered refreshments."

Not true. No longer did Beata's father take an interest in the workings of his household or administration of the demesne though Durand pressed for his involvement. Apathy was his daily bread. Hopefully, Beata's return would change that and Sir George would welcome his father-in-law's participation.

Durand entered the hall ahead of the others, and what followed was the most tasteless meal he had ever pushed past his lips. Throughout, he withheld his gaze from Beata, who sat with her father on one side of her and Sir George on the other. But he knew she also lacked an appetite, Baron Rodelle entreating her to eat and once scolding her for being too thin.

Though Durand had not earlier ventured past her face, a moment before their eyes had met, he had noted her hollow cheeks.

Lord, I would not have her suffer so. Let the queen's instructions see me gone from Heath Castle this day so we may begin our journeys opposite each other.

A half hour later, they were that much nearer their parting when Baron Rodelle announced the meal's end as he had not done in months.

Sir Julien was among the first to rise. "Baron Rodelle, it is time I discharge my duty to Her Majesty so Sir Durand may be discharged of his."

Then my wish is granted, Durand thought. *This day I leave her. Once I am many leagues distant—and years—I shall be glad.*

"As the queen's missive is of a sensitive nature, Sir Durand," the knight continued, "it is to be delivered in private."

"Surely it is not for my eyes alone?" Durand was certain Baron Rodelle ought to be privy to it. And Beata and Sir—

Nay, they knew what the queen required. Just as Durand knew without reading Eleanor's words.

"It is not," Sir Julien agreed. "Her Majesty but advises the gathering be intimate and include Baron Rodelle, Lady Beata, Sir George, and any other you think will make the transfer of Wiltford to its successor more palatable."

Sir Elias cleared his throat. "If you would allow it, Sir Durand, I shall join you."

He wanted to refuse, but though he might deny himself the comfort of having a friend near, he could not deny Beata the same, especially after the storm weathered in her father's arms.

"So be it," he said and stepped from his chair.

Not until halfway across the hall, the steward's quarters his destination, did he realize he had once more forgotten one of the most basic lessons taught him at Wulfen. He had not thought through his actions. Considering the last time he had been in that room with Beata, they should not go there. Better he had cleared the hall. But it was done.

The steward being absent, Durand crossed to the writing desk lit by candles and turned to watch the others enter. Elias came last and closed the door, positioned himself behind Beata who stood with down-turned face between her father and the next Baron of Wiltford, and placed a hand on her shoulder.

Sir Julien halted alongside Durand and withdrew the missive.

The wax seal was not entirely intact, having journeyed far, but enough to evidence none before Durand had set eyes on the queen's words.

He broke what remained of the seal, and as he straightened the parchment, once more betrayed his resolve by giving his gaze to Beata. Her own was fixed on the floor.

Lord he silently prayed, *give us the strength to accept what cannot be changed.*

Turning to the side, less the need to direct candlelight onto the parchment than an excuse to conceal emotions that might shame him—worse, once more loose Beata's emotions—he read what was written by Eleanor's own hand.

I, Eleanor, by the grace of God queen of England, duchess of Normandy and Aquitaine, and countess of Anjou, to Sir Durand Marshal. Greetings. By these words know our determination is final. Do the Rodelles wish the barony of Wiltford to remain inheritable, it is possible only through Lady Beatrix Fauvel, and then if she weds one of whom we approve. We can do no more for that family and will not. However, we shall do the lady one further kindness in allowing her to choose between two we deem worthy.

Two? Durand glanced at Beata.

Did she know the missive's contents? Nay, that was not the way of Eleanor who believed a lesson taught was of little value. It must be learned. In this she was like Baron Wulfrith—on the surface. It was no game the latter played. His lessons were for the betterment of the knight in training and those dependent on him. The queen's lessons as much, if not more, benefitted her. As Durand had himself assumed, Beata likely thought Sir George's accompaniment indicated he was Eleanor's choice of a husband. But there was another possibility.

Conscious of how tightly he gripped the missive for how much he longed to gather its every edge into a fist, he continued reading.

The first who has proven loyal to his sovereign is Sir George Pichard who travels with Lady Beatrix. We have long known his sister and consider him the better choice of husband for his calming influence upon the lady that made it rare for us to correct her during her stay at court.

Durand did not believe it, certain a subdued Beata had more to do with how difficult these months had been.

The second choice of a husband is the same as one of those whose name was written in the missive lost at sea, which directed Baron Rodelle as to whom we approved to wed his daughter in the event of his infant son's death. Regrettably, we expect Lady Beatrix will choose this knight over Sir George, depriving us of the services of one with whom we might not otherwise part. His name is Sir Durand Marshal.

A loud breath escaped Durand, threatening to empty him of all sense of time and place—worse, reality.

Hands quaking, he gripped his left around the desk's edge and, praying he did not deceive himself, swept his gaze back to the beginning of this section of the queen's missive.

He read it again, rasped, "Dear Lord," and looked to Beata.

Her chin was up, fear flying from her eyes.

He nearly called her to him, but the queen had more to say, and it could bode ill to assume only good was in the rest of the missive. Feeling every pound of his heart, he continued reading.

See, our gallant monk, we told we would find a wife for you, and so we have. Though our Lord Husband expresses doubt over matching you with the lady, we have decided the lands she brings to the marriage are adequate compensation for the trials such a wife will prove. That is, providing she chooses the one whose letter of love I am told she keeps upon her person.

He frowned. No letter of love had he written Beata. Thinking an explanation would be given in Eleanor's final words, he returned to the missive.

And now we laugh, delighting in how well we know our subjects. Unless Lady Beatrix is witless, it is your ring she shall wear, and that ring we have entrusted to Sir Julien that the lady shall ever be reminded of her gratitude for the lifelong gift we bestow. As for Baron Soames, we must share that his name was written alongside yours in the lost missive. Woe to him and Baron Rodelle, though we also believe Lady Beata would have chosen you over him. Do not delay in sending a reply, our gallant monk who shall no longer be untouchable, and as we expect you to bring your wife to court this year, do not too soon get her with child. Fare well.

Chest so bound it was difficult to draw enough air to speak, Durand released his hold on the desk and turned to Beata.

He had kept her waiting too long. Face washed of color, she quaked so visibly Elias had pushed a place for himself between Sir George and her and put an arm around her shoulders.

"Say aye," Durand rasped.

Her eyes flicked to the missive. "Durand?"

"Say aye, Beata." He sounded desperate, but he did not care.

"Go to him, dear lady," Elias said and released her.

She stepped forward, but Baron Rodelle caught her arm and demanded, "What is this, Sir Durand?"

Beata pulled free. With measured steps, as if to move any faster would dash her feet out from under her, she crossed the room. "Is it really so terrible?" she whispered. "I behaved. I vow, I did."

Durand longed to take her in his arms and assure her they were not forever destined to cross paths and ache over each hopeless crossing—but his emotions were so stirred he could not think how to say it, especially with an audience.

She touched his sleeve. "Durand?"

"All is well." He held out the missive.

She took it, and her fingers touched his, the contact too lingering to be accidental.

"We have time aplenty, Beata," he said low.

Her frown increased, but she bent her head and began to read.

Her subtle reactions allowed him to track her place among the words, but there was nothing subtle about her response to his name written there. She went very still as if re-reading that section as he had done, then something between a gasp and a cry parted her lips and her knees failed.

Durand caught her up and pulled her to him, crumpling the missive between them. As she pressed her face against his chest and began sobbing, he looked to the three before the door.

Sir George appeared confused, Elias pleased, and Baron Rodelle outraged.

Durand returned his gaze to his friend, pointedly looked between the men on either side of him, and inclined his head.

"Come, Baron Rodelle...Sir George," Elias said. "Lady Beata and her betrothed are in need of privacy."

"Betrothed?" her father exclaimed. "My daughter will not wed a landless knight."

"Landless no more," Elias said and, with Sir Julien's aid, cleared the steward's quarters.

When the door closed, Durand swept Beata into his arms with too little effort. Silently vowing he would see her back to a good weight, he carried her to the armchair near the brazier and settled her on his lap.

She continued to cry, every ache of these past months wringing itself out. And all he could do as he waited for her to exhaust herself was savor the feel of the woman he had first encountered across a frozen field—a vexing lady he would never have believed he would want more than any other.

At last, she drew up a handful of skirts and wiped her face, but when she looked to him, uncertainty bruised her eyes. "Ever you were a choice. Ever 'twas you. Unless... Pray, tell me Eleanor does not play with us. I cannot bear to be happy if it is not to last."

"Not a game, Beata love." He eased the wrinkled missive from her fingers. "I shall read the rest to you."

When he finished, there were more tears, but she smiled through these. "We are home, Durand. We are both of us home."

He dropped the missive and cupped her face. "A longer road I have not traveled."

Shifting around, she slid her hands over his shoulders and around his neck, but as she leaned up to offer her mouth, he said, "Letter of love?"

She flashed her prettily gapped smile. "He is of few years. He is warrior enough to protect. He is man enough to provide the joy of children. He has heart enough to love and be loved. He is my greatest—my only—chance at happiness."

Recalling the ink of those words left on her that had been visible for days thereafter, Durand silently thanked the Lord for allowing her to drag him into her mess and prove she was worth more than all the trouble of making her his own.

He chuckled. "Is that what I wrote?"

Now her mouth was so close he felt her smile. "You know 'tis, Durand Marshal, but if you must verify, I do keep upon my person the copy gifted me by the queen."

He lifted his lids, with his own eyes drank deep the bright green of hers. "I begin to remember."

She gave a murmur of approval, but when she touched her lips to his, he dropped his head back. "You forget yourself, my lady. Ere we proceed, I require an answer."

She laughed. "Aye, I will wed you. Aye, I will protect your heart—beware, most fiercely. Aye, I will bear your children. Aye, I will love and be loved. Aye, Durand. Aye."

He pushed fingers through her hair, loosed the last of her braid, and drew her mouth back to his. "I love you, my beautifully vexing Beata."

34

Barony of Wiltford, England
May, 1162

LOTHAIRE SOAMES. AT the eastern end of the meadow bordering the wood, the baron sat tall in the saddle and yet loose, as if to avoid appearing the adversary. Providing he had good cause to be upon Wiltford, especially on this day, Durand had no quarrel with him. But he would not be surprised if a quarrel was in the making.

"Three warriors to our seven," Elias mused as they neared those whom Heath's men-at-arms had encountered while patrolling the land and wood surrounding the castle.

Abel grunted. "Were our numbers reversed, still we would have the advantage. The question is—where are the rest of Soames's men?"

As Durand also wished answered. It was fool enough to pass near Heath, but with so few? Resenting the baron's trespass that, though discreetly revealed to the new Lord of Wiltford, had made it necessary for the groom to excuse himself from the wedding feast, Durand said, "I neglect my bride. Let us hear the tale he weaves and be done with it."

Abel on one side of him, Elias on the other, they spurred forward and reined in before the Baron of Lexeter and his men who kept close company with those who had intercepted them.

"Sir Durand Marshal." Soames dipped his head, causing the hank of hair Durand had months past freed from its leather thong to slip forward, evidencing too little time had passed for it to remedy its length. "I am not displeased to see you again."

An interesting means of lying, but a lie, and not only because of how they had left off outside the church at Epswich.

Durand settled his hands atop his saddle's pommel. "I believe you are aware you interrupt a wedding celebration."

"I am, though 'tis not my intention."

"Is it not?"

"This I vow. My men and I but pass through on our return to Lexeter. Many a league of hard riding is saved in going by way of Wiltford."

Abel gave a grunt of laughter.

Soames shot his gaze to him. "You think I lie?"

"I do not dispute your trespass across another's lands will more quickly deliver you home," Abel said drily, "only your purpose on Wiltford."

A muscle ticked at the baron's jaw. "You are?"

"Sir Abel Wulfrith."

"Wulfrith." Soames looked back at Durand. "You keep good company, Sir Durand."

"Now *Baron* Marshal," Elias entered the conversation, a harsh edge to his voice that told he held Soames as responsible for his tainted drink as he had Beata's father.

A slight smile taking the stiff out of Soames's mouth, he considered the gold, heavily embroidered tunic Beata had fashioned for Durand's wedding day finery, next the side-laced leather boots whose soles would become worn when Durand danced his wife around the hall this eve. "And so this day we are made equals," he said and sighed. "A pity."

Durand raised his eyebrows. "A pity?"

"Selfish me. I truly hoped to gain your sword arm so I might better my own—even after you stole my bride."

"Now and evermore *my* bride."

"I do not argue that. Did I, I would have contested the annulment rather than testify that vows which should not have been spoken were unconsummated."

Durand inclined his head. "We are grateful this day was all the sooner possible for you having seen your error."

Soames shifted in the saddle, squinted against the sunlight of a day absent clouds—providing one did not cast him in that role. "My error..." He returned his regard to Durand. "It was ill of me to force Lady Beata to speak vows. But I was angry, the same as you would be did you learn after twenty years of silence that your father was murdered, and by one of the family with whom you sought an alliance."

"That *I* cannot argue," Durand said.

"Good. Then you will understand there is something I want, which is far less than what is due my family."

"Speak."

"The location of my father's body so he may be removed from whatever unconsecrated ground Baron Rodelle dumped him in. Properly buried, my grieving mother may begin to heal."

The request was not unexpected. The only surprise was it had not come sooner. Expecting it, Durand had tried to persuade Beata's father to tell where he had buried the baron, but he would not discuss it.

"We understand your mother was not as willing to accept the dissolution of your marriage," Durand said.

Soames's nostrils flared. "The people of Lexeter have suffered much since the murder of its baron. Hence, my mother's need to heal. And you need to give an answer, *Sir* Durand."

Now he looked the adversary, threat in his posture, voice, and the slighting of his equal's title.

"Be assured, I seek an answer," Durand said. "When I have it, you will receive it."

"Make it soon," Soames said, then smiled so broadly the expression was almost believable. "Now, I shall allow you to return to the wedding celebration. Tell your bride I wish her all happiness."

"I shall." Durand motioned to the men-at-arms. "Heath's guard will ensure no ill befalls you across Wiltford lands."

Offense flickered in the man's eyes, but he said, "An escort. You are too kind."

Durand reined around.

Abel and Elias did the same, but the former paused and said across his shoulder, "Methinks I would enjoy giving you lessons, Baron Soames, beginning with courtesy. Do you grow the courage to be instructed, come to me at Wulfen."

Then the three put spurs to their mounts and set off across the meadow. Back to Durand's wedding celebration. Back to his bride.

Ignoring the restless shifting of his men and escort, Lothaire breathed deep and exhaled much of his anger. He did want his father's body returned for proper interment, but of greater import *this* day was that he fool Sir Durand. He had not, but neither had the new baron discovered his equal's true purpose on Wiltford.

Lothaire had not trespassed to do Marshal and his wife harm but to keep them from harm. And so he had, as evidenced by those he and a half dozen men had taken to ground shortly before the approach of Heath's guard. Blessedly, he had received enough warning to allow him and two of his men to lead their pursuers astray.

Inwardly, he groaned. Silently, he berated the Lady of Lexeter. If he did not wish to make a lifelong enemy of Durand Marshal—and his friend, whose offer of Wulfrith instruction ought to greatly offend—he would have to control his mother better.

"Tell your bride for what her groom slipped from the donjon and was gone for half an hour."

Surely they were not words Durand expected to hear once the door closed behind those who put the couple to bed to ensure consummation sealed the marriage, but the question had pecked at Beata for hours.

Her husband, who moved his appreciative gaze down her where she sat beside him amid stacked pillows, looked up. "You, Lady Beata Marshal, were to be too distracted by the jongleur and his dancing dogs to note my absence."

She smiled. "But note it I did, as well as that of Sirs Elias and Abel who followed you out of doors within minutes of each other."

He grimaced.

Angling toward him, she looked nearer on the man who was more bared than she, and for which she had shown maidenly modesty in the presence of those who had delivered him to the nuptial chamber. His chest and abdomen were thickly muscled as she had known from their embraces. What she had not expected was how terrible the scar that started at his lower rib and coursed his side to disappear beneath the waistband of his braies—doubtless, the life-threatening injury sustained in saving Beatrix Wulfrith's life.

"*Now* you allow yourself to be distracted," he murmured.

She swept the green of her eyes to the golden-brown of his. "Ah, but at last I am where I so longed to be that I should be ashamed of how impatient I grew to see day into night."

He raised an eyebrow, drew her left hand onto his lap, and pressed a thumb to her inner wrist. "You are saying all this jumping beneath your skin is but impatience?"

Though her face warmed, she said, "Excitement as well."

He chuckled, but soon turned serious. "What of unease?" At her frown, he said, "I speak of that accursed physician."

Tears pricked, not for what had been required of her but for his concern. "Not only has it been months and months, but I am not so vestal I do not know that becoming one with you will be as different from that humiliation as hope is from hopelessness." She shifted nearer. "As Lady Helene assured—methinks she also feared my impatience was unease—the night ahead will be the most beautiful of all. *The first knowing,* she called it."

"The first knowing," he mused, then raised her hand to his mouth. As candlelight played among the facets of the sapphire given by Eleanor to see the widow made a wife and the vestal undone, he kissed each finger.

Sensations shivered through her, tempting her to allow her question to remain unanswered. "You seek to further distract me, Husband. And you are almost succeeding."

He pressed her hand to his heart. "You will not be content with being only my wife and the mother of our children, will you, Beata?"

"I would be by your side in all things—not only the good."

"Then all the more vigilant I shall have to be in protecting you."

"As long as it keeps you near, I will not complain. Now tell, why did you leave your bride in the midst of our celebration?" A celebration attended by Baron Wulfrith and his wife, and which Lady Gaenor had assured Beata by way of a missive that her husband and she would have attended had she not recently given birth.

Durand sighed. "Abel, Elias, and I rode out to meet Soames."

She startled. "The baron was here?"

"He and two men were intercepted near Heath. Soames told he was upon Wiltford only to shorten the ride to Lexeter, and that may be, but I thought it best to provide him an escort off the barony."

"Then he did not ask for the return of his father's body?" Certain his family would wish a proper burial, it was long expected—and dreaded. Though since Beata's return, her sire's disposition had improved, he refused to speak further about the murder.

"At the end of our discussion, he asked for it," Durand said, "and I assured him that when I learn its location, he will receive it."

"He could not have been pleased to learn it remains unknown."

"He was not. Regardless, he said I should tell you he wishes you all happiness. And I believe he was sincere."

"As proved, he is not all bad—perhaps not bad at all." She rose onto her knees beside her husband. "And now, methinks, we ought to see his wish granted."

Durand smiled, slid a hand over the side of her neck, and slowly drew his fingers through the tresses she wore like a mantle. "Do you know how many times I longed to undo all of your braid and see your hair down around your shoulders?"

She laughed. "And now you shall every night, Baron Marshal. But tell, what is to follow?"

Fixing his gaze on hers, he also rose to his knees. "Better I show you." As he loosened the laces of her chemise that coursed from neck to waist, he lightly touched his mouth to hers. Too lightly, since he had shortened his beard to the length when first they had met.

Beata leaned in and deepened the kiss, and he responded as ardently. But as if reminding himself to proceed slowly, he stilled hands that had begun to raise her chemise, lifted his head, and breathed deep. "My lady, methinks *the first knowing* ought to be savored."

Wanting his lips on hers again, his hands where she had yet to feel them, she said, "Methinks it just ought to *be*," and drew back a space, further loosened her laces, and let the chemise fall from her shoulders and down around her knees.

He stared, said low, "My lady!"

Beata slid her arms around his neck. "Do not say it, Husband."

"What?"

"Behave."

He laughed, pulled her near. "Forsooth, I was thinking the opposite." He kissed her brow and nose and said against her lips, "Do *not* behave, my love."

The Awakening

Age Of Faith: Book Seven

Releasing Winter 2017/18

Prologue

Barony of Owen, England
Spring, 1152

Beware the Delilah, my son. Beware the Jezebel.

That warning again, ever near though it did not belong in the space between this young woman and him. She was no Delilah. No Jezebel. Were she, his mother would not have chosen her for the heir of Lexeter.

She was pure and only pretty enough to please him so he would not stray from vows they would exchange a year hence when she attained her fifteenth year and he his nineteenth. Only pretty enough to ensure those who sought to make a cuckold of him would not be overly tempted to make a harlot of her.

He nodded.

She laughed. "If you are done conversing with yourself, Lord Soames…" She leapt in front of him and danced backward to allow him to maintain his stride. "…mayhap you would like to converse with me."

Lothaire scowled amid the embarrassment warming his face. "You are too expressive, Lady Laura."

She arched eyebrows above eyes so dark they might haunt did they not sparkle like stars on a moonless night. "You make that sound a bad thing. Fie on you! I shall not be ashamed I am pleased to see you again." She bobbed her head forward. "And more so without your mother."

He halted. "What is wrong with my mother? You do not like her?"

She stilled her own feet, clapped a hand over her mouth, and smiled on either side of it.

The sight of her—so pretty and happy—made his heart convulse. And stirred his body as it should not. "Lady Laura!"

She dropped her hand but not her smile. "Do not take offense, Lord Soames. I did not say I do not like her, severe though she is. I am simply glad to be alone with you."

Only possible because the Lady of Lexeter had taken ill. Despite his mother's attempt to sit the saddle, they had barely gained the drawbridge before she became so light of head she had to accept he alone would journey to visit his betrothed. Lothaire had been secretly pleased, hating her constant attendance that made him seem a boy.

"As we are to wed," Lady Laura continued, "we ought to know each other better, and now we can." She threw her arms wide, dropped her head back, and whirled. "'Tis a beautiful day to fall in love!"

Appalled, yet entranced, he stared. Such frivolity had not been apparent six months past when his mother accompanied him to the barony of Owen to determine if the girl fostered by Lady Maude D'Arci would make a suitable wife.

For hours, the young lady who was to bring a generous dowry to her marriage had sat quietly with hands folded and slippered feet tight against each other, speaking only when spoken to. She had seemed shy, and only twice had he caught her looking at him. What had happened these past months that she thought it appropriate to behave in such a manner? And speak of love!

She ceased whirling, released a long breath. "I will make you talk to me, Lord Soames. I vow I shall! And you will laugh, as I know you wish to do."

"My lady!"

She held up a hand. "If we are to wed, you must accept that though I shall be the gracious noblewoman in the company of others, when 'tis you and me, I shall be... Well, I shall be me, as I would have you be you. Now the question is"—she stepped nearer, tilted her head—"who are you?"

He could hardly breathe for how close she stood. More, for how much he wanted to put his arms around her and match his mouth to hers.

She raised an eyebrow. "I wait."

He swallowed loudly, said tightly, "I am your betrothed, the man for whom you will bear children and keep a good household."

She groaned. "That is not who you are. Lady Maude assured me 'tis not."

"Lady Maude?"

"She said once you are away from your mother, you will not be dull as I told her I feared—"

"I am not dull!"

She scowled prettily. "I believe what I see and feel, not merely what is told me. So show me, Lord Soames, the life we share will be blessed with far more laughter than tears."

Again, he stared. Again, his body stirred.

She swung away. "Chase me!"

"What?"

"I wish to be chased," she called over her shoulder, "and caught." Hitching up her skirts, she ran, unbound hair flying out behind her, sunlight gliding over strands of auburn amid rich brown.

"This is unseemly, Lady Laura!"

More laughter, but not mocking. It called to the boy in him he had thought shut away. Still, he held his feet to the beaten path that led to the pond she had assured him lay just beyond the castle walls.

That had been his first mistake, allowing her to persuade him to leave the garden. And his second mistake he would make if he gave chase. But she grew distant and would soon go from sight.

A lady alone in the wood. *His* lady.

He gripped his sword hilt and ran.

Though swift, his legs long and muscled, she made it even easier for him to overtake her, staying just far enough ahead to reach the bank of the promised pond.

She spun around, propped her hands on her hips, and past an open-mouthed smile, said, "Methinks Lady Maude is right. You are not dull."

He should have drawn up far short, but his feet carried him to within an arm's reach of her. "Lady, we must return to the castle."

"We shall, but first..." She stepped near, laced slender fingers with his that had never seemed so large and clumsy. But before he could find words to correct her for being so familiar, she turned and lightly settled her shoulder against his.

"Look, Lothaire. Is it not lovely?"

She was lovely. Not simply pretty as was required.

"I am fond of this place," she said as he followed her gaze across and around the pond. "When I was little, Lady Maude brought her son and me here on the hottest of days and we swam and played in the water."

"You speak of Simon?" he said to distract himself from the soft hand he should not be holding. He knew it was Simon, Lady Maude and her departed husband's only child. Though Lothaire liked the lady's stepson, who was now Lord of Owen, there was something about the half-brother that bothered—something beyond the feeling Simon D'Arci did not like him. Their one encounter this day had been brief since the young man was preparing to return to the lord from whom he received knighthood training, but it had disturbed. And Lothaire was glad when Simon had departed two hours past.

He frowned. "Surely you do not still swim here with Lady Maude's son?"

His betrothed looked up, made a face. "I do not. 'Twould be improper now we are no longer children."

His mother would not like that Simon and she had ever frolicked here, and neither did he, but though that could cause Raisa Soames to reject this young woman, Lothaire was now a man. *He* would determine what was acceptable.

"But once you and I are wed..." she made a song of her words and angled her head toward the pond. "Methinks it permissible for husband and wife to swim together."

The thought of going into the water with her once more making him overly aware of their bodies, he told himself to release her hand and distance himself.

Told himself.

Her sparkling eyes returned to his. "Perhaps even bathe together, hmm?"

He caught his breath, heard his mother's words again—*Beware the Delilah, my son. Beware the Jezebel.*

He cast off her hand. "You should not speak thus, Lady. 'Tis sinful!"

She blinked rapidly as if surprised by a slap, and as the light in her eyes fell to earth alongside her smile, whispered, "Forgive me." She sidestepped. "Oh, Lady Maude shall be disappointed. I am a lady. Truly, I am. I just..." She peeked at him from beneath her lashes. "I am pleased you wish to take me to wife, Lord Soames. You are young and handsome, and I am certain you are kind. I but wish to make you as happy with me as I am with you."

Still, his mother would not overlook such behavior, but the man he was decided she could be forgiven. She was very young and would mature much before they wed—especially once Lady Maude was made aware of her ward's deficiencies and set to correcting them.

Lady Laura lifted her chin, and he saw her eyes sparkled again, but not with joy or mischief. "You are not pleased with me, are you?"

Struggling against the impulse to pull her close and wipe away her tears, he clenched his hands at his sides. "I make allowances for your age, my lady, confident a year hence you will be nearer a woman than a girl."

His words offended, as told by a different sort of light in those dark eyes, but it faded and she said, "Much can happen in a year. Be patient, and I shall not disappoint you or Lady Maude who has been so good to me."

The lady *had* been generous, fostering Laura since the age of five following her mother's passing that had left her husband with one female child to raise among six males.

"You..." She moistened her lips, and he saw they trembled. "...will not be too harsh in telling Lady Maude of my failings, will you? She will count herself responsible, and she is not. Ever I have been excitable." A tear spilled over, and she clapped a hand to her cheek as if to hide it. But another fell. "Oh, how the tiny things upon the summer air irritate my eyes!"

Dear Lord, Lothaire silently appealed, *she should not so captivate.*

But she did, and he had only himself to blame when he breached the space between them and set his mouth on hers. He had kissed a few chambermaids—the extent of his carnal sin—but he was familiar enough with the intimacy to know this was different. The taste of Laura was more than pleasant. It was sweet, like the honey milk of his childhood.

It was she who ended the kiss. Dropping from her toes he had not realized he had dragged her onto, she breathed, "I like that, Lord Soames. But now I must prove Lady Maude has made a lady of me."

"Very good," he said as if he but tested her. If only he did! How many hours must he spend praying for forgiveness?

"My lord?"

"My lady?"

She was smiling again, though more demurely, and her cheeks were softly flushed. "Methinks you ought to release me."

He lurched back, and had only a moment to miss the press of her body before what sounded like a large insect passed between their faces and skittered across the pond.

He snapped his head around, considered the rippled surface. "What was that?"

"Simon?" she called, question and rebuke in that one's name.

Lothaire turned and followed her gaze to the trees between the pond and castle. "You think 'twas him?"

"I..." She looked sidelong at Lothaire, pressed white, even teeth into her lower lip.

"He is gone from Owen," he reminded her, then wondered if he erred when he recalled the slingshot looped over the young man's belt—of note since Lothaire was also fond of that childhood weapon. Though these past years of training at arms were mostly spent mastering the sword, he was certain he could still make his mark.

"You are right, it cannot have been him," she said firmly, as if to convince herself. "Do you think 'twas a dragonfly?"

He studied the trees again. No movement. No sound that did not belong there.

Might it have been only a dragonfly? Possible. Regardless, it would have struck him in the temple had he not released his betrothed.

"We ought to return," he said and stepped past her. And halted.

We are going to wed, he assured himself. *She will be my wife. We will swim together. Mayhap even bathe together.*

He peered over his shoulder and met her wary gaze. Longing to see the sparkle returned to it, he reached to her.

There. So much light shone from her he felt its rays pass through him. And as she slid her hand over his palm and worked her fingers through his, he was so warmed he discovered places within him he had not known were cold.

It *was* a beautiful day to fall in love. Mayhap he would.

As they walked side by side, skirts brushing chausses, dark brown hair caressing muscled forearm, neither saw the one who pressed his back hard to the bark of an ancient oak. Neither saw the calloused fingers gripping straps of leather whose missile should have turned *Lord Soames's* dark blond hair red…knocked him to his knees…made him cry like a boy…

Neither heard him rasp, "She is mine. Shall ever be mine! She promised."

1

Barony of Owen, England
April, 1163

A<small>WAKEN</small>, L<small>AURA</small>. I<small>T</small> *is time.*

She shook her head, felt the lingering caress of hair across her cheeks, nose, and throat.

Open your eyes, the voice persisted.

She squeezed her lids tighter, ignored the ache of lungs that had expelled their last breath.

Do not do it for you. Never you. For Clarice.

She sprang open her lids, peered at the clouded, candle-lit ceiling. It *was* time. Past time. But she was not yet clean.

That made her laugh, causing a bubble to burst from her lips and further distort the ceiling.

Her lungs lied. She had breath—in the deepest of her.

And *she* lied. Never would she be truly clean, no matter how hard she scraped at her scalp or urged her maid to scrub her flesh until it was so abraded pricks of blood surfaced.

A moment later, that woman appeared above—wide-eyed and disapproving.

Pushing her feet against the tub's bottom, Laura slid up its side with a great slop of water.

Tina jumped back. "Oh milady! Ye got me skirts. Again!"

Water streaming her face and shoulders and over breasts she knew more by weight than sight, Laura managed one of the few smiles of which she was capable—that of apology. "I was in need of air."

"Then ye shoulda come up sooner." Tina snorted. "Sometimes ye worry me no end."

Laura flicked water from her fingers, dragged a hand across her eyes. "I come up when I must."

"As Lady Maude said, ye are a creature of the water."

Maude. Gone six months now. And every day of those months felt.

It was true. She *must* awaken. For Clarice, who needed her mother now that the woman she had not known was her grandmother had died. But there was something else Clarice needed more—a father. Rather, a provider.

And so I shall sell this used body to the highest bidder, she silently vowed. It mattered not if he was young or old, only that he had sufficient income to support a wife and child and could be trusted to treat Clarice well.

It seemed easily attainable, as if she would have many to choose from, but she would be fortunate to find one, and only then were she given aid. Would Queen Eleanor help her distant cousin who had borne a child out of wedlock, so shaming her family they had disavowed her?

No chance if the truth of Clarice was withheld, but now that Maude was gone...

"Come, milady, give me your back."

Laura scooted forward and lowered her chin in preparation for the stiffly bristled brush.

Tina gathered her lady's wet tresses, piled them atop the back of her head, and began working the brush over a shoulder blade.

But that voice reminded Laura it was time.

She peered over her shoulder. "Not the brush, Tina. A washcloth."

The maid's eyes grew so round, Laura knew that in her first life—before Clarice—she would have laughed. "I do not know I heard right, milady. Did ye say to use a washcloth?"

"I did."

"Huh!" She dropped the brush to the floor and snatched up the cloth she had earlier worked over her lady's face and hands.

It was so lightly felt that twice Laura looked around lest she imagined the soft fibers.

"Are ye comin' into sickness, milady?"

Laura lowered her chin again, caught her reflection in water so clouded with soap she could see no more than the outline of her torso and limbs—just as she preferred.

"I am not." She stared into eyes one would never know had once shone with happiness. "'Tis just that…" She nearly said it was time, but that would make as little sense to Tina as the washcloth. "I am clean enough."

Rather, she could get no cleaner. She was sullied. Would ever be. More, were she able to capture a husband, he would expect soft skin, not raw. And well after vows were spoken, for the sake of Clarice's future, she would have to keep him content. Especially in bed.

Bile shot into her mouth, and she convulsed.

"Ye *are* ill, milady!"

Laura swallowed hard, grimaced as the acid burned its way down. "It is only something I ate."

After a long moment, Tina said, "Or something ye did not eat. I saw ye nibble all 'round your bread, and did you even taste the soup? Methinks not!"

Though Laura's appetite was often lacking, it had been absent this eve after the most recent incident with Clarice and the son of the lady of the castle shoved her in a direction she had not yet accepted she must travel.

Laura sat back. "I am done with my bath. Pray, bring a towel near."

Tina rose, shook out the large cloth, and stretched it between her hands to all the sooner enfold her lady.

Gripping the tub on either side, Laura put her chin up and stood. Another thing she must overcome—distaste for an unclothed body. As difficult as it was to look upon her own, how was she to look upon that of a husband?

More bile, but she was prepared, and Tina did not notice her lady's discomfort as she wrapped her in the towel.

"I shall get ye into your chemise and braid yer hair, then to bed with ye."

"Clarice—"

"Oh *tsk,* milady. Worry not, I shall go for her and see her soon upon her pallet."

The one alongside Laura's bed, which her daughter had rarely used before Maude's passing. Most nights the girl had slept in her grandmother's chamber. Though Laura told herself it was because of her own restlessness once sleep clasped her close, that was a lie. Clarice had loved her grandmother more. And still did, with good cause.

But I am awake now, she assured herself.

Yet another lie. But she was awakening. Would do right by her daughter as had not seemed necessary until now. Maude had made it too easy for her to live inside herself—to be more a creature of the water than the air.

Guilt had done that to the lady. And love for Clarice.

I am sorry, Laura sent her thoughts in search of the dead. *I did not say it often enough, but you were too good to me. I should have been stronger for Clarice. Should have been a mother not a... What was I? What am I? Not even a sister.*

She returned to the present when Tina pressed her onto the stool before her dressing table. And in a moment of unguardedness, she caught her reflection in the mirror.

Forcing her awakening self to confront the stranger there, she wondered how she was to capture a husband. Though with Maude's guidance and encouragement she had maintained the facade and carriage of a refined lady, these past months had been less kind to her appearance than all the years before. She was thin and pale, eyes shadowed, lips low, shoulders bent.

Awaken, Laura. That voice again. *For Clarice.*

She opened her eyes wider, lifted her chin higher, raised her slumped shoulders, and watched as Lady Laura's hair was gently combed and worked into braids.

A quarter hour later, Tina swept the covers atop her, fussed over the placement of the braids upon the pillow to ensure the crimps lay right when she uncrossed them in the morn, then snuffed all but one candle.

"Sleep in God's arms, milady," she said and pulled the door closed.

Laura stared at the ceiling, thought how much more she liked it seen through water. "God's arms," she whispered. "Ever too full to hold me. Lest I drop Clarice, I shall have to hold myself."

2

Barony of Lexeter, England
Mid-May, 1163

King Henry was returned, and with him his Eleanor. For four years, he had occupied his French lands, not once setting foot in his kingdom. But now he was everywhere, traveling across England at a furious pace, setting aright wrongs, and—it was said—increasingly disillusioned with his old friend, Thomas Becket.

The archbishop, a favorite to whom the king had entrusted the education of his heir, was not behaving. At least, not how Henry wished Thomas to behave.

As for Eleanor, she was also making her presence felt. In this moment. Inside these walls.

"What does that harlot want?"

Lothaire stiffened. He had heard footsteps, but as they had not scraped or landed heavily as they were wont to do, he had thought they belonged to a servant come to prepare the hall for the nooning meal. When his mother wished to be stealthy, she made the effort to lift her feet and softly place them.

Setting his teeth, he turned.

She stood before the dais upon which the lord's table was raised. Wisps of silver hair visible beneath her veil, an imperious lift to her chin, lips pinched, she arched thin eyebrows above eyes so lightly lidded they seemed unusually large.

"I asked a question, my son."

And he would answer when he answered. They were years beyond her ability to intimidate and dominate him, but ever she tried to take back ground lost ten years past after his first betrothal was broken.

Resenting that even a glancing thought for that lady could still feel like a blade between the ribs, he rolled the missive and slid it beneath his belt.

His mother stared at what he denied her grasping hands and greedy eyes, the color blooming in her cheeks proving blood yet coursed beneath her skin.

"I am summoned to court, Mother."

She drew a sharp breath. "For?"

"What we knew would call me to Eleanor's side if I failed to find a bride with a sizable enough dowry to make Lexeter whole."

She lunged onto the dais and would have dropped to her knees did he not catch her arm and pull her up beside him.

Gripping his tunic, she said, "You have not searched far enough." Her saliva sprayed his face. "Now see, our future is in the hands of that French harlot!"

She was not entirely wrong. Since the annulment of his unfortunate marriage to Lady Beata Fauvel a year ago, he could have searched harder, but the thought of awakening beside a woman he wanted only for the wealth she brought her husband had put him off the hunt. Too, when he himself was not working the land to turn it profitable, he pursued his only other passion—becoming a warrior worthy of donning a Wulfrith dagger.

Of that his mother remained unaware, though not for lack of trying to discover where twice now he had gone for three and four weeks, where he suffered humiliation after humiliation and sometimes at the hands of mere squires, where he was to have gone a sennight hence. Wulfen Castle.

Much to Abel Wulfrith's displeasure, Lothaire had slammed his pride to the ground and accepted the man's offer to train him into a formidable knight. He had known it was but a taunt, but he had dared, and Sir Abel's brother, Everard, had sighed and said if the offer was made, it must be fulfilled.

Despite all the pain and humiliation visited upon him, Lothaire had discovered a liking for the two brothers, and even the eldest, Baron Wulfrith. More surprising, Sir Abel had become easier in his pupil's company during the second visit. They could never be friends, Lothaire having no use for such, but there was something appealing about spending time with men his own age with similar interests.

Now he would have to send word he would not avail himself of Wulfrith training this next month. More unfortunate, even if he returned from court with a wife, it would be months before he could resume training since he would have to wait until next Sir Abel relieved one of his brothers of the task of training up England's worthiest knights.

"I shall accompany you," his mother broke into his thoughts. "King Henry's wife will know exactly what you require in a wife—a sizable dowry, pretty, but not too pretty—"

"I go alone." Lothaire unhooked his mother's hands from the material of his tunic.

"But my son—"

"Nay." Ensuring she had her balance, he stepped back. "You shall remain here, and if the queen does provide a wife, you will relinquish the title of Lady of Lexeter without protest else I will see you settled on your dower property." Which he would have done years ago if not for her poor health.

Light leapt in her eyes, but naught resembling the sparkle of stars on a moonless night. This was fire—so hot it would disfigure any who drew near. And here came the threat that was the greatest control she wielded over him.

"Becca will go with me. You know she will."

His older, unwed sister had only her mother to live for, though twice Lothaire could have secured a husband for her had their mother not deemed a lowly knight beneath her daughter.

"For years that has worked, Mother, most notably last year when you defied me and risked all of Lexeter by sending men to murder Lady Beata and her new husband. It will be different if you threaten *my* wife."

"Foolish, foolish boy!" she spat. "You do not see the Delilah, do not see the Jezebel. But I do and would not have you suffer again as that—"

"Enough!" Lothaire stepped from the dais and tossed over his shoulder, "You may wish me to be a boy, but I have not been since—"

"Since that harlot made a cuckold of you, just as over and again your father made a betrayed wife of me."

He halted. She spoke of his first betrothed, though neither had the woman he wed after Laura been pure. Tempted though he was to feign ignorance, he turned and waited.

"You still think on her," she scorned.

Do I hate my own mother? Lothaire wondered. Certes, he disliked her.

"You would like that, hmm?" he said and smiled. "For me to regret more not heeding your advice than that she lay with another."

"You should have listened to me! How many times did I warn—?"

"I did listen to you. You said she would be a fitting wife."

"Until time and again she called you back to her, like a siren seeking to drag you down into the dark. Into sin!"

It was as his mother wished to believe, though he knew her objections thereafter were rooted in jealousy. She had never fully recovered from the wasting sickness that prevented her from accompanying him to Owen for his second visit with his betrothed. Hence, four more times he had visited Laura unchaperoned, and each time was sweeter than the last.

Nay, not the last. That was when he learned the truth of her. Even now, ten years gone, he could see her standing before the pond. Alone, but not entirely alone.

"Leave it be, Mother," he said and strode to the stairs.

He closed himself in the solar and, when his breathing calmed, read the queen's missive again. He did not like the wording. It begged too unsettling a question. Did she or did she not have a wife for him? She said she did, and yet in closing she wavered.

We shall expect you within a fortnight, Lord Soames. Do you present well, we believe you will gain the hand of the lady who brings to her marriage the relief many a lord seeks to save his lands. Do not disappoint us.

3

Windsor Castle, England
Late May, 1163

SHE KNEW SHE was awake, but it seemed more a dream she inhabited as she stared at the lady before her.

It was the finest mirror, with so little distortion she wondered if she had truly seen herself before. Ever the pond she had not visited since Clarice's birth had offered the truest reflection when it was at its stillest, but she had never presented as clear as this.

She did not think herself beautiful, but she was quite fair, especially after a month beneath the watchful eye of the queen who oft sighed over all that must be done to transform her guest from sickly to...desirable.

Laura closed her eyes. She hated that word. It told of things that happened in the dark whether a woman wished it or not.

"Milady?"

She opened her eyes, looked to the maid beside her. "Am I ready, Tina?"

"Oh, lass." She stepped near, patted her lady's cheek. "More ready than ever I have seen you. And it has been six years since Lady Maude gave ye into my care, hmm?"

Six years—following the visit to Simon's half-brother whose wife had nearly suffered the same as Laura.

How she adored Michael and Lady Beatrix. How she wished she could accept their offer for Clarice and her to live at Castle Soaring. The temptation was great, but she had known that were she to accept, she would not fully awaken as she must. And she was determined she would not be a burden to anyone again—excepting whomever she wed, but he would have payment enough in the bedroom.

She almost smiled at the realization her throat did not burn with bile. She was growing accustomed to the idea of violation. And that was good, for a poor marriage it would be—and of detriment to Clarice—if the man whose ring she wore learned how she felt about what he did to her.

Still no bile.

"Six years, Tina. I pray we have many more."

And she would, Maude's stepson having agreed the maid could leave Owen, and Queen Eleanor having concurred that Laura's husband would accept Tina's services to his wife.

"'Tis time," the maid said.

Laura slid her palms down the skirt of one of dozens of gowns gifted her by Maude over the years.

The queen had been pleased with the quality and colors of Laura's wardrobe, surely having expected the royal coffers would bear the cost of clothing her in finery needed to capture a husband.

Though some of the gowns were not as fashionable as once they had been, a seamstress had been engaged and altered their fit and design.

Were I happy, Laura thought, *I would feel like a princess.*

"I am ready," she said and followed Tina to the door of the luxurious apartment that had been hers these past weeks. Soon she would leave it, collect her daughter from Michael D'Arci and Lady Beatrix, and journey to wherever she would spend the remainder of her life with the man to whom she would give herself to provide her daughter a good future.

Now to see who so badly needed funds he would pay the price of a used lady newly awakened.

Which one was she?

The tall lady whose eyes rushed about the hall as if in search of someone? The heavily freckled lady who twisted at a tress of red hair tucked behind an ear? The beautiful blond lady who was of an age several years beyond his own? What of the lady with hair the color of burnished bronze?

Lothaire looked nearer upon that last. She stood in profile, but there was no doubt she was lovely, albeit thinner than he liked.

He grunted. Though given a choice he would choose a wife passing pretty and pure of body, what mattered most was that whoever he wed possess lands or dowry enough to return Lexeter to the prosperity it had enjoyed before his father's murder twenty-two years past.

He stiffened, pushed that reminder aside. Though determined to learn where his father was buried so Ricard Soames could be moved to consecrated ground, he was here to secure a wife.

He looked to the queen who had yet to grant him an audience though he had arrived at Windsor last eve. Likely, she was still displeased with him for wedding Lady Beata Fauvel without her permission, forcing her to see the unconsummated marriage annulled before she could wed her favorite—Sir Durand Marshal—to the lady.

As he started to move his gaze from Eleanor, she settled hers on him. And smiled.

That he did not expect. Though he did not like her, he returned the smile.

She inclined her head and pointedly looked toward a gathering to her left.

The lady with the burnished bronze hair, then. And she had added another nobleman to her audience.

He was not displeased with the queen's offering. Of all those whose unveiled hair proclaimed them unwed, she was among the few with whom he would have sought an acquaintance. Young enough to bear children, but not so young he would suffer the foolishness of a girl who believed her maturing body made her a woman. Though more pleasing to the eye than he liked, he would simply have to be vigilant. As for her weight, once she knew he was not the sort who found half-starved women desirable, she would eat more.

He looked back at Eleanor, and she frowned and gestured for him to approach the lady.

Wishing he had a name by which to call her, he strode forward. As he neared, he studied her face in profile and revised his opinion. Given a choice, he would not seek to make this lady's acquaintance. Too much she resembled his first betrothed, albeit more mature. Unfortunately, he dare not further displease the queen, and he needed to wed a lady who brought a goodly amount of coin to the marriage.

He was several strides distant when she tapped the air between her and a nobleman of middle years and said, "Fie on you, Lord Benton."

Now he had a name, one that stopped him and blew warm breath into his cold places. But it could not be. She had no dowry, her father having disavowed her.

At what did the queen play? This was no coincidence. Eleanor had to know that once he had been betrothed to this lady. Was this punishment for his defiance?

Feeling his chest and shoulders rise and fall, hearing the thrum of blood in his veins, he looked to Eleanor.

She raised her eyebrows, impatiently motioned him to resume his approach.

Dear Lord, he silently beseeched, *make me stone. Open wide a path to sooner see me away from her.*

Continuing forward, he altered his course and inserted himself between Lord Benton and another nobleman. He had only a moment to take in the lady's lovely face before shuttering his own.

Lids fluttering, breath catching, she stumbled back and dropped her chin.

"Lady Laura?" Lord Benton gripped her arm to steady her.

"Forgive me!" she gasped. "I believe the heel of my slipper has failed." Though she put forward its toe, it provided no evidence of that which remained beneath her skirts.

She sighed, looked up, and as if Lothaire were not a flicker of the eyes away, smiled at Lord Benton. "Pray, excuse me." She moved her smile to the others. "I shall remedy the situation as soon as possible and return."

"Do not forget your promise to sit with me at meal," said a short but handsome man to Lothaire's right.

"I shall not, Lord Gadot." She swung away and, lacking a hitch in her step, moved toward the stairs.

Lord Benton looked to Lothaire. "You are?"

"Baron Soames."

The man's brow lowered. "Another rival? Or just passing through?"

"Rival?"

"For the lady's hand," Lord Gadot said and winked. "Quite the surprise she is so lovely, eh? I was certain she must be the freckled one, else the lady nearing the end of her child-bearing years, but the Lord is kind. I would very much like Lady Laura in my bed."

For a moment, Lothaire did not know himself. But a reminder of who she was—a Jezebel from the top to the bottom of her—kept his hand from his dagger's hilt and the fist he made of it at his side.

"Ah, but whoever wins her must needs watch her closely," said the third nobleman who, were he capable of wielding a sword, would find his swing hindered by an excess of weight. He sighed. "I have no wish to be made a cuckold."

As the others murmured agreement, it occurred to Lothaire the comment was meant to discourage the other rivals. Still, ache lanced him that her sin was so well known. Blessedly, none looked upon him in any way to indicate they knew he was a victim of that lady's cuckolding.

"Are you a rival, Baron Soames?" Lord Benton asked again.

"Just passing through." Lothaire pivoted opposite the three who sought to wed the woman he had once wanted for his own. But no more. Not ever again. As soon as he could gain an audience with the queen, he would make it known Lady Laura was unacceptable. If she insisted on finding a wife for him, it would have to be another.

Upon reaching a sideboard, he accepted a goblet of wine from a servant. Once his face was composed as much as possible and cooled of angry color, he turned.

The queen remained seated. Though she conversed with one of her ladies, her eyes shifted to him.

She liked this game of hers—wanted to watch the players dance on their twisted and knotted strings. But he would not, and eventually she would weary of her sport and summon him.

Unless she had another lady able to raise Lexeter out of its financial difficulties, he would depart on the morrow, ride for Wulfen, and make good out of bad by sharpening his sword skill with the anger coursing his veins.

Abel Wulfrith's opponent would prove far more worthy. And deadly.

About The Author

TAMARA LEIGH HOLDS a Master's Degree in Speech and Language Pathology. In 1993, she signed a 4-book contract with Bantam Books and began writing full time. Her first medieval romance, Warrior Bride, was released in 1994 and nominated for a RITA award. Continuing to write for the general market, she was published with HarperCollins and earned awards and spots on national bestseller lists.

In 2006, Tamara's first inspirational contemporary romance, Stealing Adda, was received with critical acclaim. In 2008, Perfecting Kate was optioned for a movie and Splitting Harriet won an ACFW Book of the Year award.

In 2012, Tamara returned to the historical romance genre with the release of Dreamspell: A Medieval Time Travel Romance, followed by the Age of Faith series, which will include the seventh book, The Awakening, in winter 2017/18. Baron Of Blackwood, the third book in the #1 bestselling The Feud series, is now available. Among Tamara's #1 Bestsellers are her general market romances rewritten as Clean Reads, among them: Lady at Arms, Lady Of Eve, and Lady Of Conquest. The final rewrite, Lady Betrayed, releases Summer 2017.

When not in the middle of being a wife and mother, Tamara dips her writer's pen in ink and nose in a good book. She lives near Nashville with her husband, a Doberman who bares his teeth not only to threaten the UPS man but to smile, a German Shepherd who has never met a squeaky toy she can't destroy, and a feisty Morkie who keeps her company during long writing stints.

Connect with Tamara at her website www.tamaraleigh.com, Facebook, Twitter, and email tamaraleightenn@gmail.com.

For new releases and special promotions, subscribe to Tamara Leigh's mailing list: www.tamaraleigh.com

Made in the USA
Lexington, KY
28 May 2018